STORYTELLING
REFLECTING ON ORAL NARRATIVES AND CULTURES

Written and edited by Anne Goding

SUNY—New Paltz

cognella
San Diego, CA

Bassim Hamadeh, CEO and Publisher
Christopher Foster, General Vice President
Michael Simpson, Vice President of Acquisitions
Jessica Knott, Managing Editor
Kevin Fahey, Cognella Marketing Manager
Jess Busch, Senior Graphic Designer
John Remington, Acquisitions Editor
Jamie Giganti, Project Editor
Brian Fahey, Licensing Associate

First published in the United States of America in 2013 by Cognella, Inc.

Trademark Notice: Product or corporate names may be trademarks or registered trademarks, and are used only for identification and explanation without intent to infringe.

Printed in the United States of America

IISBN: 978-1-60927-097-1

www.cognella.com 800.200.3908

CONTENTS

INTRODUCTION

Many years ago, I sat in a story circle with a Native American man, Gheezhis Mokwa, who told the following intertribal story:

How Stories Began (The Storytelling Stone)

Long ago, in a time before our grandfathers' grandfathers could remember, there lived a young hunter in a village at the edge of the woods. Each morning, just before sunrise, he ran along a path through the woods until he came to the edge of the prairie. Just when he got there, the warmth of the sun touched him, and he was happy. He prayed, giving thanks for his life, and for all of life, and he asked permission to go out on the prairie and take a life in order to continue his own.

On one particular morning, he then shot a rabbit with his arrow, gave thanks for the food he would take home, and turned to go back through the woods. As he came to a certain place along the path, he heard a voice, which said, "Young Man." The voice seemed to come from a boulder next to the path.

The young hunter stopped to listen, and heard the voice again. "Young Man, if you give me that rabbit, I'll tell you a story."

"What's a story?" the young hunter asked.

Grandfather Stone replied. "A story is a wise and ancient teacher. It's a companion on cold winter nights. It's a sign, helping you decide which way is right. It's a path to a time before the world began. A story is a friend."

The young hunter wanted to hear a story, so he put the rabbit on the great stone and sat down to listen. He heard a story of wisdom and courage. At the end, he stood, thanked the great stone, and returned to his village. He had no food to give his wife, but he had a story, and they were happy.

The next day, the young hunter went to the prairie again, and arrived just as the sun began to warm the earth, and he could smell the perfume of the flowers and herbs and grasses, and he was happy. He prayed, giving thanks for his life and for all of life, and he asked permission to take a life in order to continue his own. That day, he shot a grouse. Then, giving thanks for the food, he turned to the path through the woods. As he approached the great stone he slowed his run, just in case. Yes, the Grandfather Stone spoke again, saying, "Young Man, if you give me that grouse, I'll tell you another story."

The young hunter put the grouse on the great stone and sat down to hear a story of beauty and love. He thanked the stone and returned to the village, but again, he had no food for his wife. But he had a new story, and so the two were happy.

The next morning, the young hunter understood that on that day, he would have to take the lives of two animals, one for the great stone, and one for himself. When he reached the prairie, the sun's warmth shook the grasses and leaves, and their music blended with birdsong, and the young hunter was happy. He prayed, asking permission to take two lives in order to continue his own. That day, he shot two rabbits, and again gave thanks for the food. When he reached the Grandfather Stone, it spoke again, saying, "Young Man, if you give me one of those rabbits, I'll tell you another story."

And so the young hunter sat down to hear a story filled with an understanding of Creation. That day, he brought his wife food and a story, and they were very, very happy.

Every day that the young hunter went to the prairie, he always stopped to learn a new story from the great stone. But over the years, young hunters become middle-aged hunters, not quite as swift on their feet as younger men. And middle-aged hunters become old. They become slower, and their eyesight dims. Sometimes they miss their shot, or even lose an arrow. And the time finally came when our young hunter could no longer go to the prairie to provide for his needs. But by then, he himself had learned to say, "Young Man, if you give me that rabbit, I'll tell you a story." And thus, our young hunter became the first human storyteller.

....

By listening to this story, we can come to learn a great deal about some of the Native American cultural beliefs and values. First and most obviously, tellers of this story embody an awareness of the earth, the natural world. Our young hunter takes the time to greet the morning, feeling the warmth of the sun, hearing the music of the earth, and breathing the fragrant breath of nature. Not only do the storytellers embody the awareness, but also feel a deep connection, kinship, and respect for all of life. In remembering to ask permission to take a life, the storytellers and the hunters acknowledge the finality of the acts they are about to commit, and the importance of the natural world in providing for their needs.

Second, tellers of this story embody reverence and an awareness of the world of spirit, and in a prayer for a humble rabbit, acknowledge that spirit animates even the smallest among animals.

Third, tellers of this story embody an awareness of the duality of nature: Earth and spirit intertwined, life and death, youth and age, speaking and listening, beginnings and endings.

Folktales from all cultures carry within them the beliefs, values, experiences, expectations, hopes, and meanings that are central to the culture of origin. This is why, in this textbook, we will seek to learn about other humans through their folktales and other stories.

Why should we care about storytelling? These are modern times, after all, and we now have books, electronic readers, computers, and all kinds of communication devices. Journalists, filmmakers, and other media professionals now produce what we call digital storytelling. We no longer have to wait for others to gather. We no longer need to have patience in waiting for a story to unfold. We can gulp down information at will at our private desks. Yet there are reasons to value face-to-face storytelling:

- It contributes to social cohesion, reducing the isolation of competitive, individualistic work.
- It brings to us many layers of meaning not available in databases.
- It brings us closer to what it means to be human.
- It provides new ways of understanding the past and present.
- It reminds us that there are millions of people, like ourselves, whose lives are profoundly different.
- It offers alternative ways of understanding the nature of Creation.
- It offers an opportunity to share an experience with others.

Here's a comparison:

ORAL TRADITION	LITERARY TRADITION	ELECTRONIC GENERATION
Originated in pre-literate societies, where face-to-face transmission of cultural lore generated social cohesion and shared understandings.	Reading and writing are both solitary activities. The words are frozen into sequences that do not respond to audience involvement. Ownership of stories is exerted through copyrights.	Stories are mediated by electronic devices. Viewing and listening are solitary. A cultural context is often missing, and some stories are altered in order to "make a better movie."
The experience of the story is shared collectively with others who hear the same stories at the same time and in the same ways.	At best, the experience is not direct, but vicarious, and is not shared with others, unless the story is read aloud. Different readers may read differently.	Experience is vivid, but vicarious, with many layers of professional expertise, technology, equipment, and electrical energy between the story and the audience.
The audience relies on imagination for visual images.	Readers rely on imagination for visual images unless there are photos or illustrations.	No imagination is necessary. Images are provided.
Memorable stories are durable. Powers of recollection develop.	Stories are fragile. When the paper record is destroyed, the story is gone.	Stories are ephemeral. With no book and no human memory involved, one must find an electronic record.
Old-time storytellers could recall Norse sagas and Navajo Creation stories that could last many days. Ray Bradbury's book *Fahrenheit 451* acknowledges the capacity to remember.	Sometimes the literary tradition comes to our service. For example, the discovery of cuneiform clay tablets recording *The Epic of Gilgamesh* means much of the epic could be recaptured even after 3000 years.	Often, a picture is worth a thousand words. Television and other visual media can do things that a human storyteller can't do alone.

This table emphasizes the power of human connection, in which the lonely can become less lonely, the individual can find a place in the stream of humanity, and human differences can be bridged.

The scholar Walter Fisher also emphasized human connection in Fisher's *Narrative Paradigm*. By way of explaining it, he contrasts what he calls the narrative paradigm with the rational-world paradigm.

RATIONAL-WORLD PARADIGM	NARRATIVE PARADIGM
Humans are essentially rational beings.	Humans are essentially storytelling beings.
Some people argue that the only discourse that is truly informative is scientific discourse. They argue that only it is really factual. Such a paradigm would direct our understanding and inquiry in specific directions, such as systematic observation and perhaps experimentation, in order to discover facts.	It can also be argued that people are often motivated by concepts other than facts. We are motivated by love, beauty, desire, imagination, courage, and many other things that are not measurable. We can be "transported" by literature, mythology, rhetoric, and other nonscientific human creations.
Argument follows clear-cut inferential patterns and structures (such as syllogism).	We create and communicate symbols ultimately as stories meant to give order to human existence.
The world is a set of logical puzzles that can be solved through systematic analysis and the application of reason.	Metaphor counts as a way of relating "truth" about the human condition.

Walter Fisher insists that humans are storytelling creatures, and his view of storytelling is broad. It is found in many kinds of human discourse. Our conversations are full of all kinds of accounts. Television news refers to news pieces as stories. They are narrative, sequential accounts that include characters, events, and meanings.

Humans make decisions based on good reasons, says Fisher, and "history, biography, culture, and character determine what we consider good reasons." In other words, what makes sense to us might appear dangerous, stupid, or even unethical to people in some other cultures. The way we understand the world is learned through cultural experience. For instance, living in an individualistic or in a collectivist culture influences the way we decide what's important. We will address individualism and collectivism in Chapter 1.

While the term storytelling has come to refer to many kinds of communication activity (such as news reporting, film making, social networking and the like), here the emphasis is on the face-to-face oral narrative as a practice that strengthens cultural beliefs, attitudes, and values. The very circumstance of being together in the presence of the storyteller maintains social cohesiveness where it already exists, and has enormous potential to establish it where needed. Hence, the title *Storytelling: Reflecting on Oral Narratives and Cultures* narrows the focus of this book to the unmediated interpersonal sharing of cultural ideals through traditional folktales.

The meanings to be discovered in stories can be profoundly important. By now, much of the world is literate, but not all. Some languages have no written form. Other languages have written forms, but the people who speak those languages must rely on their power of listening and recalling. Our hominid ancestors relied wholly upon listening and recall when they learned their own histories, their spiritual truths, and their strategies for subsistence. Their educations relied on stories.

Today, though we can write lists, read instructions (when all else fails), and communicate through the written word, we still have important ways of using stories. We find storytelling used in counseling, hospice care, drug abuse prevention and recovery, bullying prevention, and team building within business and other kinds of organizations. The characters represent courage, or virtue, or wisdom. The other symbols represent authority, resilience, unity, or transformation. The actions inform us of our choices and empower us to find our own wisdom.

There are ancient stories, legends, explanatory stories, ghost stories, and fun stories. We will be exploring some of each, drawing from many cultures.

HUMAN EXPERIENCE

Ultimately, however, this volume is as much about real live human beings as it is about the oral tradition. We're concerned about the cultural experience, the ways in which different cultural groups experience their cultural milieu and the larger world. While there is an overarching American culture, we cannot claim that all Americans find it comfortable.

Mainstream American Culture

In general, we live in a society that values certain things, such as privacy, the right to vote, opportunity for success, financial security, youth, looks, style, technology, and upward mobility. You need only to assess the advertising in print and in the media to identify the overarching values. However, not all Americans are young and good-looking. Not all Americans have access to a good education, and many have no financial security, but these remain cultural preoccupations nonetheless. Clearly, there are generational and co-cultural differences in what people value.

Let's consider the cultural differences between Manhattan, New York, and Manhattan, Kansas. Manhattan, Kansas, is in the American heartland, almost exactly in the middle of the contiguous United States. In 2009, there were just under 53,000 residents in that city. By contrast, Manhattan, New York, one of five boroughs in New York City, is the home of nearly 1.6 million people. It is a coastal city, which contributes to its reputation as an international and cosmopolitan center, and a center of fashion, finance, tourism, entertainment and the arts. If we suddenly transplanted someone from New York to Kansas, they would most likely be disoriented and would have difficulty knowing how to make a life in this new place. Likewise, if we took someone from Kansas and let them out in New York, it would be equally bewildering and difficult to understand.

Co-cultures

Co-cultures are smaller groups within the overarching culture. These groups tend to have values that differ from that of the larger culture, but are not necessarily in conflict with them. If you attended a high school of any size, you are already acquainted with some co-cultures. You co-existed with athletes ("jocks"), technical wizards ("geeks"), "Goths," "preppies," "tree-huggers," and others. Typically, these communities clustered together with the like-minded, but were still tolerant of the other groups. This does not mean there was no discord in high school; it simply means that many differences were accepted.

Larger co-cultures are easily identified in places like Washington, D.C., Hollywood, Aspen, and Lancaster County, Pennsylvania. They can be found in all branches of the military, the giant financial institutions, the research universities, and the many diverse religions. Each co-culture embraces a specific set of shared values. Let's consider the cases of the Lancaster Amish and the culture of Hollywood, with its motion picture industry. We would find that the Amish would reject the glamour, the noise, and the competition that typify Hollywood, and instead, embrace obedience to God. These are almost entirely opposite the values that would be embraced in Hollywood.

We also know of groups whose values are in direct conflict with the overarching society. Some of these groups are hobos, Hell's Angels, illegal drug distributors, and so on. However, before we lump them together as similar, we need to be aware of some fundamental differences. Hobos, for instance, are simply unwilling to conform to the voracious expectations of the economy. They prefer not to be trapped in 30-year mortgages. But many have served in the military and have skills, which they use in making an income in their itinerant lives. In fact, we know of one hobo who traveled about working as a high school math teacher. When asked for his address, he gave it as "1993 Ford Road." We're reminded of the mnemonic saying: A hobo travels and works; a tramp travels and doesn't work; a bum doesn't travel and doesn't work. Therein we already detect countercultural differences. Hobos have a highly developed culture, which includes a specific code of ethics concerning the treatment of others and their own self-presentation.

The Hell's Angels are organized outlaw motorcycle gangs. They choose to be guided by their own laws and principles—which they do have, though it might not be obvious to most of us. They're highly cohesive and loyal to each other and others they regard as friends. But if they perceive a threat, they can be dangerous. Hell's Angels have their own styles of highly symbolic self-presentation.

We should remember that being a member of a co-culture is not necessarily stigmatized. There are well-regarded, well-represented co-cultures, such as the Mormon Church, NASA, New York City firefighters, athletes, and others who are members of

Underrepresented cultural groups: Groups that have distinctive cultural characteristics that have often been used to exclude them from full participation in social, economic, political, legal, or educational institutions. These cultural characteristics can be ethnic, racial, or religious.

In the United States, some of these cultural groups are African American, Native American, various Hispanic cultures, Native Hawaiian, Native Alaskan, Creole, Amish, Gypsy, Arab American, and many immigrant groups.

When we refer to certain cultural groups as underrepresented, we mean, for example, that they don't appear as members of Congress in the same proportions they occupy in the general population. They often have limited access to quality education and health care. Sometimes they receive unequal treatment in the legal system. If they're poor, they're stigmatized. Moreover, other consequences have included prejudice, stereotyping, discrimination, misinformation, mistrust, hostility, hate speech, and neglect.

respected co-cultures. These special groups have their own codes of ethics, bodies of knowledge, social roles, and stories. They decide their own heroes based on their specific cultural values.

There are, however, many people in underrepresented cultural groups.

One way to illustrate underrepresentation is to compare the number of members of a cultural group in the general population with the number in particular institutions. For instance, the Census Bureau tells us that 12.9% of the U.S. population was African American in 2009, but we know that there have been only two African American justices in the U.S. Supreme Court. There have been 112 Supreme Court justices since its beginning in 1732, and if the proportion of African American justices matched the general population, we should have seen eight or nine African American justices by the year 2000. By the same token, we should have had at least one Native American justice, but we have had none. They are numerically underrepresented in the U.S. Supreme Court.

However, numeric underrepresentation is not simply a matter of numbers. It turns out to be a matter of historical relationships with the dominant culture. Although some effort has been made to include Blacks, Native Americans, women, and others into the mainstream of American experience, the results are disappointing, and we're often at a loss to explain why. We believed that after the Emancipation Proclamation, free Black people would enjoy the benefits of American society equally, but they have not. Even the oral literature of African Americans was sometimes dominated by agendas not of their own making.

When we consider the African American folktales available to us, we need to use some judgment. From the *Storytelling Encyclopedia*, we find:

> Among the best known of all African American folklore are the Uncle Remus tales, collected by journalist Joel Chandler Harris and first published in the Atlanta *Constitution*. Harris published the tales collectively in 1880 in *Uncle Remus, His Songs and His Sayings: The Folklore of the Old Plantation*, and later in *Nights with Uncle Remus and Brer Rabbit*. Brer Rabbit is a classic trickster figure in these tales, a rascally character playing hoaxes on a host of less cunning creatures who cross his path. ... As well known as these stories are, however, they do not give a complete or even very accurate picture of African American

folklore. As a collector of folklore, Harris, as a Euro-American, faced at least two problems. First, he was working in a period in which many white folklorists were invested in perpetuating the myth of the "happy slave," a position suggested by Harris's invented framework of the contended African slave telling nursery stories to white children. And second, the fact that Harris was a white collector of these tales probably affected both which tales the informants told, as well as how they told them. (19)

Reading any authoritative works on African American history, we quickly find that there has not been such a thing as a "happy slave," and, in fact, some scholars argue that African American people are not naturally or inherently slaves. This is a view expressed by Dr. Karanja Carroll, a scholar and professor of Black Studies, who explains that the fact that they were enslaved means that their role ran opposite their fundamental nature, and that in fact, all enslaved people lived miserable lives without the dignity, autonomy, or citizenship, and often, without even the basic human necessities. Moreover, they have been underrepresented in the profoundest ways. In fact, in the 17th and 18th centuries, churches and political institutions delineated their subordinate positions. After slavery was abolished, political structures still maintained their positions as nonvoters and nonprofessionals.

We are fortunate, however, to find some examples of stories that appear realistic. Some of these stories are in more recent voices than that of Joel Chandler Harris. The following tale illustrates African-American under-representation in a stark way. It's a tale Daryl Cumber Dance learned from her mother.

Jim Crow Laws: These laws prohibited contact between white and black people in the Southern and border states between 1876 and 1965. They enforced the "separate but equal" status for Black Americans. Although facilities for Black people were legally required to be equal to white facilities, they were not.

Jim Crow laws were overruled by the Civil Rights Act of 1964. However, this act did not stop de facto segregation, which could still be achieved through rules about neighborhood school attendance, for instance, in many cities.

The earlier Civil Rights Act of 1866 gave freedmen some legal rights, but not the right to vote. The 14th and 15th Amendments to the Constitution guaranteed civil rights and the right to vote. However, as late as 1965, even after the Civil Rights Act of 1964, other measures were used in order to prevent the Black vote. The Alabama Literacy Test was required of Black citizens. The test was long and asked for several obscure answers about American government. Wrong answers were taken as evidence that the individual could not read sufficiently to vote. The test is no longer used.

The term Jim Crow comes from an early minstrel show blackface character/caricature that became widely popular.

I'll Go As Far As Memphis

This Black man had lived in Mississippi all his life, but times had gotten so bad there with Jim Crow and lynching and all that he decided that he would go North like a lot of his people. So he went North and he was doing fine. I mean he had gotten to the top. Then one of his friends called him and begged him to come back to Mississippi and help his folks because times were so hard. So he thought and he thought. Finally he said, "I'm going to have to talk to the Lord about it."

So his friend called him again, and said, "Well, what did the Lord say?"

He said, "I told the Lord that my friends in Mississippi needed my help and I asked Him if He would please go back South with me."

"So what did God say?" his friend inquired.

He said, "The Lord told me, 'I'll go as far as Memphis.'" (55)

This anecdote expresses a cynical frame of mind in which even the Lord finds it difficult to cope with the racism and brutality still ongoing in the South.

Among the most salient underrepresented groups are African Americans. Roger Abrahams, anthropology professor and collector of tales from the Black tradition, says, "Humorous and often subversive, these [African American] stories commonly report an especially brazen or subtle act in the face of Old Master's authority ... " Furthermore, he points out a perception at the bedrock of stereotypes: " ... one of the most virulent white stereotypes of blacks was the imputation of stupidity to the slaves, especially with regard to their supposed inability to employ language effectively. ... " He then provides us with a humorous and "openly hostile black-white stor[y]."

John Outruns the Lord

You know, before surrender Old Massa had a slave named John, and John always prayed every night before he went to bed. His prayer was for God to come get him and take him to Heaven right away. He didn't even want to take time to die. He wanted the Lord to come and get him just like he was—boots, socks, and all. He'd get down on his knees and say: "O Lord, it's more and again your humble servant, knee-bent and body-bowed, my heart beneath my knees and my knees in some lonesome valley, crying for mercy while mercy can be found. O Lord, I'm asking you in the humblest way I know how to be so pleased as to come in your fiery chariot and take me to your Heaven and its immortal glory. Come, Lord, you know I have such a hard time. Old Massa works me so hard, and doesn't give me time to rest. So come, Lord, with peace in one hand and pardon in the other, and take me away from this sin-sorrowing world. I'm tired and I want to go home."

One night, Old Massa passed John's shack and heard him begging the Lord to come get him in his fiery chariot and take him away; so he made up his mind to find out if John meant it. He went on up to the big house and got himself a bed sheet and came on back. He threw the sheet over his head and knocked on the door.

John quit praying and asked: "Who's that?" Old Massa said: "It's me, John, the Lord, coming with my fiery chariot to take you away from this sin-sick world." Right under the bed John found he had some business. He told his wife: "Tell him I'm not here, Liza."

At first Liza didn't say anything at all, but the Lord kept right on calling John: "Come on, John, and go to Heaven with me where you won't have to plow any more furrows and hoe any more corn. Come on, John." Liza said, "John isn't here, Lord. You have to come back another time."

The Lord said, "Well then, Liza, you'll do." Liza whispered and said, "John, come out from underneath that bed and go on with the Lord. You've been begging him to come get you. Now go on with him."

John was back under the bed not saying a mumbling word. The Lord is out on the doorstep, and he kept on calling.

Liza said, "John, I thought you were so anxious to get to Heaven. Come out and go on with God." John said, "Didn't you hear him say, 'You'll do'? Why don't you go with him?"

"I'm not going anywhere. You're the one who's been whooping and hollering for him to come get you, and if you don't come out from under that bed, I'm going to tell God you're here."

Old Massa, still pretending he was God, said, "Come on, Liza, you'll do." Liza said, "O Lord, John is right here underneath the bed." "Come on, John, and go to Heaven with me to immortal glory." John crept out from under the bed and went to the door and cracked it; and when he saw all that white standing on the doorstep, he jumped back. He said, "O Lord, I can't go to Heaven with you in your fiery chariot in these old dirty britches; give me time to put on my Sunday pants."

John fumbled around a long time changing his shirt, and then he went back to the door, but Old Massa was still on the doorstep. John had nothing else to change into so he opened the door a little piece and said, "O Lord, I'm ready to go to Heaven with you in your fiery chariot, but the radiance of your countenance is so bright, I can't come out with you right there. Stand back just a little way please." Old Massa stepped back a little.

John looked out again and said, "O Lord, you know that poor humble me is less than the dust beneath your shoe soles. And the radiance of your countenance is so bright I can't come out by you. Please, please, Lord, in your tender mercy, stand back a little bit farther." Old Massa stepped back a little bit more.

John looked out again and said, "O Lord, Heaven is so high and we're so low; you're so great and I'm so weak: and your strength is too much for us poor suffering sinners. So once more and again your humble servant is knee-bent and body-bowed asking you one more favor before I step into your fiery chariot and go to Heaven with you and wash in your glory—be so pleased in your tender mercy as to stand back just a bit farther."

Old Massa stepped back a step or two more, and out that door John came like a streak of lightning. He ran all across the pumpkin patch, through the cotton, over the pasture. John ran and here comes Old Massa right behind him. By the time they hit the cornfield John was way ahead of Old Massa.

Back in the shack one of the children was crying and she asked Liza. "Mama, you reckon God's going to catch Papa and carry him to Heaven with him?"

"Shut your mouth, talking that foolishness!" Liza answered the child. "You know the Lord can't outrun your pappy—specially when he's barefooted at that." (278–280)

It's easy to follow the action and find the humor in it, but the hostility is salient as well. The reference to the white sheet starkly reminds the audience of the Ku Klux Klan and its implacable hatred of Black, Jewish, Native American, and other groups. It is not God at all chasing John, but an ungodly white man in a white sheet, and John is quite willing to outrun him in the story, though historically, African Americans have not been so lucky. Even after the end of slavery, they have found that there are still obstacles uniquely in place for them.

Racism, simply put, is the belief in the inherent superiority of a particular race and the inferiority of others. The expression of racism takes various forms: hate speech, hate crimes, avoidance, discrimination, racial "jokes," and tokenism.

We might be tempted to think of racism and discrimination as things of the past, but modern forms continue. These new forms are more pernicious than older forms of blatant racism because they are framed in subtler ways, making it more difficult to criticize them.

Before moving on, let's clarify what racism is.

Overturning the Melting Pot

We often hear the United States referred to as a "melting pot," but that term is now undergoing some serious scrutiny. The term seems to assume that when people arrive in this country, they should quickly toss away all traces of their former culture to Americanize themselves as quickly and fully as possible. In this way, it might be assumed, we can all conform to a homogeneous American model.

In the first place, we should not assume everyone wants to walk away from their identities, traditions, and values. The various cultures all have their celebrations, their customs, and their other practices that might differ from those of our mainstream, but might provide a good model for us. For instance, the daily family table that was once the pattern in the United States is fading away for reasons connected to the changes around us: the need for the second job, the after-school activities of the children, the professional expectations that impact family life. However, in many immigrant families, the family table is where they meet, acknowledge, and support each other as family; strengthen their social and religious values; and reaffirm their emotional connection.

There are other terms that have been proposed as replacements for "melting pot." The term "pluralism," for instance, attempts to emphasize a context of enriched by cultural difference. However, it's easy to assume it refers to a context in which all cultural groups are equally accepted and vibrant. However, our own creations of the Chinese Exclusion Act, the Japanese American internments after Pearl Harbor, and the Alabama Literacy Test of 1965 show that not all groups are equally treated. Finally, another term that has been proposed is "cultural mosaic." While not perfect, this is the term that seems to imply that there are many cultures in many stages of development: some just beginning to develop their communities, some reaching full cultural vitality, and some past their peak and in decline. Of the three terms, this seems the most representative of the reality we have now.

When we begin examining the folktales from traditions beyond our own, it can be confusing and bewildering. We may want to find the common ground that unites all people. However, we will find we must admit that our experiences have been too diverse, our assumptions about creation are too different, and our values too varied to allow us to find that common ground so easily. Instead, we should find that the differences are fascinating and enriching. It's in the differences that we can learn the most about the breadth of human experience. It's in the differences that we can find out our choices in how to live. It's in accepting, even celebrating, the differences that we begin to understand the deep importance of cultural diversity.

Modern racism, or "reasonable" racism: This is a pernicious type of racism wherein an individual denies being racist while having racist attitudes. It occurs as much among educated people as among the uneducated. People who deny that they are racist have learned how to verbalize their prejudice in a "reasonable" way.

One example of reasonable, or subtle, racism occurs with the desegregation of schools in some cities where busing is proposed as a way to distribute cultural and racial diversity among several schools. Parents might say they support diversity but oppose busing their children (usually to largely Black schools) because they don't want their child spending so much time on the bus.

Another example occurs in some cases of prejudice against immigrants. No objection to ethnicity is overtly expressed, but opposition to non-English speakers or illegal aliens is expressed and defended. Scholar Neil Brick explains that one place where modern ("reasonable") racism appears is the English-only movement. He says that movement "justifies racist and nativist biases below a cover of American patriotism." Nobody argues against the usefulness of knowing the language spoken where you are. However, the English-only emphasis would provide an undeserved barrier to those who have not yet had a realistic opportunity to learn the language. Other instances of modern racism occur when people express the misguided opinion that "aliens" pay no taxes, but only burden our schools and welfare system.

From *Crow and Weasel* by Barry Lopez

"I would ask you to remember only this one thing," said Badger. "The stories people tell have a way of taking care of them. If stories come to you, care for them. And learn to give them away when they are needed. Sometimes a person needs a story more than food to stay alive. That is why we put these stories in each other's memory. This is how people care for themselves. One day you will be good storytellers. Never forget these obligations." (60)

REFERENCES

Afro-American Folktales: Stories from Black Traditions in the New World. (1985) (Ed.) Roger D. Abrahams. New York: Pantheon Books.

Brick, N. (2008). "Modern Racism and Its Psychosocial Effects on Society—Including a Discussion About Bilingual Education." Retrieved April 2011. http://bilingualeducationmass.wordpress.com/category/modern-racism-and-its-psychosocial-effects-on-society-including-a-discussion-about-bilingual-education/

Carroll, K. K. (personal communication, August 2010).

Fisher, Walter (1987). *Human Communication as Narration: Toward a Philosophy of Reason, Value, and Action.* (Studies in Rhetoric/Communication) University of South Carolina Press.

"I'll Go as Far as Memphis." (2002) In (Ed. Daryl Cumber Dance) *400 Years of African American Folklore from My People: An Anthology.* New York: W. W. Norton.

Lopez, Barry (1990). *Crow and Weasel.* New York: Farrar, Straus and Giroux.

"Race, Racism and the Law: Examples of Jim Crow Laws." University of Dayton School of Law. Retrieved April 2011. http://academic.udayton.edu/race/02rights/crow02.htm

Storytelling Encyclopedia: Historical, Cultural, and Multiethnic Approaches to Oral Traditions Around the World. (Ed.) David Adams Leeming. (1997). Phoenix: Oryx Press.

U.S. Census Bureau QuickFacts. Retrieved April 2010. http://quickfacts.census.cov/qfd/states/00000.html

"We the People: American Indians and Alaska Natives in the United States. Census 2000 Special Reports." Issued February 2006 by Stella U. Ogunwole. U.S. Census Bureau. Retrieved April 2011. http://www.census.gov/population/www/socdemo/race/censr-28.pdf

CHAPTER ONE

The Meaning of Culture

Cultural differences enrich the human experience. Although a visit into a culture where everything is different can feel disorienting and frustrating, an understanding of those differences can provide a window to the vast variety of worldview and creative genius embodied in human beings.

At the outset, it must be said that culture is human-created. If it were merely instinctive, the differences would disappear, and with some variations provided by environmental and population pressure, there would be essentially one culture. From birth, we learn our various cultures from our surroundings: our family, our linguistic contexts, and our experience. Samovar, Porter, and McDaniel explain the process of enculturation when they say, "From infancy, members of a culture learn their patterns of behavior and ways of thinking until most of those patterns become internalized and habitual. What is special about this 'learning process' is that any normally healthy infant can be placed into any family on earth and will learn its culture and accept it as his or her own." Evidence of this process is found in the many cases of children adopted from other countries and brought up in American families. They become so thoroughly enculturated in their new families and communities that most would be mystified and unable to negotiate daily life if they suddenly returned to the cultures of their birth.

Enculturation: The process of becoming a member of a culture. Scott & Marshall say, "[I]ndividuals have constantly to learn and use, both formally and informally, the patterns of cultural behavior prescribed by that culture" (189).

A culture is a relatively coherent pattern of beliefs, attitudes, values, institutions, and behaviors. We will address beliefs, attitudes, and values in Chapter 2.

Samovar, Porter, and McDaniel tell us that "The three most enduring and influential social organizations that deal with the deep structure issues are (1) *family*, (2) *state (community)*, and (3) *religion (worldview)*. These three social organizations, working in concert, define, create, transmit, maintain, and reinforce the most crucial elements of every culture" (49). From these social organizations, we learn what's "true," what's "important," and what's "valuable." We learn, for instance, the "truth" that competition leads to excellence. Clearly, this is a truth taught within an individualist society. In a collectivist society, we might learn an equally true truth that cooperation leads to excellence. We will find other cultural contrasts too, where in one culture, individual achievement and success are important, while in another, family stability is more important. We will look at differences in values in Chapter 2.

Family, community, and religion are among the institutions that change slowly over time and in response to changing environments. Hence, they provide stability for cultural members.

Institutions: The term is widely used to describe social practices that are regularly and continuously repeated, are sanctioned and maintained by social norms, and have a major significance in the social structure. Abercrombie, Hill, and Turner have identified five complexes of institutions (124).

There are five broad categories of institutions in nearly all cultures. They are the economic, political, stratification, kinship, and cultural institutions. Let's take a look at each.

Economic institutions serve to produce and distribute goods and services. In the United States, these institutions drive business, banking, credit, and taxes. In some cultures, however, economic practices can include such things as reciprocity, or the return of favors, and collectivist land distribution, wherein the land is owned by the collective, and farming plots are distributed to families.

Economic institutions sometimes involve kinship obligations. For instance, in the wet rice farming tradition of Senegal, there are villages where a farmer gives shares of his best rice to his mother-in-law, another share to his parents, and keeps the rice with broken grains and mixed rice for himself and his children. It is a system by which nobody in the village goes hungry no matter whether or not they are able to share in the work. Elders are thereby thanked for the work and sacrifices of the past, and they are shown that they are valuable people in the community. This is far different from a common Western pattern of economics by which competition and economic advantage determine the distribution of goods and services.

A traditional Korean tale shows one perspective on the distribution of goods and services:

The Brother Who Gave Rice

Long ago, there were two brothers. They grew rice in a field.

The brothers worked hard, but they grew enough rice to fill only a few bags. Each brother took some rice home.

Younger Brother had a big family. He needed rice for his wife and children. They ate many bowls of rice each day.

Older Brother lived alone. He had only two bags of rice, but that was enough for him.

He worried about Younger Brother. "They need more rice than I do," Older Brother thought.

Then one day he had an idea.

That night, Older Brother took a bag of rice from his house. He carried it quietly to Younger Brother's house. The bag was heavy, but Older Brother did not stop.

He left the bag by the door.

Older Brother went home. He had less rice now, but he was happy. He thought about his brother's family. He slept well that night.

When Older Brother woke up the next morning, he was surprised. He still had two bags of rice!

Older Brother shook his head. He did not understand.

That night, Older Brother decided to try again. He took another bag of rice from his house. He carried it to Younger Brother's house. Again, he left the bag by the door.

Then Older Brother went home. He was tired, but he felt good. He slept well that night.

When Older Brother woke up, he saw two bags of rice again!

Older Brother thought, "This is very strange!"

That night, Older Brother took another bag of rice from the stack. He began to walk up the path.

But then he did something different. He hid behind a rock.

The moon was bright. Older Brother saw a man far away. The man was walking down the path. He was carrying something.

The man was Younger Brother! He had a bag of rice.

"YOU were bringing rice to ME!" Older Brother said.

"YOU were bringing rice to ME!" Younger Brother said.

Now the brothers understood. They were both trying to help each other!

The brothers went back to their houses. They slept very well that night.

The next night, Younger Brother's wife made a big dinner. Older Brother came to visit. Everybody sat at the table and ate many bowls of rice!

The story is not simply about the distribution of goods, but also cultural values and the importance of family as part of a social support system. As we work our way through this textbook, we'll find that many meanings can emerge from the same story. As we saw earlier, social organizations work in concert with each other to teach us the social behaviors that come to be the norm. The behavior we see in the Korean story is driven by a cultural conception of family, where family is not merely the source of our DNA and last name, but is a fundamental unit to whom we owe love, loyalty, and cooperation.

Western economic institutions emphasize capitalism, and we find that this form of economics can achieve a great deal that can't be achieved on a small scale. Within capitalism, work and production are done for pay rather than for meeting personal need. On a large scale, wealth can be concentrated in financial institutions where it becomes available for loans, investments, and industry, and where the continued accumulation of wealth is an end in itself. But as we saw in the Korean tale, the accumulation of wealth isn't equally important to everyone.

Dr. Muhammad Yunus is a Bangladeshi economist who won the Nobel Prize in Economics in 2006, after working with others to establish the Grameen Bank, a bank devoted to providing low-interest micro-loans to the very poor. The recipients of those micro-loans were then able to begin an industry or business that lifted them out of grinding poverty. Many of the early loan recipients could neither read nor write and had no collateral, so filling out application forms was out of the question for them, but overwhelmingly, they repaid the loans and continued the economic activities that kept them from relapsing into poverty.

Without knowing Dr. Yunus personally, we should be able to infer that his relationship with wealth differs from that of most financial institutions in the West, where the accumulation of wealth is an end in itself.

Political institutions regulate the use of, and access to, power. Here we find kings, chieftains, emperors, presidents, dictators, soldiers, the law, and the courts. In the Western world, we typically find the places of greatest power or authority at the national level, followed by state, regional, and local seats of authority. By now in the 21st century, most lands have been consolidated into nations that usually have a similar hierarchy. However, not all nations are headed by a president. For instance, there are still nine nations with kings. A few nations are theocracies, and in those nations, religious law is the law of the land. There are other nations yet where a head of state becomes a dictator who remains in power as long as possible, regardless of political law. In such situations, the will of the leader can be in brutal conflict with the will of the people. But what we generally seek in government is stability, well-being, and voluntary participation.

This is easier said than done, however. Dee Brown provides this example of how the political institutions worked among the Seneca:

Godasiyo the Woman Chief

At the beginning of time when America was new, a woman chief named Godasiyo ruled over an Indian village beside a large river in the East. In those days all the tribes spoke one language and lived in harmony and peace. Because Godasiyo was a wise and progressive chief, many people came from faraway places to live in her village, and they had no difficulty understanding one another.

At last the village grew so large that half the people lived on the north side of the river, and half on the south side. They spent much time canoeing back and forth to visit, attend dances, and exchange gifts of venison, hides, furs, and dried fruits and berries. The tribal council house was on the south side, which made it necessary for those who lived in the north bank to make frequent canoe trips to consult with their chief. Some complained about this, and to make it easier for everybody to cross the rapid stream, Godasiyo ordered a bridge to be built of saplings and tree limbs carefully fastened together. This bridge brought the tribe close together again, and the people praised Godasiyo for her wisdom.

Not long after this, a white dog appeared in the village, and Godasiyo claimed it for her own. Everywhere the chief went the dog followed her, and the people on the north side of the river became jealous of the animal. They spread stories that the dog was possessed by an evil spirit that would bring harm to the tribe. One day a delegation from the north bank crossed the bridge to the council house and demanded that Godasiyo kill the white dog. When she refused to do so, the delegates returned to their side of the river, and that night they destroyed the bridge.

From that time the people on the north bank and those on the south bank began to distrust each other. The tribe divided into two factions, one renouncing Godasiyo as their chief, the other supporting her. Bad feelings between them grew so deep that Godasiyo foresaw that the next step would surely lead to fighting and war. Hoping to avoid bloodshed, she called all members of the tribe who supported her to a meeting in the council house.

"Our people," she said, "are divided by more than a river. No longer is there goodwill and contentment among us. Not wishing to see brother fight against brother, I propose that those who recognize me as their chief follow me westward up the great river to build a new village."

Almost everyone who attended the council meeting agreed to follow Godasiyo westward. In preparation for the migration, they built many canoes of birch bark. Two young men who had been friendly rivals in canoe races volunteered to construct a special watercraft for their chief. With strong poles they fastened two large canoes together and then built a platform which extended over the canoes and the space between them. Upon this platform was a seat for Godasiyo and places to store her clothing. extra leggings. belts. robes, moccasins. mantles, caps. awls, needles and adornments.

At last everything was ready. Godasiyo took her seat on the platform with the white dog beside her, and the two young men who had built the craft began paddling the double canoes beneath. Behind them the chief's followers and defenders launched their own canoes which contained all their belongings. This flotilla of canoes covered the shining waters as far as anyone could see up and down the river.

After they had paddled a long distance. they came to a fork in the river. Godasiyo ordered the two young canoeists to stop in the middle of the river until the others caught up with them. In a few minutes the flotilla was divided, half of the canoes on her left. the others on her right.

The chief and the people on each side of her began to discuss the advantages and disadvantages of the two forks in the river. Some wanted to go one way. some preferred the other way. The arguments grew heated with anger. Godasiyo said that she would take whichever fork her people chose, but they could agree on neither. Finally those on the right turned the prows of their canoes up the right channel. while those on the left began paddling up the left channel. And so the tribe began to separate.

When this movement started, the two young men paddling the two canoes carrying Godasiyo's float disagreed as to which fork they should take, and they fell into a violent quarrel. The canoeist on the right thrust his paddle into the water and started toward the right, and at the same time the one on the left swung his canoe toward the left. Suddenly Godasiyo's platform slipped off its supports and collapsed into the river, carrying her with it.

Hearing the loud splash. the people on both sides turned their canoes around and tried to rescue their beloved chief. But she and the white dog, the platform, and all her belongings had sunk to the bottom, and they could see nothing but fish swimming in the clear waters.

Dismayed by this tragic happening. the people of the two divisions began to try to talk to each other, but even though they shouted words back and forth, those on the right could not understand the people on the left. and those on the left could not understand the people on the right. When Godasiyo drowned in the great river her people's language had become changed. This was how it was that the Indians were divided into many tribes spreading across America. each of them speaking a different language. (71–74)

....

The Seneca Nation, from which this story came, is an Iroquoian nation where it was common for women to be placed in the highest levels of political authority. For many generations, it was the women's councils that decided who would be chief. They were among the most powerful agents of diplomacy with other tribal groups, often deciding that the human cost of war was too great. To this very day, clan mothers still have influence in the decisions that will have an impact on the people. As we saw in the story, Godasiyo made the decisions she thought would benefit everyone. First, she had a bridge built to bring the people together. When the bridge was destroyed, Godasiyo took steps to avoid bloodshed between brothers, and moved her village. Even then, Godasiyo agreed to do the will of the people. This enactment of political authority is far unlike many of the decisions made in institutions, such as legislatures and the Internal Revenue Service, that now function to organize American society. We disagree, and we take sides within political parties, much like the people who divided themselves at the fork in the river. In the 21st century, we seem to be no better in finding agreement.

The courts are another manifestation of political institution. Because in the West we live in an adversarial society, when a suit is taken to court, one side wins and the other side loses. The outcome is never entirely positive, since one side will be dissatisfied. However, in smaller societies, when there is conflict, people go to the elders to decide how harmony can be restored to the community. For instance, if someone's cows destroy another person's garden, the council of elders will try to find a reasonable and effective way for the injured party to be compensated without bringing economic ruin to the owner of the cows. To the degree they are successful, harmony is restored. Clearly, this approach is unusual in a society where there must be official records of who is right and who is wrong.

<u>Stratification institutions</u> determine the distribution of social position and resources. Stratification institutions regulate jobs, prestige, privilege, power, pay, promotion, and wealth. Education is therefore one of our stratification institutions. Traditionally, an education from a prestigious university could pave the way to a prestigious, well-paying job. But such an education is expensive, and is out of reach to some people. Thus, we are stratified into social groups that can and cannot afford to earn a degree at the highest-ranked universities. Within the lowest quintile of our economy, there are people who, because of the dire need to work for a wage, never finished high school.

In the United States, we have a normative value of equality. This means that equality is a value we believe we should embrace. In colonial times, we rebelled against a set of royal institutions that perpetuated inequality. We probably do sincerely value the ideal of equality, but in a competitive, individualist society, we find that our economic institutions give us neither equality nor security, so we also must compete for the best educations, the best jobs, and so on.

Inequality is a reality, however much we value equality. Underrepresented groups find themselves at the bottom levels of a stratified society in all respects. Underrepresented groups are those that have distinctive cultural characteristics that are often used to exclude them from full participation in social, economic, political, legal, or educational institutions. These cultural characteristics are often ethnic, racial, or religious.

Some of these underrepresented groups are African Americans, Native Americans, Native Alaskans, Native Hawaiians, American gypsies, Arab Americans, Cajuns, Creoles, Hispanics, and other cultural groups. There are also recent immigrants, the poor, the homeless, the mentally ill, and the disabled, who find themselves very far from the levels of influence, and even self-determination. For instance, an individual who, through no fault of his or her own, must ask for assistance has to work their way through bureaucratic channels that are cumbersome and discouraging. These bureaucracies,

Race: Race is the categorization of people based on their appearance (skin, hair color and texture, facial characteristics, etc.) rather than on any legitimate genetic differences. These categories might have useful application in explaining patterns of poverty, health, employment, and other social experiences. They are not useful, however, in predicting characteristics such as intelligence, personality, attitudes, work ethic, or other values (Scott and Marshall, 543).

Racism, simply put, is the belief in the inherent superiority of a particular race and the inferiority of others. The expression of racism takes various forms: hate speech, hate crimes, avoidance, discrimination, racial "jokes," and so on.

Institutional discrimination: J. R. and C. B. Feagin tell us this term "refers to practices having a negative and differential impact on minorities and women even though the ... norms or regulations guiding those actions are carried out with no prejudice or no intent to harm ... " (31). Often carried out without intent or awareness, it is still the unfair and unequal treatment that is so entrenched in basic social institutions that it defies recognition or change.

then, are institutions of stratification, specifically organized to keep records and control the amount of assistance anyone gets.

Furthermore, there is some evidence that socially advantaged people have greater access to good health care, education, and lawyers, when they need them. We find that among prison inmates, convicts are disproportionately poor. In the United States, they might have been assigned a lawyer for the purposes of a "fair and speedy trial," but financially, they couldn't sustain a more vigorous defense.

Moreover, much as we might dislike it, racism is still alive and influential.

Racial dynamics are so complicated and intertwined that positive change has been slow in coming. First, many are confused about what racism is; they often believe any form of discrimination is racism. Moreover, there are abundant misperceptions about the purpose of Affirmative Action, and those misperceptions lead to further misperceptions about whether Affirmative Action is fair. Too often, it is believed that Affirmative Action gives unfair advantage to the undeserving and the unqualified.

Scholar Bonilla-Silva explains:

Nowadays, except for members of white supremacist organizations, few whites in the United States claim to be "racist." Most whites assert they "don't see any color, just people"; that although the ugly face of discrimination is still with us, it is no longer the central factor determining minorities' life chances; and finally, that like Dr. Martin Luther King Jr., they aspire to live in a society where "people are judged by the content of their character, not by the color of their skin." More poignantly, most whites insist that minorities (especially blacks) are the ones responsible for whatever 'race problem" we have in this country. They publicly denounce blacks for "playing the race card," for demanding the maintenance of unnecessary and divisive race-based programs, such as affirmative action, and for crying "racism" whenever they are criticized by whites. Most whites believe that if blacks and other minorities would just stop thinking about the past, work hard, and complain less (particularly about racial discrimination), then Americans of all hues could "all get along." (1)

Bonilla-Silva shows us how many unrealistic and naive perceptions are compounded into a view that is entirely unhelpful. Yet the truth is complicated, and many don't understand that institutional racism does a great deal more than personal racism in presenting obstacles to nonwhite groups.

How does institutional discrimination exert itself, even when individuals are not racist? An example will be helpful in explaining this. Institutional discrimination occurs when banks and other mortgage lenders follow institutional policies that assess "risk," and then give favorable terms to white borrowers and unfavorable terms to applicants of color, who have lower incomes and are seen as less likely to repay a loan. For instance, white borrowers typically get lower interest rates and pay a lower down payment, especially if they're buying a home in a "good neighborhood." The impact of even a small difference in interest rate means a difference of many thousands of dollars over the life of the mortgage. Furthermore, home buyers of color are generally steered toward more or less segregated neighborhoods. A similar phenomenon exerts itself when renters seeking housing in predominantly white neighborhoods encounter resistance when they are told that the vacant apartment was just leased to someone else. In this case, however, it is probable that personal bias could be a factor. These processes do exist, and they are commonplace. They do not accord with our normative value of fairness.

Our normative values of equality and fairness are reflected in this Burmese story from Sharon Creeden:

The Fisherman and the King's Chamberlain

Once there was a King who could not eat any meal unless it included a dish of fried fish. One day, there blew a great storm, and fishermen could not catch any fish. The King could not eat any breakfast because there was no fried fish, and he was very annoyed. Lunchtime came, but there was no fish, and the King was very angry. Dinnertime approached, but still there was no prospect of any fried fish, and the King now grew desperate. "Let it be announced by beat of gong and drum," ordered he, "that the fisherman who brings me but one single fish will be given any reward that he may name." However, the storm continued to rage, and the waters remained turbulent.

At last at dusk, a Fisherman, trying with a mere line and hook, caught a fat and oily fish, and he ran with all his might to the King's palace. The guards, seeing the fish in the Fisherman's hand, threw open the gates, and the Fisherman reached the King's chamber without hindrance. But at the chamber door, the Chamberlain said, "Promise me half your reward and I will let you in."

"One-tenth," promised the Fisherman.

"Oh, no," said the Chamberlain, "One half, and no less."

"Agreed," replied the Fisherman, and in great glee, the Chamberlain announced to the King the arrival of a Fisherman with a fish. The King, in great joy, seized hold of the fish, and the Fisherman's hand, and rushed into the kitchen.

After the fish had been fried, the dinner laid before the King, and the King had eaten, he sat back hugging his well-filled stomach, and asked, "Fisherman, name your reward. Do you want to have a priceless ruby, or a well-paid post, or a pretty maid from the queen's bower?"

"No, Sire, no, Sire," replied the Fisherman, falling on his knees. "I want twenty lashes with your cane."

"The poor fellow is flabbergasted," mused the King, "and he does not know what he is saying." So he said gently to the Fisherman, "My man, you mean twenty rubies, or twenty elephants, or even twenty horses."

"No, Sire, no, Sire," replied the Fisherman. "I want just twenty lashes with your cane."

"I am sorry," sighed the King, "But I must keep my promise and give you what you ask." So saying, he took up a cane and beat the Fisherman gently.

"No, Sire, no, Sire," said the Fisherman, "not so soft, Sire, please hit me hard." The King, feeling annoyed, wielded the cane with some vigor, but when he had given the Fisherman ten lashes, to his astonishment he saw the Fisherman jump away.

"Have I hit you too hard?" the King inquired with concern and pity.

"No, Sire, no, Sire," explained the Fisherman, "but the remaining ten lashes are your Chamberlain's share."

The poor Chamberlain now had to confess what he had done, but pleaded, "My Lord, I asked for a half share of his reward, and not of his punishment."

"But this is my reward and not my punishment," argued the Fisherman. The King sent for the Princess Learned-in-the-Law to come and decide the case.

"My Lord King," said the Princess Learned-in-the-Law after she had arrived and listened to the two litigants. "The Chamberlain and the Fisherman were partners in a business, to wit, to supply a fish to the King, and they agreed to share. But my Lord, in a partnership, the agreement to share does not mean that only the profits are to be shared, but it means that gain and loss, income and expenditure, success and failure, reward and punishment, are to be equally shared."

The King accepted the judgment of the Princess, and gave the Chamberlain ten good lashes with his cane. Then he said, "The partnership is now dissolved, as the business has ended. As a consequence, however, I order that the Chamberlain be dismissed for corruption and disloyalty, and the Fisherman appointed in his place." (43–44)

This story is an example of the supremacy of law; even the King was obligated to obey. Further, it was established law. The king could not simply change the law at will. In addressing questions about the law, he turned to a young woman whose expertise was greater than his, though she also lacked the authority to change the law. Whether or not such relationships actually exist any longer in Burma, now called Myanmar, the social arrangement appears to be traditional. More recently, however, the government of Myanmar is a military government in which political dissent is not tolerated.

Early in this chapter, we found that at the bedrock of culture, institutions were slow to change. How, then, did the kingdom of Burma so swiftly become the Union of Myanmar? Political upheaval, as we can see in the history of Russia and China, is a brutal experience for people when the old, reliable patterns and institutions are swept away, and those who are slow to adapt suffer greatly.

Kinship institutions deal with marriage, the family, and the socialization of the young. In the Western world, nuclear families, consisting of two married, heterosexual parents and their biological children, are considered the ideal pattern. The ideal persists, even though modern realities now present us with other family configurations. We now find single parents, remarried couples and their stepchildren, gay parents, adoptive parents, and grandparents bringing up their grandchildren. Whatever configuration a family takes, it is still the major source of teaching about cultural realities. The rules of human interaction are first taught here, where table manners are taught, along with the rules about not interrupting others, and the use of acceptable language in front of grownups. Moreover, gender expectations are impressed in no uncertain terms. Here is where we learn that a boy may not cry or run away from a fight, and that girls may not get angry and beat up boys—it's not ladylike. We learn that boys are better at math and science, and that girls are better at the humanities. Fortunately, these ideas, too, change gradually, and we find that the daughters of Rosie the Riveter are encouraged to take much wider latitude in following their intellectual talent.

Cultural institutions are concerned with religious, scientific, and artistic activities. These institutions include churches, music, arts, medicine, and scientific research. Earlier we saw that Samovar, Porter, and McDaniel emphasized the central importance of religion (worldview). From that, we can infer that even people who do not see themselves as religious still have a worldview, or a view of the larger reality that explains its events. Later chapters will look at religion and medicine. Here, we consider music and art.

Music and the arts have such a central presence in the West that even 30-second media commercials must have music and drama. The central character might be a car, but it's a heroic car, a car that dramatically prevails over all terrains, all weather, and all other cars.

However, we can also find interconnections between music and art and political pageantry. The ceremonial swearing-in of a new president is followed by a rousing rendition of "Hail to the Chief." In Europe, we might find processions of royals and popes—all accompanied by music composed especially for the occasion, and surrounded by stained glass, banners, and other symbols signifying highly developed and culturally specific meanings.

Inequality: This term usually refers to social inequality, or the ways in which economic rewards, access to education and health care, and fair treatment within the legal system benefit some social groups more than others. Scott and Marshall emphasize that in human society and in capitalism, inequality is inevitable, but that view ignores the scarcity of rewards for people of color (306).

Inequality is closely linked to the concept of life-chances, or the likelihood that an individual can achieve social advancement, given his or her demographic circumstances at the outset. Advancement depends on a number of variables, and these include many social realities, such as race, poverty, and educational attainment (363). Other obstacles might include discrimination, wherein people of color are hired only to low-paying jobs. It would be an error to believe that the presence of a single person of color in a high social position means that all life-chances are equal. For example, even though we have a Black President, there are still many obstacles against the advancement of other people of color.

Scott, J. and Marshall, G. (2005). *Oxford Dictionary of Sociology*. New York: Oxford.

Cultural institutions develop over centuries and tend to endure. They are the bedrock of culture. We find that other cultural phenomena seem to emerge rapidly and fade away, but these events—events such as the Agricultural Revolution, the Industrial Revolution, the shift from feudalism to mercantilism, and so on—are not at the fundamental bedrock. They are important changes, but do not contribute to social or cultural stability. The Industrial Revolution, for instance, increased the pace of urbanization, undermined cottage industries, and had deadly impacts on environmental conditions more quickly than medical knowledge developed to counteract the effects of crowding and disease.

Still more ephemeral change happens in the field of electronic technology. Computer technology, not widely available until the late 1970s, has gone through many incarnations, and now the industry no longer supports technology that was new only 40 years ago. Surprisingly, these developments impact human behavior. For instance, a whole new generation of students does not know how to put a sheet of paper into a typewriter, a crucial piece of equipment for a student only 30 years ago. But these contraptions are not at the foundation of culture. They will not endure; innovation will continue.

REFERENCES

Abercrombie, N., Hill, S., and Turner, B. (1988). *Dictionary of Sociology*. New York: Penguin.

Bonilla-Silva, E. (2010). *Racism Without Racists: Color-Blind Racism & Racial Inequality in Contemporary America*. Third Edition. New York: Roman & Littlefield Publishers.

Brown, D. (1993). *Dee Brown's Folktales of the Native American Retold for Our Times*. New York: Henry Holt and Company.

Creeden, S. (1994). *Fair is Fair: World Folktales of Justice*. Little Rock: August House.

Feagin, J. R. and C. B (1978). *Discrimination American Style: Institutional Racism and Sexism*. Englewood Cliffs, NJ: Prentice-Hall.

Samovar, L., Porter, R., and McDaniel, E. (2010). *Communication Between Cultures*. Boston: Wadsworth Cengage.

Scott, J. and Marshall, G. (2005). *Oxford Dictionary of Sociology*. New York: Oxford University Press.

Yang, D. J. (no publication date). *The Brother Who Gave Rice*. Carmel, CA: Hampton-Brown.

CHAPTER TWO

The Purposes of Story

Most of the people who have ever lived learned through what we refer to as the oral tradition. Before the development of cuneiform and other ancient kinds of writing, the transmission of learning was done with speech and listening. Hominids and humans later learned the location of herds and pasture. They learned about the creation of the world and its human and nonhuman inhabitants. They listened to stories about important historic events, of gods and spirits, of great migrations, and of heroes and wise ones. They learned why things are the way they are.

Through the spoken word, they learned how to live, how to cooperate for hunting and farming, how to share. They learned how to make families and how to communicate with the world of spirit. They learned the important events of the past. Almost all knowledge was shared through the spoken word.

Most languages by now have written forms, but it was not always so. Before writing developed, information, instruction, history, opinion, propaganda, hero stories, and folktales were transmitted face to face. Interim steps on the way to writing were the symbolic markers in sacred or significant places. Many petroglyphs, or rock paintings, are still visible on rock faces in North America, Australia, North Africa, Europe, and

China. The meanings of the symbols were still explained through the spoken word. Even after writing was invented, it followed a general pattern wherein the educated classes could read and write, but ordinary people did not—and for a long time, books were copied by hand, and were so expensive that they were far out of reach.

In pre-literate times, stories contributed most heavily to the cohesiveness of human societies. While some stories were histories, genealogies, and hero stories that strengthened the cultural identities of individuals, a few provided moral guidance, but many others simply brought people together to be entertained. The gathering of people is significant, for the shared experience of story, time, and place contributed to the social cohesiveness of a community. It contributed to cultural vitality, coordination, cultural identity, and survival (Cole, xvii).

Theodor Gaster tells us that among the oldest stories was *The Epic of Gilgamesh*, a story thought to have been written on cuneiform clay tablets as early as 1700 BC. In the city of Uruk, Gilgamesh was a glorious, intelligent, powerful, radiant king, but his brutality was breathtaking. The cultural reality in Uruk was a steep hierarchy in which only the gods were more powerful than the king. Although only fragments of the epic were retrieved, we know the story addresses the issues of power, loss of innocence, loneliness, and the human milieu, and its messages about inner character reverberate even now.

We know that Homer recorded stories that were older than he. We know he worked in the bardic tradition, which means that he sang or chanted his tales. The *Iliad* and the *Odyssey* were old stories of mythic heroes and must have evoked pride in cultural identity. We know little about Homer, but it is said that he was blind, so we don't know how he would have written those stories he passed down from his ancestors to the descendants of his generation, but we are fortunate to have that cultural treasure.

Beowulf is another hero epic from Norse tradition, in which the monster Grendel had virtually superhuman power for evil, yet was defeated by a courageous and powerful man. We believe the saga was composed sometime between the 7th and 10th centuries. Interestingly, Grendel's mother also had to be overcome. Perhaps this is an allegory or a cautionary message about confronting not just the face of evil, but the root of evil as well. If so, we could consider the epic to be not only a hero story, but also a moral tale.

At the same time, traditional stories perpetuated in China, Ireland, Africa, India, Australia—wherever there were people who shared a language. Scholar Jack Zipes describes and explains the backdrop for the creation and perpetuation of these stories. He tells us that "folk tales were autonomous reflectors of actual and possible normative behavior which could strengthen social bonds or create more viable ones" (6). Moreover, "the folk tale was (and still is) an oral narrative form cultivated by non-literate and literate people to express the manner in which they perceived and perceive nature and their social order and their wish to satisfy their needs and wants. ... [T]he folk tale originated as far back as the Megalithic period and ... both non-literate and literate people have been the carriers and transformer of the tales" (7). He goes on to point out "a shift in the narrative perspective and style which not only altered the original folk perspective and reinterpreted the experience of the people for them but also endowed the contents with new ideology" (10). When stories were committed to print, they served literate people and excluded those who could not read. Print transformed original meanings and sought to "legitimize the aristocratic standard of living ... " (10). This goes far to explain the many versions of stories collected by the Brothers Grimm. Many of us would be astounded by a reading or a hearing of the oldest versions of Little Red Riding Hood. Orenstein tells us that "Once upon a time, hundreds of years ago, 'Little Red Riding Hood' was a bawdy morality tale for adults, quite different from the story we know today" (3).

Shakespeare, alternatively referred to as the Bard of Avon and great storyteller, found older folktales as the focus for several of his plays. Patrick Ryan retold several, connecting them to Shakespeare titles. "The Devil's Bet" was the inspiration for "The Taming of the Shrew," and "The Hill of Roses" provided the story line for "Romeo and Juliet." Many readers and playgoers find the themes and characters enduring. There is no question that Shakespeare's characterizations were vivid, contributing greatly to entertainment.

We finally reach the likeliest truth, that there were all kinds of stories, and that they served many functions, including that of establishing and perpetuating core cultural values, but they also transmitted histories, comforted, inspired, cautioned, created social cohesion, and entertained. Hero stories cannot be overlooked, for they also had a role in the formation of cultural identity. The Irish hero Cuchulainn is portrayed, as Leeming explains, as "an archetypal superhuman of the epic epic tradition, [and] is said to have lived about the first century A.D. The story of this hero's birth is an ambiguous affair. According to one version, the King of Ulster's daughter, Deichtine, becomes pregnant under mysterious circumstances. People in Ulster believe that King Conchobor is the father. During a dream, however, the Celtic god Lugh (or Lug) speaks to Deichtine and says that she is pregnant by him. ... Other tales suggest that King Conchobor is Cuchulainn's uncle, his mother's brother" (129). Cuchulainn demonstrates his might at the age of six when he is able to defeat 150 boys at various games, and goes on to defend various castles alone against armies. There is no doubt that he was a splendid character, and that those who heard the stories of Cuchulainn might have believed that such a hero could have come only from Ireland. Such a feeling of connection becomes an element in cultural identity. Hero tales exist in virtually all cultures, promoting cultural identity.

When we think of stories, we think of many varieties: folktales, fairy tales, legends, fables, allegories, parables, and myths. Here, we emphasize folktales, the tales about ordinary characters with whom we can identify. Some characters are animals, but even they embody human characteristics. These tales do not

Cultural identity: This is an important component of self-concept. Many people in the U.S. do not think of themselves as having a culture or cultural heritage and might simply think of themselves as "American." That, however, is an identity laden with beliefs, attitudes, and values that are embedded in American history. Our pioneering history, for instance, has contributed to the ethos of being "rugged individualists."

Scholars Samovar, Porter, and McDaniel explain that "identity is an abstract, complex, and dynamic concept" (154). Klyukanov, emphasizing the abstract character of identity, says, "cultural identity can be viewed as membership in a group in which all people share the same symbolic meanings" (122). They and others caution, however, that when people build a positive association with a group, part of their positive feelings about their membership group can lead to ethnocentrism and the perpetuation of stereotypes.

always end happily ever after in reconciliation and peace. Often we find that the "good guy" prevails at the expense of the "bad guy," who forever suffers the humiliation of having been foiled by his enemy. Like fairy tales, folktales often contain extraordinary elements, such as superhumanly powerful characters. There are enemies, or there are obstacles to overcome, such as the powerlessness and poverty of John Henry, the steel-driving man and hero of the once-popular song. Here is one variation of the story, as recalled from having heard it within the oral tradition. What follows is a short summary of a story widely told and sung:

John Henry

When the slaves were freed, John Henry was also freed. Born into slavery, he rose above his circumstances and performed amazing feats. He was a tall and powerful man, and he could work harder and longer than anyone. As a free man, he began working for the Chesapeake and Ohio Railroad as a steel driver, a worker who drilled the holes in rock so that explosives could be set. In this way, tunnels could be drilled through mountains for train tracks. It is said that John Henry used two sledge hammers, one in each hand. When he swung a hammer through the air, it made thunder, and when the hammer struck the steel, it made lightning.

John Henry could have worked anywhere, he was so famous. But he worked on the railroad at the Big Bend Tunnel pounding steel and drilling as no other man could. But one day, his boss brought a steam-driven machine to blast through the rock. John Henry saw this as a challenge and he raced the machine. By the end of the day, he won, and then he died, saying, "A man ain't nothing but a man."

As explained earlier, not every folktale ends happily ever after, and this one ends profoundly sadly. Why would such a story live on for more than 100 years? John Henry, after all, was a poor, Black, uneducated man, not someone you would expect to become a hero. Was John Henry a real person, or was the story made up?

Historian and scholar Scott Reynolds Nelson decided to investigate how much of John Henry's story was true. During his five summers of research, he discovered a 19th-century backdrop of cultural realities: social rank, gender expectations, economic ventures, and racial attitudes—in short, a cultural milieu that was well established and still echoing in the 21st century.

To his surprise, Nelson also discovered a real man named John Henry. John Henry was a common name, but Nelson was able to identify the John Henry of tale and ballad, the Black folk hero. He found that John Henry was 19 years old at the time of the Emancipation Proclamation, and after only two weeks, was arrested for "taking something" from Wiseman's Store. Nelson could not discover what it was that John

Henry had been accused of stealing, but he was incarcerated anyway in the Virginia State Penitentiary.

The prison was not supported by the state, and the warden had to find ways of raising revenue in order to feed the inmates. He leased three hundred and eighty black inmates to the Chesapeake and Ohio Railroad. These inmates worked as a chain gang doing back-breaking, dangerous work, for no pay. It essentially was slavery under a different master. Nelson claims that 48 Black inmates died working for the railroad in 1872, and that number represented nearly 10% of the prison population of Virginia State Penitentiary. This puts the prison population at close to four hundred, and it probably means that fewer than one hundred inmates were White, or at least not Black. We saw in Chapter 1 that underrepresentation is the result of a variety of social practices and institutional arrangements, and it seems likely that the large proportion of Black inmates had to do with limited access to equal access to the protection of the law. Moreover, in his unpaid chain gang, again, the men had little or no access to the protection of the law concerning forced labor—the very thing the Emancipation Proclamation had sought to end.

Many prisoners working on the railroad died of silicosis, a lung disease caused by silicon particles in the air, raised by the steam drills. It was a gruesome death, and again, unequal access to health care played a large part.

Given the evidence uncovered by Nelson, how can we explain why a 19-year-old Black man of a stature of 5'1" and probably in poor health be celebrated in a hero tale? One possible explanation is that the hero story served two communities: the African American community and White railroad workers and miners. Miners were the first group to benefit. The ballad of John Henry acknowledged the fundamentally important work of the poor and powerless. It created social cohesion among miners and White railroad workers. At the end of each day when miners went to the tavern to rest and have a beer, they could celebrate a "low-born" man who "made good." It boosted morale.

It took several years before John Henry became acknowledged as a Black hero. Here again, the idea that a Black man can be a hero provided a glimmer of hope that one's Blackness does not forever condemn him or her to an anonymous, unfulfilling existence. The oral tradition makes for social cohesion, wherein the members of a community, ethnic group, or occupation can celebrate themselves together.

Dan Yashinsky, a storytelling veteran, suggests the power of stories, saying that as storytellers, we "must have the compulsion to bring those stories to people isolated, not by weather and rough terrain but by a world where the sense of community relentlessly erodes, where we lost the signal from our shared history and forget how to imagine a common future (236)."

In other stories, cultural values are emphasized. When we read or hear stories from the people of other cultures, we are sometimes surprised by the narrative. Here is an example from "Arab Folktales," as translated by Iner Bushnaq:

The Price of Pride

A Beduin [sic] once had business in the cattle market of a town. He took his young son with him, but in the confusion of the place he lost track of his boy and the child was stolen.

The father hired a crier to shout through the streets that a reward of one thousand piasters was offered for the return of the child. Although the man who held the boy heard the crier, greed had opened his belly and he hoped to earn an even larger sum. So he waited and said nothing.

On the following day the crier was sent through the streets again. But this time the sum he offered was five hundred piasters, not a thousand. The kidnapper still held out. To his surprise, on the third day the crier offered a mere one hundred piasters. He hurried to return the boy and collect his reward. Curious, he asked the father why the sum of money had dwindled from day to day.

The father said. "On the first day my son was angry and refused to eat your food; is that not so?" "Yes," agreed the kidnapper. "On the second day he took a little, and on the last he asked for bread of his own accord." said the father. It had been so, the kidnapper agreed. "Well." said the father, "as I judge it, that first day my son was as unblemished as refined gold. Like a man of honor, he refused to break bread with his captor. To bring him back with his pride untarnished, I was ready to pay one thousand piasters. On the second day, when hunger made him forget the conduct of a nobleman, he accepted food at your table, and I offered five hundred piasters for him. But when he had been reduced to begging humbly for food, his return was worth but one hundred piasters to me."

First, we should remember that this is an English translation of an Arab story, and that some meanings are bound to be lost. Before we react to the word "pride," or hubris, the attitude that goes before the fall, we should remember that we might define pride differently from Arab definitions. It seems in this story and other Arab stories that pride is a kind of dignity that arises from keeping one's behavior impeccable and in refusing to yield to weakness. Through American eyes, pride might seem more closely related to vanity than to virtue, but to a culture where honor is among the most valuable of currencies, and where you know a person by his or her behavior, virtuous behavior is important.

However, in the story, we find the kidnapper, whom we assume is also Arab, is surprised that the child's father values the son's conduct more highly than his safety. Given that the two main characters think in such different ways, are we able to make any assumptions about Arab values? Perhaps we can, to the extent that the value system of a dishonorable man in any culture must be different from that of an honorable one.

Hence, the story in some ways reflects the structure of Western tales that feature a good character in opposition to a bad one.

Another anthologist, Nuweihed, shows us in a story titled "Hajji Brumbock" that haughtiness, a much different kind of pride, is an unacceptable attitude in Palestine and Lebanon. In that story, a young woman refuses to marry a man who accidentally drops a pomegranate on the rug and picks it up to eat it. She exclaims, "He behaves like a beggar, or like a beast rather." This, after all, is the kind of contempt that divides people. In the largely arid stretches of land occupied by Arab cultures, survival depends on trust. One cannot extend hospitality to a traveler if one sees other humans as beasts, and hospitality is a strong cultural value in Arab culture.

How are beliefs, attitudes, and values reflected in "John Henry" and in "The Price of Pride"? They are reflected in John Henry's fundamental goodness. They are also reflected in the Arab father's tenacious adherence to honor as the basis for his decisions. This is one of the points at which we should consider differences in cultural values, and even cultural definitions. For an American, we would consider the physical safety of a child to be the highest priority. Nothing else would make more sense to us. However, in other cultures such as Arab cultures, honor might be considered more fundamentally important as a condition of life. Each tale reflects culturally important values within the context of the story.

VALUES AND MEANINGS IN STORIES

The meaning of a story emerges from the context, both within the story and within the listener. The success of a story depends on the clarity and relevance of its message to the audience. Regardless of the story's purposes (teaching, entertainment, cultural preservation, and so on), it will not work if the audience derives no meaning from it.

Beliefs, attitudes, and values

A **belief** is the conviction that something is true. For instance, people who believed that women are inherently less capable and less intelligent than men profoundly influenced the social arrangements that have reechoed through the ages. Klyukanov tells us, "Belief structures, as mental constructs, can be quite complex and abstract, especially when the connection between things is perceived very indirectly." Therefore, we can hypothesize that a belief in the inferiority of women was possibly derived from a combination of religious teachings, social interaction, one's experience as a privileged individual in a society dominated by men, and by positive cultural identity as a man.

An **attitude**, to quote Klyukanov again, "is a predisposition to respond positively, negatively, or neutrally to certain objects and practices." Beliefs contribute to attitudes, and, extending the example of women, with the belief that women are weaker and possibly emotionally fragile, an attitude of disdain can arise, and certainly has many times in the past and present. The attitude then contributes toward practices that isolate women.

Values are "shared ideas within a culture about what is important or desirable." Many values are deeply held and difficult to change, partly because of the powerful influence that culture has in shaping our reality and experience. It shouldn't be surprising, then, that there have been many women who agreed that men were "better suited" to go out into public and exert his influence, and that a woman's "place" is to maintain the home fires in order for the man to take his own place in the world.

All communication should be viewed as an audience-centered process. Whatever is said should be said with the intent to benefit the audience. Our knowledge of the audience is therefore central to the enterprise.

The messages that merge from the successful telling of traditional tales have to do with the human milieu: who we are, how the world came to be the way it is, how we should live. People of different cultures have different conceptions of what is true in all these respects. Therefore, stories told in some cultures will contain messages about obedience, duty, wisdom, and patience, stories from other cultures emphasize courage, heroism, and daring, or some other combination of virtues.

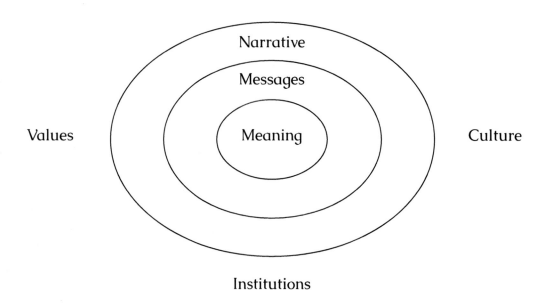

Messages and Meanings Model

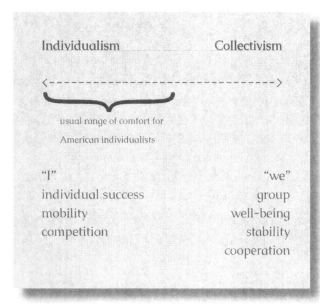

In this model, we find that a story is located in the context of culture. Within each culture are institutions, beliefs, and world views such as those conceived by Kluckhohn and Strodtbeck, as discussed in Chapter 1. Each of these cultural elements has an impact on what subtle but important messages will be embedded in a story. This model consists of three layers, analogous to layers of an onion. The elements inside the circles are strongly connected to the cultural context.

Folktales and other kinds of stories are seated in cultural context. Even stories that are heard in dissimilar cultures are adapted to reflect the relevant cultural assumptions and values. As Klyukanov tells us, values are things we consider to be good or worthy. For instance, values differ dramatically between individualist and collectivist cultures. Members of individualist cultures tend to value autonomy, individual success, competition, and mobility, while in collectivist culture, people usually prefer strong social connections, group success, cooperation, and stability. There are, of course, exceptions in every culture, and there are times when a cultural group might shift to another position on the individualism–collectivism continuum.

First, we must recognize that no culture exists entirely in the extreme individualist or collectivist position (Gilbert). Cultures occupy a preferred range along the continuum.

Although many Americans tend to feel most comfortable in the bracketed range posited in the model above, there are times when we willingly shift into a different part of the continuum. For instance, in the months following Hurricane Katrina, many American students gave up their spring vacations and, at their own expense, went to New Orleans to help other Americans. This was a clear shift from a preoccupation with personal individual "I" interests to a concern for the well-being of the larger "we," those living in New Orleans who counted heavily on help from outside the devastated area. Many returned home feeling that they hadn't accomplished very much, but still felt that they had done what they wanted: volunteering in New Orleans instead of basking on the beaches of Cancun. Quickly, these same students found it important to shift their interest back to their academic studies, their jobs, and their usual lives.

In addition, there are differences of opinion among various cultures about the value of family, spirituality, duty, chastity, wealth, intelligence, truth, faith, and many other values. It is by knowing what a culture's values have historically been that we best understand the meaning of stories that come from that tradition. When we lack knowledge of a culture's values, we often find we don't "get" the story, and we miss out on appreciating the many messages that underlie the story line.

With careful judgment, we can make similar generalizations about beliefs. Beliefs have extraordinary variety among cultures. Belief is the conviction that something is true. In some cultures, people believe that souls are reincarnated through many lifetimes, regardless of whether their behavior has been good or bad. In each lifetime, they have the opportunity to do the things they failed to do in the previous life, and to come closer to enlightenment. In other cultures, people believe that they have only one opportunity to live a worthy life, and that if they don't botch it too badly, they'll go to heaven when they die. Again, of course, many exceptions exist in every culture.

Institutions, as shown on the model, include such things as religion, family, university, government, corporation, and so on. These institutions might take different forms in different cultures. For example, we find that a normatively ideal family is configured one way in individualist Western traditions, but entirely differently in collectivist cultures. This example shows how cultural institutions can undergird the meanings of folktales in several ways. First, in collectivist cultures, we find the inclusion of elders to be experienced as valuable. Youngsters commonly love and respect their elders, interacting with them simply as a matter of course. However, in an individualist culture, accommodations for an elder's needs might be grudgingly provided and viewed as a hassle. Within the institution of family, then, we find that expected relationships bear important meanings that can change the meanings of a folktale. Is the character good because they are patient with an elder, or in contrast, are they good because they take the elder's advice seriously?

Returning to the outer ring of the "Messages and Meanings" model above, we find the story: the basic story line. It is the narrative that makes sense and means something to the audience, as Walter Fisher would agree. The narrative is the glue that holds the story together, whether there is dialog or not. It tells the audience what happened, sometimes even explaining the situation. The narrative, including dialogue between characters, holds the story together. Within the narrative, the motivations of characters explain the actions events and move the story toward its conclusion.

Character motivation should be consistent with cultural origin. They are either constrained by cultural norms, or they defy them, which should be clearly represented in the narrative. Let's say that we have a Native American story in which a young woman is of age to be married. In her collectivist society, efforts to include her into the community as an adult are exerted. Her parents might watch for a suitable husband for her. The eligible unmarried men might do what they can to present themselves in the best light. For instance, they might exert themselves to serve the needs and the well-being of the village through hunting, healing, or leadership. However, let's imagine the young woman is selfish and vain. All these motivations trigger decisions and behaviors, and they are the makings of the narrative. Perhaps the message is that vain and selfish young women might end up without husbands and end up alone, having alienated most people in that collectivist society.

From the second ring in the "Messages and Meanings" model emerges a message deeply connected to cultural beliefs and values. The second layer is a message, sometimes overt and sometimes subtle, embedded in the action and motivation. Symbols and archetypes deliver a culturally relevant message, such as the importance of respecting elders. Respect for elders, though it does exist in American culture, is not as pronounced here as it is in Korea, for instance. The wise old woman is the mono-dimensional archetype representing the idea of wisdom. She doesn't need the full character development of an ordinary character because she represents a concept well understood in her culture. We expect that her wisdom and speech will reflect cultural ideals.

In a much different culture, Jack, the mischievous slave boy, tricks the Massa. Again, he doesn't have to be complex; he only has to represent the hope that one day, African American slaves will no longer be under the heel of the master's overseer. Essentially, the archetype is symbolic, just as there are other symbols, such as swords, doors, books, rainbows, and other items that convey meanings to members of a given culture.

Finally, in the center of the model is the meaning, which is highly personal. Though the story delivers a shared cultural message, in a deeper sense, the meaning of the story has to do with what it means privately to each listener. The meaning might be deeply personal to each listener, negotiated between him- or herself, the story, and his or her own cultural experience. For instance, Hans Christian Andersen's story "The Ugly Duckling" will resonate with some listeners more than with others, and for different reasons. Will the story have the same meaning to a woman and a man? Will an elder understand the story in the same way as a high school student? Will the story carry the same meanings for a survivor of the Great Depression as it does for a young person born into advantage? Though a fundamental message might be shared, the deep meaning might differ between individuals.

Some listeners relate to the mother duck who will not forsake her child. Other listeners will relate to the ugly, socially rejected young bird who is an outcast. Yet others will chafe at what they will view as a "herd mentality," in which a group victimizes an individual for his failure to conform. Still others, viewing themselves as "late bloomers," will see themselves in the duckling, and they might well feel vindicated by the ending of the story. Much depends on the cultural experience of the individual, even in a collectivist setting.

Are Folktales True?

We generally take folktales to be fictive works of imagination, developed over time and generations to express things that are culturally understood as true. In other words, they don't have to be true in order to contain truth.

May We Tell Any Story We Wish?

In some cultures, it's considered respectful, if you've heard a good story, to ask permission to learn it and tell it to others. Joseph Bruchac, an Abenaki storyteller, explains that "all too many non-Native storytellers still get their American Indian tales only from books and not from the mouths of native tellers themselves. Moreover, even when they do hear stories told by native tellers, there is often a lack of understanding about the place of those stories and about the responsibilities involved in telling them or the knowledge and permission which are often required in native cultures before one tells the stories of another" (93). There is no question that the risk of misunderstanding is always present. We tend to dilute the meanings of actions we don't really understand, and in conveying the story, we risk missing the point entirely.

When we undertake to tell stories that come to us from other cultures, one way of showing respect for the culture and the story is to investigate the core values and historic experience of people in that culture. Another part of our responsibility is to avoid cheapening the story by telling it in an inappropriate style.

American history has been a history of conquest and acquisition, and all too often, it seems natural to take things that attract us even when they might not be ours to take—stories, for instance. The very best thing we could conceivably do is to approach a keeper of a culture's lore and ask how to get permission to tell that story. However, this is not realistic for all of us, so we go to a next-best strategy: learn as much as you can about that culture, and understand it deeply.

Since Bruchac also tells us "it is standard practice to credit the person who told it to you," your stories should begin by acknowledging the source. Following is an <u>example</u> of an introduction and a folktale from African American tradition:

INTRODUCTION TO "HOW NEHEMIAH GOT FREE"

My story today is from African American tradition. The title is "How Nehemiah Got Free." The story was collected by Virginia Hamilton, a well-known scholar of folktales, myths, and legends, in her book *The People Could Fly*.

Many African Americans are still underrepresented to this day in the areas of education, good jobs, good neighborhoods, health care, environmental justice, and access to equal treatment by the police and courts. A vicious cycle still exists for many urban African Americans. Because of financial constraints, they often live in undesirable neighborhoods and have access to less successful schools than wealthier people. They often suffer from environmental dangers, such as peeling lead-based paint, smoke and fumes, toxic contaminants, garbage, and noise. All these factors impact health and make it even more difficult to maintain health, be successful in school, to have a successful career, or to improve one's own social situation. It is still a very difficult cycle to break, and the odds are stacked against African Americans to this very day.

I chose this story because of the history of slavery. My own (white) ancestors benefited from the existence of slavery even though they owned none. Rather, their prosperity was built upon the textile mills of New England, which used cotton, the product of forced labor. This story shows the faith, the humor, the wit, and the hope that enslaved people deployed in order to cope with the harshness of their lives. The name Nehemiah comes from a book in the Old Testament, as many African and African-American names do. This kind of child-naming shows the faith in the Lord urgently needed by the slave people in order to carry on under the burden of the whip, the back-breaking forced work, the abuse, and the absence of rights that characterized their lives.

In this story, Nehemiah outwits a succession of owners until he gains his freedom.

How Nehemiah Got Free

In slavery time, there was smart slaves and they did most what they wanted to do by using just their wits. Hangin around the big house, they kept the slaveowners laughin. They had to "bow and scrape" some, but they often was able to draw the least hard tasks.

Nehemiah was a one who believed that if he must be a slave, he'd best be a smart one. No one who callin himself Master of Nehemiah had ever been able to make him work hard for nothin. Nehemiah would always have a funny lie to tell or he made some laughin remark whenever the so-called Master had a question or a scoldin.

Nehemiah was always bein moved from one plantation to another. For as soon as the slaveowner realized Nehemiah was outwittin him, he sold Nehemiah as quick as he could to some other slaveholder.

One day, the man known as the most cruel slaveowner in that part of the state heard about Nehemiah.

"Oh, I bet I can make that slave do what I tell him to," the slaveowner said. And he went to Nehemiah's owner and bargained for him.

Nehemiah's new owner was Mister Warton, and he told Nehemiah, "I've bought you. Now tomorra, you are goin to work for me over there at my plantation, and you are goin to pick four hundred pounds of cotton a day."

"Well, Mas, suh," Nehemiah says, "that's all right, far as it goes. But if I make you laugh, won't you lemme off for tomorra?"

"Well," said Warton, who had never been known to laugh, "if you make me laugh, I won't only let you off for tomorra, but I'll give you your freedom right then and there!"

"Well, I declare, Mas, suh, you sure a good-lookin man," says Nehemiah.

"I'm sorry I can't say the same about you, Nehemiah," answered the slaveowner.

"Oh, yes, Mas, you could," Nehemiah said, laughin. "You could if you told as big a lie as I just did."

Warton threw back his head and laughed. It was a long, loud bellow. He had laughed before he thought. But true is true and facts are facts. And Nehemiah got his freedom. (147–150)

In this example, following Bruchac's good advice, the source of the story was acknowledged fully. After that, the introduction provides a very brief but honest, unexaggerated picture of the cultural experience of urban African Americans before explaining the purpose of the emancipation story—to strengthen the hope of the community that there could be a better future. All of the content in that short introduction is provided in order to help the audience understand the story as fully as possible. As we already know, storytelling is an audience-centered activity, and to serve the audience as well as we can, we should acknowledge the chain of humanity who brought the stories to us.

We also recognize the differences in personal meanings among audience members: Some listeners may have grown up in places where slavery drove the economy. Other listeners might be African American. Yet others are likely to have political ideals, as did Rev. Dr. Martin Luther King Jr., that would allow them to understand the story in other ways.

Before leaving this chapter behind, let's look at the role of face-to-face storytelling as a choice, along with other modes of storytelling.

ORAL TRADITION	LITERARY TRADITION	TELEVISION STORYTELLING
Face-to-face transmission contributes to social cohesion.	Reading is often a solitary activity.	Private viewing has the potential to isolate individuals in families.
The experience of hearing a story is shared with others in real time and in a real place.	Unless reading is done out loud for an audience, even a vicarious experience is not shared.	In solitary viewing no experience is shared with others.

The audience relies on the gestures of the storyteller and on their own imaginations for visual images.	Readers largely rely on their imaginations for visual images even when books are illustrated.	No imagination is required. All images are provided. The capacity for imagination may erode.
Stories are durable because they are remembered.	Stories are as fragile as the books from which they come.	Stories are ephemeral. They are not easily recalled. We rely on recordings.
The novel and motion picture *Fahrenheit 451*, ironically, shows how the absence of books motivated people to begin remembering their stories.	On the other hand, a written record could preserve a story, such as *The Epic of Gilgamesh*, a Babylonian story recorded on cuneiform clay tablets.	Though we rely on expensive and quickly outdated technology, electronic tools can do some things that can't be done any other way. Often, a picture is worth a thousand words.

The three delivery systems in this model provide ways to reach out. Where there is a shortage of experienced storytellers, people may rely on books or electronics. Where reading skills tend to be weak, storytellers and television can fill in. Where access to television and computers is limited or absent, then traditional storytelling and reading will suffice.

In recent times, the effects of face-to-face storytelling have been discussed in a number of venues. We find that storytelling can bring comfort to families of patients in hospice care. In a very different setting, businesses and corporations use storytelling in team building. Some school anti-bullying programs have also made use of storytelling. Storytelling has been an ingredient in the counseling of abused or at-risk children. Even the U.S. Department of Health, Education, and Welfare has chimed in. Their 1978 publication, "Come Closer Around the Fire: Using Tribal Legends, Myths, and Stories in Preventing Drug Abuse," makes the point, first explored in prisons, that when an individual is isolated from his or her community and traditional stories, there is a danger that social isolation can lead to the abuse of alcohol and other drugs. The publication quotes Keen and Fox's explanation that

> For a variety of historical reasons (the emergence of machines, cities, anonymity, money, mass media, standardization, automation) we've lost awareness of storytelling as a way to dramatize and order human existence. ... We feel nameless and empty when we forget our stories, leave our heroes unsung, and ignore the rites that mark our passage from one stage of life to another. (3)

REFERENCES

Abu Jmeel's Daughter and Other Stories: Arab Folk Tales from Palestine and Lebanon. (2002) Retold by Jamal Sleem Nuweihed. New York: Interlink Books.

Arab Folktales. (1986). Translated by Iner Bushnaq. New York: Pantheon Books.

Boccaccio. *Stories of Boccaccio (The Decameron).* London: Published for the Trade.

Bruchac, J. (1996). "The Continuing Circle: Native American Storytelling Past and Present." In *Who Says? Essays on Pivotal Issues in Contemporary Storytelling.* Eds. C. Birch and M. Heckler. Little Rock: August House.

Cole, J. (ed.) (1982). *Best-Loved Folktales of the World.* New York: Anchor Books.

Gaster, T. (1952). *The Oldest Stories in the World.* Boston, Beacon Press.

Gilbert, R. (1992). Course lecture in Intercultural Communication.

Gudykunst, W., & Kim, Y. (2003) *Communicating with Strangers: An Approach to Intercultural Communication.* New York: McGraw-Hill.

Hamilton, V. (1985). "How Nehemiah Got Free." In *The People Could Fly: American Black Folktales.* New York: Alfred A. Knopf.

Klyukanov, I. (2005). *Principles of Intercultural Communication.* Boston: Allyn and Bacon.

Leeming, D. A. (1997). *Storytelling Encyclopedia: Historical, Cultural, and Multiethnic Approaches to Oral Traditions Around the World.* Phoenix: Oryx Press.

Nelson, S. R. (2006). *Steel Drivin' Man: John Henry: The Untold Story of an American Legend.* New York: Oxford University Press.

Nuweihed, J. S. (2002). *Abu Jmeel's Daughter and Other Stories: Arab Folk Tales From Palestine and Lebanon.* Brooklyn, NY: Interlink Books.

Orenstein, C. (2002). *Little Red Riding Hood Uncloaked: Sex, Morality, and the Evolution of a Fairy Tale.* New York: Basic Books.

"Shakespeare's Storybook: Folk Tales That Inspired the Bard." (2006) Retold by Patrick Ryan. Cambridge, MA: Barefoot Books.

U.S. Department of Health, Education, and Welfare. (1978). *Come Closer Around the Fire: Using Tribal Legends, Myths, and Stories in Preventing Drug Abuse.* Public Health Service.

Yashinsky, D. (2008). "Stealing Wisdom, or the Education of a 'Storm Fool.'" In *Storytelling, Self, Society: An Interdisciplinary Journal of Storytelling Studies.* Vol. 4, no. 3, pp. 235–244.

Zipes, J. (1979). *Breaking the Magic Spell: Radical Theories of Folk & Fairy Tales.* Lexington: University Press of Kentucky.

CHAPTER THREE

Characters

Most stories have characters: human characters, gods, ghosts, fairies, dragons and other animals, the wind, and so on. The more we know about the cultural background of a story, the more we know about the characters. Furthermore, the more we know about the characters, the more we understand and remember a story.

A good example to show us the connection between character and cultures are the familiar tales "Little Red Riding Hood" and "Little Red Cap." They are essentially the same story, but they are located in different cultures. Orenstein tells us that "fairy tales are among our most powerful socializing narratives. They contain enduring rules for understanding who we are and how we should behave" (10). She further explains that Charles Perrault first wrote the story of Little Red Riding Hood in the court of Louis XIV where sexual indiscretions were commonplace (24). However, affairs were dangerous, and when a girl lost her virginity (or was euphemistically "devoured by the wolf"), her prospect for a good marriage was reduced substantially. Hence, many scholars view the Perrault story as a cautionary tale, one that admonishes young women to be obedient and chaste, or they will be devoured.

We also learn from Orenstein that "the Grimms' 'Little Red Cap,' with its patriarchal lesson in female obedience, easily found purchase in the social landscape of Victorian Europe, and the heroic rescue by the hunter echoed the social protection that the nineteenth-century man—father, then husband—represented" (60). Yet the Grimms, who reframed many tales for different audiences, had another ending to the story, in which Little Red Riding Hood and her grandmother devised a plan to trap and kill the wolf without need of a man to rescue them.

The important thing to note is that the main character in both versions matched the cultures and historic eras in which they were told. The French aristocratic court in the second half of the seventeenth century presented a different set of morals and cultural assumptions than did the German Brothers Grimm more than a century later. Therefore, the main character in each version was portrayed differently, and upon the character rested the story outcomes.

What conclusions can we reach from this cursory look at the familiar tale of Red Riding Hood? First, we can say that perceptions of the worldview differ from culture to culture, and that therefore, characters differ as well. Second, we can say that in order to show fidelity to a culture, you must know something about its fundamental assumptions in order to know what kinds of characters enact its stories. The French Little Red Riding Hood, in other words, behaves differently from the German one. Third, we can say that we must resist the assumption that our own cultural assumptions are pretty typical. We must investigate the worldviews of people in other cultures, much as Kluckhohn and Strodtbeck did, and we should particularly contemplate the human nature dimension of their model.

In their model, Kluckhohn and Strodtbeck acknowledge that different cultures either embrace or reject the possibility that humans are perfectible (mutable). We should not forget, however, that mutability also suggests the possibility not only for perfectibility, but also for the degeneration of moral character. In the two versions of Little Red Riding Hood, we detect a world view that allow some characters to be fundamentally good and decent but corruptible, while others are irredeemably evil.

Kluckhohn and Strodtbeck offer the following array of views about the character of humans. We find, for instance, that in cultures that view humans as basically good, some believe humans can be corruptible, while people in other cultures believe the basic goodness of humans underlies the events, temptations, and misfortunes that befall an individual (11–12).

HUMAN NATURE	BASICALLY EVIL	NEUTRAL/MIXTURE OF GOOD AND EVIL	BASICALLY GOOD
	Mutable/Immutable	Mutable/Immutable	Mutable/Immutable

The relationship between culture, character, motivation, and story outcome is not trivial. Take the following story from the Tlingit people of Alaska as an example.

How Selfishness Was Rewarded

A young warrior came to the coast with his wife and mother one summer and settled in the place where Sitka now stands. It was a summer of hardship for the family because the fish stayed away from the coast and the game had moved far away over the mountains. The warrior set traps and laid nets in the water and wandered many miles hunting for food, but he found nothing. The family had to eat berries and green sprouts and dig for roots to eat. Even so, there was barely enough each day to keep the family going.

The old mother, who was nearly blind, began to lose health and strength as the days went by with little food. In sharp contrast to this was the pretty young wife, who stayed strong and healthy and just picked at her meal each evening. This puzzled the young warrior, who felt himself losing his vigor as the days went by, but he could find no reason for her good health in this time of adversity.

Then his old mother came to her son very early one morning and told him a sad and cruel story. The old mother had awakened the night before from a dream of cooked fish to smell the reality in the air. She opened her old eyes and saw a fish roasting on a small, flickering fire. The starving old mother saw her son's wife crouched near the fire and she heard the girl eagerly chewing the hot fish. The old mother cried out to her son's wife to give her a morsel, but the girl was selfish and told the old woman that the fish she smelled was just a dream. When the old mother begged for just a single bite of fish, the girl denied her request. The old woman kept up her cries until the selfish girl took the bare bones from the last fish and thrust them into the old woman's hands, burning her flesh. Then the old mother wept bitter tears and retreated back to her corner.

When he heard his mother's story, the warrior cautioned her to say nothing to the wife. When the selfish girl awoke, the warrior treated her in his customary manner, but he kept watch to see what she would do. That night, when she thought everyone lay sleeping, the young wife crept down to the shore and summoned a school of herring to the shore using a magic spell. She swept two of the largest fish into her basket and took them back to the lodge to cook.

Unbeknownst to her, the warrior had followed his wife. He took care to memorize the strange words of his wife's spell, and then slipped quickly back to the lodge and into his blankets before she returned. He lay so still that the girl never suspected that he was watching as she cooked and ate the fish, carefully burying the bones so that her family would not know what she had done.

In the morning, the warrior went out hunting and caught a fat seal. That evening, the whole family feasted on the rich meat, and soon the selfish young wife lay fast asleep in the lodge. At midnight, the young warrior rose and went to the shore. Using his wife's spell, he summoned the herring and filled a basket with the largest of the fish. When the girl woke in the morning, she saw her husband and his mother eating roast fish beside a crackling fire. The old mother savored each mouthful and kept darting triumphant looks at the selfish young girl. Then the young wife knew that her shameful behavior had been discovered.

After greeting her husband pleasantly, the young girl left the lodge and walked casually toward the woods. As soon as she was out of sight, she took to her heels, running as fast as she could toward the mountains, fearful of her husband's wrath. She heard the warrior call her name, and she heard him running after her. She flung herself up the mountainside, clambering up a large boulder that stood in her way. As the girl climbed, she felt her body growing smaller and smaller. She gasped in fear as she realized that the magic she had used so selfishly was turning against her in punishment for the crimes she had committed against her starving family. She felt feathers sprouting from her arms and face, and when she cried out, the only sound she could make was a soft hooting noise.

By the time the young warrior reached the boulder, the girl's transformation was complete. He found himself face to face with a small owl that gazed up at him with his wife's large, pleading eyes. He reached out to her, not knowing what to do or say. The owl backed away from his hand, and he saw the humanity fading from its eyes. The owl shook itself, stretched its wings, and flew away into the forest, hooting plaintively.

The warrior gazed after his transformed wife sadly. He had planned to treat her gently, to woo her away from her selfishness with his love and kindness. But the evil forces she had used so selfishly had taken her and there was nothing he could do but return to his lodge and tell his old mother what had happened.

To this day, the plaintive hoot of the owl may be heard in the woods of Alaska, reminding those of us who hear it of the price a young girl once paid for her selfishness.

....

We notice in this story that none of the characters had personal names. They might represent Everyman or Everywoman with our human strengths and weaknesses. We find in this story the possibility that humans embody good, but also bad. The end seems tragic to a non-Native reader or listener, for our cultural experience tells us that we are mutable, perfectible. The young wife should have tried harder, we're tempted to think. But the story, without personal names, is about values.

Characters can be archetypes, or they can be more complex. An archetype is a simplified, mono-dimensional, "pure" character type that comes to symbolize some human characteristic or motivation. The motivations of these archetypes produce the story outcomes—for instance, such outcomes as the triumph of good over evil, the heroic rescue of a victim, or the self-sacrifice of a hero in order to save his or her people.

Robert Louis Stevenson's classic novel, *Dr. Jekyll and Mr. Hyde*, provides us with two exaggerated archetypal models. The main character of the story accidentally reveals his hidden side by testing a new medicine on himself before prescribing it to others. Both aspects of his personality form archetypes in opposition to each other.

DR. JEKYLL		MR. HYDE
respected research scientist		depraved and destructive man
amiable and attractive		hateful and unkempt
thoughtful and responsible	*non-nuanced, absolute opposites, or ndispensable counterparts*	selfish and abusive
seeks ways to help humanity		seeks ways to brutalize humans
virtuous		corrupt

In this model, character and motivation are closely intertwined. There are other archetypal opposites, including David and Goliath, Robin Hood and the Sheriff of Nottingham, Obi-Wan Kenobi and Darth Vader, the virtuous Sir Galahad and the dastardly Sir Mordred, or, from African American tales, "Jack and the Massa."

Not all archetypes have opposites: some include the dreadful Captain Ahab, Hiawatha, Don Quixote, Molly Pitcher, the tragic Hester Prynne, Faust, Ichabod Crane, John Henry, and the variously named fire 'n' brimstone preachers.

Further, not all characters are archetypes. Some will have traits typical of ordinary people in their culture, usually constrained by the values and expectations of their culture. What makes them main characters in a story is their motivation as they enact the story. Is the main character a defiant woman who lives to learn a lesson? Or does she instead liberate her people from an ancient curse? Or is the main character a wise old man who refuses to be bought off in order to please the king? There are many possible main characters, and their motivations evoke the dramatic clash with either another character, or with a larger enemy—perhaps represented by a giant or a dragon.

Archetype: Symbolic characters found in many stories. They embody a coherent and predictable set of characteristics. They tend to be simplified, mono-dimensional types that symbolize various kinds of human motivations. For instance, Coyote represents human foolishness: mischief, lust, manipulation, and trickery. An opposite example might be Sir Galahad of the King Arthur cycle: a knight whose virtue and spiritual faith are unshakable.

There many male and female archetypes, and their inner character and motivation shape the outcome of the story.

Motivation

Animal characters can be considered human insofar as their motivations represent human characteristics. Often, they are really stories about humans, often used in order to gently chastise a misbehaving child or adult. In a Native American story, for instance, Coyote is a character who represents human resourcefulness, the human capacity for ethical flexibility and mischief, and the many moments of human foolishness. By the same token, Aesop's tortoise and hare represent other kinds of humans whose motivations inevitably lead to the outcome of the story.

Action

Some actions, fueled by dire motivations, have dire consequences. This Chinese story is provided by Haiwang Yuan:

A Forsaken Wife and Her Unfaithful Husband

Long ago, there lived in Central China a scholar named Chen Shimei. Living with him were his invalid, elderly parents; his loving, caring wife Qin Xianglian; and their two young children, a boy and a girl. While Chen Shimei devoted himself to studying for the coming imperial examination, Xianglian took care of the family. Life was hard, but she looked forward to the day when her husband would have passed the examination and returned home with fame and fortune.

When the examination season came, Chen Shimei bade farewell to his parents, wife, and children. He promised to come back to them as soon as he obtained a lucrative government position upon his success in the exam. In tears, Xianglian told him, "Don't worry about us. I will take care of your parents and our children. Come back to us no matter whether you succeed or not. We all wish you good luck!"

Three years passed, but not a single word came from Chen Shimei. Qin Xianglian and his parents were worried, wondering if he had encountered some misfortune. Xianglian wished to go to the capital, where she knew the examination took place every year, to find out what had happened to him. But in addition to the long distance and cost of such a trip, she had to look after her young children and her aged parents-in-law, whose health was deteriorating with each passing day.

As if Qin Xianglian's misery were not enough, a serious drought hit her region and soon resulted in a famine. Xianglian had to sell her belongings to purchase medicine for her parents-in-law. She could not prevent worry, hunger, and sickness from ruining their lives. When her parents-in-law died, like a dutiful daughter, Xianglian managed to give the elderly couple a decent burial before she became penniless. Having no idea what would become of her and her children, she placed all her hope on finding her missing husband. On many occasions, she indulged in the wishful thinking that her husband had succeeded in the imperial examination and become a high-ranking official. He must have been too busy to come home for a visit. If he had known that disaster had devastated his home-town and took the lives of his parents; if he had known his wife and their children were at the brink of starvation, surely he would have returned?

One day, while she was out begging, a neighbor came up to her and told her something that gave her a glimmer of hope. He said that he had been to the capital lately and seen her husband there.

"My husband is still alive?" asked Qin Xianglian, both happy and incredulous. The neighbor suspected that the new *fuma* (emperor's son-in-law) must be her husband, Chen Shimei.

"Are you sure? Misidentifying an emperor's relative is not a joke!" Xianglian warned.

"I don't think I can mistake him, because I grew up with him and know him too well, don't I? I know how he looks, talks, and moves. I can recognize him even though he is in an official's robe."

"Did you talk to him?" Xianglian asked impatiently.

"Who am I to speak to an emperor's son-in-law?" retorted the neighbor. "I could not even come close to him while he was surrounded by his guardsmen."

Qin Xianglian decided to pay the *fuma* a visit at any cost, particularly when she had nothing to lose. The next day she set out for the capital, taking along her two children. Assuming that what the neighbor had said was true, Xianglian was going to have a talk with her husband and try to convince him to help his family.

The emperor's son-in-law was indeed Chen Shimei. He had not only passed, but excelled at the examination. His performance caught the attention of the emperor, who wanted to marry his daughter to this new *zhuangyuan* (The Scholar). Finding him to be in his late twenties, the emperor hesitated, for at his age, he must have been a married man, or he could be so abnormal that he was simply unmarriageable. When asked about his marital status, Chen Shimei said that he was a widower without children. He told the emperor that he had remained single since the death of his wife so that he could concentrate on his studies. Desperate for wealth and rank, Chen Shimei took the risk of lying to the monarch, a capital offense at the time. His marriage to the princess made him one of the most powerful and wealthy men in the country.

Qin Xianglian and her children begged their way to the capital. When they finally approached the mansion of the fuma, two guardsmen blocked their entrance. When they heard Xianglian's story, however, they relented and let them "break in" and "chased" them to the fuma's living room. The sudden appearance of his wife and children startled Chen Shimei.

"How dare you break into a *fuma*'s mansion?" yelled Chen Shimei, treating them as if they were total strangers. He almost relented when his two children clung to his sleeves and called him "Dad," but he immediately recollected himself, thinking, "I must be iron-hearted, or my head could roll." He could not afford to let the emperor and the princess know that he had lied to them. He did not want to give up what he had: the princess, the money, the power, and the prestige. He had his wife and children ejected from his mansion before the princess could find out what was going on.

The sympathetic guards told Xianglian secretly that the only person who might be able to help her was the old Prime Minister. They said he was one of the few high-ranking officials in the capital who had a sense of justice.

"A Prime Minister is next only to the emperor in power and prestige. No one else would be in a position to confront the *fuma*," they added.

"But I know nobody in the capital. How can I get in touch with the Prime Minister?" Xianglian asked.

The guards paused a few seconds, and one of them came up with an idea. He said, "The Prime Minister goes to the court every day along the same route. You can stop him on his way and tell him your story then and there."

The next day, Qin Xianglian did as the guards had suggested. The interruption irritated the Prime Minister at first, but when he heard her story, he was shocked by the *fuma*'s betrayal and deceit. He knew Chen Shimei had committed a capital crime, but he would not want to ruin him, thus making his wife widowed and his children fatherless. He wanted to help the *fuma* avoid capital punishment, if he would tell the truth. He hoped to see the family reunited. He told Qin Xianglian what to do.

The next evening, the Prime Minister invited Chen Shimei for dinner at his mansion. In the middle of the feast, the Prime Minister suggested that they have some fun while eating. When a ballad singer was ushered in, a *pipa* (lute) in her arms, Chen Shimei recognized Xianglian. He realized that the Prime Minister had tricked him. Enraged, he wanted to leave on the pretext that he was not feeling well. The Prime Minister, however, pretended not to know anything about the relationship between his two guests and insisted that Chen Shimei stay and listen.

At the request of the Prime Minister, Qin Xianglian gave a few plucks on the pipa and began to sob out her sufferings and the fate of her parents-in-law while her husband was away taking the imperial examination. The Prime Minister meant this to be a subtle way of educating Chen Shimei so that he could change his heart and avert fatal consequences. Chen Shimei, however, would not heed the Prime Minister's kind admonishment. Instead, he stormed out of the mansion, accusing the Prime Minister of poking his nose into a *fuma*'s affairs. Xianglian thanked the embarrassed and indignant Prime Minister for doing what he could. Despondent over her husband's cold-heartedness, she left the capital with her children, not knowing where to go.

Chen Shimei saw his wife and children as liabilities. He feared that as long as they existed, they could come to ruin his life at any time. So he hired an assassin named Han Qi, lying to him by saying that Qin Xianglian was his former lover who had come to blackmail him. He wanted Han Qi to kill the family on their way back home. Before Han's departure, Chen Shimei demanded, "Come back to me when you finish. I need you to show me their blood on your sword. If you fail, I'll have you destroyed with your own blade."

Chen Shimei had not anticipated that Han Qi was an honest and righteous man. When Han Qi learned the truth from Xianglian, he spared the family's lives by taking his own, knowing that he would lose it anyway at the hands of Chen Shimei for betraying him. At his request, before his death, Xianglian took his bloodstained sword as evidence and returned to the capital. She was going to bring the murderous Chen Shimei to the High Court.

In those days, officials were largely corrupt, and they often shielded one another. Judge Bao Zheng of the High Court was allegedly the most upright in his time. Qin Xianglian's case, however, was not an ordinary one because it involved the royal family. Fully aware that the arrogant fuma would deny everything in the courtroom, Judge Bao Zheng came up with an idea. He invited Chen Shimei to chat in his office, in the hope of reasoning him into admitting his wrongdoing. When Chen Shimei came, he found it to be another trap. Bao Zheng calmed him down and assured him that he would get him a lenient sentence if he reconciled with his wife, Qin Xianglian. "I hope that you won't reject my offer." Bao Zheng said, "You have to understand that each of your offenses—lying to the emperor, neglecting your parents, and committing a murder—each deserves capital punishment."

"I don't think you can do anything about it even if this woman's allegations are true," retorted Chen Shimei in an overbearing manner. "Tell you what: I've already told my story to the princess and her mother before I came here. They've already pardoned me and don't want the wicked woman and her children to tarnish our royal reputation."

"I'll believe it when I see it!" the indignant Bao Zheng exclaimed. He ordered Chen Shimei to be arrested and brought to his courtroom. Sure enough, both the princess and her mother were waiting there to ask for Chen Shimei's release.

"How dare you stand in front of the royal family? Drop to your knees and show respect to Your Highness!" demanded the princess, flaring up at the sight of Qin Xianglian, who entered the courtroom with her children behind Judge Bao Zheng.

"By tradition," Xianglian began, composed, "you are but a concubine in our family. You ought to kowtow to me because I am the legal wife!" Her smart retort enraged the princess, who would have torn this insolent countrywoman into pieces but for Judge Bao Zheng's intervention.

Before long, the Chief Eunuch (the emperor's closest attendant) brought up the emperor's decree of pardon to the court. As the pressure was mounting, Judge Bao Zheng thought it wise to seek a compromise. He offered Qin Zianglian a decent sum of money and asked her to drop the case. Qin Xianglian was terribly disappointed. She chided the judge. "I heard that you were the most just and brave judge in the country, but now I've finally learned that crows are black everywhere." Before Judge Bao Zheng could say anything in his defense, she continued, "How can you, a man known for his integrity, bribe me into forgiving such a heinous murderer as this man?"

Qin Xianglian's taunt struck Judge Bao Zheng as a wakeup call. Taking off his hat and putting aside his seal—both symbols of his office—he said with determination, "I would rather give up my position or even my life to uphold justice than protect a criminal, no matter who he is." He then sentenced Chen Shimei to death and had him executed. (97–100)

Here we're astonished by such an exceedingly different sense of justice from that with which we are familiar. Wasn't it justice for Qin Xianglian we expected? Why was it a crime for Chen Shimei to abandon his parents, but not his wife and children? How is it that lying to the emperor deserves the same consequence as the murder of his parents through neglect?

This tale provides a modest window into another world. In the Confucian view of order and harmonious relationships, society was organized along a steep political and gender hierarchy. Moss Roberts explains,

The Confucian philosophers who dominated the Chinese state conceived of relationships as a harmonious balance of obligations. ... By and large, the Confucians were the voice of the superior orders—emperor, father, husband.

The emperor transmitted his influence across the land directly through the imperial bureaucracy and indirectly through the great landowning clans, sometimes called the local gentry or nobility. Official positions (the goal for every clan's sons) were obtained through a series of qualifying examinations based on the sacred books of Confucian doctrine, ritual, ethics, metaphysics, and history. An ambitious young man could rise by passing three successive levels of examinations, the county, the provincial, and the metropolitan. Each of the degrees brought its holder various immunities, exemptions, and privileges, though not always an actual office. The system was designed to delegate the responsibilities of government to upright and learned men, to scholar-officials would rule with judgment. ...

However, these tales deal with practice, not theory, and in reality the bureaucracy was a cumbersome, often corrupt structure in which official appointment was determined by a mixture of factors that included patronage and bribery as well as scholarship. (xv–xvi)

Within such a system, it might seem to make sense to ignore the personhood of the self-sacrificing wife, Qin Xianglian, and the princess, whose name we never learn. They are merely part of the story's context. It's the male characters who have the power and authority to set events into motion. We find that because of the prestigious rank earned by the husband, he is able, at least for a while, to deflect criticism. It's difficult for most of us to identify a moral lesson or a satisfying resolution. On one hand, this seems like an assault on our American sense of justice. On the other hand, however, it clarifies the traditional assumptions that to this day influence Chinese culture. For us, the addition of Taoism is easier to accept, for as Roberts again explains, "The Taoist view found vivid expression in popular literature. ... Indeed, one of the purposes of this genre, typically scorned and even banned by Confucian authorities, was to publicize the crimes of the mighty and the injustices suffered by the subordinate order, including children, women, and animals" (xv).

Stereotype: A simplified generalization we make about an actual person. We might treat a person the way we would treat a stereotype. Everyone has stereotypes, and we acquire these stereotypes socially, through things we read or watch on television, from our neighbors, other kids at school, and even our families. For instance, many people have a stereotype of the used car salesman, or of the athletic young African American male.

The difficulty with stereotypes is that they fail to acknowledge the variety and complexity of the human mind and experience. Even "positive" stereotypes do people a grave disservice. For instance, when we say that Asian students are very smart, we imply that their intelligence makes academic life "easy" for them. We fail to acknowledge that many are studying advanced concepts in a language not their own, that they are living halfway around the world from their social support systems, and that here, everything is different and unfamiliar.

Stereotypes defy change, even when we are aware of them. We're obligated to try to identify our own stereotypes, examine them, and know that they do not represent real people. In this way, we can reduce the danger of treating others through our stereotypes of them.

Crones

Crones are old women, representing power embodied. For instance, a fairy godmother, or a witch who can grant wishes is an example of a wise, kind, mature, principled woman who has become influential. Cinderella is rescued from her loneliness and despair by her fairy godmother. On the other hand, crones can be scary and threatening, and just as powerful. In Russian tales, Baba Yaga is a witch, and one that can cheerfully devour an innocent child who haplessly wanders within her reach. Mayer describes Baba Yaga, saying, "Deep in the birch forest, in a small clearing, lives the ancient, the terrible Baba Yaga. No one knows how old she is; she has always been there in the forest. Baba Yaga is very tall, and thin as a skeleton, though she never stops eating. Humans are Baba Yaga's favorite food, and she is always hungry ... " (1). Within stories about Baba Yaga, we often find virtuous characters portrayed as beautiful and intelligent, while bad characters are portrayed as coarse and ugly, selfish and abusive. They are archetypes.

Of crones, Walker says, "The 'Crone' may have descended from Rhea Kronia as Mother of Time. ... Because it was believed that women became very wise when they no longer shed the lunar 'wise blood' but kept it within, the Crone was usually a Goddess of Wisdom. Minerva, Athene, Metis, Sophia, and Medusa provide typical examples" (187).

Stories containing crones usually are stories that celebrate human virtues and disparage human weakness. On the one hand, Cashdan tells us, "Of the many figures who make their presence felt in a fairy tale, the witch is the most compelling. She is the diva of the piece, the dominant character who frames the battle between good and evil. The witch has the ability to place people in deathlike trances—and just as easily bring them back to life. Conjurer of spells and concocter of deadly potions, she has the power to alter people's lives ... " (30). But this is only one possibility for a crone. Leeming, on the other hand, describes the fairy godmother, also a crone, as a "supernatural being, especially prevalent in fairy tales, who provides protection, assistance, or the fulfillment of a deserving character's desires. Although fairy godmothers are benevolent beings, these supernatural figures originate with the Fates (also called the *Norns*), a group of three crone-like beings who bestow good or ill fortune upon a child at birth ... " (171).

Tricksters

Leeming further tells us that a trickster is a "dual-natured figure prevalent in oral traditions around the world. The trickster is usually a male, lecherous, a cheat, careless about taboos, amoral, and outrageous. He can be human, semi-human, or take on an animal form which varies with the fauna of the area. Tricksters clearly represent chaos and disorder. However, tricksters are also inventive and creative culture heroes who are often a great help to human beings" (475).

Virtually every culture has at least one trickster character, and although Leeming expresses the similarities among most of them, there are also differences. For instance, some tricksters are female. A Spanish-American trickster, for instance, is Hermana Zorra (Sister Fox). San Souci describes the place of trickster stories which "are popular the world over. The folklore of countries from America to Africa is filled with tales of sly, clever, sometimes heroic, sometimes dastardly, always resourceful fellows such as Br'er Rabbit, Anansi the spider, Coyote, Raven, and many others. Not as well known—but every bit the equals of their male counterparts are the females ... " (7).

To illustrate how widespread the trickster character is, a few names are Wiley Coyote of cartoon fame, Iktomi, Kokopelli, Wisikajak, the Monkey King of many Asian cultures, Texcatlipoca, Captain Jack Sparrow, Robin Hood, and Bart Simpson. Kitsune the fox inhabits many Japanese tales, Maiu is Polynesian, and Hermes has plied his wiles in Greek mythology. Finally, Loki, the Norse god of mischief, can't be overlooked, but he is malicious where others are not.

One of the most popular of tricksters is the Native American trickster Coyote. He is a complicated character: reckless, promiscuous, curious, and clever. He is also antiauthoritarian, always breaking the rules. He's at the mercy of his huge appetites. He is a liar, a manipulator, a glutton, a fornicator, and a thief. He is chaotic, disorganized, and irrational. He's astoundingly clever, but quickly forgets what he has learned. His pranks backfire. But somehow, in spite of his boastful foolishness, and in spite of himself, he sometimes becomes a hero and a benefactor, mostly by accident.

The following Klamath (Native American) story from western Oregon illustrates the dual character of Coyote the trickster. This story was collected by Erdoes and Ortiz:

Coyote Steals Fire

There was a time when people had no fire. In winter they could not warm themselves. They had to eat their food raw. Fire was kept inside a huge white rock that belonged to Thunder, who was its caretaker. Thunder was a fearful being. Everybody was afraid of him. Even Bear and Mountain Lion trembled when they heard Thunder's rumbling voice.

Coyote was not afraid of Thunder. He was afraid of nothing. One day, Thunder was in an angry mood and roared and rumbled his loudest, so that the earth trembled and all animals went into hiding. Coyote decided that this was the time to get the fire away from Thunder. Coyote climbed the highest mountain on which Thunder lived. Thunder was at home. "Uncle," said Coyote, "let us play a game of dice. If you win, you can kill me. If I win, you will have to give me fire."

"Let us play," said Thunder.

They played with dice made from the gnawing teeth of beavers and woodchucks. The beaver teeth were male dice. The woodchuck teeth were female dice. A design was carved on one side of these teeth. The teeth were thrown on a flat rock. If the male teeth came up with the carved sides, they counted two points. If the female teeth came up with the carved sides, they counted one. If the dice came up uneven, they did not count. There was a bundle of sticks for counting, for keeping track of the points scored.

Now, Coyote is the trickiest fellow alive. He is the master at cheating at all kinds of games. He continuously distracted Thunder so that he could not watch what Coyote was up to. Thunder was no match for Coyote when it came to gambling. Whenever Thunder took his eyes off Coyote's hands, even for just the tiniest part of a moment, Coyote turned his dice up so that they showed the carved sides. He turned Thunder's dice up so that they showed the blank sides. He distracted Thunder and made him blink. Then, quick as a flash, he took a counting stick away from Thunder's pile and added it to his own. In the end, Thunder was completely confused. Coyote had all the counting sticks, Thunder had none. "Uncle, I won," said Coyote. "Hand over the fire." Thunder knew that Coyote had cheated but could not prove it.

Coyote called upon all the animals to come up to the mountaintop to help him carry the big rock that contained the fire. That rock was huge and looked solid, but it was very fragile, as fragile as a seashell. So all the animals prepared to carry the rock away. "Not so fast," growled Thunder, "Coyote won the game and so I gave him the fire. But he cheated, and for that I shall take his life. Where is he so that I can kill him?"

Now, Coyote had read Thunder's mind. He had anticipated what Thunder was up to. Coyote could pull the outer part of his body off, as if it were a blanket, so he put his skin, his pelt, his tail, his ears—all of his outside—close by Thunder, and with the inside of his body, his vitals, moved a distance away. Then he changed his voice so that it sounded as if it were coming not from a distance, but like from just a few feet away. "Here I am, Uncle," he cried. "Kill me if you can." Thunder picked up the huge rock containing fire and hurled it at what he thought was Coyote. But he hit only the skin and fur. The rock splintered into numberless pieces. Every animal took a little piece of the fire and put it under its armpit or under its wing, and they hurried all over the world, bringing fire to every tribe on earth. Coyote calmly put on his outer skin and fur again. "Good-bye, Uncle," he said to Thunder. "Don't gamble. It is not what you do best." Then he ran off.

• •

This story, of course, oozes with irony. Using the honorific *Uncle,* Coyote manipulates and finagles rather than striking an honorable bargain and seeing it through. It is at the end when we find out that Coyote knew all along that Thunder was an inept gambler—and he taunts him.

The point in this story, however, is that in the kerfuffle, Coyote ends up the benefactor, bringing life-sustaining fire to all humanity. Even that makes sense, for fire is also a dangerous gift, just as coyote is an unpredictable character.

There are hundreds of Native American stories about Coyote, and those stories have lasting value in Native communities, for Coyote is the embodiment of foolishness. Many Native American families correct their children's behavior without punishment, often by telling a story that shows how foolish the same behavior is when enacted by Coyote. The children know, or are told, that if they don't want to be thought of as foolish, they will refrain from behavior that would be seen as foolish by the people in the collective community. In a collectivist society, such a story suffices to teach a child.

Heroes

How heroes are defined will vary from culture to culture. What constitutes heroism? Courage? Virtue? Honesty? The ability to overcome the seemingly impossible? Joseph Campbell, the eminent scholar, tells us:

... [T]he makers of legend have seldom rested content to regard the world's great heroes as mere human beings who broke past the horizons that limited their fellows and returned with such boons as any man with equal faith and courage might have found. On the contrary, the tendency has always been to endow the hero with extraordinary powers from the moment of birth, or even the moment of conception. The whole hero-life is shown to have been a pageant of marvels with the great central adventure as its culmination. (319)

We find another scholar, John Roberts, with a view of heroes that emphasizes cultural identity. He explains:

We often use the term "hero" as if it denoted a universally recognized character type, and the concept of "heroism" as if it referred to a generally accepted behavioral category. In reality, figures (both real and mythic) and actions dubbed heroic in one context or by one group of people may be viewed as ordinary or even criminal in another context or by other groups, or even by the same ones at different times ... the heroes that we create are figures who, from our vantage point on the world, appear to possess personal traits and/or perform actions that exemplify our conception of our ideal self. ... In other words, a hero is the product of a creative process and exists as a symbol of our differential identity ... (1)

These ideas echo in the folktale of John Henry, a man of nearly superhuman physical power who overcame bodily limitations. Certainly, the real John Henry did no such thing. In fact, he was unable even to reach equality with other human beings. But the poor and powerless man was not the ideal hero. Hence, he had to be re-created in order to be a hero for African Americans and other subordinate groups. Roberts identifies specific heroes for various periods of Black history: John, the clever boy, and Br'er Rabbit, imported from West Africa used trickery to oppose the powerful Massa or other strong enemy; the male or female plantation conjurer, the comforter, interpreter, and avenger of wrong; the Christian preacher, using the power of spiritual music to uplift, inspire, and unite people in the fellowship of Jesus; and the outlaw hero, acting in defiance against the tyranny of white rules and social structures and eluding capture. Consider how time could be a factor in the perception of the hero:

About 1619–1865	Enslavement of captive Africans and indentured white servants
	Heroes were:
	Br'er Rabbit
	Jack, the clever boy
	The conjure man or woman
1784	Methodists deem slavery "contrary to the laws of God"
Early 1800s	African traditions are viewed as "loathsome pagan idolatry" and are forbidden. **Conjure** continues in secret.
1865	Emancipation Proclamation
	New hero: **The Preacher Man**
1875	Civil Rights Act of 1875 is enacted to protect the rights of African Americans and guarantee them justice.
1890s to very recently	**The Outlaw hero**

We find that John Henry doesn't fit neatly into any of these hero archetypes. Hence, he is a hero without being an African American archetype.

Women/Beauty

It's virtually impossible to read folktales and fairy tales without some exposure to the idea that beauty is important. However, the definition of beauty by one culture might differ dramatically from the definition by another. Even here in the U.S., beauty was once found in the frail and delicate features of young women. However in more recent times, there are many who would look upon such beauties as too pampered and useless to be really attractive. Now we idealize women who work out, are athletic and physically fit, and are capable. There are, of course, men of legendary attractiveness too, but we're accustomed to beauty as a value we seek in female characters and real women.

Many stories emphasize beauty, but meanings can differ. In many Western stories, beauty is symbolic of virtue. We know this from such stories as the Story of Esther in the Bible, and in the story of White Buffalo Calf Woman. However in other cultures, beauty can be a liability. For instance, we find that in some stories, such as the Moroccan folktale "The Sultan's Daughter," beauty symbolizes power, manipulative power and the power to make demands. A man who had once loved her finally said, "Oh, what cruelty can lurk beneath such beauty!" (18)

Beauty in some stories can represent various kinds of danger. For instance, we find that in the story of Cinderella, beauty instigates jealousy. The story of Samson and Delilah, the story of Lilith, and the Japanese story of Yuki-Onna represent beauty as a disguise for deceitful character. Yuki-Onna's own husband learns who she is when he tells her, " ... [T]hat was the only time that I saw a being as beautiful as you. Of course, she was not a human being ... " (117)

As you prepare stories for presentation on paper or aloud, it's extremely important to investigate the culture and context of the story so you can understand the characters in a way consistent with their context, whether your characters be tricksters, wise old women, or heroes.

REFERENCES

Campbell, J. (1949). *The Hero With a Thousand Faces*. Princeton, NJ: Princeton University Press.

Cashdan, S. (1999). *The Witch Must Die: The Hidden Meaning of Fairy Tales*. New York: Basic Books.

Erdoes, R., and Ortiz, A. (1998). *American Indian Trickster Tales*. New York: Viking.

"How Selfishness Was Rewarded." From American Folklore. Retrieved 1/17/2011. http://americanfolk-lore.net/folklore/2010/09/how_selfishness_was_rewarded

Leeming, D. A. (1997) *Storytelling Encyclopedia: Historical, Cultural, and Multiethnic Approaches to Oral Traditions Around the World*. Phoenix: Oryx Press.

Matthews, J., and Matthews, C. (2008) *Trick of the Tale: A Collection of Trickster Tales*. Cambridge, MA: Candlewick Press.

Mayer, M. (1994). *Baba Yaga and Vasilisa the Brave*. New York: Morrow Junior Books.

Orenstein, C. (2002). *Little Red Riding Hood Uncloaked: Sex, Morality, and the Evolution of a Fairy Tale*. New York: Basic Books.

Roberts, J. (1989). *From Trickster to Badman: The Black Folk Hero in Slavery and Freedom*. Philadelphia: University of Pennsylvania Press.

Roberts, M. (1979). *Chinese Fairy Tales & Fantasies*. New York: Pantheon Books.

San Souci, R. D. (2006). *Sister Tricksters: Rollicking Tales of Clever Females*. Little Rock: August House.

"The Forsaken Wife and Her Unfaithful Husband," in *The Magic Lotus Lantern and Other Tales from the Han Chinese*. By Haiwang Yuan. (2006). Westport, CT: Libraries Unlimited.

"The Sultan's Daughter," in *Moroccan Folktales*. Translated by Jilali El Koudia and Roger Allen. (2003). Syracuse: Syracuse University Press.

Walker, B. (1983). *The Woman's Encyclopedia of Myths and Secrets*. San Francisco: Harper & Row.

"Yuki-Onna," in *Kwaidan: Stories and Studies of Strange Things*. Lafcadio Hearn. (1971). Boston: Tuttle Publishing.

CHAPTER FOUR

Relationship with Audiences

AUDIENCES IN THE ORAL TRADITION

Before there was writing, there was the spoken word, and the spoken word was used for many vital purposes: to warn someone of danger, to convey information, to coordinate efforts among people, to predict, to explain, to make decisions, and to teach. One way humans teach is through the use of stories. Every culture has stories of how the world began, and many other stories about how it came to be peopled, and why things are the way they are. Moving in from the macro scale, we have migration stories that address the history of a people, we have family stories, and personal stories of something that happened yesterday.

Walter Fisher's Narrative Paradigm says that humans are storytelling beings.

FISHER'S NARRATIVE PARADIGM:

Walter Fisher insists that humans are storytelling creatures. His view of storytelling is broad, and includes much of human discourse. Our conversations are full of all kinds of accounts, he says. Even television news refers to news pieces as stories. They are narrative (sequential) accounts that include characters, events, and meanings.

Fisher contrasts two views of discourse:

The Narrative Paradigm	The Rational-World Paradigm
Humans are essentially storytelling beings.	Humans are essentially rational beings.
We create and communicate symbols ultimately as stories meant to give order to human existence.	Argument follows clear-cut inferential patterns and structures (such as syllogism).
Rationality is determined by the nature of persons, their inherent awareness of narrative probability, what constitutes a coherent story, and their constant habit of testing narrative fidelity, whether or not the stories they experience rings true with the stories they know to be true in their lives.	Rationality is determined by subject matter knowledge, argumentative ability, and skill in employing the rules of advocacy.
Metaphor counts as a way of relating truth about the human condition.	The world is a set of logical puzzles that can be solved through analysis and the application of reason.

It appears that in the rational worldview, there are those who argue that the only discourse that is truly informative is scientific discourse, which emphasizes fact. On the other hand, however, Fisher's Paradigm suggests that people are also motivated by concepts other than facts. We are motivated by love, beauty, desire, imagination, courage, and many other things that are not objectively observed and measured. This paradigm allows us to be transported by literature, mythology, rhetoric, and other nonscientific human creations.

The Midwife and the Cat

Many years ago, there was a midwife named Miriam, an older woman who supported herself by delivering the babies of Zakho, her town. At the end of one particular day, a day which had been very busy with births, Miriam got right into bed. She was just about to drift off to sleep when she saw a red-haired cat at the foot of her bed. The cat was obviously pregnant.

I wonder how the cat got inside? It's really a beauty, Miriam thought. *I wish I could deliver its kittens.*

And because she was so tired and didn't have the energy to get up out of bed, she let the cat go on its way and fell asleep. She had not been asleep long, when she was awakened by a loud knocking on the door.

"Oh, not another baby who wants to come into the world in the middle of the night," murmured Miriam, pulling herself out of the warm bed to answer.

There was a man she did not recognize at the door. "Can you come with me and help with a birth?" he asked.

"Of course," Miriam answered. "Wait here while I dress."

The man led Miriam to a carriage pulled by two goats. Miriam and the stranger traveled through the streets of the town and out into the country, down the familiar road. They traveled for a long time until they came to a stone bridge Miriam had never seen before. On the other side was a field filled with men and women dancing around one very beautiful woman who looked ready to give birth.

The man who had brought her seated Miriam next to the woman. "This is the woman you are to assist," said the man. "But be careful not [to] eat or drink anything these demons offer you or you will become one of them."

Demons! So that was it! That explained the strange journey and this celebration in the field, Miriam realized.

"But why have you chosen to bring me here?" whispered Miriam. "Surely, demons do not usually call on a human midwife?"

"No, but you requested to be present at this birth."

"I did?" said Miriam. Then she looked closely at the pregnant woman, at her silky reddish hair, the way she moved her body, the shape of her face.

Oh, my, thought Miriam. *This woman resembles that cat I saw just before I fell asleep!*

"I have never before seen a demon," said Miriam. "Have you told me all I must know? Only that I shouldn't eat any of their food or drink anything?"

"Yes," answered the man. "And you will be safe."

So Miriam began to make preparations for the delivery all the while listening to the sounds of the dancers. They were chanting these words, "If it is a healthy baby, we will give her great gifts, but if it is not, it will be her end."

Suddenly Miriam realized the dancers were talking about her! She knew she was a good midwife, but whether a baby was born healthy or not? That was in God's hands.

And so was she! Miriam tried to concentrate on her preparations. If she let her thoughts wander, she would not be able to do her best.

Luckily, she did not have to wait long. The demon woman gave birth soon, and to a healthy little boy!

What merriment there was among the demons! They ate and drank, laughed and danced around. They offered Miriam food and drink, but though she was there for many hours, she was careful not to taste one morsel of food or one drop of drink.

In order not to offend the demons. Miriam told them she could only eat food she prepared herself because she kept the laws of kashrut.

When the dancing and merriment came to an end, Miriam took her leave of the demon mother and baby, and asked to be taken back to Zakho.

"First you must tell us what gift you would like," said her hosts.

"I performed a good deed." said Miriam. "That is a gift in itself."

"No! No!" they insisted. "You must take a gift!"

"Well, then, give me that bunch of garlic I see near your fire," she said.

So the demons gathered up the garlic and gave all of it to her. Miriam got into the carriage pulled by two goats with the same stranger who had brought her.

When she reached her home, she was so tired, she just tossed the garlic by the woodpile, intending to get rid of it in the morning. She knew [she] could not eat it. The strange man had warned her of that. And she went to bed.

In the morning, one of her grandchildren woke her up. "Grandma, where did you get all the gold?" she asked.

"What gold are you talking about, child?" asked Miriam. "Show me."

The child led Miriam by the hand outside the house to the woodpile. There, to Miriam's great surprise, she saw that the child was right! The garlic had changed into gold! Miriam took the golden garlic and divided it up among her children and grandchildren. And from that day to this, Miriam's descendants have been blessed with good health and fortune.

· ·

It can be argued that narrative, as Fisher frames it, provides an audience with an opportunity for vicarious experience, whether or not the story rings true to ordinary life. Barbara Goldin provides this example of a Jewish story in an improbable context, and yet, we might become as engaged in the narrative as we would a factual story:

One of the notable points in this story is its absence of the rational-world paradigm. It's clearly within the narrative approach, and we find a clear and specific example in Miriam's belief that the health of the baby was in the hands of God. Since this belief is the fundamental element organizing our character's world view, we have to ask whether the truth of her belief can be observed or measured. Since it can't, it's an example of the narrative paradigm.

The other notable point is that the narrative transports the audience to another time and place where reality is different, and where things and events do not coincide with our ordinary lives. Whether the story is historically true or not, it has narrative fidelity, and it reflects a cultural truth, the truth that God protected Miriam.

We know that audiences have been around longer than there have been stories. There are many ancient stories that were transmitted orally to pre-literate audiences. Homer gave us examples of epic stories, passed along by word of mouth from storyteller to storyteller. There are even older stories that seem to have no specific author—stories like *Beowulf*, like *The Epic of Gilgamesh*, like the tenth-century Japanese *The Tale of the Shining Princess*, and many others.

Professional storytellers were exemplified by musician bards in Europe and the Middle East and *griots* in West Africa. Their skills were carefully cultivated and refined. Most of what they knew was unwritten but important knowledge needed by the communities they served, and they served different functions.

> **Bard:** Storytellers in the bardic tradition often play lutes or other stringed instruments while they sing or recite heroic tales of ancient times. Many believe that Homer was a bard who performed ancient stories but did not create *The Iliad* or *The Odyssey* in the first place. It is thought that he was following a bardic tradition.
>
> **Griot:** A musician from a West African culture who sings the seven-generation history of a tribal group or family. They have vast amounts of memorized knowledge, which they deliver in singing while playing huge stringed instruments. Griots are almost exclusively men.

TREATING YOUR AUDIENCE WITH RESPECT

Audiences are diverse. In most instances, a presenter will attempt to analyze the audience in order to learn how to serve that audience best. When there are variables shared among all or nearly all audience members, the task isn't difficult. For instance, if the audience consists of all retirees, all engineering majors, all advertising executives, or all Episcopalians, you can identify areas of shared understanding—areas where you can address their interests. Using your best judgment, you would not contrive jokes aimed at their demographic group.

Most audiences, however, are diverse. They contain women and men of all sexual persuasions and economic conditions. They include all cultural groups (Native American, African American, Anglo American, Asian American, and so on). The people in an audience can be a wide mixture of ages, body types, occupations, religions, and political persuasions. An audience is a big responsibility, and it matters how we humans treat each other. Most of us would never consider offending the audience on purpose. However, now we must be mindful that we can offend them by accident, and that we must strive with conscientiousness and intent not to offend them. When they're assembled to listen to us, they trust us to be honorable.

We can't ever be 100% certain that nobody will find fault with what we say, but there are some things to keep in mind about audiences:

- Assume your audience is intelligent, ethical, and responsible.
- Assume your audience has feelings.
- Assume your audience is deserving of a well-prepared, thoughtful presentation, even if it's done for fun.

Respect: Unconditional positive regard, courtesy and restraint from making assumptions or reacting to stereotypes.

- Assume the members of your audience have developed sets of values
- Assume that the members of your audience have widely varied worldviews.
- Assume the people in your audience would like to have their dignity respected, and watch your language.

As the same authors also say, "Although you have no ethical responsibility to hold everyone in high esteem, during your interactions you should display respect for the dignity and feelings of all people."

Immigration has been a controversial topic in recent years, with vitriolic rhetoric flung at the groups who attempt to find a new life in America, much as many of our own ancestors did. Many people are troubled by the potential impact of immigration on the quality of life here. However, we should try to remember that unless we are Native American (Navajo, Cherokee, Iroquois, Blackfeet, or the like), our own ancestors were immigrants, and we would not be here without their journeys. Like our ancestors, most contemporary immigrants are also seeking a new home where they can participate in society and take care of their families. Being mindful of these realities—not simply knowing, but being mindful—can help you refrain from committing subtle slights with your choices of words.

Political correctness is a concept that has received a certain amount of sneering contempt over time, but it still seems better than carelessness with our verbal behavior. Political correctness does not mean that we treat each other better in any substantial way. For instance, referring to someone as "mobility impaired" instead of "handicapped" doesn't mean that we're considerate of their needs or appreciative of their contributions. Moreover, ignoring the people in such a group does not acknowledge their basic human dignity. You should give respectful attention and eye contact to all parts of your audience, and not disconfirm anyone simply by refusing to look at them.

Cultural identity is a concept that refers to group inclusion. According to Klyukanov, "cultural identity is the way we see ourselves; it is our self-image. For example, people from the United States might identify with characterizations of themselves as hard-working, friendly, tolerant, and freedom-loving." In a broad way, cultural identity provides us with a place in the stream of humanity, but in an interpersonal way, "cultural identity can be viewed as membership in a group in which all people share the same symbolic meanings" (12). The reason to have this awareness is to recognize that all humans have meanings and worldviews. We don't have to agree with everyone, but we should assume that the worldviews of others are legitimately acquired through their own cultural experience. An awareness of cultural identity and its presence in the audience equips a storyteller with a mindset toward rhetorical sensitivity, a willingness to be respectful of differences.

Rhetorical sensitivity: Galanes and Adams explain it as "speaking and phrasing statements in such a way that the feelings and beliefs of the listener are considered; phrasing statements in order not to offend others or trigger emotional overreactions" (118). This does not mean the speaker simply says what he or she believes others want to hear. What it means is that the speaker is honest, but sensitive to the dignity and self-worth of others.

STORY SOURCES AND ETHICS

Samovar, Porter, and McDaniel tell us, "Ethics refers to judgments that focus 'on degrees of rightness and wrongness, virtue and vice, and obligation in human behavior.'" In storytelling, we have a double obligation: We must treat our diverse audience with respect, and we must extend respect to the sources of the stories we tell.

It's a tradition among many storytellers to acknowledge the sources of the stories they present. This shows respect for the cultural or the individual source. However, it demonstrates mindfulness to carry this practice a step further by learning something more about the source, so that your knowledge can help you present the story in as authentic a way as possible.

My story today is from African American tradition. The title is "How Nehemiah Got Free." The story was collected by Virginia Hamilton, a well-known scholar of folktales, myths, and legends, in her book *The People Could Fly.*

Many African Americans are still underrepresented to this day in the areas of education, good jobs, good neighborhoods, health care, environmental justice, and access to equal treatment by the police and the courts. A vicious cycle still exists for many urban African Americans in spite of laws that were enacted to prevent discrimination. Because of financial constraints, they often live in undesirable neighborhoods and have access to less successful schools. They also suffer from environmental dangers, such as peeling lead-based paint, smoke and fumes, toxic contaminants, garbage, rats, and noise. All these factors impact health, and make it even more difficult to be successful in school, have a successful career, or improve one's social situation. It is a difficult cycle to break.

I chose this story because of the history of slavery. The story shows the faith, the humor, the wit, and the hope that enslaved people used to cope with the harshness of their lives. The name Nehemiah comes from a book in the Old Testament, as many African and African American names do. This kind of naming shows the faith in the Lord needed by enslaved people in order to carry on under the burdens of the whip, the back-breaking forced work, the abuse, and the absence of rights.

In this story, Nehemiah outwits a succession of owners until he gains his freedom. It is a hopeful story.

What are the important things you should acknowledge about the culture of a story's origin? It depends largely on the story itself, but you shouldn't forget the actual people to whom the story belongs. Here are some examples of hypothetical introductions that show respect for the intelligence for the audience and for the cultural sources of folktales and other stories:

My story today is called "Daft Sandy and the Mare's Egg." It comes from the *Penguin Book of Scottish Folktales* edited by Neil Philip.

For at least 3000 years, Scotland has been at the mercy of people from other cultures. We know that the Romans arrived during their political and military height, but even earlier, strangers appeared from Denmark, France, and Norway. The Isles came to be inhabited by the Normans, Angles, Picts, Jutes, and Saxons.

More recently, when King Edward I ruled England, he declared Scotland to be part of his kingdom, and installed English knights in Scottish castles and lands. Through them, he ruled Scotland. We know through the story of William Wallace ("Braveheart") that Scotland was not happy with the arrangement, and there were many Scots willing to throw themselves into battle to regain their independence. The rigid social hierarchy that favored the titled English was insufferable, so during the reign of Edward II (in 1314), under the Scottish king Robert the Bruce, England was driven from Scotland.

Even after Scotland was returned to the Scots, life and survival were often difficult. May of the folktales revealed a sense of humor that helped them cope. Sandy, the trickster in this story, brings us an example of that humor.

Such an introduction considers the audience's need to be oriented so they can understand the many layers of meaning found in the story itself. After this introduction, a

My story today has been in my family for a very long time. It's a story about a preacher in the early days of American settlers. I first heard the story from my grandmother Mattie Jennings.

At the time this story took place, there were very few doctors as educated as they are now. People depended on midwives, bone-setters, and people who knew how to use herbs, and their authority came from having been successful enough in the past. Though they might not have been able to save every patient, they at least had not been accused of killing anyone. For most people, these practitioners were their only source of help.

Another situation existed at the time this story took place: people were very religious—understandable in light of their medical vulnerability. Preachers sometimes claimed that the suffering people experienced was punishment for sin. Many people believed it, and many people looked up to the preacher as a role model who dedicated his life to God and refrained from sin.

In this story, the preacher must confront his own sin, committed so long ago, before he can preach again about other people's sins, or God will know he's a hypocrite.

. . . .

storyteller can present the folktale in an appropriate way and provide a way for it to be understood appropriately as well.

Here's another example:

What if you acquire your folktale or other story in a traditional way rather than from a book or website? Further, what if you can find no recorded version of that story? Here's one example of how to introduce it:

In this example, the cultural realities are an important part of preparing the audience to hear and understand the story. By providing them this information, you are attentive to their needs.

BEING PREPARED

Choosing a story involves thinking about the audience. What stories are suitable for audiences that might include children? How can you avoid stories that could frighten recent immigrants? How long can your audience pay attention? What is your purpose? Do you want to entertain, to honor a group, or to teach? You should attempt to answer these questions when you choose a story.

If, for instance, you want to honor the Navajo Code Talkers of World War II, you should find a story that doesn't rest on too many concepts that will be unfamiliar to the audience. You should also be prepared to explain who the Navajo are, who the Code Talkers were, and what the Code Talkers did for America. And we should _not_ rely on John Woo's motion picture *Windtalkers* for a

Navajo Code Talkers: During World War II, the United States needed a way to communicate in a code that could not be broken by the Japanese. The solution came with a specially-trained group of native speakers of the Navajo language. They developed a second layer of code by referring to armored tanks as turtles, and so on. It is believed that the participation of the Code Talkers altered the course of the war.

After the war, many of these Code Talkers returned to their reservation only to find that there was no work for them. Off the reservation, they had little success in getting hired for whatever jobs were available.

realistic account. Instead, you could refer to the History Channel DVD titled *Navajo Code Talkers*. While the History Channel is not authoritative in the same sense as a scholarly work, they provide a DVD with more accurate representations than the motion picture.

Another sensitive area involves "ownership" of a story. From whom must you get permission before presenting a story? In many cases, stories have long been in the public domain, and your main responsibility is to acknowledge the source. However, there are stories that contain additional layers of unfamiliar meaning, and such stories should not be used without examining their appropriateness, without reexamining your purpose in telling the story, and without examining the ethical question of trespass. We should take every step to keep from devaluing a significant story and from misrepresenting the culture or the meanings of the story.

Furthermore, there are reasons for protecting certain stories, and these reasons are not readily apparent. Joseph Bruchac, a widely respected storyteller of both Abenaki and Slovak descent, says:

> Some kinds of Native American stories, like jokes, circulate freely among the community, but even where such stories are concerned, it is standard practice to credit the person who told it to you. The acknowledgement of sources and the understanding that something very much like a copyright exists in Native American oral tradition is another overlooked or totally unknown aspect of American Indian stories for many non-Native tellers. Some stories, in fact, clearly belong to a particular individual or a particular family. No one is to tell those stories without the direct permission of that person or that family. How can non-Indian tellers know which stories fall into this category? They usually cannot tell it when they get a story from a book. But when they hear a Native teller relate a story that they would like to tell themselves, it is their responsibility to directly ask permission of that Native teller. And if permission is refused, they must understand that it would be irresponsible for them to then tell that story. There are certain stories which I have been given permission to tell which I do not tell at large public gatherings where many non-Natives are present because I know that there will be people in that audience, even when I caution them not to do so, who will steal that story and even publish their own version of it … (96)

Cultural theft: The co-optation of cultural art forms, artifacts, or practices for the purpose of making money. As Joseph Bruchac noted, non-Native people have stolen Native stories, taken them without permission, and published their own versions of them. This is not only theft, but presents a risk of distorting the integrity of a story, often without the awareness that one has done so.

Another example of cultural theft is the reenactment of others' ceremonies, which have perhaps been witnessed or even experienced, but for which no legitimate training or teaching has been sought. The thief is ignorant of the symbolic gestures, songs, and objects, but might allow himself or herself to be viewed as someone knowledgeable and authorized to be conducting Native ceremonies.

How sad it is that even in the 21st century, non-Native people still assume the right to acquire what little remains of significant Native culture.

Knowing the Cultural Source

If you've identified a story from a given culture, such as the Lakota people, you have an obligation to understand some basic things about that culture in order to understand the messages in the story. For example, you should not refer to your source as "the Native American culture." There is no overarching Native American culture. Navajos are as distinct from Inuits as Seminoles are from Mohawks. Secondly, you should do whatever you can to learn about their relationship to Mother Earth, their historical experience after the arrival of the Europeans, and their current socioeconomic condition. You should probably be able to identify at least one or two outstanding past and contemporary members of that culture who do not fit the stereotypes about the cultural group.

Every culture is full of heroes. The underrepresented culture heroes do not appear in school textbooks at the same rate as the heroes of the dominant culture, but they are there, and they have done extraordinary things against great odds. For instance, in early African American history, we know about the abolitionist and writer Frederick Douglass, activist Harriet Tubman, the scholar W. E. B. Du Bois, the prominent figures of the Harlem Renaissance: Langston Hughes, Zora Neale Hurston, Ralph Ellison, Rev. Martin Luther King Jr., and others. Thurgood Marshall was the first Black justice in the U.S. Supreme Court. Rosa Parks fought for racial justice in Montgomery, Alabama, and triggered a bus strike in 1955. There are also contemporary heroes: LeBron James, Winton Marsalis, James Earl Jones, Maya Angelou, and many, many others.

We also have other culture heroes: Wovoka (Paiute), John Ross (Cherokee), Tecumseh (Shawnee), Chief Washakie (Shoshone), Osceola (Seminole), Tsali (Cherokee), Chief Joseph (Nez Percé), Sacajawea, and many others whose names you might not recognize, but their strength in the face of cultural upheaval serves even today as a model to Native people. Contemporary heroes include Winona LaDuke, Walter Echo Hawk, Sherman Alexie, and many others.

We should think beyond the easily identifiable groups, however, to keep in mind all the people, past and present, who have worked for justice for all people: Mahatma Gandhi, Muhammad Yunus, Margaret Sanger, Bono, Eleanor Roosevelt, Charles Schurz.

Knowing and acknowledging these exceptional people will do two things: it will show respect for people in that cultural group, and it will show respect for people in your audience who also belong to the group or feel a connection. Moreover, knowing and acknowledging them will teach members of your audience that exceptional people are in every cultural group.

The greater and deeper your knowledge is about a culture, the better you understand the folktale, and the better you can present it. When you're presenting other people's folktales, you are borrowing something important from that culture, and you have an obligation to do your best when you present to an audience. Since you're also asking for your audience's attention, you owe it to them, too, to do your best and be prepared.

Know the Characters

We first looked at the issue of authentic characters in Chapter 3. Character distinctiveness is also an important element in the coherence of your presented story. You audience must never become confused about which character in your story is speaking or acting. You should take steps to create clear images of each of your main characters: their appearance, their age, their posture, their attitude, and their voice. When you develop a clear description of your character, your story also becomes clearer and more animated. It's more likely to engage the audience.

Many stories don't provide details about a character's appearance, age, way of walking, or attitude, so as a storyteller, you have to develop these details for yourself.

Let's imagine one of your story characters is a **Younger Sister**:

> **Physical description**: She is about 14, girlish, and not yet womanly in either physical or mental development. She is slender and average-looking when quiet, but when arguing, she tends to bend forward at the hips and thrust her face forward, or to stand up very straight with her arms folded and her shoulders raised. She also clamps her jaw.

Assuming that another character has a profoundly different physical description, you should be able to assume each posture in turn during the unfolding of the story, and your audience will have an easy time knowing when Younger Sister is speaking or acting. Now let's consider her hypothetical motivations:

> **Personality**: Younger Sister exhibits a need to always be right. Inherently, therefore, the other character in the story must be wrong. However, if the other character isn't wrong, Younger Sister takes an attitude of superiority. She believes herself to be smarter and more insightful than others. She is very competitive with her sisters. Her one saving grace is that she does listen to elders, for it is obvious that they outstrip her in experience and knowledge.

If you can imagine a character motivated in this way, it shouldn't be difficult to present her personality as you present the story. Let's also consider the possibilities for her voice:

> **Vocal Quality**: Younger Sister speaks in a tone that's sharp, decisive, and strident, even when not in a dispute. She's not loud or harsh, but is simply sure she is right.

If there is a Younger Sister, of course, there must also be an Older Sister or an Older Brother. It's equally important to develop that other character in a way that's consistent with the message in the story, and is consistent with the culture from which the story is drawn, but is distinctive from Younger Sister.

When you present stories from cultures other than your own, it's crucially important to avoid developing your characters as stereotypes. In some stories, archetypes might be useful, since they are simplified, mono-dimensional characters that represent an idea—for example, Lisa Simpson, the girl nerd; or Hester Prynne, the ultimate victim in Hawthorne's *The Scarlet Letter*. However, using simplified stereotypes of under-represented cultures would be insensitive because it becomes a way of perpetuating negative views. Sadly, our media have perpetuated some skewed images of the family dynamic in Black and Hispanic cultures.

Know the Story

Many students believe that knowing a story means memorizing it. That isn't the best approach for most people. If you memorize a story as a sequence of words, you can get in trouble if, during a presentation, you forget a word.

Knowing a story means more than memorizing a sequence of words. It means knowing the characters, the cultural context, and perhaps the cultural message embodied in the story. Is the story heroic? Or is it funny, spiritual, or scary? Will it challenge the assumptions of the audience? Or will it offer an example of courage? Understand the story before you attempt to learn the narrative.

The perspective of the storyteller and the understanding of the story itself will shape the way a story is presented. Therefore, it's a considerable responsibility to treat a story with the attention and respect it deserves. This means, for one thing, that you can't hurry through your preparation. Your relationships with the story and with your audience require your best efforts even if the purpose of the story is to entertain.

Writer and masterful storyteller Carol Birch explains:

> "Who says?" asks a child, arms akimbo and chin thrust out. We've all witnessed this scene of a youngster deciding what she'll do—or not do—after she has weighed the reliability and authority of both who is standing before her and who is being quoted as having "said" so! Adults just grow more subtle. Yet, I believe receptive audiences are actively evaluating the reliability and authority of the storyteller standing before them. They want to know who says also. It affects their choices to stay or go, how closely they will listen, how fully they will trust the teller and the tale. (107)

Being an Audience Member

This chapter is about the relationship with the audience, which implies that both the speaker and the listeners have a role and responsibility. Your audience wants to know you as a credible presenter, even if the story is fantastical. But they should also extend the basic courtesy of listening receptively.

As Americans, we tend not to be good listeners. In our daily lives, we often find ourselves wishing that a speaker would hurry up and get to the "bottom line." We learn to prefer the kind of stand-up comedy that delivers a punch a minute over the subtly unfolding story. We're impatient. Our culture has taught us that time is important and must be used efficiently. But that isn't the kind of listening a story calls for. Storytelling coach Doug Lipman speaks of its importance:

Like so many of us, I used to take listening for granted, glossing over this step as I rushed into the more active, visible ways of being helpful. Now, I am convinced that listening is the single most important element of any helping relationship.

Listening has great power. It draws thoughts and feelings out of people as nothing else can ... (48)

Long ago, the philosopher Aristotle believed that the entire responsibility for the effectiveness of a presentation resided with the speaker. Since then, the view has changed. We now see communication as a transaction between or among people—a transaction in which each side has a responsibility. Walter Fisher might say that the thing that brings the two together is the shared symbolism carried in the story.

REFERENCES

Birch, C., and Heckler, M. (1996). "Who Says??" *Essays on Pivotal Issues in Contemporary Storytelling.* Little Rock: August House.

Fisher, W. R. (1989). *Human Communication as Narration: Toward a Philosophy of Reason, Value, and Action.* University of South Carolina Press.

Galanes, G., and Adams, K. (2010). *Effective Group Discussion.* Boston: McGraw-Hill.

Hamilton, V. (1985). "How Nehemiah Got Free," in *The People Could Fly: American Black Folktales.* New York: Alfred A. Knopf.

Klyukanov, I. (2005). *Principles of Intercultural Communication.* Boston: Pearson Education.

Navajo Code Talkers. (1998). DVD. The History Channel.

One Hundred and One Jewish Read-Aloud Stories. (Ed.) Goldin, B. D. (2001) New York: Black Dog & Leventhal Publishers.

Penguin Book of Scottish Folktales. (1996) Ed. P. Neil. New York: Penguin.

Samovar, L., Porter, R., and McDaniel, E. (2010). *Communication Between Cultures.* Boston: Wadsworth.

CHAPTER FIVE

Family, Love, Jealousy, Courtship, and Marriage

In Chapter 1, we learned that institutions are in the deepest foundations of culture. They are the continually repeated patterns of social behavior sanctioned by a culture and strengthened by repetition. They are enduring, and they change only in response to changing needs and conditions very slowly over a long time. Religion is one of those institutions, as we will see in Chapter 7. Another is family, an institution that probably developed long before the Agricultural Revolution 12,000 years ago. For in order to have social organization for hunters and gathers or for pastoralists, there had to be rules about who was responsible for whom, who could marry whom, and who could inherit from whom.

Marriage is most often the basis for family, and marriage has not always considered romantic love as its required underlying condition. In fact, many people in the world have prospered in arranged marriages, marriages that strengthened connections between families. These marriages, when successful, contributed to social cohesion, social status, the consolidation of wealth, and other advantages. In a few societies, the betrothal of infants is enough to create social cohesion and cooperation, and in these cases, a child grows up knowing he or she already has a wife or a husband. When it's time for them to marry, they follow the local cultural rules about place of residence, dowries, and degree of authority each spouse has in a household.

Most of us, however, expect to choose our own spouses, based on a combination of factors, including age, attraction, love, religion, the potential for security, professional status, and so on. However, in the Western world, we rarely encounter such wifely devotion as Amore and Shinn offer in providing this Hindu story:

Savatri and the God of Death

Ashvapati, the virtuous king of Madras, grew old without offspring to continue his royal family. Desiring a son, Ashvapati took rigid vows and observed long fasts to accumulate merit. It is said that he offered 10,000 oblations to the goddess Savatri in hopes of having a son. After eighteen years of constant devotion, Ashvapati was granted his wish for an off-spring even though the baby born was a girl.

The king rejoiced at his good fortune and named the child Savatri in honor of the goddess who gave him this joy to brighten his elder years.

Savatri was both a beautiful and an intelligent child. She was her fa-ther's delight and grew in wisdom and beauty as the years passed. As the age approached for Savatri to be given in marriage as custom demanded, no suitor came forward to ask her father for her hand—so awed were all the princes by the beauty and intellect of this unusual maiden. Her father became concerned lest he not fulfill his duty as a father and incur disgrace for his failure to provide a suitable husband for his daughter. At last, he instructed Savatri herself to lead a procession throughout the surrounding kingdoms and handpick a man suitable for her.

Savatri returned from her search and told her father that she had found the perfect man. Though he was poor and an ascetic of the woods, he was handsome, well educated, and of kind temperament. His name was Satyavan and he was actually a prince whose blind father had been displaced by an evil king. Ashvapati asked the venerable sage Narada whether Satyavan would be a suitable spouse for Savatri. Narada re-sponded that there was no one in the world more worthy than Satyavan. However, Narada continued, Satyavan had one unavoidable flaw. He was fated to live a short life and would die exactly one year from that very day. Ashvapati then tried to dissuade Savatri from marrying Satyavan by telling her of the impending death of her loved one. Savatri held firm to her choice, and the king and Narada both gave their blessings to this seemingly ill-fated bond.

After the marriage procession had retreated from the forest hermitage of Savatri's new father-in-law, Dyumatsena, the bride removed her wed-ding sari and donned the ocher robe and bark garments of her ascetic family. As the days and weeks passed, Savatri busied herself by waiting upon the every need of her new family. She served her husband, Satyavan, cheerfully and skillfully. Satyavan responded with an even-tempered love which enhanced the bond of devotion between Savatri and himself. Yet the dark cloud of Narada's prophecy cast a shadow over this otherwise blissful life.

When the fateful time approached, Savatri began a fast to strengthen her wifely resolve as she kept nightly vigils while her husband slept. The day marked for the death of Satyavan began as any other day at the hermitage. Satyavan shouldered his axe and was about to set off to cut wood for the day's fires when Savatri stopped him to ask if she could go along, saying "I cannot bear to be separated from you today." Satyavan responded, "You've never come into the forest before and the paths are rough and the way is very difficult. Besides, you've been fasting and are surely weak." Savatri persisted, and Satyavan finally agreed to take her along. Savatri went to her parents-in-law to get their permission saying she wanted to see the spring blossoms which now covered the forest. They too expressed concern over her health but finally relented out of consideration for her long period of gracious service to them.

Together Satyavan and Savatri entered the tangled woods enjoying the beauty of the flowers and animals which betoken spring in the forest. Coming to a fallen tree, Satyavan began chopping firewood. As he worked, he began to perspire heavily and to grow weak. Finally, he had to stop and lie down telling Savatri to wake him after a short nap. With dread in her heart, Savatri took Satyavan's head in her lap and kept a vigil knowing Satyavan's condition to be more serious than rest could assuage. In a short time, Savatri saw approaching a huge figure clad in red and carrying a small noose. Placing Satyavan's head upon the ground, Savatri arose and asked the stranger of his mission. The lord of death replied, "I am Yama and your husband's days are finished. I speak to you, a mortal, only because of your extreme merit. I have come personally instead of sending my emissaries because of your husband's righteous life."

Without a further word, Yama then pulled Satyavan's soul out of his body with the small noose he was carrying. The lord of death then set off immediately for the realm of the dead in the south. Grief stricken and yet filled with wifely devotion, Savatri followed Yama at a distance. Hours passed yet hunger and weariness could not slow Savatri's footsteps. She persisted through thorny paths and rocky slopes to follow Yama and his precious burden. As Yama walked south he thought he heard a woman's anklets tingling on the path behind him. He turned around to see Savatri in the distance following without pause. He called out to her to return to Satyavan's body and to perform her wifely duties of cremating the dead. Savatri approached Yama and responded, "It is said that those who walk seven steps together are friends. Certainly we have traveled father than that together. Why should I return to a dead body when you possess the soul of my husband?"

Yama was impressed by the courage and wisdom of this beautiful young woman. He replied, "Please stop following me. Your wise words and persistent devotion for your husband deserve a boon. Ask of me anything except that your husband's life be restored, and I will grant it."

Savatri asked that her blind father-in-law be granted new sight. Yama said that her wish would be granted, and then he turned to leave only to find that Savatri was about to continue following. Yama again praised her devotion and offered a second, and then a third boon. Savatri told Yama of the misfortune of her father-in-law's lost kingdom and asked that Yama assist in ousting the evil king from Dyumatsena's throne. Yama agreed. Then Savatri utilized her third boon to ask that her own father be given one hundred sons to protect his royal line, and that too was granted by Yama.

Yama then set off in a southerly direction only to discover after a short while that Savatri still relentlessly followed him. Yama was amazed at the thoroughly self-giving attitude displayed by Savatri and agreed to grant one last boon if Savatri would promise to return home. Yama again stipulated that the bereaved wife could not ask for her husband's soul. Savatri agreed to the two conditions and said, "I only ask for myself one thing, and that is that I may be granted one hundred sons to continue Satyavan's royal family." Yama agreed only to realize, upon prompting from Savatri, that the only way Satyavan's line could be continued would be for him to be restored to life. Although he had been tricked by the wise and thoughtful Savatri, Yama laughed heartily and said, "So be it! Auspicious and chaste lady, your husband's soul is freed by me." Loosening his noose Yama permitted the soul of Satyavan to return to its earthly abode and Savatri ran without stopping back to the place where Satyavan had fallen asleep. Just as Savatri arrived at the place where her husband lay, he awoke saying, "Oh, I have slept into the night, why did you not waken me?" (28–33)

....

From this story, it's clear that a great deal of self-sacrifice is or was highly valued in a wife. Devotion, piety, wisdom, purity, obedience, and hard work were all parts of Savatri's way of serving her husband and his family. Most of these qualities, such as obedience, would not be considered essential in a Western marriage—or at least not in such extraordinary proportions. Remembering the influence of such important institutions over time, we should consider the probability that the same characteristics are still admired. However, in the face of changing international and economic realities, gender roles must have expanded to include gainful employment for many women and more child care for men.

Gender expectations vary widely across India. Traditionally, women were relied on for duties of household maintenance and child rearing, but had little influence in the political and economic life of the community. In fact, some Indian people say, there is a prayer in which a man gives thanks that he was not born a woman (Mathur). This long-established sentiment is passing very slowly, just as the institutions of the caste system linger long after their statutory nullification. We recall from Chapter 1 that in the deep structures of culture, changes in long-standing institutions take place only very slowly over time. It's therefore not a surprise that old attitudes about the roles and statuses of women fade away slowly, even in the face of extraordinary achievements by Indian and Indian American women. A case in point is Dr. Kalpana Chawla, who was born in India and received her first academic degree in aeronautical engineering there. After moving to the United States, she received her MS and PhD in aerospace engineering, and sadly, was an astronaut aboard the space shuttle *Columbia* when it disintegrated in 2003. She was far from alone as a woman with high academic and intellectual achievement, and yet the images of India before modernity persist. Like Savatri, Dr. Chawla was married, but chose her own non-Indian husband rather than having an arranged marriage. It is highly unlikely that she served the daily needs of her husband's parents in the way Savatri did.

We find that traditionally, women in many parts of India, especially in the North, experience marriage as less than joyful. Kirin Narayan tells us that "across castes, marriage for women is seen not as a choice but as a necessary, natural destiny. Urmilaji [an informant] once commented, 'A girl is goods that belong to her husband's family, not to her parents.' Women are almost always subject to marriages arranged by their elder relatives and so have little control over the choice of a partner. Also, because of the principle of village exogamy—marrying out—women are routinely married into families far from the home of their birth ... " (30–31)

It would be reasonable to think in terms of many Indians. In the Northern areas, traditions survive, contributing to social stability, but limiting the choices for both women and men. In the South, however, we encounter modernization, change, choice, and an international role in technology that was first developed in the West. This situation paves the way for educational opportunity and wider marriage options—including remaining single longer than would be traditional.

Turning now to another theme, jealousy, we find the following tale from S. E. Schlosser:

Pele's Revenge

Ohi'a and Lehua loved each other from the moment they first saw each other at a village dance. Ohi'a was a tall strong man with a handsome face and lithe form. He was something of a trickster and was first in all the sports played by all the young men. Lehua was gentle and sweet and as fragile as a flower. Her beauty was the talk of the island, and her father was quite protective of his only child.

When Lehua saw the handsome, bold Ohi'a speaking with her father beside the bonfire, she blushed crimson, unable to take her eyes from the young man. At the same moment, Ohi'a glanced up from his conversation and his mouth dropped open at the sight of the beautiful maiden. He was not even aware that he had stopped speaking right in the middle of his sentence, so overwhelmed was he by the sight of the fair maiden across the fire from him.

Lehua's father nudged the young man, recalling him to his duties as a guest. Ohi'a stuttered and stammered apologies, trying to continue his conversation while keeping one eye on the fair Lehua. Lehua's father was amused by the young man's obvious infatuation with his daughter. He quite liked this bold trickster, and so he offered to introduce Ohi'a to his daughter. The young man almost fell over in his haste as they walked across the clearing to where Lehua stood with her friends.

From that moment, there was no other woman for Ohi'a but Lehua. He had eyes only for her, and courted her with a passion and zeal that swiftly won her heart. Her father gave his only daughter gladly into the keeping of the strong young man, and the young couple lived quite happily for several months in a new home Ohi'a built for his bride.

Then one day the goddess Pele was walking in the forest near the home of the handsome Ohi'a and spied the young man at work. Pele was smitten by him, and went at once to engage him in conversation. Ohi'a spoke politely to the beautiful woman, but did not respond to her advances, which infuriated Pele. She was determined to have this young man for herself, but before she could renew her efforts, Lehua came to the place her young husband was working to bring him his midday meal.

When he saw his lovely wife, Ohi'a's face lit up with love. He dropped everything at once and went to her side, leaving a fuming Pele to stare in jealous rage at the young couple. Dropping her human disguise, the goddess transformed into a raging column of fire and struck Ohi'a down, transforming him into a twisted ugly tree in revenge for spurning her advances.

Lehua fell to her knees beside the twisted tree that had once been her husband. Tears streaming down her lovely face, she begged Pele to turn him back into a man or else turn her into a tree, as she could not bear to be separated from her beloved. But Pele ignored the girl, taking herself up to the cool heights, her anger satisfied. But the gods saw what Pele had done to the innocent lovers and were angry. As Lehua lay weeping in despair, the gods reached down and transformed the girl into a beautiful red flower, which they placed upon the twisted Ohi'a tree, so that she and her beloved husband would never more be apart.

From that day to this, the Ohi'a tree has blossomed with the beautiful Lehua flowers. While the flowers remain on the tree, the weather remains sunny and fair. But when a flower is plucked from the tree, then heavy rain falls upon the land like tears, for Lehua still cannot bear to be separated from her beloved husband Ohi'a.

Here we find a story in which love is so powerful that the level of passion would seem impossible to sustain over time. Love at first sight is rare to find among ordinary mortals, but in this case, it even has the capacity to strike the young man nearly mute. It's a story in which one character is a goddess, so we make some allowances for accepting the extraordinary capacities of the other characters as well. After all, the story takes place in Hawaii, where volcanoes erupt and where rogue waves are known to sweep up a shoreline and sometimes sweep someone out to sea. Hawaii is the exemplar of violent earth geography, and we find intensity not only in the natural setting, but in characters as well. The goddess Pele is the goddess of volcanoes, and no one can doubt their explosive force, but even Pele's intensity does not suffice to destroy eternal love, for the love between Ohi'a and Lehua is also intense like the natural world around them.

Jealousy often runs rampant through stories with which we're familiar. The jealously of Snow White's vain stepmother triggered a sequence of events from which Snow White miraculously escaped. In the Russian tale "King Frost," we find that a stepmother's jealousy leads to the death of her own daughter. Greek mythology brings us Hera, the jealous wife of the god Zeus, who wreaks havoc as cataclysmically as Pele. We get a similar values message from these stories, that jealousy is selfish. It is destructive, not only of others, but of the soul of the one who is jealous. It is almost universally forbidden and held in contempt, even **taboo**. In fact, even the Christian Bible forbids it in the Ten Commandments, though in that context, it appears to be aimed primarily at males: "Thou shalt not covet thy neighbor's house, thou shalt not covet thy neighbor's wife, nor his manservant, nor his maidservant … nor anything that is thy neighbor's" (Exodus 20:17).

The near-universal taboo against adultery challenges Pele and reveals her as a complicated character. First, she is a goddess, accustomed to making volcanoes erupt, yet cannot charm Ohi'a. Second, she is overwhelmed by jealousy. How often do goddesses become overwhelmed by anything? Being overwhelmed isn't a condition we normally attribute to the powerful. Third, she has serious character flaws, at least from a Western point of view. She's selfish, malicious, narrow-minded, undisciplined, and destructively jealous. We find that in most stories, jealousy is a deadly flaw, taboo, and few characters

Taboo: A taboo is a serious injunction against some action or type of food (such as pork, among Muslims and Jews). The injunction is so serious that it is felt that when a taboo is broken, there is serious harm to the individual violator or to the community. If something is taboo, it means either that it isn't allowed at all, or that it isn't allowed to ordinary people.

An example of a taboo that is nearly universal is adultery, fornication with another person's spouse. In some societies, it is thought the ultimate betrayal of a spouse, and it generates such intense anger that danger to individuals and communities is a pressing concern. Therefore, adultery, as defined by most societies, is generally taboo. In some societies, the injunction rests more heavily on women than men.

In some societies, the mere circumstance of being caught alone with another person's spouse is enough to be called adultery, and the punishments and other consequences of violating a taboo are set in motion. On the other hand, there are societies where a married individual may give their blessing to a dalliance between their spouse and a close friend on a given occasion. In this rare and specific situation, the dalliance is not considered adultery, and is not taboo.

The Catholic Catechism expounds on the Sixth Commandment: You shall not commit adultery. "You have heard that it was said, 'You shall not commit adultery.' But I say to you that every one who looks at a woman lustfully has already committed adultery with her in his heart" (Part 6: 619). The Catechism goes on to explain: "Adultery is an injustice. He who commits adultery fails in his commitment. He does injury to the sign of the covenant which the marriage bond is, transgresses the rights of the other spouse, and undermines the institution of marriage by breaking the contract on which it is based ... " (Part 6, 632). The Catechism also forbids polygamy, incest, and "free union." Further, it forbids the regulation of birth by "morally unacceptable means," or contraception.

Hence, we find a great many taboos concerning intimate behavior, which both the Catholic Catechism and the Qur'ān acknowledge as an innate human urge.

Menstrual taboo

The Qur'ān provides instruction about menstruation and marriage: "They also ask you about (the injunctions concerning) menstruation. Say 'It is a state of hurt (and ritual impurity), so keep away from them during their menstruation and do not approach them until they are cleansed. When they are cleansed, then (you can) go to them inasmuch as God has commanded you (according to the urge He has placed in your nature, and within the terms He has enjoined upon you). Surely God loves those who turn to Him in sincere repentance (of past sins and errors), and He loves those who cleanse themselves'" (Part 2, Sūrah 2: 222, Ali Ünal).

overcome it to finally become virtuous, as we see in the folktale "Pele's Revenge."

There are many triggers for jealousy—wealth, power, and beauty among them. In many stories, including the story of Savatri and the story of Ohi'a and Lehua, beauty is emphasized. Beauty is emphasized in so many tales that it's worth a brief look, for the meanings of beauty range widely between different cultures.

In the Western world, we often feel the tyranny of looks. The standards imposed on both women and men are often experienced as cultural imperialism. Who decides what is beautiful? In what generation do they decide it? In keeping with issues of gender power, men are big and strong and women are slender and dainty. Men and women in the western world spend enormous amounts of money on beauty salons, baldness remedies, fitness, breast implants, cosmetic surgery, and fashion. Age is the enemy, since the loss of one's looks can be a scary specter. Beauty is power, the power to be taken seriously, and the loss of beauty seems like the loss of that power to count as a worthy person. The boundaries between natural and achieved beauty fade and blur. Another story from India, "The Prostitute Who Lost Her Charm," emphasizes "the transitoriness of all things, including a woman's beauty" (Amore and Shinn).

The Prostitute Who Lost Her Charm

Once when the Buddha was teaching in the area of Rajagaha, the famous prostitute of the area, Sirima, happened to visit a lay woman's house at the very time that the Buddha was giving instruction to lay people. Hearing some of the instruction from the Master, Sirima converted and became a devoted and generous supporter of the Buddhist Order of monks. With the wealth she had accumulated from her high-priced services Sirima was mistress of a mansion and many servants. Whenever Buddhist monks came by for alms she would personally serve them food fit for a king. Soon she became as famous for her food gifts to the monks as she had been for her sexual prowess among the laymen.

One young monk overheard another monk praise Sirima's food and physical appearance in great detail one night and determined to see her for himself. He arranged this on a day when she happened to be so seriously ill that her servants had to carry her on a cot to a point where she could salute the monks. The young monk fell hopelessly in love with her—even though she had been too weak to dress up properly in jewels and fine clothing. He was so lovesick that he did not eat for several days. During this time Sirima died and the king, at Buddha's request, had her nude body put on display at the burning grounds, rather than being cremated. Again acting upon Buddha's request, the king ordered all his subjects to view Sirima's decomposing, maggot-infested body. "Who will pay one thousand pieces of money for Sirima's body," the town criers called out. When there were no takers, the price was lowered and lowered and lowered until at last no one would have Sirima for free, though men had formerly paid one thousand a night! The lovesick monk was cured and the teaching of the Buddha about the transitoriness of all things, including a woman's beauty, was impressed upon the minds of the people of Rajagaha.

. . . .

The power that accompanies beauty is often a two-edged sword. For instance, "The Sultan's Daughter" tells of a sultan's youngest and most beautiful daughter who was her father's favorite. Though she promptly received anything she wanted from her father, her sisters became jealous, and took steps to make her life difficult, even taking steps to destroy her relationship with a young man. Koudia translated this Moroccan folktale:

The Sultan's Daughter

 . . . .

Long, long ago there lived a sultan who was well respected by his people. God had endowed him with three daughters, but he had no son. The youngest daughter was the most beautiful and was her father's favorite. All her requests were promptly granted. Naturally, her sisters because very jealous of her and started making her life hard. And so, in order to live in peace with them, she asked her father to build her a palace of her own and to provide her with servants. Once her wish had been fulfilled, she allowed no one to approach her palace, having made up her mind to live as a hermit.

In the neighboring country, the son of another powerful sultan heard the story of the beautiful damsel living alone in her palace. He sent her a message, but she ignored it. He started frequenting her palace and managed to make clear his desire to marry her. She accepted, but only with many conditions. He had to provide her with one hundred of every-thing she asked for. When he had fulfilled all the conditions, she still did not allow him to make public visits to see her; instead, he had to dig a tunnel under her palace and visit her only during mealtimes. All this was not impossible for a sultan's son, especially since he was so in love with her. Thus, their meetings became more regular.

Despite the total secrecy, rumors of what was happening reached her sisters' ears. Their curiosity was roused: how did the young man look, and why did he come through a secret tunnel? They begged their father and then sent their sister a message, saying how very much they had missed her and how they longed to see her. At these words her heart melted, and she believed that their jealousy was a thing of the past. So she forgave them and allowed them to pay her a visit.

After agreeing on a plan they went to see her. They suggested tak-ing her to the *hammam*, the public bath, and she liked the idea. Once there, they pretended they had forgotten something. Leaving her with the servants, they hurried back to her room to get a glimpse of the young man. They had made their precise calculations to coincide with his visit. Upon investigation they discovered that the tunnel was made of glass. When they heard him making his way through the tunnel, they started throwing stones. A sharp piece of broken glass went straight into his eye and did him a serious injury. Furious at what had happened, he retreated in agony.

The sisters quickly rejoined their sister at the bath and helped her wash. She thanked them and returned home, assuming that her visitor would be waiting for her. But he was not there. She waited for a long time. When he did not show up, she began to suspect that something had happened to him. She went into the tunnel to see if he had left her a message, and there she found pieces of broken glass and drops of blood. For just a moment she paused for thought, and then it dawned upon her that her sisters had conspired against her during their brief absence from the bath. She realized that, unfortunately, neither time nor distance can cure jealousy.

Leaving the palace she found an old beggar woman who always sat around the corner. She invited the woman in and talked to her in her private room. After exchanging clothes, she left her palace and went in search of her future husband disguised in dirty, tattered garments.

During the day she walked a few miles and at night she lay down to sleep under a willow tree. Two pigeons took refuge for the night in the same tree. Perching just above her head they started talking about two lovers and how the sisters of the young woman had interfered to destroy their relationship. They said the young man was in grave danger of losing his sight forever. The two pigeons concluded their night talk by saying that the only cure for the young man was the ash of their feathers.

The two pigeons fell sound asleep. She meanwhile climbed the tree and caught them. Then she proceeded to pluck most of their feathers, burn them, and collect the ash in a piece of cloth. Next morning she continued her search for her lover's palace. Taking her for a beggar or madwoman, the palace guards stopped her at the entrance, but she insisted on seeing the sultan, saying she was bringing him an urgent message. When she told them that she had the cure for his son, she managed to convince them. A messenger was sent to tell the sultan about the mission of an old woman. He immediately received her.

In the sultan's presence, she cleaned his son's eyes with warm water, then sprinkled a few pinches of the ash on them. She advised him to keep them shut for at least an hour. When the sultan offered her a reward, she declined, saying that it was a cure from God.

She returned hurriedly to her palace and entered, still in disguise. She thanked the old woman and gave her plenty of gold and silver. Once the old beggar had left, the young woman ordered her cook to make a special cake that looked exactly like her. Then she laid her replica in bed and covered it in a clean white sheet, leaving only the face uncovered.

After about two hours the sultan's son opened his eyes. He was feeling no pain whatsoever, and had completely regained his sight. Overjoyed, he asked to see the old woman who had cured him, but he was told she had already left. Taking his sword he jumped on his horse and went in search of the girl he thought had betrayed him. He was determined to take his revenge.

When he arrived at the palace, he entered secretly through the tunnel and headed straight for the bedroom on tiptoe. There he saw her, lying comfortably in her bed and smiling as she slept. "Oh, what cruelty can lurk beneath such beauty!" he thought to himself. Unsheathing his sword, he chopped off her head. When a piece of pastry popped into his mouth, he realized he had been deceived once more. He stood on guard and looked around, but everything was quiet and all the doors were locked. As he bent over to uncover the false woman, suddenly someone jumped on his neck and started kissing him. Then she told him what her sisters had done to her and how she had come by the cure for his injuries. When he learned the whole truth, he fell tearfully into her arms. And they lived together in complete happiness ever after.

Aside from the message that a single event can be perceived and interpreted differently by different people, there is the expression of conflicted ideas about beauty. We've all heard the message that inner beauty is more important and honest than outer beauty, but we've seen evidence that it is outer beauty that gives some people a social and professional advantage. Beauty can inspire love, courage, admiration, devotion, jealousy, mistrust, frustration, treachery and revenge.

Other dangers also accompany beauty. A beautiful appearance disguising evil shows up in stories such as the Bible story of Samson and Delilah, the story of Lilith, and the story "Yuki-Onna," in which a beautiful but dangerous woman nearly kills her own husband, and only the presence of their children prevents it (Hearn).

How important is beauty? Do beautiful people make more money than ordinary people? Do they have more opportunities? Are they more likely to marry "well"—that is, in a direction of high social status? The answer depends on culture. We have already said that culture must change in response to the realities around and within it, so it shouldn't be a surprise that in the time of Charles Dickens, wealth was much more important than looks, and a woman without money would be unlikely to attract an educated or otherwise influential husband. In fact, one feature of the institution of marriage was that in those times, the wife's property would automatically become the property of her husband. Even if he abandoned her later, the property would still be his. Physical beauty simply didn't count.

So far, we've linked together the concepts of marriage, beauty, jealousy, danger, and power. We can finally look at beauty in the light of morality. Desire and temptation threaten cultural values even when beauty is valued. In the Christian Bible, we find the story of David and Bathsheba, a story in which a king loses his standing through desire, temptation, adultery, deceit, manipulation, and murder.

We also find that beauty makes both women and men vulnerable. In the ancient story of Gilgamesh, we meet the radiant and splendid king of Uruk. His physical beauty and magnificence is a liability, we find, for he has no compunctions against having his way with maidens. We also find female beauty as a locus of power when a beautiful woman goes to the wilderness to seduce the wild man Enkidu, the only human who is the equal of Gilgamesh in strength and intellect. He is distracted and ensnared by the woman who then captures him to bring him to the city of Uruk and to the presence of the monarch Gilgamesh. Within the story, we find the virgins of Uruk vulnerable to the desires of Gilgamesh on their wedding day, even before they have spent a single night with their husbands. And within this one ancient Babylonian story, we find the embodiment of beauty as power, and also as vulnerability in the face of the tyrant Gilgamesh.

Other cultures bring us stories concerned less with beauty than with inner qualities. The following Hasidic tale comes from the Hasidic Stories home page. We find that it wasn't beauty that enriched the life of this husband; it was righteousness.

> **Baal Shem Tov:** A Jewish mystic rabbi said to be the founder of Hasidic Judaism.

Take a moment and bask in the beauty of that story.

The Three Laughs

Once, the disciples of the Baal Shem Tov decided to prepare him a special Sabbath. They worked for days to make sure that everything would be just as it should be, so that the spirit of the Sabbath would descend as it never had before.

At last, a few minutes before sundown on Friday night, they were all seated around a long table with the Baal Shem Tov at the place of honor at the head. The disciple who had been chosen for the special honor of lighting the Sabbath candles stood up and began to light the candles and say the blessing.

"Ha! Ha-ha!" Suddenly, the Baal Shem Tov gave a loud laugh.

The disciple lighting the candles looked around to see what was wrong—if there was something amiss with his clothing, perhaps—but everything was as it should be.

Later, they began the Sabbath meal. They gave the Baal Shem Tov the first bowl of the soup they had labored so long over.

He tasted it.

"Heh, heh, heh, heh!" He laughed and laughed.

The disciples were appalled. They rushed to taste the soup, but there was nothing in it that tasted … humorous.

Still later, they were singing the Sabbath songs:

Oh, what strength a righteous woman has!
There is no treasure rarer than this!
Happy is the heart that relies on her,
For such a heart can lack for nothing …
Yai, dai, dai, dai, dai, dai, dai, dai …

As they sang, the Baal Shem Tov began to laugh and laugh, as though he could not contain himself.

It was the custom of the disciples that, on Saturday night, after the spirit of the Sabbath had departed, they would choose one question between them, and present it to the Baal Shem Tov.

This Saturday, there was no debate as to what question they would ask. "Holy master, why did you laugh during the Sabbath—three times?"

All the disciples crowded into the Baal Shem Tov's carriage. He drew the curtains over the windows, and they began to travel swiftly.

Several hours later, when he opened the curtains, they were in a distant village. None of them had ever been there before.

The Baal Shem Tov went to the leaders of the village. "Bring everyone to the village square. Now."

When the Baal Shem Tov stood looking out over that crowd of faces, he said, "There is still one family missing."

After a few minutes, the people realized, "It must be the old bookbinder and his wife. They live on the edge of town; they must not have gotten the word."

When this old man and this old woman entered the village square, and the old man saw who it was who was calling for him, he began to wring his hands. "Oh, Holy Master. I know I have committed a great sin. I only ask forgiveness."

"Bookbinder, tell my disciples and these people gathered here how you spent your Sabbath."

Fearfully, the old man glanced at the illustrious students of the Baal Shem Tov and began to speak. "I am an old bookbinder. In my youth, I could earn enough that we had what we needed during the week, and something special to greet the Sabbath. But as I have grown older, there has been less and less.

"Finally, this Sabbath—for the first time—we had no Sabbath candles—and only a few crusts of bread for a Sabbath meal.

"My wife was determined that we would observe the Sabbath as well as we were able. And so, just before sundown, she went through the motions of lighting candles that were not there.

"As she did, I saw … a flash of light. And I understood for the first time that the light that I had thought came only from candles was also coming from her. I shouted out, 'I love you'—in the middle of the holy blessing.

"I got control of myself, and went back to observing the Sabbath with due respect.

"But then later, we were beginning our humble meal. We had only warmed water for soup. But I tasted it. I felt … nourished.

"At that moment, I realized that the nourishment—which all these years I had thought came only from the soup—actually came also from her, from our being together through so many Sabbaths.

"And before I realized what I was doing, I jumped up. I kissed her!

"Shocked at my own behavior, I sat back down. I stayed in my seat properly until later, when we sang the Sabbath songs.

Oh, what strength a righteous woman has!
There is no treasure rarer than this!

"Singing these words, I realized what a great strength she was in my life.

Happy is the heart that relies on her,
For such a heart can lack for nothing …

"Suddenly, I knew that, in spite of our great poverty, while I had her in my life, I lacked for nothing.

"And then, before I knew what I was doing, I jumped up. I grabbed her by the arms. We began to sing and dance together.

Yai, dai, dai, dai, dai, dai, dai, dai;
Yai, dai, dai, dai, dai, dai, dai, dai, …

"At last, I got control of myself and sat back down.

"Holy master. I know I have defiled the Sabbath. Please, tell me: what must I do to be forgiven?"

The Baal Shem Tov looked at his disciples. "When this man and this woman spent their Sabbath in such deep and holy love, I was there with them, and I shared in their joy.

"And when he spoke his love for that woman, not only I but the angels in heaven heard—and they smiled. And when he got up and kissed that woman, acting on that deep love—the angels in heaven saw them, and they laughed.

"And when the two of them joined their hands and sang and danced their joy, the angels themselves began to sing and to dance. And the Eternal Heart itself heard them, and it was warmed.

"On a Sabbath of such perfect joy, who wouldn't laugh?"

. . . .

Then, notice that the characters in the story didn't have personal names. They didn't need them. Instead, the story conveys that possibility that the depth of joy in virtuous love can exist for anyone. Though this is a Jewish story, and although their Sabbath began at sundown on Friday, we saw in the Sabbath song that it celebrated the strength of a righteous woman; it did not specify a Jewish woman, although it's safe to assume it was a Jewish woman they had in mind at the time. The story was told without Jewish or other names. Does this mean that the story intentionally invites non-Jewish people to find meaning in it? We don't know for sure, but the astonishing openness of Jewish people toward including non-Jewish guests at Passover and Chanukah suggests that non-Jewish people are welcome to find meaning in this story as well.

We learned of a strong Hasidic value in righteousness, whatever the circumstance. This should not be a surprise, since we know that in the brutal and dangerous context of the Holocaust, Jewish people celebrated the Sabbath in secret, often without any of the consecrated places or symbolic objects that usually focalized their worship. Like the wife in the story, the people would symbolically

Monogamy is marriage between two people. This kind of marriage is emphasized in cultures where sexual equality and rights are valued. When parents are expected to provide education for both sons and daughters, monogamy serves to limit the number of children, make it possible to provide for each, and to accumulate wealth. Monogamy also exists when equal rights are marginalized, and where the poor might not accumulate wealth.

Polygamy is marriage to more than one spouse. Though illegal in the United States, it's legal in parts of the Middle East, India, Africa, and Indonesia. It is a functional arrangement where families primarily educate their sons, and where a spouse can afford to support many dependents.

Polygyny is marriage with one husband and usually two to four wives. The wives may or may not be sisters. The assumption is that all wives will be treated equally, and that all children will have equal access to their multiple mothers.

Polyandry is marriage between one woman and several husbands. Virtually always, the husbands are brothers, and the woman is not permitted to marry outside their family. This form of marriage has several practical functions as well. It keeps land collectively owned by the husbands instead of being split up into marginal farms. It militates toward collective labor on all the land. It also means that all the children born to the wife are related to all her husbands. She may or may not tell anyone who is the father of an individual child. The dominant pattern is that all her husbands invest in the upbringing and wellbeing of the child. This form of marriage occurs most often in remote, rugged areas that are isolated from population centers.

Arranged marriage is generally decided by parents, and their children may or may not have a say. Sometimes children are promised in infancy, and grow up knowing they already have a husband or a wife. Arranged marriage happens for several reasons. First, arranged marriage strengthens the ties between two families. Second, arranged marriage helps families accumulate wealth and engage in cooperative enterprise. Third, arranged marriages between prestigious families help maintain social standing. In some cases, marriages are arranged when children are older. In those cases, some parents strive to match their children in happy marriages. Sometimes the children have a choice in whether or not they are willing to marry a particular individual.

"Walking Marriage" is a misleading term for a form of matrilocal marriage in which everyone lives throughout their lives in the family in which they were born. The Musuo people, a small ethnic minority in China, practice this kind of marriage. Within a

perform the ceremonies, using the prayers and songs in order to strengthen the people.

Marriage is a fundamental institution in all cultures, but it takes many forms considered ideal in different cultural contexts.

The definition of marriage is of crucial importance in all cultures. The relationships between adults and their children are fundamental to decisions about who may marry whom and who inherits from whom. In the Western world, there is more freedom to decide how to distribute wealth upon our demise. However, in many cultures, the rules about kinship and the distribution of wealth are grounded in ancient tradition.

Family is the most fundamental of the institutions embedded in the deep foundations of culture. However it is defined, it is where cultural values are taught and where individual identities are forged. It is thought that the first awareness of self that children have is gender, in that a child as young as three months old knows whether she is more like her mother, or he is more like his father. As a child becomes older, he or she becomes aware of the other institutions: those of worldview (religion) and community or state. Hence, a child becomes a member of his immediate and extended family, a member of a religious community, and a citizen of local and national identification.

It's good to resist stereotypes and other kinds of determinism, however. Not all individuals conform to the cultural patterns available to them. There are defiant women, and there are men who break the rules. Here is a story collected by Nathan Ausubel.

The Woman Who Buried Three Husbands

....

Homah, the great grand-daughter of Rabbi Yehuda, was famed for her beauty, but she was also a coquette. She had been married twice and she had seen both of her husbands buried. Each died a short time after he had married her.

It so happened that Rabbi Abbai, who was then getting on in years, fell in love with her. His friends tried to dissuade him from his intention to marry her. They warned him that it was dangerous to marry a woman who had already buried two husbands. But Abbai dismissed their fears as foolish. He married Homah. However, a short while later he too died.

After Homah had become a widow for the third time she went to the House of Judgment to petition Rabbi Raba to give her material assistance.

"Please give me money for food." she asked.

So Rabbi Raba fixed a sum sufficient for her food.

"And now give me money for wine." she added.

Rabbi Raba was surprised.

"I never knew that wine had been drunk in the house of your last husband Abbai."

Homah replied: "I swear by your life, Rabbi, that we used to drink wine from tall goblets as high as—." And speaking thus she rolled up her sleeve and measured upon her arm the length of the goblets.

The moment she exposed her naked arm a bright radiance filled the room—so beautiful she was!

Her impudence offended Raba, and he angrily left the House of Judgment. And as he went he rejoiced that at home there was waiting for him his true and virtuous wife.

Arriving home, Raba embraced his wife with greater tenderness than was usual with him, so that she was filled with wonder.

"What is the reason for this?" she asked.

"Homah appeared today in the House of Judgment," he answered and lowered his eyes.

typical family, a girl gets her own private bedroom when she's fourteen or fifteen years old so she can have a lover. Young women are likely to be the assertive sex, and will take the lead in choosing who her lover will be. Her lover visits her at night, and then returns to his own family household. When the woman's children are born, they are members of her family's household, not that of their father. This form of pairing has several advantages. First is stability. Each person in the couple continues to live in a household where they enjoy the continued support of other family members. Second, there is no need for an expensive private home for a couple. Third, children are nurtured by all the members of their mothers' households. Fourth, if a rift occurs between the mother and father, the disruption is minor: they do not need to divide property, decide custodial issues or issues of parental rights and responsibilities, or move their residence.

Hearing her husband speak thus, Rabbi Raba's wife picked up a large iron key and went out into the street. She found the wanton and ran after her crying, "You've buried three husbands already, do you want to bury a fourth one now?"

And with this cry she followed Homah everywhere she went until she had driven her from the town.

. . . .

Two interesting symbols appear in this story. First, there is the overt display of physical beauty that offended Raba and sent him to the embrace of his beloved and virtuous wife. It is rare that we find a character repelled by beauty, but as we know, modesty is much more highly valued in some societies than in others. Second, there is an iron key picked up by Raba's virtuous wife as she pursued the beautiful and dangerous Homah. We find in the Hebrew Bible (Chronicles 9:27) that the iron key is symbolic of authority to open and to close palace gates. In this story, Raba carried the key as she drove Homah from the city, perhaps to lock her out, to ostracize her from the community she had offended with her dangerous sexuality.

Though we rarely find sex overtly singled out as a function of culture, we find stories that address not only gender roles, but the importance of regulating the power of sex, a power both generative and destructive. Regulation takes many forms. Marriage, gender roles, societal norms, rewards for conformity and consequences for defying those norms are embedded into stories. Investigating the symbolic objects and behaviors we find in stories can help give us a fuller picture of a culture's beliefs, attitudes, and values.

REFERENCES

Amore, R., & Shinn, L. (1981). *Lustful Maidens & Ascetic Kings: Buddhist and Hindu Stories of Life*. New York: Oxford. (p. 39)

Ausubel, N. (Ed.) (1974). "The Woman Who Buried Three Husbands" in *A Treasury of Jewish Folklore*. New York: Crown Publishers. (p. 173)

Catechism of the Catholic Church. Revised in Accordance with the Official Latin Text Promulgated by Pope John Paul II. (1995) New York: Doubleday.

Hearn, L. (1971). *Kwaidan: Stories and Studies of Strange Things*. Boston: Charles E. Dutton Co.

Lipman, D. "The Three Laughs." Retrieved February 2011. http://www.hasidicstories.com/Stories/The_Baal_Shem_Tov/three_laughs

Mathur, S. and Mathur, K. (2005). Personal communication.

Narayan, K. , in collaboration with Urmila Devi Sood. (1997). *Mondays on the Dark Night of the Moon: Himalayan Foothill Folktales*. New York: Oxford.

Schlosser, R. E. (2010). "Pele's Revenge." Retrieved February 2011. http://americanfolklore.net/folklore/2010/10/peles_revenge.html

"The Sultan's Daughter." Translated by J. Koudia. (2003). *Moroccan Folktales*. Syracuse University Press. (pp. 15–18)

Ünal, A. (2010). *The Qur'ān, with Annotated Interpretation in Modern English*. Clifton, NJ: Tughra Books.

CHAPTER SIX

Youth and Innocence, Age and Wisdom, Foolishness, and Values

This chapter addresses the intersection of story message and listener. We've already looked at the ways in which characters, and especially archetypes, are symbolic of certain clusters in of ideas that are culturally shared. For instance, in some cultures, characters that exemplify virtue will be apparent. In other cultures, many courageous characters will be evident. However, no culture is so narrowly focused that it values only a few kinds of human behavior. Cultures value large complexes of human qualities. Milton Rokeach was one of the earliest scholars to examine these complexes, and further work has been done since his seminal work.

Rokeach also makes a strong case that values are linked to behavior, saying, "the kinds of behavior we will be especially interested in are those that are exhibited in connection with a wide variety of issues that we all confront in contemporary American society—civil rights, religion, politics, the war in Vietnam, the hippie life style, and the occupations we choose … " (123). His study, however, was done in the early 1970s and extended only to social and professional groups within the United States. Since then, a great deal has happened: The proliferation of communication technology and the expansion of international travel have made intercultural contact far more frequent than ever. So how are values and behaviors linked in the newer reality?

Values: Rokeach, one of the early researchers, defined this term. He said, "A *value* is an enduring belief that a specific mode of conduct or end-state of existence is personally or socially preferable to an opposite or converse mode of conduct or end-state of existent. A *value system* is an enduring organization of beliefs concerning preferable modes of conduct or end-states of existence along a continuum of relative importance" (5).

Peterson offers another definition: "Cultural values are principles or qualities that a group of people will tend to see as good or right or worthwhile" (22). Samovar et al., quoting Nanda, explain that the significance of values is that they provide the "system of criteria by which conduct is judged and sanctions applied" (188).

It's important to note some important differences in the prevalence of specific values in different cultures. For instance, in the United States, we are more likely to be preoccupied with copyrights and other property rights than in more traditional nations, where the social mingling of the sexes is simply forbidden.

One possible example would be the general contrast between youth-oriented America and the relationship of filial piety in China.

Without an understanding of filial piety, we risk being critical of traditional family configurations of Chinese families when they immigrate into the United States. When we witness the strong authoritarian control taken by Chinese mothers when their children are young, we are astonished. The writings of Maxine Hong Kingston and Amy Tan included models of mothers who, by U.S. standards, seemed demanding and unreasonable. More recently, Amy Chua found herself surrounded by controversy because of her book, *Battle Hymn of a Tiger Mother*, which was excerpted in the *Wall Street Journal* under the editorial title "Chinese Mothers are Superior." While Ms. Chua didn't write the headline, she certainly did receive powerful reactions to it. She had allowed her daughters "no play dates, no sleepovers, no school plays, and no whining about no school plays," and A-minuses were unacceptable. The mother is preparing her children for a world they must navigate successfully as adults. In the fullness of time, it is thought, the young adult comes to understand and appreciate parental sacrifices in their behalf.

In the United States, parents are to guide and teach their children, but it is also expected that parents nurture. In doing these things, including the nurturing, parents prepare a child for independence, for leaving the nest and striking out on their own, but not staying close to home in order to accommodate the eventual needs of aging parents.

In this example, the value of filial piety contrasts dramatically with the value of independence, making fertile ground for misunderstanding and criticism. The following Chinese story, collected by Joanna Cole, shows the harshness of the consequences that can occur when it's perceived that someone fails to render filial piety, respect, and obedience.

Faithful Even in Death

....

The village of the Liang family and that of the Chu family were close together. The inhabitants were well-to-do and content. Old excellency Liang and old excellency Chu were good friends. A son was born to the Liang family, who was given the name Hsienpo. Being an unusually quick and clever child, he was sent to the school in the town.

At the same time a daughter was born to the Chu family, who, besides being very clever, was particularly beautiful. As a child she loved to read and study, and only needed to glance at a book to know a whole sentence by heart. Old Chu simply doted on her. When she grew up, she wanted to go away and study. Her father tried in vain to dissuade her, but eventually he arranged for her to dress as a boy and study with Hsienpo.

The two lived together, worked together, argued together, and were the best of friends. The eager and zealous Hsienpo did not notice that Yingt'ai was really a girl, and therefore he did not fall in love with her. Yingt'ai studied so hard and was so wrapped up in her work that her fellow students paid no attention to her. Being very modest, and never taking part in the children's jokes, she exercised a calming influence over even the most impudent. When she slept with Hsienpo, each lay on one side of the bed, and between them stood a bowl of water. They had arranged that whoever knocked over the bowl must pay a fine; but the serious little Hsienpo never touched it.

When Yingt'ai changed her clothes, she never stood about naked but pulled on her clean clothes under the old ones, which she then took off and finished dressing. Her fellow students could not understand why she did this, and asked her the reason. "Only peasants expose the body they have received from their parents," she said; "it should not be done." Then the boys began to copy her, not knowing her real reason was to prevent their noticing that she was a girl.

Filial piety: This is a sense of obligation instilled in Chinese people since ancient times. One's obligation was to respect the parents and ancestors. The *concept* of filial piety seems to be based on the view that parents, through their toil, their care, and their moral investment in their children had earned the respect and accommodation of their children. The *behavior* that expresses filial piety is attentiveness to parents as they grow elderly, providing for their needs, and taking responsibility for their financial, medical, domestic, and other needs.

In modern times, it is increasingly difficult to fulfill filial obligations. A person's profession might take them to a location far from where the parents live. Children are then less able to assist them with daily tasks. As parents age, their medical costs are likely to increase, putting another strain on the finances of the children. As it sometimes works out, under the one child policy adopted in China, some young couples would find themselves alone responsible for two sets of parents. These circumstances limit the fulfillment of filial piety in modern times.

Then her father died, and her sister-in-law, who did not approve of Yingt'ai's studying, ordered her to come home and learn housework. But Yingt'ai refused and continued to study.

The sister-in-law, fearing that Yingt'ai had fallen in love with Hsienpo, used to send her from time to time babies' things, swaddling clothes, children's clothes and covers, and many other things. The students became curious when they saw the things, and Yingt'ai could tell them only that they were the things she herself had used as a child, which her sister-in-law was now sending her to keep.

The time passed quickly. Soon Yingt'ai and Hsienpo were grown up. Yingt'ai still dressed as a man, and being a well-brought-up girl, she did not dare to ask Hsienpo to marry her; but when she looked at him, her heart was filled with love. His delicate manner attracted her irresistibly, and she swore to marry him and none other.

She proposed the marriage to her sister-in-law, who did not consider it suitable, because after her father's death they had lost all their money. Against Yingt'ai's will the sister-in-law arranged a match with a Dr. Ma, of a newly rich family in the village. Yingt'ai objected strongly, but she could do nothing about it. Day after day she had to listen to complaints: she was without filial piety, she was a shameless, decadent girl, a disgrace to the family. Her sister-in-law still feared she might secretly marry Hsienpo, and she urged the Ma family to appoint a day for the wedding. Then she cut off Yingt'ai's school money, which forced her to return home.

Yingt'ai was obliged to hide her misery. Weeping bitterly, she said good-bye to Hsienpo, who accompanied her part of the way home. As they separated, Yingt'ai sang a song which revealed that she was a girl and that she wanted to marry him. But the good, dense Hsienpo did not understand her hints. He did not see into Yingt'ai's heart, and tried to comfort her by telling her that one must return home some time and that they would soon meet again. Yingt'ai saw that everything was hopeless, and went home in tears.

Hsienpo felt very lonely without his companion, with whom he had lived day and night for many years. He kept on writing letters to Yingt'ai, begging her to come back to school, but he never received a reply.

Finally he could bear it no longer, and went to visit her. "Is Mr. Yingt'ai at home?" he asked. "Please tell him his school friend, Hsienpo, has come and wants to see him."

The servant looked at him curiously, and then said curtly, "There is no Mr. Yingt'ai here—only a Miss Yingt'ai. She is to be married soon, and naturally she can't leave her room. How could she speak to a man? Please go away, sir, for if the master discovers you, he will make a complaint against you for improper behavior."

Suddenly everything was clear to Hsienpo. In a state of collapse he crept home. There he found, under Yingt'ai's books, a bundle of letters and essays which showed him clearly how deeply Yingt'ai loved him and also that she did not want to marry any other man. Through his own stupidity, his lack of understanding, the dream had come to naught.

Overcome by remorse, he spent the days lost in tears. Yingt'ai was always before his eyes, and in his dreams he called her name, or cursed her sister-in-law and Dr. Ma, himself, and all the ways of society. Because he ceased to eat or drink, he fell ill and gradually sank into the grave.

Yingt'ai heard the sad news. Now she had nothing more to live for. If she had not been so carefully watched, she would have done herself some injury. In this state of despair the wedding day arrived. Listlessly she allowed herself to be pushed into the red bridal chair and set off for the house of her bridegroom, Dr. Ma. But when they passed the grave of Hsienpo, she begged her attendants to let her get out and visit it, to thank him for all his kindness. On the grave, overcome by grief, she flung herself down and sobbed. Her attendants urged her to return to her chair, but she refused. Finally, after great persuasion, she got up, dried her tears, and bowing several times in front of the grave, she prayed as follows: "You are Hsienpo, and I am Yingt'ai. If we were really intended to be man and wife, open your grave three feet wide."

Scarcely had she spoken when there came a clap like thunder and the grave opened. Yingt'ai leaped into the opening, which closed again before the maids could catch hold of her, leaving only two bits of her dress in their hands. When they let these go, they changed into two butterflies and flew up into the air.

Dr. Ma was furious when he heard that his wife had jumped into the grave of Hsienpo. He had the grave opened, but the coffin was empty except for two white stones. No one knew where Hsienpo and Yingt'ai had gone. In a rage the grave violators flung the two stones onto the road, where immediately a bamboo with two stems shot up. They were shimmering green, and swayed in the wind. The grave robbers knew that this was the result of magic, and cut down the bamboo with a knife; but as soon as they had cut down one, another shot up, until finally several people cut down the two stems at the same time. Then these flew up to heaven and became rainbows.

Now the two lovers had become immortals. If they ever want to be together, undisturbed and unseen, so that no one on earth can see them or even talk about them, they wait until it is raining and the clouds are hiding the sky. The red in the rainbow is Hsienpo, and the blue is Yingt'ai.

Clearly, this is another tale in which we must suspend disbelief in order to listen to the narrative, which, if magic were possible, would make sense in the way Walter Fisher describes in his Narrative Paradigm. Furthermore, this is a tale in which certain cultural values are explicitly addressed. Yingt'ai said to her schoolmates, "Only peasants expose the body they have received from their parents […] it should not be done." This comment, understood by all who we imagine heard her, acknowledged the obligation to honor the parents, to show respect for their wishes and their dignity. Even more directly to the point, "Day after day she had to listen to complaints: she was without filial piety, she was a shameless, decadent girl, a disgrace to the family." Within this story, at least, there was no room for complaint from a girl, for her role was to be obedient to the needs of the family.

A word of caution, however: Even though we look to folktales for insight into cultural institutions and values, we should not assume that Chinese values are accurately represented here. We know that the children's stories with which we grew up were laden with exaggeration and hyperbole, magic, and drama for the sake of an attention-riveting story. Subtle details are ignored. If we simply recall the story of John Henry, the steel-driving man, we know that nothing of the kind actually happened, and yet his story is important and he is a hero.

What does ring true in the story of Yingt'ai and Hsienpo is that China is still a collectivist society. One is likely to put aside his or her personal wishes for the sake of the family or other group. In his *Study of Human Values*, Richard Kilby refers to Hsu's 1967 book titled *Under the Ancestor's Shadow*.

> ... Centuries ago the Chinese evolved the conception that the dead enter a spirit world, there to remain for a long period of time before eventual rebirth on earth. While in the spirit world the given spirit may either be tortured and damned in a sort of Chinese version of hell (and later be reborn a lowly animal or miserable human), or be treated well and have a comfortable life in a city of the dead, or even be made an honored official or sort of divinity of the spirit world and spared rebirth entirely. The Chinese came to believe further that the fate of the spirit in the other world is in good part determined by the prayers and other observances and acts in its behalf by living sons. Failure here would cause the spirit to be damned. (Kilby, 58)

This was the state of affairs in prerevolutionary China. And if a Chinese listener had heard this story, he or she must have believed in the possibility that Yingt'ai and Hsienpo had the prayers of people who believed in love, not just marriage. In China, the institution of marriage and family depended on the birth of sons who would pray for the well-being of ancestors. Kilby further tells us, "Hsu mentions ... that there was no romantic tradition as we understand it, for the purpose of marriage was not to find a love-mate and life's companion for the son, but rather to find a mother for his children; hence an estrangement existed between the sexes ... " (58). But, Kilby adds, "There is a romantic tradition in Chinese literature going back thousands of years."

We should also avoid assuming that the influence of the past entirely overwhelms the present. In fact, Chinese culture has adapted in many ways to emerging global realities, allowing women to become educated and have careers, for example. And, as earlier noted, occupational relocation creates difficulties in caring for elderly parents, which means that some Chinese families are simply unable to fulfill filial obligations in the way that was once expected.

Filial piety is an alien value to many Western people. Looking at commercial advertising reveals what some of our Western values are: mobility, autonomy, financial well-being, health and fitness, style, and technology, to name a few. We do not tend to value obedience, duty, modesty, humility, and chastity as much. Rokeach, whose studies focused on American respondents, posited two sets of values: instrumental values and terminal values. Instrumental values are values such as ambition and capability that, when enacted, are instrumental in our reaching our terminal values, or states of existence, such as self-respect, happiness, and freedom.

The crucial thing to remember is that different cultures have different sets of values, but that the most important, though different, values are equally compelling in all cultures. Klyukanov offers an example:

> The interaction between the Native American tribes and the oil company was not ... successful. Negotiation was difficult because the cultures attached entirely different values to the same land. While for the oil company the canyon's worth consisted of millions of dollars in profit, for the tribes the value of the canyon was as a holy spot, connecting them to their past and inestimable in monetary terms. (83)

We have no doubt that the violent conflict that so often erupted between tribal groups and corporations was motivated and escalated by deeply held values on both sides. Samovar et al. explain the process by which values are translated into behavior. They say:

> ... [V]alues tell a member of a culture what is normal by identifying what things are good and bad, or right and wrong ... For example, the outlook of a culture toward the expression of affection is one of the main values that differ among cultures. In the United States, people are encouraged to express their feelings openly and outwardly and are taught not to be timid about letting people know they are upset. ... This positive American attitude toward the public expression of emotion is very different from the one found in China. As Gao and Ting-Toomey note, "Chinese are socialized not to openly express their own personal emotions, especially strong negative ones." (189)

Clearly, values are expressed in behavior, and behavior can be easily misinterpreted through various cultural lenses. In the following Mexican story collected by Bierhorst, we find that assumptions and misinterpretations can emerge even from people considered learned, ethical, and careful. We find one character is human, and the other is the Lord.

St. Theresa and the Lord

The Lord went walking with St. Theresa one day and they came to a house that had an open window. There in the window, for all to see, a husband and wife were kissing. The Lord noticed this and refused to give them his blessing.

They walked on, and they came to another pair of lovers, this time unmarried, and the lovers hid when they saw them coming. As the Lord passed, he gave them his blessing. St. Theresa was puzzled, but she didn't say a word.

They kept on, and they came to a humble little inn, a place so poor there was just one mug for the four people who were the customers, and two of them were fighting over it. The Lord went in and took away the mug, which made St. Theresa wonder. They went on and came to an expensive inn, and the Lord stopped and gave the mug to the innkeeper.

"Lord, tell me," said St. Theresa, "why did you bless those people who weren't married, and why did you take the mug from that poor little inn-keeper?" The Lord said, "If you want to know, travel the main highway, and soon you'll find out."

St. Theresa went on by herself. She came to the highway and settled down at a mule drivers' stopping place. After a while a man on horseback came along and pulled up to rest. He fell asleep, and when he awoke it was well after nightfall. In the dark he was frightened and confused. He jumped on his horse and rode off so fast he left his money on the ground where he had been sleeping.

Now, in that town there was an old man who had the habit of begging food from a certain lady, who would always give him a few little *gordas* to keep him from starving. He came along, then, and sat down to build a fire to heat up his *gordas*. By the firelight he saw the purse that had been left by the horseman who had fallen asleep. In his excitement he forgot about the *gordas* and went off counting the money and praising the Lord.

When he had gone, a mule driver pulled up. He was a poor man who had been traveling three days without food, and when he saw the *gordas* that had been left there for anyone to take he sat down and toasted them over the fire. He was a man who never remembered his Maker, yet on this occasion, when he was so badly in need, he praised the Lord over and over again. At just that moment the horseman who had left the money came back and heard the prayer of thanks. Enraged, he demanded his money.

"But, sir," said the mule driver, "I didn't see any money, only this fire and these little *gordas*." The other man said, "You're a liar. Hand over the money or I'll kill you." The poor mule driver kept protesting that he had seen no money until finally the exasperated horseman strangled him and rode away.

After witnessing all this, St. Theresa went back to the Lord and asked for an explanation.

The Lord said to her, "I blessed the lovers because they feared me. I did not bless the married couple because they were shameless.

"And the mug, I took it because the innkeeper allowed fighting and stealing, and I gave it to the other innkeeper because in him I found nothing to blame.

"And I took the money from the man on the horse to save him from damnation.

"And the old beggar who found the money, I allowed him to have it because I knew he would not forget me.

"And the mule driver who was killed, I permitted it to happen because he never remembered me until this day. I took his life to keep him from sinning again."

. . . .

This story provides an example of confusion and misunderstanding in the character of St. Theresa, a human character. Whether you are Christian or not, the story gives pause, for what are we to think of the horseman who lost his money to save his soul, and then God strangled the mule driver? Is this a flaw in the story, a break from the narrative sense-making that Fisher describes in the Narrative Paradigm? Or is it a break in a logic that can remind the listener that we humans can never have a complete understanding of the complicated world of human emotions or divine intent? Since the story doesn't explain it, it is our responsibility to find the meaning for ourselves. Earlier, in the "Messages and Meanings" model, we saw that stories are messages, but meanings are negotiated between the story and the private world of the listener.

In that tale, we also found characters we might consider foolish: the married couple, the customers fighting over a mug, and the horseman. But in other tales, we find characters who seem to behave in foolish ways, but who might embody some wisdom. In Larson's collection of Gypsy tales, we find the following story:

In this story, who is foolish? The townspeople thought it was Piccolo. Piccolo thought it was God. God thought it was the dignified, somber townspeople. The story tells us

Piccolo

. . . .

Long ago, far over the water, the people of a certain town were sober and industrious. They busied themselves every day, baking serious bread, making proper cheese, and raising well-behaved onions and peppers. These people were very proud of themselves.

But the citizens of that town never sang or danced and they had forgotten how to laugh. God was displeased with them because they were vain and as sour as vinegar.

One night, as he slept, God had a dream. In that dream, he saw a Gypsy boy capering and dancing in fast shoes, bringing laughter to all who saw him.

At dawn, when dreams turn into reality, God brought that Gypsy boy to life. He dressed him in a coat with bright patches, a soft hat, and fast shoes.

"Go and dance, because that is what I made you for," God said, setting the boy on the road to the town.

The Gypsy boy started down the road, then turned and called to God. "What is my name?" he asked."

"You are Piccolo, because you are a little bit of nothing," God chuckled.

Piccolo arrived in the town and went straightaway to the market square. The sun shone brightly and the square was crowded with shoppers.

Piccolo chose a spot before a fruit vendor's stall and began to dance, singing a merry tune and clapping his hands.

Passers-by stared at him in horror.

"Stop at once!" the fruit vendor cried.

Piccolo stopped.

"I can see that you are a stranger here, so I will give you good advice," the fruit vendor said. "You must not dance like a fool, but behave as others do. If you do not, you will have no friends. It is clear that you do not understand how things work in this world."

Piccolo excused himself and hurried from the town and down the road to the place he had left God.

There was God.

Piccolo addressed him politely. "You do not understand how things work in this world," he said. "I cannot dance and caper about. If I am not like everyone else, I will have no friends."

God said gently, "I am your friend. Go and dance."

Piccolo returned to the town square, selected a spot before the stall of a baker who was selling very serious bread, and began to dance.

"Stop at once!" the baker cried. "Because you are new here, I will give you good advice. If you hold your head high and smile at no one, you will be considered a fine fellow. You will gain respect. By dancing like a fool, you are making a mistake."

Piccolo listened carefully, then excused himself and hastened from the town to the place where he had left God.

There was God.

"See here," Piccolo called as he approached, "you have made a mistake. If I dance and act the fool, I will get no respect."

God sighed, then said patiently, "I made you to dance. If you do not do as I say, you will not respect yourself."

Piccolo scowled. It was clear to him that God did not know what he was talking about.

Again, Piccolo entered the town. This time, he stopped before the stall of an onion vendor and began to dance half-heartedly, seeing frowns on the faces of all the passers-by.

"Stop that foolish dancing, you good-for-nothing boy," the onion vendor ordered. "Go and earn an honest living or you will starve. You don't know anything!"

The crowd that had gathered hooted and jeered at Piccolo.

Piccolo hid his face in shame and sped from the town to confront God. God was there.

"You don't know anything!" Piccolo shouted. "If I dance, I will starve!"

"Then starve!" roared God, for he was out of patience.

Piccolo was bewildered.

God would say no more, so Piccolo turned and walked slowly toward the town, trying hard to understand all that had happened.

But as he went, it seemed to Piccolo that he heard music, as if from some far-off place, beyond the horizon. Though he tried to step along in a dignified manner, he could not keep his fast shoes from dancing, so that by the time he reached the down he was dancing and singing and snapping his fingers like castanets.

Even before Piccolo reached the market square, a line of children had formed behind him, and all of them danced as if they heard the music too.

It would be pleasant to report that all the townspeople changed their sour ways for songs and laughter. That was not the case. Many years passed before music was once again heard in that town.

But Piccolo went from place to place, capering and dancing, and God smiled on him.

. . . .

that of course God was the only one who could see the larger picture of human experience, but Piccolo came to understand that he must take his dancing to those who would embrace it—the children.

Piccolo's relationship with God also brings a surprise. Piccolo doesn't believe God understands how the world works. Surely, in most religions, we would assume that God the Creator would be in full awareness of how it all works, but Piccolo did not. It took three trips to town before Piccolo would submit to his purpose. Here, the number three is significant because it's a religious number signifying the Father, the Son, and the Holy Spirit. It's a magical number in many tales where important things happen three times, where there is a choice to take one of three roads to follow, or where three attempts are required in order to succeed in some endeavor. Piccolo endured the admonishment of the fruit vendor, the bread vendor, and the onion vendor and survived. His survival was accompanied by music.

So far, we've referred to these people as Gypsy, but they prefer to call themselves Rom. Historically, they've been misunderstood, disparaged, and excluded in regions and neighborhoods. However, among the Rom cultures, we find fully developed values, and a culture's values are central to the way they live. Because of the widely believed stereotype that Roma are dirty, it is surprising to many people that cleanliness is a strong value among these people. In their spotless homes, there are many practices that are not apparent to the *gadjo* (non-Gypsy) eye. The Roma think of cleanliness as crucial both physically and spiritually, so that one's surroundings and their behaviors must be clean. Beginning with physical cleanliness, the Roma view the upper half of the body as potentially clean, but the bottom half, by virtue of its nearness to the organs of elimination, can never be clean. They are therefore inclined, when bathing, to use one washcloth and one towel for the top half and a separate washcloth and towel for the bottom. Whenever possible, these items are kept separate. Likewise, in the Rom kitchen, the sink is only for the preparation of food and washing dishes. It is not for hand washing. Washing one's hands in the kitchen turns it into a bathroom.

The spiritual side of cleanliness helps to explain why the Roma are reluctant to mingle with *gadjo* people. Most apparent is the idea that one does not expose him- or herself too much to people who behave in unclean ways. Generally speaking, *gadjo* are often more sexually liberated than the Roma choose to be, and since the bottom half of the body is considered unclean, people who are sexually active are viewed as unclean. The tendency of these cultures to keep their distance from others amplifies the mystery around them, and many Roma prefer it that way. They simply prefer to protect their privacy. Unfortunately, this is too often understood as secrecy.

As a consequence of their self-imposed isolation, "superstitions about the Gypsies abound: accused in centuries past of witchcraft, child theft and cannibalism, today they are still disparaged ... " (Windling, 1). They were also the targets of the Nazi holocaust, enslaved in Romania, and forced into settlement camps during their history. It is no wonder that they now wish to remain together in their own communities, separate from a society that has so often held them in contempt. Despite that history of disparagement and exclusion, however, the many Rom cultures still thrive. It is important to remember that not all Roma are the same; they have developed many cultures. We might use an analogy with Native American people who also are not all the same. A Hopi Indian is vastly different from a Northern Plains Lakota as an Inuit is from a Mohawk. Rom cultures are different, too. Occupationally, the horse traders of older times have given way to trading used cars, but some groups still maintain traditional occupations, such as jewelry-making or music performance.

In many Gypsy tales, we find evidence of belief in an approachable God, very different from the distant, though loving God. In fact, it is thought that Gypsy culture began in India and spread to other parts of the world with Gypsies adapting to local religion wherever they went. No longer Hindu only, they embraced Catholicism and other religious practices where they sojourned. This is evidence that they are adaptable, and also religious as well as spiritual.

Before leaving this chapter behind, we should remember that storytelling has been used in many societies at many times toward character education. Through stories, it is possible to teach respect, honesty, industry, and so on. Many Native American traditions used storytelling as an educational tool rather than scolding or lecturing a child.

Jane Yolen provides this African American story about self-respect:

"Knee-High Man" is one of those stories someone might tell a child who feels bad about being smaller than other children his or her age. Children can feel bad about

Knee-High Man: Height Does Not Make a Hero

In a swamp not far from here lived Knee-High Man, and he was as little as his name sounds. He was knee-high to a reed and knee-high to a hoptoad. He was a small man, but he wanted to be sizable.

So one day, he decided to go calling on the biggest critter in the neighborhood to find out how to make himself big.

Off he went to visit Mr. Horse.

"Hey, brother," he cried out in his knee-high voice, somewhere between a squeak and a squawk, "how can I grow as big as you?"

Horse turned his great head till he eyed Knee-High Man. "Eat a whole mess o' corn." he said. "Then run all day." He whinnied and went back to his eating.

Well, Knee-High Man did just what the horse advised, but it was no dang good. The corn hurt his little belly, and the running hurt his little legs. Instead of getting bigger. why, the Knee-High Man was sure he'd gotten smaller.

"That brother didn't do me any favors," said the Knee-High Man. "I'd better get advice from somebody else."

So he went off to visit Mr. Bull.

"Hey, brother." he cried out in his knee-high voice, somewhere between a whisper and a whimper. "How can I grow as big as you?"

Bull looked down till they were eye to eye. "Eat grass." he said, "and learn to bellow."

Well, Knee-High Man did just what the bull advised, but it still was no dang good. The grass hurt his little belly, and the bellowing made his little throat sore. Instead of getting bigger, why, the Knee-High Man was sure he'd gotten even smaller.

"That brother didn't do me any favors," said Knee-High Man. "I'd better get advice from somebody else."

So off he went to visit Mr. Owl. Owl was known for his wisdom, even though he wasn't near that big himself. He was a preacher, too, which made him somebody important.

"Hey. brother," Knee-High Man cried out in his knee-high voice, somewhere between a hough and a howl.

"Whooooo are you?" asked owl.

"I am Knee-High Man," Knee-High Man explained. "But I am tired of being small. How can I grow big? I want to be sizable. like Mr. Horse or like Mr. Bull—only not made to eat corn and run all day, or to eat grass and bellow."

Owl looked at Knee-High Man with his great eyes. "Why do you want to be big, brother? Is it because folks are picking fights with you all the time?"

Knee-High Man shook his head. "No."

"Is it because you want to see a long way?" asked Owl.

"No."

"Because you want to carry heavy objects?" asked Owl.

"No."

"Well," Owl said. "there's no reason to be bigger in the body than anyone else, Knee-High Man. But there's reason enough to be bigger in the brain!" He flapped his wings—soft and silent—and flew off.

Knee-High Man thought about that, and the more he thought, the bigger in the brain he became. till at last he was well satisfied. Then he went back to his swamp, never to mind his height again.

themselves for so many reasons. They might feel they are not fast enough, not smart enough, or not pretty enough. They might feel self-conscious about being fat, wearing glasses, or having a scar or speech problem. Even more, a child of color in a setting where most other children are white often feels frightened, overwhelmed, and nonstandard. If a person with age or wisdom notices the sadness and self-disdain, perhaps they can find a story to help the child cope with the foolishness of others. It's not surprising that so many have resonated with Hans Christian Andersen's story "The Ugly Duckling," the story of a cygnet (young swan) being judged by duck standards and enduring the derisive taunts of ducks. Because at the end of the story, the so-called ugly duckling is transformed, a child hearing the story can find a new belief in his own worth.

Many stories have foolish characters, and these stories are valuable tools for teaching. Nobody wants to look foolish, and hearing a story about a foolish character encourages a listener to consider their behavior before acting. The following Cheyenne story comes from Barry Lopez and is as relevant to adult foolishness as it is to children's foolishness:

Many listeners laugh out loud when they hear that story. The image of such goofy behavior at the end of the story provokes glee. However, the important part is that Coyote defied a clear set of rules, and though he was able, as usual, to save himself from his predicament, he ended up looking very foolish. This is not just a message for children; it is just as much, or more, a story for adults who might be tempted to take

The Eye-Juggler

One day Coyote was going along and he saw a man throwing his eyes up into a tree.

The man said. "Eyes, hang on a branch." and his eyes left him and hung on a branch high up in a tree where they had a good view of the country. When he wanted them back. the man called for his eyes to come back.

Coyote immediately wanted to know how to do this and asked the man to teach him.

The man agreed and taught him, but he warned Coyote not to do the trick more than four times in one day.

As soon as the man was gone Coyote threw his eyes up into a tree. Then he called them back. He could see a great distance out across the land when his eyes were in the top of a tree and he was glad to have learned the trick.

Coyote thought he could do the trick as often as he wanted and on the first day he did it four times. When he said, "Eyes, hang on a branch" the fifth time, the eyes went into the top of a tree; but they did not come back when he called them. Again and again Coyote called, but his eyes stayed up in the tree. Coyote pleaded with his eyes to come down, but they remained fastened to the limb. As the day got hotter his eyes began to swell and spoil and flies began to gather on them.

Coyote called for his eyes to come down all day and into the night, but they never moved. Finally Coyote lay down to sleep.

A mouse ran over Coyote's chest. Coyote was going to brush him away, but then he had an idea. He lay very still. The mouse came across Coyote's chest to Coyote's head and began to cut the hairs on Coyote's head for its nest. Coyote did not move at all. While the mouse was busy cutting the hair, its tail happened to slip down into Coyote's mouth. Coyote quickly closed his mouth and he had the mouse.

Coyote told the mouse what had happened. The mouse said that he could see Coyote's eyes up in the tree and, indeed, they were puffed up to an enormous size. He offered to go up and fetch the eyes for Coyote, but Coyote would not let him go. The mouse struggled to free himself from Coyote's grasp but it was impossible. Finally the mouse asked what he would have to do to go free. Coyote said he would have to give him one of his eyes.

This the mouse did. Coyote took the eye and let the mouse go. The eye was very small and it fit way back in Coyote's eye socket and he could not see very well with it.

There was a buffalo grazing nearby that had been looking on all this time. "This buffalo has the power to help me in my trouble," thought Coyote.

The buffalo asked Coyote what he wanted. Coyote told him he had lost one of his eyes and that he needed another. The buffalo took one of his eyes out and put it in Coyote's other socket.

Now Coyote could see again, but he couldn't walk straight. The buffalo eye was so big most of it was outside the socket. The other eye was rolling around way back inside.

Coyote went around like that, with his head tilted to keep that one eye from rolling out.

. . . .

shortcuts, cheat, or bend the rules of the culture and society. We might be able to worm our way out of some of the consequences, but there is an enduring consequence, which is that we did a foolish thing that impacts our own self-concept and the views of the people who know us. Our dignity is compromised, and we need another story to help us find our way back.

REFERENCES

Bierhorst, J. (Ed.) (2002). *Latin American Folktales: Stories from Hispanic and Indian Traditions*. New York: Pantheon Books. (pp. 118–120)

Cole, J. (1982). *Best-Loved Folktales of the World*. New York: Random House. (pp. 531–534)

"The Eye-Juggler." (Ed.) Lopez, Barry (1977). *Giving Birth to Thunder, Sleeping With His Daughter: Coyote Builds North America.* New York: Avon. (pp. 59–60)

Kilby, R. W. (1993). *The Study of Human Values.* Landham, MD: University Press of America.

Klyukanov, I. E. (2005). *Principles of Intercultural Communication.* Boston: Pearson.

"Knee-High Man: Height Does Not Make a Hero." (Ed.) Yolen, J. (2003). *Mightier Than the Sword: World Folktales for Strong Boys.* New York: Harcourt, Inc. (pp. 36–38)

Larson, J. R. (2000). *The Fish Bride and Other Gypsy Tales.* North Haven, CT: Linnet Books. (pp. 1–4)

Peterson, B. (2004). *Cultural Intelligence: A Guide to Working with People from Other Cultures.* Boston: Intercultural Press.

Rokeach, M. (1973). *The Nature of Human Values.* New York: Collier Macmillan.

Samovar, L., Porter, R., and McDaniel, E R. (2007). *Communication Between Cultures.* Seventh edition. Boston: Wadsworth Cengage.

Wildling, T. "The Road That Has No End: Tales of the Traveling People." Retrieved August 2009. http//:Endicott-studio.com/rdrm/forgypsy.html.

CHAPTER SEVEN
Worldview and Conceptions of Virtue, Good, and Evil

This chapter attempts to address perceptions of reality that grow from the deep structures of cultures. Our beliefs about the purpose of life, the birth of evil, and the meaning of death all rise from those deep structures, regardless of their direction of change and alteration.

Religion is a fundamental institution in culture that instructs humans in what we must do to "overcome" our humanness and fulfill the purpose of a creator. But different religions have different things to say about reality. For instance, do we believe in the existence of a single, omnipotent God who is in charge of every event in our lives? Do we believe instead that there is a creative force that set the world in motion and now simply takes note of our behavioral choices? On the other hand, do we believe, as some native people do, that spirit exists in all living things, and that spirit can be called on to teach and to help us? Or do we believe in a pantheon of powerful forces that are sometimes in conflict, giving rise to a chaotic appearance to events?

In medieval Europe, some philosophers conceived of creation as a "well-oiled machine," wherein existence was orderly and in compliance with a divine plan. René Descartes gave us the ladder-like view of a hierarchy in which, typically, humans were at the top. It goes something like this:

God	The male authority highest in the hierarchy.	God can be cited in support of human agendas.
Humans Humans are entirely dependent on all the life forms "below" them in the hierarchical scale. They clearly needed the animals and plants, but the need for such things as oxygen was not yet known.	**Respectable Anglo-Saxon men** Elders Married women Single but respectable women Children Servants The poor People of color "Primitive" people	The main proponents of this view of Creation. This ranking of people reflects the positions they tended to occupy in a hierarchical society. The rich and powerful defined this organization, and the poor and powerless found themselves at the bottom.
Animals Interestingly, humans saw themselves as "owners" of the very things they depended on. When an animal or organism was unpleasant or threatening, it was relegated to the bottom.	**Domesticated animals** Animals bred for beauty and status Work animals Wild, but "harmless" animals Dangerous animals Pests Parasites	The ranking of animals sometimes changed according to their perceived usefulness.
Plants	Profitable cultivated crops Trees for wood Trees for fruits Plants for usufruct Trees considered beautiful Medicinal herbs Culinary herbs and spices Weeds Noxious plants (poison oak, stinging nettles, thorny plants)	Again, members of this group are ranked according to the perceived benefit for people.
The Elementals (wind, water, earth, and fire)	Water, when useful for irrigation, sea travel, medicine, and later, cleanliness. Fire for heating homes, forging swords, making plowshares, and founding cook pots and church bells. Earth as property, often cultivated, landscaped, or used recreationally. Wind, for sea travel, and after the need for oxygen was discovered by Joseph Priestly. Water when it creates floods, danger, messes, or inconvenience. Fire when it causes injury or damage.	These elementals are important to humans, but humans are not important to them. In fact, they exist vibrantly in the absence of human meddling.

This organization of creation was extremely useful, and was reflected in many of the stories found in the Bible. We must remember that culture is human-made, and that the way a society chooses to organize its knowledge makes life predictable and manageable. In this model, God is clearly at the very top, and there is no authority above Him. This idea helps a society muster around the teachings of scripture: the story of Adam and Eve, the Ten Commandments, and the parables. In other words, it contributes to the stability of other institutions besides religion. It becomes the basis for law, education, politics, and domestic relations. Whether or not we agree with the main thrust of this model, we can see its relevance to the cohesiveness of many cultural groups.

The Genesis story of Adam and Eve in the Garden of Eden has had profound influences on cultural truths. The Christian Bible teaches that God alone created everything. The first 25 verses of Genesis describe all the elements of the natural world, which God brought into being, and it is not until verse 26 that people were placed into the world. As they were made in the likeness of God and given dominion over the earth, they are in charge of a great deal, but God is still the ultimate authority. In essence, it seems that all of Creation was put in place for the pleasure and well-being of humans, often thought of as the pinnacle of Creation. Many people believe this gives humans a special set of responsibilities to be obedient to the Creator's intentions. There is no general agreement on exactly what those responsibilities are. The Catholic Catechism explicitly delineates a set of behavior and attitudes that resemble the Harmony with Nature worldview, yet at least in the Western world, we see overwhelming evidence of the Mastery over Nature orientation, or dominion, in the structure of cathedrals and in the real estate orientation toward the earth. This shows us how undecided we can be within the complex culture of Christianity.

There are other ways that cultures have organized their own views of Creation. Probably not unique to Native Americans is the view of the Great Spirit within and throughout everything. One model, which was taught by some Native American teachers, looked somewhat like the diagram to the right:

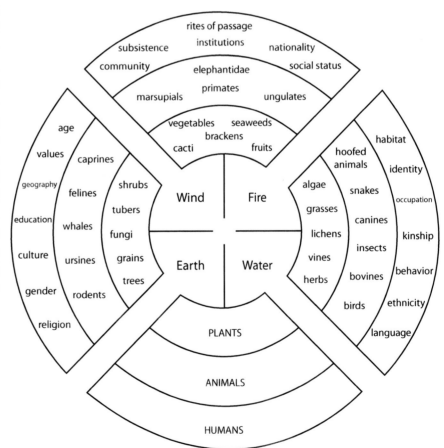

At the center of this model, we find the elementals: wind, water, fire, and earth. They could interact with each other, and they could exist quite well without depending on humans or other biological beings. Around the center, we find the wild plants. They need the elementals, but do not rely for their existence on humans or animals. Though some plants now depend on insects for pollination, in some situations, the wind can accomplish it. In the next ring outside are the animals. They depend on both the plants and the elementals. Many animals eat plants only, and some eat other animals. Some predators might eat humans, but as a whole, animals in their natural state do not depend on humans. In the outside ring, humans depend on the elementals, the plants, and the animals, yet seem to have the least to contribute. Finally, spirit animates all life, including the elementals.

Many people would see the relationship this model expresses, but might not link it to the organization of culture. However, the spiritual life of many cultures reenacts these relationships through ritual and art. The Buddhist *mandalas* and the Navajo sand paintings are examples of the ways of expressing the spiritual in art. But the relationship among Creation's components is also expressed in this Tibetan tale from *Tibetan Folk Tales*:

The Creation

In the beginning was voidness, a vast emptiness without cause, without end. From this great voidness there arose gentle stirrings of wind, which after countless eons grew thicker and heavier, forming the mighty thunderbolt scepter Dorje Gyatram.

Dorje Gyatram created the clouds, which in turn created the rain. The rain fell for many years until the primeval ocean Gyatso was formed. Then, all was calm, quiet, and peaceful; the ocean because clear as a mirror.

Slowly the winds began to breathe once more, gently moving over the waters of the ocean, churning them continually until a light foam appeared on the surface. Just as cream is churned into butter, so were the waters of Gyatso churned into earth by the rhythmic motion of the winds.

The Earth rose like a mountain, and around its peaks murmured the wind, ever moving, tireless, forming cloud upon cloud from which fell more rain, only this time heavier and full of salt, giving birth to the great oceans of the universe.

The center of the universe is Rirap Lhunpo (Sumeru) the great four-sided mountain made of precious stones and full of beautiful things. There are rivers and streams on Rirap Lhunpo and many kinds of trees, fruits, and plants, for Rirap Lhunpo is special—it is the abode of the gods and demi-gods.

Although this story goes on for several pages, we find no mention of humans until later in the narrative. Further, this first part of the narrative reflects a circular shape in which the wind is the first character to appear. Afterward, we find water and earth, and fire is suggested in the presence of a thunderbolt. Whether or not we can accept a view of gods and demigods, we see that in this narrative, the divine beings preceded people.

The next piece of the creation story reveals an important Tibetan cultural value:

> Around Rirap Lhunpo is the great lake, and encircling the lake a ring of golden mountains. Beyond the ring of golden mountains is another lake, it too encircled by mountains of gold, and so on, seven lakes, seven rings of golden mountains, and outside the last ring of mountains is the lake Chi Gyatso.
>
> It is in Chi Gyatso that the four worlds are found, each like an island, with its own particular shape and distinct inhabitants. The world of the East is Lu Phak and is shaped like the half moon. People of Lu Phak live for five hundred years and are peaceful; there is no fighting in Lu Phak. The people have bodies like giants and faces shaped like the half moon. They are not as fortunate as us, however, for they have no religion to follow.

So we find a story from a belief system very different from the Western view, which is complex, value laden, and peopled not only with people, but with a pantheon of gods and demigods inhabiting the same places.

In contrast, an Onondaga story, offered by Caduto and Bruchac, gives us another view:

The Earth on Turtle's Back

> Before this Earth existed, there was only water. It stretched as far as one could see, and in that water there were birds and animals swimming around. Far above, in the clouds, there was a Skyland. In that Skyland there was a great and beautiful tree. It had four white roots which stretched to each of the sacred directions, and from its branches all kinds of fruits and flowers grew.
>
> There was an ancient chief in the Skyland. His young wife was expecting a child, and one night she dreamed that she saw the Great Tree uprooted. The next morning she told her husband the story.

He nodded as she finished telling her dream. "My wife," he said, "I am sad that you had this dream. It is clearly a dream of great power and, as is our way, when one has such a powerful dream we must do all that we can to make it true. The Great Tree must be uprooted."

Then the Ancient Chief called the young men together and told them that they must pull up the tree. But the roots of the tree were so deep, so strong, that they could not budge it. At last the Ancient Chief himself came to the tree. He wrapped his arms around it, bent his knees and strained. At last, with one great effort, he uprooted the tree and placed it on its side. Where the tree's roots had gone deep into the Skyland there was now a big hole. The wife of the chief came close and leaned over to look down, grasping the tip of one of the Great Tree's branches to steady her. It seemed as if she saw something down there, far below, flittering like water. She leaned out further to look and, as she leaned, she lost her balance and fell into the hole. Her grasp slipped off the tip of the branch, leaving her with only a handful of seeds as she fell, down, down, down, down.

Far below, in the waters, some of the birds and animals looked up.

"Someone is falling toward us from the sky," said one of the birds.

"We must do something to help her," said another. Then two Swans flew up. They caught the Woman From the Sky between their wide wings. Slowly, they began to bring her down toward the water, where the birds and animals were watching.

"She is not like us," said one of the animals. "Look, she doesn't have webbed feet. I don't think she can live in the water."

"What shall we do, then?" said another of the water animals.

"I know," said one of the water birds. "I have heard that there is Earth far below the waters. If we dive down and bring up Earth, then she will have a place to stand."

So the birds and animals decided that someone would have to bring up Earth. One by one they tried.

The Duck dove down first, some say. He swam down and down, far beneath the surface, but could not reach the bottom and floated back up. Then the Beaver tried. He went even deeper, so deep that it was all dark, but he could not reach the bottom either. The Loon tried, swimming with his strong wings. He was gone a long long time, but he, too, failed to bring up Earth. So it seemed that all had tried and all had failed. Then a small voice spoke.

"I will bring up Earth or die trying."

They looked to see who it was. It was the tiny Muskrat. She dove down and swam and swam. She was not as strong or as swift as the others, but she was determined. She went so deep that it was all dark, and still she swam deeper. She went so deep that her lungs felt ready to burst, but she swam deeper still. At last, just as she was becoming unconscious, she reached out one small paw and grasped the bottom, barely touching it before she floated up, almost dead.

When the other animals saw her break the surface they thought she had failed. Then they saw her right paw was held tightly shut.

"She has the Earth," they said. "Now where can we put it?"

"Place it on my back," said a deep voice. It was the Great Turtle, who had come up from the depths.

They brought the Muskrat over to the Great Turtle and placed her paw against his back. To this day there are marks at the back of the Turtle's shell which were made by Muskrat's paw. The tiny bit of Earth fell on the back of the Turtle. Almost immediately, it began to grow larger and larger and larger until it became the whole world.

Then the two Swans brought the Sky Woman down. She stepped onto the new Earth, and opened her hand, letting the seeds fall onto the bare soil. From those seeds the trees and the grass sprang up. Life on Earth had begun. (25–26)

⋯⋯

There are many examples of both folktales and sacred stories showing the importance of the female principle in the creation and maintenance of the world. The following dialog comes from the Ekoi people of the Calabar Coast of Africa. Courlander's compendium offers this:

Obassi Nsi and Obassi Osaw

"Who is Obassi Nsi?"

"He is Obassi who is kind to us."

"Where does he live?"

"Under the earth. There is a world beneath the earth whose king is Obassi Nsi."

"Which do you think the more powerful—Obassi Nsi or Obassi Osaw?"

"Both are powerful, but Osaw is cruel and Nsi is kind and good."

"Why then do you pray to Obassi Osaw?"

"Obassi Nsi told us to do so, that Osaw might spare our lives, for the latter always seeks to kill us."

"How do you know that Osaw is fierce and cruel?"

"Because he tries to kill us with thunder and in many other ways. Also, he is not so loving and near to us as Obassi Nsi, for he cannot receive our offerings. We sometimes throw things up into the air for him, but they always fall back again to the earth. Obassi Nsi draws them down; that shows he is more powerful."

"How do you know that Obassi Nsi is good?"

"He never shows us terrifying things as Osaw does, such as thunder or lightning, nor the sun which blazes so hot as to frighten us sometimes, and the rain which falls so heavily at others as to make us think there will be no more sunshine. Nsi ripens our yams, cocos, plantains. etc.. which we plant in the ground. When we are dead we are buried |in the| ground. and go to the world under the earth. to our Father Obassi Nsi."

"What do you think happens to you when you are buried?"

"When a man's body decays. a new form comes out of it. in every way like the man himself when he was aboveground. This new shape goes down to its Lord, Obassi Nsi, carrying with it all that was spent on its funeral in the world above."

"You said that Obassi Nsi told you to make offerings to Obassi Osaw. Why then does he draw them down to himself. as you say he does?"

"He draws them back because he is greater than Osaw. Besides. he wants the latter to come to him. that they may divide the offerings between them. They are, of course, friends."

"Does Obassi Nsi ever want to kill you?"

"No, he would like us to live always: but when Osaw kills us, Nsi takes us to his country under the earth."

"You said that you were told to make offerings to Osaw, in order that he might spare your lives. How then can Nsi, who does not want you to die, partake of these?"

(Hesitation and shy laughter.)

"I told you that they are friends. They talk together and eat together. I think that Obassi Nsi is really our mother and Osaw our father. For whenever we make offerings we are taught to say Nta Obassi (Lord Obassi) and Ma Obassi (Lady Obassi). Now I think that the lord is Osaw and the lady Nsi. Surely Nsi must be a woman, and our mother, for it is well known to all people that a woman has the tenderest heart."

. . . .

Courlander's notation of "hesitation and shy laughter" suggests a cultural Ekoi reluctance to speak indelicately of the generative forces that are sexual. Clearly, the presence of the gods is the important thing. The allocation of male and female sex, while important, is spoken of last of all, and only under the right circumstance. Even when the sexual difference is revealed, it is still framed in terms of the way they talk and eat together. Even when we find that "everyone knows" a woman has the tenderest heart, without more knowledge of the culture, we still don't know exactly what that means. Is she tender toward her counterpart, allowing new life to be generated? Or does she feel tenderness for the humans?

The indirect, tentative nature of the last passage suggests the Ekoi are a high context culture. They are likely to be homogeneous, with such agreement about human society that some understandings don't even have to be uttered. The Japanese have also traditionally been such a high-context culture. They speak politely, delicately, tentatively, and sparingly. The feelings of the listener are taken seriously. Direct, aggressive, or extreme opinions are very rarely uttered.

Anthropologist Edward T. Hall developed the idea of high context and low context communication patterns and wrote about them in his 1976 book, *Beyond Culture*. Some cultures, where there is one widely shared culture, are thought of as high-context cultures because the culture itself provides so much information that ordinarily, few words need to be used. Many things are simply understood. The term "high context" can be confusing, for it is not a comment on the development of the culture, but on the role of culture in conveying knowledge that most people readily understand. In contrast, looking at large societies that contain many cultures, no single culture is able to provide understandable meanings. Hence, a low-context culture provides low context, or a meager basis for mutual understanding. Instead, more verbal exchange tends to be required.

The United States is a low-context culture. It's a culture where there is no one context that applies to people across the spectrum of Americans. We are simply too heterogeneous. We tend to speak directly, concretely, and decisively, and we use many words so that nothing has to be assumed. Silence is not understood as a sign of polite respect; it is often understood as disinterest, stupidity, or hostility if verbal exchange is expected. The feelings of the listener are considered less important than the meanings of the speaker.

HIGH-CONTEXT CULTURE USUALLY CULTURALLY HOMOGENEOUS (E.G., EKOI, JAPANESE)	LOW-CONTEXT CULTURE USUALLY CULTURALLY HETEROGENEOUS (E.G., AMERICAN, GERMAN)
There is much shared understanding and perspective.	There is little shared understanding and perspective.
Few words are used.	Many words are used.
The dignity and feelings of the listener are important.	The meanings of the speaker are most important.
Speech is indirect.	Speech is direct.
Speech is polite.	Speech is concrete.
Speech is tentative.	Speech is decisive.
Speech might avoid delicate topics.	Speech addresses all topics.

In some societies, topics related to reproduction might be considered delicate and uncomfortable to the degree that people don't even converse with the opposite sex unless they're related to each other. However, in some cultures, the sacredness of the generative forces is spoken of with the greatest respect, and the generative principles, male and female, are framed in sacred ways in sacred stories. This is an example from John Fire Lame Deer.

White Buffalo Calf Woman Brings the First Pipe

One summer so long ago that nobody knows how long, the *Oceti-Shakowin*, the seven sacred council fires of the *Lakota Oyate*, the nation, came together and camped. The sun shone all the time, but there was no game and the people were starving. Every day they sent scouts to look for game, but the scouts found nothing.

Among the bands assembled were the *Itazipcho*, the Without-Bows, who had their own camp circle under their chief, Standing Hollow Horn. Early one morning the chief sent two of his young men to hunt for game. They went on foot, because at that time the Sioux didn't yet have horses. They searched everywhere but could find nothing. Seeing a high hill, they decided to climb it in order to look over the whole country. Halfway up, they saw something coming toward them from far off, but the figure was floating instead of walking. From this they knew that the person was *wakan*, holy.

At first they could make out only a small moving speck and had to squint to see that it was a human form. But as it came nearer, they realized that it was a beautiful young woman, more beautiful than any they had ever seen, with two round, red dots of face paint on her cheeks. She wore a wonderful white buckskin outfit, tanned until it shone a long way in the sun. It was embroidered with sacred and marvelous designs of porcupine quill, in radiant colors no ordinary woman could have made. This *wakan* stranger was *Ptesan-Wi*, White Buffalo Woman. In her hands she carried a large bundle and a fan of sage leaves. She wore her blue-black hair loose except for a strand at the left side, which was tied up with buffalo fur. Her eyes shone dark and sparkling, with great power in them.

The two young men looked at her open-mouthed. One was overawed, but the other desired her body and stretched his hand out to touch her. This woman was *lila wakan*, very sacred, and could not be treated with disrespect. Lightning instantly struck the brash young man and burned him up, so that only a small heap of blackened bones was left. Or as some say that he was suddenly covered by a cloud, and within it he was eaten up by snakes that left only his skeleton, just as a man can be eaten up by lust.

To the other scout who had behaved rightly, the White Buffalo Woman said: "Good things I am bringing, something holy to your nation. A message I carry for your people from the buffalo nation. Go back to the camp and tell the people to prepare for my arrival. Tell your chief to put up a medicine lodge with twenty-four poles. Let it be made holy for my coming."

This young hunter returned to the camp. He told the chief, he told the people, what the sacred woman had commanded. The chief told the *eyapaha*, the crier, and the crier went through the camp circle calling: "Someone sacred is coming. A holy woman approaches. Make all things ready for her." So the people put up the big medicine tipi and waited. After four days they saw the White Buffalo Woman approaching, carrying her bundle before her. Her wonderful white buckskin dress shone from afar. The chief, Standing Hollow Horn, invited her to enter the medicine lodge. She went in and circled the interior sunwise. The chief addressed her respectfully, saying: "Sister, we are glad you have come to instruct us."

She told him what she wanted done. In the center of the tipi they were to put up an *owanka wakan*, a sacred altar, made of red earth, with a buffalo skin and a three-stick rack for a holy thing she was bringing. They did what she directed, and she traced a design with her finger on the smoothed earth of the altar. She showed them how to do all this, then circled the lodge again sunwise. Halting before the chief, she now opened the bundle. The holy thing it contained was the *chanunpa*, the sacred pipe. She held it out to the people and let them look at it. She was grasping the stem with her right hand and the bowl with her left, and thus the pipe has been held ever since.

Again the chief spoke, saying: "Sister, we are glad. We have had no meat for some time. All we can give you is water." They dipped some *wacanga*, sweet grass, into a skin bag of water and gave it to her, and to this day the people dip sweet grass or an eagle wing in water and sprinkle it on a person to be purified.

The White Buffalo Woman showed the people how to use the pipe. She filled it with *chan-shasha*, red willow-bark tobacco. She walked around the lodge four times after the manner of *Anpetu-Wi*, the great sun. This represented the circle without end, the sacred hoop, the road of life. The woman placed a dry buffalo chip on the fire and lit the pipe with it. This was *peta-owihankeshini*, the fire without end, the flame to be passed on from generation to generation. She told them that the smoke rising from the bowl was *Tunkashila's* breath, the living breath of the great Grandfather Mystery.

The White Buffalo Woman showed the people the right way to pray, the right words and the right gestures. She taught them how to sing the pipe-filling song and how to lift the pipe up to the sky, toward Grandfather, and down toward Grandmother Earth, to *Unci*, and then to the four directions of the universe.

"With this holy pipe," she said, "you will walk like a living prayer. With your feet resting upon the earth and the pipestem reaching into the sky, your body forms a living bridge between the Sacred Beneath and the Sacred Above. Wakan Tanka smiles upon us, because now we are as one: earth, sky, all living things, the two-legged, the four-legged, the winged ones, the trees, the grasses. Together with the people, they are all related, one family. The pipe holds them all together."

"Look at this bowl," said the White Buffalo Woman. "Its stone represents the buffalo, but also the flesh and blood of the red man. The buffalo represents the universe and the four directions, because he stands on four legs, for the four ages of man. The buffalo was put in the west by Wakan

Tanka at the making of the world, to hold back the waters. Every year he loses one hair, and in every one of the four ages he loses a leg. The Sacred Hoop will end when all the hair and legs of the great buffalo are gone, and the water comes back to cover the Earth.

"The wooden stem of this *chanunpa* stands for all that grows on the earth. Twelve feathers hanging from where the stem—the backbone—joins the bowl—the skull—are from *Wanblee Galeshka*, the spotted eagle, the very sacred bird who is the Great Spirit's messenger and the wisest of all who cry out to *Tunkashila*. Look at the bowl: engraved in it are seven circles of various sizes. They stand for the seven ceremonies you will practice with this pipe, and for the *Ocheti Shakowin*, the seven sacred campfires of our Lakota nation."

The White Buffalo Woman then spoke to the women, telling them that it was the work of their hands and the fruit of their bodies which kept the people alive. "You are from the mother earth," she told them. "What you are doing is as great as what warriors do."

"And therefore the sacred pipe is also something that binds men and women together in a circle of love. It is the one holy object in the making of which both men and women have a hand. The men carve the bowl and make the stem; the women decorate it with bands of colored porcupine quills. When a man takes a wife, they both hold the pipe at the same time and red cloth is wound around their hands, thus tying them together for life."

The White Buffalo Woman had many things for her Lakota sisters in her sacred womb bag: corn, *wasna* (pemmican), wild turnip. She taught how to make the hearth fire. She filled a buffalo paunch with cold water and dropped a red-hot stone into it. "This way you shall cook the corn and the meat," she told them.

The White Buffalo Woman also talked to the children, because they have an understanding beyond their years. She told them that what their fathers and mothers did was for them, that their parents could remember being little once, and that they, the children, would grow up to have little ones of their own. She told them: "You are the coming generation, that's why you are the most important and precious ones. Some day you will hold this pipe and smoke it. Some day you will pray with it."

She spoke once more to all the people: "The pipe is alive; it is a red being showing you a red life and a red road. And this is the first ceremony for which you will use the pipe. You will use it to pray to Wakan Tanka, the Great Mystery Spirit. The day a human dies is always a sacred day. The day when the soul is released to the Great Spirit is another. Four women will become sacred on such a day. They will be the ones to cut the sacred tree, the *can-wakan*, for the sun dance."

She told the Lakota that they were the purest among the tribes, and for that reason Tunkashila has bestowed upon them the holy chanunpa. They had been chosen to take care of it for all the Indian people on this turtle continent.

She spoke one last time to Standing Hollow Horn, the chief, saying, "Remember: the pipe is very sacred. Respect it and it will take you to the end of the road. The four ages of creation are in me; I am the four ages. I will come back to see you in every generation cycle. I shall come back to you."

The sacred woman then took leave of the people, saying: "*Toksha ake wacinyanktin ktelo,* I shall see you again."

The people saw her walking off in the same direction from which she had come, outlined against the red ball of the setting sun. As she went, she stopped and rolled over four times. The first time, she turned into a black buffalo; the second into a brown one; the third into a red one; and finally, the fourth time she rolled over, she turned into a white female buffalo calf. A white buffalo is the most sacred living thing you could ever encounter.

The White Buffalo Woman disappeared over the Horizon. Sometime she might come back. As soon as she had vanished, buffalo in great herds appeared, allowing themselves to be killed so that the people might survive. And from that day on, our relations, the buffalo, furnished the people with everything they needed, meat for their food, skins for their clothes and tipis, bones for their many tools.

• •

In the Harmony with Nature orientation, we are not surprised in seeing the transformation of a human into an animal, nor in learning the symbolism of the number four, so prominent in the natural world. However, we do encounter evil in the expressed contempt for the holy woman when the young man saw her through lustful eyes and reached out to touch her. This is a highly symbolic act, met by a highly symbolic punishment. White Buffalo Calf Woman represents, in part, Mother Earth, because she is female. Some Native people strongly feel that the way a nation treats its land is analogous to the way they treat women. Therefore, they believe, those who show contempt for the female principle are in peril of scorching the earth through acts of conquest. In contemporary times, Native Americans maintain that exploitive and extractive industries are depleting and poisoning Mother Earth. They might also say that humans are bringing this fate on themselves as well, just as the young man in this story brought about his own fate.

There are many questions to consider as parts of this sacred story. For instance, why did the two young men climb only halfway up the hill when they first saw White Buffalo Woman? Why did the holy woman carry a fan of sage leaves? Why did Chief Standing Hollow Horn address the sacred woman as Sister? Why was the medicine lodge made with twenty-four poles? Why was the pipe bowl held in the left hand, and the stem in the right? How do Lakota people think of the universe? What's the significance of the color red?

We are enriched to hear a story so laden with spiritual significance. But may we tell the story to others? Joseph Bruchac, an Abenaki storyteller, would tell us:

... many of the misconceptions about Native American stories and storytellers still exist and all too many non-Native storytellers still get their American Indian tales only from books and not from the mouths of Native tellers themselves. Moreover, even when they do hear stories told by Native tellers, there is often a lack of understanding about the place of those stories and about the responsibilities involved in telling them or the knowledge and permission which are often required in native cultures before one tells the stories of another. (93)

What we should understand, then, is that the sacred stories of others do not belong to us. We may hear them, and we may grow in understanding from them, but they are not ours until our cultural knowledge is deep and until we receive the permission of a spiritual teacher from that culture. The words of John Fire Lame Deer, whose story we've just "heard," is taken from an online source, and so it becomes available for the edification of many. The story is in his own words. With permission, it is passed along in this book. But for most people, the sacred stories of others' cultures are to hear, but not to repeat. However, you can become a voice for your own culture.

THE GREAT RELIGIONS

Christianity is monotheistic, viewing God as the eternal Creator. Jesus is embraced as the redeemer of believers. In Christianity, humans are accountable for how they live, and the uniqueness of the individual is celebrated. Salvation is achieved through effort and good deeds.

In Christianity, the understanding of the place of women has been modified since the Garden of Eden. Roskos tells us that "After Adam and Eve eat the forbidden fruit, nature becomes corrupt and humans sinful, as they are introduced to hardened labor, shame of their nakedness, and knowledge of their eventual death" (312). Death is not the end of existence; heaven exists for the virtuous and the righteous. There is no general agreement on what hell is like, or who goes there.

The designation of "great" religion has no qualitative meaning. It simply refers to religions that have endured over time, and which include the largest numbers of people. These are Christianity, Judaism, Islam, Hinduism, and Buddhism. Each religion has produced sacred texts and a rich literature describing creation and how humans should live. The literature of each religion is substantial, requiring a sustained effort over time to appreciate its depth and complexity. Therefore, what follows is a rather gross oversimplification of each religion, but acknowledging them as legitimate religions is important in conducting respectful communication among these and other diverse humans.

Islam is monotheistic, and denotes submission to Allah. Many Muslims believe life's events are predestined, but humans are still accountable for their acts. Hypocrisy will be punished in an afterlife. They embrace peace and equality as primary values. The Five Pillars of Islam are the statement of belief, prayer, charity, fasting, and pilgrimage to Mecca at least once. Samovar, Porter, and McDaniel explain that Jihad is the struggle to "strive constantly to live up to the requirements of the faith" and restrain lesser nature (127). Though women's roles vary by location, the Qur'ān requires that women must consent to marriage, that they be included in inheritance, and that men and women have equal religious responsibilities. Heaven and hell are the destinations in the afterlife.

Judaism is also monotheistic. They embrace one eternal God and the concept of the chosen people. In Judaism, people are inherently good, and are capable of obedience even though given free will. Judaism does not acknowledge original sin, but breaking God's commandments is sinful. Among the precepts of Judaism is the covenant between God and humans: it is a mutual commitment to a relationship in which humans are obedient to moral law and God will continually bless humans with insights and sustenance. Judaism also emphasizes the core importance of justice, moral treatment of others, learning, and the family as the center of religious and social life. Death is natural, and there is no clear reference to an afterlife.

Buddhism is a non-theistic "religion," a somewhat surprising concept for most Westerners. Chödzin and Kohn say that "though traditional tales from Buddhist cultures are often alive with gods, goddesses, and lesser spirits and ghosts, these are not regarded as independent entities but rather in essence as virtues and powers of mind" (4). Important values are compassion, generosity, awareness, and humor. Within Buddhism, all beings are capable of enlightenment. The Four Noble Truths address the cause, nature, and remedy for suffering, and the Eightfold Path concerns moral living. Of particular interest to the field of communication is the Path of Right Speech, which admonishes us to be truthful, harmonious, gentle, and meaningful.

Hinduism is considered the oldest religion, and it developed over many centuries and over wide geographic areas. Narayanan tells us that "Although there are few concepts that all Hindus would believe in or accept, notions of immortality of the soul, a supreme being, and karma would be accepted by most Hindus" (762). Some Hindus may never have heard the names of the sacred texts, the *Vedas*, the *Upanishads*, and the *Bhagavad-Gita*, but are nonetheless considered Hindu because they practice some of the religious rituals and other practices that are part of Hinduism. Hinduism says that death is inevitable, that the soul is immortal, and that reincarnation occurs wherein a soul begins a new life.

No disrespect is intended in giving such brief descriptions of the five great religions and in omitting the many religions that do not reach as many people. All deserve and require much fuller knowledge if we are to approach an understanding of diverse others. However, such an undertaking would require many volumes, and those already exist, set forth by scholars of each religion. The important thing for us to remember is that religion, or worldview, influences the way we interpret and find meaning in the world around us.

REFERENCES

Bruchac, J. (1996). "The Continuing Circle: Native American Storytelling Past and Present." In "Who Says?" *Essays on Pivotal Issues in Contemporary Storytelling*. Little Rock: August House.

Caduto, M., and Bruchac, J. (1988). *Keepers of the Earth: Native American Stories and Environmental Activities for Children*. Golden, CO: Fulcrum, Inc.

Chödzin, S., and Kohn, A. (1997). *The Wisdom of the Crows and Other Buddhist Tales*. Berkeley, CA: Tricycle Press.

Courlander, H. (1996). *A Treasury of African Folklore: The Oral Literature, Traditions, Myths, Legends, Epics, Tales, Recollections, Wisdom, Sayings, and Humor of Africa*. New York: Marlow & Company.

Hall, E. T. (1976). *Beyond Culture*. New York: Doubleday Anchor.

Hyde-Chambers, F. & A. (1981). *Tibetan Folk Tales*. Boston: Shambhala Publications.

Johnson, S. (2008). *The Invention of Air: A Story of Science, Faith, Revolution, and the Birth of America*. New York: Penguin.

Lame Deer, J. F. (1967) "White Buffalo Calf Woman Brings the First Pipe." Retrieved May 2009. http://www.kstrom.net/isk/arvol/lamedeer.html

Narayanan, V. (2005). "Hinduism," in *The Encyclopedia of Religion and Nature, Volume 1*, edited by Bron Taylor. (pp. 762–776) New York: Continuum.

Roskos, N. (2005). "Christian Theology and the Fall," in *The Encyclopedia of Religion and Nature, Volume 1*, edited by Bron Taylor. (pp. 312–314). New York: Continuum.

Samovar, L., Porter, R., and McDaniel (2007). *Communication Among Cultures*. Seventh Edition. Boston: Wadsworth Cengage.

CHAPTER EIGHT

Illness and Health: Doctors, Shamans, Priests, Midwives, and Medicine Men

The way we think of health and illness offers another window into our own cultural assumptions and values. Often we don't give it much thought until something happens; we break a bone, feel pain, run a fever, have sudden weight loss, or have other symptoms. Sooner or later, we are compelled to give our attention to our condition. But what is health? How do we define it?

At the outer layer, health is the absence of physical disease. As Americans, we might consider fitness to be an equivalent. Healthy people are portrayed as slender, fit, tan, attractive, kinetic, surrounded by friends, and forever smiling. They seemingly have excellent eyesight, bounding energy, lightning-fast reflexes, and good looks. But these characteristics are physical, and the usual approach to assessing health and treating disease are mostly based on the scientific knowledge discovered so far.

The emotional and social dimensions of health had been marginalized until the 1970s, when holistic approaches emphasized the mind-body-spirit model. This approach suggested that disease was not simply a matter of exposure to microorganisms and toxic/radioactive materials, but could also be influenced by emotional trauma, depression, or loneliness. This model also emphasized that lifestyle matters: that consuming too much sugar and refined foods, using alcohol and tobacco, and failure to maintain cleanliness of the body and personal space, could damage one's health.

We have yet to fully understand the role of the spiritual component of health, and that is probably because of our limited exposure to successful examples and information that makes sense to us within our own cultural lenses. We know about acupuncture without understanding how it works in the body and the emotions. We've heard of shamanism, but dictionaries give faulty definitions that undermine the attempt to understand it.

What is it that causes illness anyway?

viruses	witchcraft
bacteria	emotional shock
bad luck	genetic predisposition
malnutrition	stress
drug abuse	poverty
bad spirits	psychological violence
accidents, burns	toxins, poisons
karma	

Illness, failure to thrive, and even aging are often blamed on the perceived causes in this table. In all likelihood, we attribute our own illnesses to several of those causes, but the causes we reject as lacking validity might be central to the understanding of illness for people in other cultures. We might not even agree on what illness is.

Earlier, in Chapter 1, we took a preliminary look at Kluckhohn and Strodtbeck's Worldviews Model. Applying that model to our understandings of illness and health, we might come up with these hypothetical assumptions:

SUBJUGATION TO NATURE	HARMONY WITH NATURE	MASTERY OVER NATURE
God has ordained that I shall experience illness. I will get better, or I will die. I can only accept His wisdom.	Because I am sick, I know I must be out of harmony with Creation. When I regain that harmony, I will be healed. If I try, the spirits will help me.	I do not have time for this nonsense. I have important plans for the weekend and cannot tolerate a cold. Get me some Nyquil and vitamin C.

As we saw earlier, there is some risk of viewing the three descriptors as bounded categories. A more realistic way to view them is as stations along a continuum that includes other perspectives, such as the following hypothetical views:

| God in His infinite wisdom has chosen this experience for me. Suffering is redemptive. | I must have sinned and this is God's punishment. I must not sin. (This implies slightly more control.) | I need to learn my limits and respect them. I should know better than to defy the winter cold. | I shouldn't be so lazy with my diet and fitness regimens. | I refuse to age. I need Botox and liposuction. |

As we move along this last series of health attitudes, we find that slightly more human agency is assumed, until finally, we reach Mastery over Nature, wherein eventually we problematize and medicalize natural, and even healthy, aging processes.

Furthermore, in the Western world, we assume there is a solution for virtually every health problem. We tend to be in denial that death stands a chance in the face of our medical knowledge and institutions. Moreover, the Christian Bible refers to "life everlasting." Still, we in the Western world seek to postpone the afterlife as long as possible.

In his book *Latin American Folktales: Stories from Hispanic and Indian Traditions*, John Bierhorst offers this story from the Dominican Republic:

Death and the Doctor

This was out in the country, and there was a man who kept thinking if only he could find the right work it would make him rich. Then one day Death stood in front of him and said, "I'm going to take care of you. I'm going to make you a doctor. You'll cure the sick just by laying your hands on them, and if you see me standing at the foot of the bed, you'll know there won't be any trouble. But if I'm standing at the head of the bed, don't bother. The cure won't work."

The man went to the city and began to practice his art. Time passed. He cured thousands, and word spread through the town that there was a physician working miracles. The news reached the king, whose daughter was gravely ill, and the king sent for the doctor.

When the man arrived, the king said, "My daughter is about to give up the ghost. Save her, you'll have half my kingdom and my daughter's hand in marriage. But if she dies, you'll be hanged at the gallows." The man started to cure the princess and saw that Death had stationed himself at the head of the bed. He thought, "Disaster! Instead of working a cure I'm going to be hanged." But an idea came to him. He turned the bed so that the princess's feet were where her head had been. And Death, seeing that he had been tricked, left the room. But not without planning revenge.

When the cure was finished, the king lived up to his promise and told the man to come back the next day for the wedding. But when the doctor walked out of the palace, Death caught him by the arm and said, "You're coming with me." He took him up to the sky and showed him acres and acres of little oil lamps. He said, "You see these lamps? These are the lives of all the people on earth, and this one that's sputtering and about to go out is yours."

The man said, "All right, but just give me fifteen minutes and I'll tell you a story you'll like." Death agreed, and while the man was telling the story, he looked around him, found where the oil was kept, and poured enough of it into his own little lamp to keep it burning. Today that man is still alive. I know him.

Scientific/Biomedical Tradition: An approach to illness and healing that relies almost wholly on empirical evidence. This approach tends to set aside the influences of beliefs, life experience, and emotional condition and to treat them within the specialization of psychiatry. The scientific/biomedical tradition assesses physical symptoms predominantly, and addresses them with physical interventions such as medication, radiation therapy, and surgery.

Holistic Tradition: "Holism is concerned with the connection of mind, body, and spirit and how persons interact with their environment," Samovar, Porter, and McDaniel explain (365). Health depends on the ability of the individual to adapt and adjust to change, stress, and challenges. This idea implies the need for the individual to take proactive responsibility for her or his physical, mental, and spiritual well-being. Natural strategies are promoted in the maintenance of health, but tools from the scientific/biomedical tradition are not rejected entirely, but are reserved for cases that are unresponsive to natural treatment.

Holistic practices include such things as naturopathy, herbal medicine, chiropractic, and acupuncture.

Here we have a story in which at one moment, Death seems inevitable. It is a fatalistic view consistent with the Subjugation to Nature world view. But within only a few sentences, we find the doctor suddenly taking control and rescuing the princess from certain death. How might we account for such a rapid and dramatic shift in worldview within a single short folktale?

Several possibilities present themselves. First, perhaps the need for a happy ending plays a part. After all, the doctor fooled Death not once, but twice. Second, we must remember that the Dominican Republic itself has emerged from the political and economic ferment of colonialism that included Spain, Africa, and others. The native Taino people were exterminated but some of their stories survived, and the invading cultures blended elements of their own stories: kings, and the near-magical event of the next-day wedding. The main theme informs us that death can be delayed, and intervention can bring a return to health. The approach is not scientific; it's the magico-religious approach in this story, and in this story, that approach that sometimes coexists with the scientific medical tradition.

There are many instances in which practitioners in magico-religious, herbal, and scientific medical traditions work side by side. For example, in the outskirts of Rio de Janeiro, Brazil, there is a free clinic every week where medical doctors volunteer and where they welcome the other practitioners. Often there are practitioners from two traditions working at the same time to help a single patient. By including several approaches, they can enhance the odds that patients, whatever they believe about disease and cures, can feel reassured that the most effective things are being done for them.

Elements from more than one tradition might appear, for instance, on a shaman's work table. In a documentary video production called *Shaman of the Andes*, we find a Quechua shaman with both shamanic and Catholic religious symbols on his altar/worktable. He uses a guinea pig to diagnose disease and an injection of anti-inflammatory medicine to relieve it. It's not unusual, in many cultural settings, to find people who generally practice one set of traditions, but who include others, perhaps just to be sure, or perhaps because their worldviews embrace a wide range of realities.

Magico-religious Tradition: An approach to illness and healing in cultures where supernatural forces are seen as dominant. People in various cultural groups look to God, spirits, and shamans to participate in healing. According to Samovar, et al., some cultural groups "believe that illness is a sign of weakness, a punishment for evildoing, or retribution for shameful behavior, such as disrespect toward elders" (360). Shamanism lies within the magico-religious tradition, and specific practices are highly varied since this view sees each shaman as uniquely guided by communication with specific spirits.

We also find the same Quechua practitioner treating a young man to relieve him of bad luck. The treatment consists of herbal liquids applied to the body, puffs of blown smoke, an amulet, and prayers throughout the healing ceremony/treatment, which ends with a Catholic prayer. We find that good luck is defined as avoiding drunkenness and avoiding associations with bad people—a very different definition from the Chinese or the North American view of good luck.

In our next story, we see a different confrontation with disease and death. Because of the inclusion of a god among the characters, we might expect the story to reflect a harmony-with-nature view, but quickly find a set of mastery-over-nature responses from the pious king.

In his book titled *Folktales from India*, A. K. Ramanujan provides a Bengali tale:

A Plague Story

Once a terrible bubonic plague broke out in Asia and wiped out millions of people. The pious king of Bharat summoned all the old and wise priests of the realm to find ways to arrest the sweeping plague. He said to the assembled priests, "The plague has come very near the borders of my kingdom. Tell me what I should do to save my people." The priests conferred for a long time, and their spokesman said to the king, "My lord, this is a visitation from the great god Siva and so we must appease him by offering worship and prayers throughout the kingdom." The king at once ordered that worship and prayers be offered in every Siva temple and in every home. He paid for it all from his royal coffers.

A week after the priests began their worship, one midnight the great god Siva appeared before the senior priest and said. "What do you want?" The priest's hair stood on end, and he prostrated himself full length on the ground before the great god and stammered, "O Siva. savior of the universe, you know what we want. Save us from the plague advancing towards our kingdom." The god replied. "Done! Your prayers have pleased me. My servant Nandi will guard your country against all evils." And then he vanished.

Early next morning, the happy news was conveyed to the king, who rewarded each of the priests with twenty five milch [sic] cows and fifty bags of cowrie shells, and sent them home.

Now Nandi was posted to see that the plague did not enter the kingdom. He watched the borders vigilantly day and night. One night, as he was on his rounds along the frontiers. the grim Plague assumed a body and a shape, and appeared before him, threatening to enter the kingdom. Nandi. with his trident lifted high, shouted at him, "Get out of my sight, you villain. One step more and you'll be finished." The hideous figure would not give way so easily. and there was a monstrous scuffle between the two giant figures. It went on for days. Several hills were demolished and great trees were uprooted as the giant bodies dashed against them. At last a truce was made, and they came to terms. It was agreed that the Plague would stay only for a day in the capital and take only one man as its victim.

But the next evening, a great hue and cry was raised in the city, for it was reported that not one or two but a hundred men had died of plague. The king sent at once for the priests and asked for an explanation. They hastened anxiously to Nandi and asked him the reason. Nandi flew into a rage and ran out in search of the Plague. He met him on the dusty floor of a ruined house. He caught him by the neck and thundered, "Scoundrel! You have broken your promise. You've taken not one but a hundred victims. You'll pay for this." Even from under Nandi's grip, the Plague let out a peal of laughter and said. "Brother, I've not broken my promise. Don't be angry with me. I did actually take only one man as I promised, but the other ninety-nine died out of fear. What could I do? These people had a simple fever and a little swelling of the glands, and they mistook them for signs of my approach and they died of fear. I had nothing to do with it." Nandi loosened his iron grip and let the Plague go.

....

We find that the scoundrel Plague has not been brought to bay. In fact, he asserts his power as a fearful enemy who can strike down humans with only a threat. Plague denies responsibility for the consequences of his action; he blames the victims. Nandi, embodying the subjugation-to-nature view, releases Plague; he perceives it useless to strive against him. By looking at this story, you find that the Indian view of creation and its inhabitants is vastly complex when simultaneously they seek to intervene against disease, yet find it terrifyingly inevitable.

This is a point at which stereotypes can be deconstructed and mindfulness can be deployed. As explained in Chapter 1, mindfulness can be built on creating new, more particularized categories, being open to new information, and awareness of more than one perspective. Here we find a story from a culture where people are not entirely fatalistic, as we might mistakenly believe. Instead, the human character confronts the enemy, and although he seems not to prevail, he asserts his outrage. Still, it's a cultural setting in which modern medicine is scarce and thereby no antidote for the plague, and a fatalistic outlook is understandable.

Another way of understanding the relationship between life, illness, and death is revealed in the following Hmong (Southeast Asian) story:

> **Shaman:** Jeremy Narby and Francis Huxley, quoting Alfred Métraux, tell us, "the shaman's functions include curing illnesses, charming game, interpreting signs or omens, influencing the weather, and predicting the future ... " (4). This explanation is severely simplified, however, since it doesn't address issues such as self-discipline, the numinous experience of becoming shaman, or the variations in cultural practices. There has been some criticism of the term "shaman" largely because the word comes from the Tungus (Siberian) language, which does not translate accurately into English, and might not represent what it is that practitioners do in Native cultures of the U.S.
>
> Willard Park explains that "the shaman is regarded as one who has undifferentiated priestly, prophetic, and magico-medical functions his ... main powers are connected with healing and divination ... " (8).

The Origin of the Shaman

There once lived two men, Ngionggi and Xigi. One day, while at the seashore, they saw an island in the middle of the waves. On the island sat a crane on a nest with eggs. The crane left her nest for a time, so the two men took the eggs, pierced them, and emptied out their contents. Then they put the eggs back in the nest.

When the crane returned and saw that her eggs had holes in them, she filled them with a special substance. After forty days all the eggs hatched.

Ngionggi and Xigi saw what happened and they took some of the special substance because they thought that they could wake the dead with it. They tried it first on the corpses of an earthworm and an ant, and immediately the creatures came back to life.

The two men then went to a village where the chief had just died. They brought him back to life. The villagers, in gratitude, heaped presents on the two men. After that, the two men traveled everywhere raising the dead.

One day they decided to return to their own families. But unknown to the men, their wives and children had died long before. The bones were dry, and Ngionggi and Xigi were not able to revive them. Mad with grief, they threw their special medicine into a cave and decided that they, too, should die. Their countrymen tried to stop them from doing this but were not able to convince them. Ngionggi and Xigi consoled the people by saying, "After our death a spirit shall appear to some of you in your dreams. This spirit will make some of you shamans and teach you how to cure the sick. Consult these shamans when you are ill and you will be cured." Since that time, the Hmong have consulted their shamans whenever they get sick.

In the magico-religious tradition, we find that spirits are implicated in virtually all of human affairs—illness, cures, death, volcanoes, floods, and flourishing food sources. Many Hmong people left Southeast Asia for the United States during the Vietnam War, and brought with them their beliefs in spirits and shamanism. Dr. Anne Fadiman learned that:

… Hmong epileptics often become shamans. Their seizures are thought to be evidence that they have the power to perceive things other people cannot see, as well as facilitating their entry into trances, a prerequisite for their journeys into the realm of the unseen. The fact that they have been ill themselves gives them an intuitive sympathy for the suffering of others and lends them emotional credibility as healers. Becoming a *txiv neeb* is not a choice; it is a vocation. The calling is revealed when a person falls sick, either with *quag dab peg* [epilepsy: the spirit catches you and you fall down] or with some other illness whose symptoms similarly include shivering and pain. An established *txiv neeb*, summoned to diagnose the problem, may conclude from these symptoms that the person (who is usually but not always male) has been chosen to be the host of a healing spirit, a *neeb*. (*Txiv neeb* means "person with a healing spirit.") It is an offer that the sick person cannot refuse, since if he rejects his vocation, he will die. In any case, few Hmong would choose to decline. Although shamanism is an arduous calling that requires years of training with a master in order to learn the ritual techniques and chants, it confers an enormous amount of social status in the community and publicly marks the *txiv neeb* as a person of high moral character, since a healing spirit would never choose a no-account host. Even if an epileptic turns out not to be elected to host a *neeb*, his illness, with its thrilling aura of the supramundane, singles him out as a person of consequence. (Fadiman, 21)

During the Vietnam War, Fadiman found that a Hmong family, recently moved to California, had a 15th child who was born epileptic. They looked to their community's shaman for help, but the child's seizures became more severe. They then took the baby to a hospital, where they expected a cure, but were terrified and confused to find that doctors removed her protective wristbands, and then began drawing blood. The parents were certain that either of these procedures would quickly kill their baby.

Again, we have an intercultural crisis wherein a family has faith in their shaman, but a confusing contradiction of beliefs about Western medicine: It should cure everything, but it can't be trusted. Moreover, without a common language, the parents were unable to understand doctors' instructions, and more often than not, used the medications incorrectly or not at all. The epileptic baby grew to be at least 22 years old, but during that time, suffered a most powerful form of seizure and it did so much brain damage that she was left paralyzed and uncommunicative.

Examining our own beliefs, attitudes and values, we find that we draw from many sources. Many of us will go to a regular medical doctor when illness occurs, and if the illness is serious or catastrophic, may also use prayer, counseling, and the support of our communities to deal with the crisis. It's not unusual for Western families to incorporate strategies from medical (scientific) institutions, religion, and community support.

Thomas A. Lambo, in his paper "Psychotherapy in Africa," tells us, "The character and effectiveness of medicine for the mind and the body always and everywhere depend on the culture in which the medicine is practiced. ... Phenomena that are regarded as opposites in the West exist on a single continuum in Africa. African thought draws no sharp distinction between animate and inanimate, natural and supernatural, material and mental, conscious and unconscious. All things exist in dynamic correspondence, whether they are visible or not" (331).

This is not evidence that all African cultures are identical; they certainly are not. Yet Lambo's explanation is a legitimate generalization. He goes on to explain that "Africans attribute nearly all forms of illness and disease, as well as personal and communal catastrophes, accidents, and deaths to the magical machination of their enemies and to the intervention of gods and ghosts. As a result there is a deep faith in the power of symbols to produce the effects that are desired" (332).

We seem to be looking at a general worldview of Harmony with Nature, in which all of nature is imbued with animating spirit, and there is therefore no real division between the natural and the supernatural. Dr. Lambo cites a specific case in which a Nigerian patient, a Cambridge-educated man, was suffering from extreme anxiety and was convinced that there was a conspiracy to kill him. In a dream, he was told that he would be relieved if he would sacrifice a goat. He sacrificed the goat, and then he recovered. He remained uncomfortable, however, because the effective strategy, the sacrifice, conflicted with what his education had taught him.

Hence, we learned that belief in the supernatural is not limited to the uneducated and superstitious. In fact, most of Western psychology finds that many emotional problems stem from the past. Moreover, though Western practitioners don't tend to use magical rituals, they do have rituals, such as taking blood pressure, asking a series of questions from a ritual standard protocol, and prescribing a medicine of which the contents are a mystery to the patient. We find part of the scientific/biomedical tradition overlapping the edges of the magico-religious tradition.

We find another example of a practice with overlapping boundaries between traditions in traditional Tibetan medicine. Practitioners follow a set of moral principles that include cultivating a compassionate mind, being attentive to their work, living a moral life, and refraining from intoxicating drink. These doctors spend 20 years in their medical educations, in which a powerful religious symbol is the Medicine Buddha. Ama

Moxabustion: A treatment from traditional Tibetan medicine that involves the insertion of an acupuncture needle and attaching a small bundle of herbs to be burned. When the herbs have burned, the needle is withdrawn.

Midwife: A female practitioner who is not a medical doctor, but is a specialist in the care of birthing mothers and their babies.

Lobsang Dolma, the first "lady doctor" in this tradition, is the daughter of several generations of doctors.

Tibetan practices take into account the physical, mental, and social condition of the patient. In the documentary *Tibetan Medicine: A Buddhist Approach to Healing*, we learn that Tibetans living in exile address their financial well-being as part of their health. The rugs woven by Tibetans in Darmsala, India, make the community cohesive, bring in revenue, and preserve traditional skills and cultural identity. In this system, we also see the use of natural medicinal herbs and diet, the development of patient records, and the use of diagnostic techniques (such as uroscopy/urinalysis and physical examinations) in common with Western medicine, and devotion to the Medicine Buddha providing us with an example of an approach that combines magico-religious, holistic, and scientific/biomedical traditions. Traditional treatment consists mainly of acupuncture, moxabustion, herbal pills and tea, and diet.

To show how important midwives are in some societies, we offer this story from Senegal, a story reflecting a harmony-with-nature worldview in which the natural and the supernatural coexist:

The Midwife of Dakar

Everyone in Dakar knows old Fatu. She is the woman who brings all the children into the world, and there is hardly a black woman who has not needed her help at one time or another. when giving birth. Her cabin was a little outside the town. where nowadays one can see nice modern streets, and houses in the fashion of the white man; but at that time, this section was just an isolated place.

One night when Fatu was sleeping, she heard a knock on the door. As she was used to being called in the middle of the night. she thought nothing of it, and answered the door. And whom should she see but a big djinn (genie)! She was so scared that she wanted to close the door quickly. but the djinn had foreseen this and seized her hand quickly, pulling her out into the street. He motioned her to follow him, and she did so. trembling all over, not because of the cold. but because of her fear. However, she did not dare to disobey, for everyone knows that you cannot escape from a djinn. So she continued following him through the lonesome roads. Besides. she could soon see that the djinn did not intend to harm her, and so, little by little, Fatu started to feel better about the whole adventure. But she could not recognize where she was, though she thought she knew Dakar inside and out. They arrived finally in front of a beautiful palace, bigger and richer than any she had ever seen. Silently she followed the genie through many courts and halls, and arrived in a room where, on a bed, was lying an extraordinarily beautiful woman genie, surrounded by a crowd of others, all very richly adorned. The queen of the genies was about to give birth, and Fatu now understood why she had been summoned.

Without delay, she started on her work, and when a short time after the little genie was born, she received it and bathed it with great care. She had hardly finished her task and handed the baby over to his smiling mother, when everything—palace and people—vanished and, to her great surprise, she found herself no longer in the chamber of the new mother, but in a dark street of Dakar near the old hospital where she had often been before.

She went back home and, upon entering her cabin, she found the table covered with many coins of gold and silver and a necklace of precious stones. She used the money to live in comfort. As for the necklace, however, she would not part with it. Many people, who had heard the story, offered her a big price for it, but she always refused to sell it, and is probably wearing it to this very day, if she is still living on this earth.

....

"The Midwife of Dakar" is clearly an example of Kluckhohn and Strodtbeck's harmony-with-nature worldview, wherein nature and supernature are not separate, isolated entities, but are instead interactive and infused within each other. Assuming the djinn represents supernatural or unseen forces, we find a humble midwife who can interact effectively and establish a good relationship with the fortune-bestowing djinn.

This does not mean that people in Senegal necessarily believe in the existence of actual *djini* (genies). It seems reasonable that the djinn was a symbol to represent a concept. Perhaps it symbolized the certainty that all humans, no matter how fortunate, will eventually encounter difficulties. Although the midwife interacted with the djinn family, and although she helped these powerful beings, she had no control over them.

We also find this example of a woman as practitioner. Fatu had the knowledge, skills, and courage to meet an extraordinary and fortunate, but terrifying challenge. She acts within a gendered role in a magico-religious tradition, interacting with the numinous or non-ordinary entities.

Another tradition in which women practitioners are prominent is the conjure tradition. The tradition also includes men as practitioners, but many of the popular images we see in modern media focus on women. For instance, the conjure woman Minerva in the quasi-autobiographical book and movie *Midnight in the Garden of Good and Evil* presents conjure in a positive light, with Minerva as creator of protective amulets and rituals in the magico-religious tradition. It brings to mind the steps taken by Enrique Velasquez in the documentary *Shaman of the Andes*. It also brings into question our definitions of health and illness. The scientific/biomedical tradition looks for symptoms, test results, and other verifiable evidence in making diagnoses. Since such things as

Conjure: Dr. Yvonne Chireau explains conjure as " … the creations that black people have woven into their quest for spiritual empowerment and meaning. It is about magic, as that term refers to the beliefs and actions by which human beings interact with an invisible reality. But it is also about religion, which may be defined as a viable system of ideas and activities by which humans mediate the sacred realm. In some African American spiritual traditions, ideas about magical and religious practice can enclose identical experiences … " (20).

" … Black Americans were able to move between Conjure and Christianity because both were perceived as viable systems for accessing the supernatural world, and each met needs that the other did not" (25).

"A range of physical afflictions were treated with conjuring methods. Pneumonia, rheumatism, and arthritis were included among the infirmities for which blacks described supernatural cures. The black novelist Charles Chesnutt observed that Conjure-related ailments among African Americans accompanied hard lives, worn bodies, and old age … " (103).

spirit influences and bad luck don't enter the scientific/biomedical cultural schemata, such claims are likely to be classified as psychological disorders.

The following folktale is a translation of a tale from *Gullah Folktales from the Georgia Coast* by Charles Colcock Jones. Translation from the Gullah (or Geechee) Creole has the effect of stripping away the flavor and spirit of the story, but it also makes it readily understandable to readers of English.

Br'er Rabbit and the Conjure Man

Br'er Rabbit was anxious to have more knowledge than other animals. He didn't like work, so he tried many tricks in order to make a living from other people.

One time he went to the wise Conjure Man to learn from him and get knowledge so he could astonish and impress other people and make them believe he is wiser than almost everybody. The Conjure Man taught him many curious things. Finally, Br'er Rabbit asked him to teach him everything he knew. The Conjure Man said, "You have enough sense already." But Br'er Rabbit begged him, so the Conjure Man answered, "If you can catch me one big rattlesnake and bring him to me alive, I will do as you ask."

Br'er Rabbit got a long stick and went into the woods. He hunted until he found an enormous rattlesnake coiled up on a log. He passed the time of day (made conversation) with him politely, and then made a bet that the rattlesnake wasn't as long as the stick he had in his hand. But Rattlesnake laughed at him and said he knew he was longer than the stick. To settle the bet, Br'er Rattlesnake stretched out full length on the log, and Br'er Rabbit measured him with the stick. Before Br'er Rattlesnake knew what happened, Br'er Rabbit quickly slipped a noose around his head and tied him to the stick. Br'er Rattlesnake struggled and twisted against the noose, but wrapped himself around the stick and couldn't get loose. So Br'er Rabbit caught him and carried him to the Conjure Man.

The Conjure Man was surprised, and he said, "Br'er Rabbit, I always hear you say you have a lot of sense, but now I know it's true. If you can fool Rattlesnake, you can have all the sense you want." So when Br'er Rabbit kept begging the Conjure Man to give him more sense, he answered, "Go fetch me a swarm of Yellow Jackets, and when you bring them to me, I promise to give you all the sense you want."

Everybody knew Yellow Jackets were worse than bees and hornets. They sting badly and, without warning, drop down on anything that comes near their nest. So what did Br'er Rabbit do? He found a big calabash and scraped it out. He cut a little hole in the side and put in some honey. Then he tied it to a pole. Then he looked for a Yellow Jacket nest. He found one, and he set the calabash down near it, and left. By and by, the Yellow Jackets smelled the honey and went inside the calabash to get it. When the calabash was full, Br'er Rabbit stopped up the hole and carried the calabash to the Conjure Man. The Conjure Man made great admiration over what Br'er Rabbit had done. He said, "Br'er Rabbit, you are certainly the smartest of all the animals. I will put a white spot on your forehead so everyone can see you have the best sense in your head." That's how Br'er Rabbit came to have a little tuft of white hair between his eyes.

....

At first it's difficult to know which of the two characters was cleverer than the other. Knowing the secret knowledge of conjure is experienced as an enormous responsibility, and most conjure practitioners would hesitate to share the knowledge indiscriminately. In the end, the Conjure Man convinces Br'er Rabbit that he already knows all the secrets of conjure and gives him a sign on his brow that others can admire. That seems to be enough to satisfy B'rer Rabbit.

Dr. Chireau also explains that in the American South, conjure is often closely associated with the Christian religion in which the freeloading behavior of Br'er Rabbit might be met with disapproval. Moreover, the freeloader can't be trusted with the arcane conjure secrets, so the Conjure Man must appear to concede, but actually prevail. Br'er Rabbit must not perceive it, though, or he will keep pestering Conjure Man.

Before moving on, we note that a major African American contribution in medical emergency response emphasized the scientific/biomedical tradition. The Freedom House Ambulance Service in Pittsburgh, Pennsylvania, grew out of a severe lack of pre-hospital emergency care, a lack keenly felt in the African American community. In the event of a medical emergency prior to 1967, one could try to find someone with a car to get the ill or injured individual to the hospital. Alternatively, one could call an ambulance and the police would arrive with a stretcher and put the patient in a paddy wagon. Police provided no life-saving intervention, and often how they treated the individual was based on their perceptions, not on any knowledge of emergency medicine.

Freedom House Enterprises undertook to provide paramedic training to more than 50 unemployed Black men. They got high-quality training in anatomy and physiology, first aid, cardiac response, CPR, intubation, establishing IV drips, and in the use of burn kits. They learned how to address gunshots, stabbings, psychotic episodes, premature babies, and domestic violence. Their skills and their appropriate responses to medical emergencies transformed the Black community. They were willing to rescue Whites as well, but their offer was rejected. Instead, White medical entrepreneurs took over the idea of emergency service and pushed the Freedom House Ambulance Service out of business, but not until after a substantial number of Black unemployed trainees had earned bachelor's degrees, a few earned master's degrees, and three were in pre-med programs.

Sadly, the contribution of the Freedom House is not acknowledged in most versions of EMT training. Yet Freedom House was clearly the innovative force in emergency medicine. One possible explanation for this omission is racism. As we recall from Chapter 6, racism is the belief in the inherent superiority of a particular race and the inferiority of others. Marginalizing or ignoring the contribution of Freedom House might be an expression of racism.

We end this chapter with an acknowledgement of the complexity of health in the Roma, or Gypsy, people. In an online paper titled "Patrin," by Anne Sutherland, we learn that they view illness as social, a concern of the community. Moreover, the strong spiritual component is present: Spiritual cleanliness, moral behavior, and food are considered especially important.

The Rom concept of cleanliness is radically different from that of the scientific/biomedical view. Cleanliness is not so much about microorganisms and toxins as it is about keeping things regarded as unclean separate from what they consider clean. For instance, they view the top half of the body as clean. The bottom half, by virtue of its nearness to organs of elimination, is unclean. Separate washcloths and towels are used for each half. Furthermore, many avoid contact with non-Gypsy people in order to avoid "pollution." Non-Gypsies, or *gadjes*, are viewed as unclean. This view complicates a hospital stay, since most physicians are not Gypsy, so the most famous physicians are requested, even when their areas of specialization are unrelated to the reason for the hospitalization. Gypsy people clearly feel they are in hostile and dirty territory at a hospital, and often go there only as a last resort, meaning they are usually very ill by the time they arrive there.

Accommodating the needs of such culturally diverse patients requires education, patience, and compromise. It would be naive to expect patient compliance with doctors' instructions if the patient doesn't understand them, or if they are at odds with cultural values or worldviews. So when we encounter concepts such as conjure, "bad medicine," or the evil eye, we should seek to understand what those terms mean before attributing superstitious ignorance to the patient.

We should not forget the impact of the Western medical perspective in its interaction with underrepresented, powerless people. For all the advancements and approaches to relieving and preventing suffering, we shouldn't forget the terrible suffering paid as the price. Dr. Harriet Washington reminds us:

The experimental exploitation of African Americans is not an issue of the last decade or even the past few decades. Dangerous, involuntary, and nontherapeutic experimentation upon African Americans has been practiced widely and documented extensively at least since the eighteenth century.

Perhaps the best-known example of involuntary nontherapeutic experimentation is the infamous Tuskegee Syphilis Study that began in the 1970s and ended in the 1990s. But we find that this kind of exploitation is nothing new. Rebecca Skloot tells us the story of an African American woman named Henrietta Lacks, who died in 1951 of a virulent cancer. Without her consent, doctors harvested her cancer cells, which have been used in tens of thousands of laboratory experiments ever since. The studies that made use of her cells have produced advancements in cancer diagnosis and treatment, but Ms. Lacks's own family remained so poor that their access to health care was severely limited.

Medical ethics now call for informed consent, but the definition of "informed" is still unclear. As we have seen in the example of Henrietta Lacks, providing information may not be the same as communicating. The component of understanding should be robust if genuine consent is expected. Conversely, we should call on ourselves to be "informed" about another's understanding of health if we offer to help. Former President Jimmy Carter has used great care to inform villagers in East Africa, and to understand *their* point of view, as he works to eradicate guinea worm disease and river blindness, two devastating diseases that no longer exist in what he refers to as "the rich world," America.

REFERENCES

Bierhorst, J. (2002). *Latin American Folktales: Stories from Hispanic and Indian Traditions*. New York: Pantheon.

Chireau, Y. P. (2003). *Black Magic: Religion and the African American Conjuring Tradition*. Berkeley: University of California Press.

Fadiman, A. (1997). *The Spirit Catches You and You Fall Down: A Hmong Child, Her American Doctors, and the Collision of Two Cultures*. New York: Farrar, Straus and Giroux.

Freedom House Street Saviors. http://freedomhousedoc.com

Kluckhohn, F., and Strodtbeck, F. (1961). *Variations in Value Orientations*. Evanston, IL: Row, Peterson and Company.

Lambo, T. A. (2000). "Psychotherapy in Africa." In *Culture, Communication and Conflict: Readings in Intercultural Relations*. Ed., Gary R. Weaver. Revised Second Edition. Boston: Pearson.

Livo, N. J., & Dia, Cha (1991). *Folk Stories of the Hmong: Peoples of Laos, Thailand, and Vietnam*. Englewood, CO: Libraries Unlimited, Inc.

Narby, J., and Huxley, F. (2001). *Shamans Through Time: 500 Years on the Path to Knowledge*. London: Thames and Hudson.

Park, W. Z. (1938). *Shamanism in Western North America: A Study in Cultural Relationships*. Chicago: Northwestern University.

"Patrin: Cross-cultural Medicine: A Decade Later" Anne Sutherland. www.geocities.com/~patrin/healthus.htm

Ragan, K. (1998). *Fearless Girls, Wise Women & Beloved Sisters: Heroines in Folktales from Around the World*. New York: W. W. Norton & Company.

Ramanujan, A. K., ed. (1991*) Folktales from India: A Selection of Oral Tales from Twenty-two Languages.* New York: Pantheon.

Samovar, L. A., Porter, R. E., and Edwin R. McDaniel (2010). *Communication Between Cultures.* Seventh Edition. Boston: Wadsworth Cengage.

Skloot, R. (2010). *The Immortal Life of Henrietta Lacks.* New York: Crown.

Tibetan Medicine: A Buddhist Approach to Healing (1985). Mystic Fire Video, Inc.

Shaman of the Andes (2003). Big Mountain Films.

Washington, H. S. (2006). *Medical Apartheid: The Dark History of Medical Experimentation on Black Americans from Colonial Times to the Present.* New York: Doubleday.

CHAPTER NINE

Poverty and Wealth, Social Status, and Power

The realities of power, wealth, and status are the root of cultural experience. Clearly, those at the top of a social or cultural hierarchy have a much different cultural experience than those at the bottom. As we found in Chapter 1, cultural institutions tend to sort people into socioeconomic groups, and ethnic and racial groups are not distributed evenly through hierarchical levels. Historically, people of color have concentrated at the bottom, while Anglo people concentrate in the middle or at the top.

We must not oversimplify the way institutions work, however. Where skin color and economic status might seem to be the determining factors, there are many other variables that also have impacts on life chances. For a great many of us, there are cognitive and emotional difficulties in facing the idea that any of our own institutions might work against an improvement in our circumstances. The myth that "anyone" can become president gives way to the reality that most people can't, often for reasons for which they are not at fault. Members of certain demographic groups are clearly underrepresented in the upper reaches of government. As a case in point, President Barrack Obama is the 44th president, and he is Black. However, if Black people were equally represented, we would have had three Black presidents by now. If 15% of our population is African American, then 15% of our presidents would be Black, given equal representation.

Life chances: The likelihood, given one's circumstances, that she or he will succeed in improving her or his socioeconomic status. Scott and Marshall maintain that the term is closely related to the idea of social mobility, saying, " ... the closed nature of a society diminishes the opportunities (chances) for advancement of social classes, women, and ethnic or racialized minorities. It includes chances for educational attainment, health, material reward, and status mobility ... " (363). Their use of the term "racialized" refers to their definition of racialism, " ... the unequal treatment of a population group purely because of its possession of physical or other characteristics socially defined as denoting a particular race. Racism is the deterministic belief-system which sustains racialism, linking these characteristics with negatively valued social, psychological, or physical traits ... " (544).

Similarly, we have had no Asian or Native American Presidents. Even in U.S. Congress, people of color are underrepresented.

Color-blind racism is a concept and a reality explained by Bonilla-Silva in his book, *Racism Without Racists*. He explains, "Whereas Jim Crow racism explained blacks' social standing as the result of their biological and moral inferiority, color-blind racism avoids such facile arguments. Instead, whites rationalize minorities' contemporary status as the product of market dynamics, naturally occurring phenomena, and blacks' imputed cultural limitations ... " (2).

Many of us who are not wealthy view the wealthy with a certain amount of suspicion. While we view our context as one of equal opportunity, we also know that some people have access to better opportunities than others. When we view rich people, we suspect they didn't become rich by going to work every day and earning a wage or salary. Our suspicions grow into stereotypes and expectations, as reflected in this story from Haiti, collected by DeSpain:

Renting a Horse

Uncle Bouki lived in Haiti long, long ago. He wasn't very rich and he wasn't very smart, but with the help of his friends, he got on in the world.

One morning, Uncle Bouki's burro ran away.

"Wah! How will I get my yams to market? I'll have to rent a horse from Mr. Royce."

Mr. Royce was the richest man in all of Haiti. Mr. Royce was the stingiest man in all of Haiti. Mr. Royce was the trickiest man in all of Haiti, or so he thought. He lived in a twelve-room mansion, high on a hill, and his huge barn was full of strong horses.

Uncle Bouki climbed the steep, dusty road to the rich man's house.

"I must take my yams to market tomorrow," he explained to Mr. Royce. "I'll need to rent a good horse. I can pay you five gourdes."

Mr. Royce smiled cruelly and said, "Ten gourdes is my price—not a centime less."

"But I have only five gourdes," said Uncle Bouki.

"Give me the five now, and the other five when your return my horse tomorrow night. You'll have plenty of cash after you sell your yams."

"But I need it for my family," said Uncle Bouki.

"And I need it for the rent on my horse," explained Mr. Royce.

Uncle Bouki gave him the money and said that he would return for the horse the next morning. He walked slowly down the steep road leading back to his small and crowded house. Something was standing in the garden eating the carrots. It was his burro! His mouth fell open in surprise. She had found her way home. Uncle Bouki was so happy, because now he wouldn't have to rent the expensive horse.

Realizing that Mr. Royce wouldn't give the five gourdes back easily, Uncle Bouki talked the situation over with his clever friend, Ti Malice.

"Don't worry your head about it," said Ti Malice. "We'll pay Mr. Royce a visit this afternoon. Play along with me and we'll get your money back, and more."

They walked back to the rich man's house and asked Mr. Royce to bring the rental horse out from the barn.

"We want to make sure the horse is suitable for tomorrow's job," explained Ti Malice.

Mr. Royce grumbled about the wasted effort, but brought the horse out anyway.

Ti Malice took a piece of knotted string from his back pocket and began to measure the length of the horse's back. Starting at the neck, he measured twelve inches down the back.

"This is where you will sit, Bouki," he said, "and since your wife is smaller than you, she will need ten inches." He marked off the ten inches.

"Your twins will fit here, six inches each," he said, measuring twelve inches more. "Now your mother-in-law is a big woman and will require at least twenty inches. That takes us right up to the tail. But wait, where will I sit? And my wife wants to go to the market, too."

"What is the meaning of this?" demanded Mr. Royce. "You can't put seven people on a horse."

"Please don't interrupt," said Ti Malice. "Let's move the twins to the horse's neck. I'll squeeze behind your mother-in-law, and my wife will sit on my lap."

"What about the six sacks of yams?" asked Uncle Bouki. "Where will we put them?"

"We'll strap them onto the horse's sides, before we all climb on."

"This is utter nonsense!" cried Mr. Royce. "You can't put seven people and six sacks of yams on my horse. It would kill him. I won't rent him to you. The deal is off."

"But you already have rented him to me," said Uncle Bouki. "I gave you half the money this morning."

"I'll give it back," said the rich man, reaching in his pocket. "Here is your five gourdes."

"The agreement was for ten gourdes," said Ti Malice. "The deal isn't off unless you give Uncle Bouki the rest. You owe him another five gourdes."

"No, no," said Mr. Royce, "that isn't fair. I won't give another centime."

Ti Malice measured the length of the horse's neck and said. "I think we can put your neighbor's three small children up here with the twins. They will enjoy a ride to the city."

Mr. Royce turned red in the face as he reached deep into his pocket. Pulling out another five gourdes. he cried, "Take it. Take it and get away from my horse!"

Uncle Bouki shared the extra money with Ti Malice. What a story they had to tell their families. They laughed all the way home.

Ti Malice (pronounced Tee Ma-LEES) is a trickster such as those represented in Chapter 3. He is a lazy character who breaks the rules of society in order to get things he wants. To him, tricking others is better than working. On the other hand, Uncle Bouki is hard-working and simple, a stock character for whom many audiences feel affection.

Returning to cultural perceptions and stereotypes, we find in this story the assumption, backed up by questionable evidence, that Mr. Royce is rich, greedy, and selfish. But we should be mindful that not everyone acquires their wealth through questionable business strategies, outright dishonesty, or theft. Some people inherit their wealth. A rare few people earn enormous wealth through their own efforts, but it does happen that oil can be discovered on someone's land, or that an author whose book becomes a movie can suddenly find him- or herself in very good financial condition. But in today's Haiti, life chances are brutally limited by the colonial history of the country, by the devastation of the earthquake in Port au Prince, by the steeply hierarchical political experience of the country, and by the scarcity of food, drinking water, and medicine for the ordinary people.

Under colonialism, Haiti was a highly stratified society with Spanish colonists, enslaved people from Africa, Portuguese and French explorers, and others who historically swept through the Caribbean, leaving the islands altered forever. In this story, we find wide differences in socioeconomic status consistent with patterns of historic political patterns of power. For example, in 1971, Jean-Claude Duvalier succeeded his father, François "Papa Doc" Duvalier, the previous ruler of Haiti. He lived a lavish lifestyle and became wealthy while poverty among Haitians was more profound than anywhere else in the Americas. Eventually he was overthrown, and he left Haiti in 1986, but the effects of "Baby Doc" Duvalier's power continue to debilitate Haiti, and recovery from the January 2010 earthquake is painfully slow.

In Chapter 1, we briefly addressed stratification institutions. Economic institutions play a part in social status as educational institutions also do. An education from a prestigious university can pave the way to a prestigious, well-paying job and prestige. In their 2005 article "Shadowy Lines That Still Divide," Scott and Leonhardt assure us that social class still matters:

Today, the country has gone a long way toward an appearance of classlessness. Americans of all sorts are awash in luxuries that would have dazzled their grandparents. Social diversity has erased many of the old markers. It has become harder to read people's status in the clothes they wear, the cars they drive, the votes they cast, the god they worship, the color of their skin. The contours of class have blurred; some say they have disappeared.

But class is still a powerful force in American life. Over the past three decades it has come to play a greater, not lesser, role in important ways. At a time when education matters more than ever, success in school remains linked tightly to class. At a time when the country is increasingly integrated racially, the rich are isolating themselves more and more. At a time of extraordinary advances in medicine, class differences in health and life span are wide and appear to be widening. (2)

The issue of education is particularly distressing. Access to a good education is difficult. Even a degree from a public institution is extremely expensive, and few have the money in hand to pay all its costs. Some people simply have no access even with the possibility of scholarships and financial aid. More distressing, however, is Scott and Leonhardt's claim that "success in school remains linked tightly to class." It's no surprise that students from professional middle-class families adapt more easily to the culture and the expectations of the academy. For a student whose parents both have college degrees and good incomes, there is a background of cultural experience that provides cognitive and emotional support. Simply put, the rarified halls of higher education provide a culture more familiar to students from a middle-class educated family than to a working-class family with high school diplomas or less. Those working-class students must work harder to adapt and succeed.

The following story from P'u Sung-ling of Chinese literature illustrates the powerful difference education makes in social status and other advantages. The story was translated by Moss Roberts.

The Scholar's Concubine

In Paoting there was a scholar who had bought himself a literary degree and was now ready to buy a position as a county magistrate. But no sooner had he packed his baggage to go to the capital for this purpose than he fell ill and could not get up for over a month. One day an unexpected caller was announced, and the sick man felt such a strange shiver of anticipation that he forgot his ailment and rushed to greet the guest. His visitor was elaborately dressed and appeared to be a man of standing. He entered making three salutations and, when asked where he had come from, replied, "I am Kung-sun Hsia, a retainer of the eleventh imperial prince. I heard that you were getting your gear ready to go to try for a position as county magistrate. If such is your intention, perhaps you would find a governor's post even more attractive?"

Not daring to be forward, the scholar declined, though he left the subject open by adding, "My sum is small, and I cannot indulge my hopes." The visitor offered to try to obtain the position if the scholar would put up half the sum and agree to pay the remainder from his profits in office. Delighted, the scholar asked the guest to explain the scheme.

"The governor-general and the governor are my closest friends," the visitor said. "For the time being, five thousand strings of cash should ensure their support. At the moment there is a vacancy in Chenting. It would be worth making a serious bid for that post."

The scholar protested that since the office was in his home province, accepting it would violate the dynasty's rule against a man's serving in his native district. But the visitor laughed cynically and said, "Don't be so pedantic. As long as you have the cash in hand, you can get across the barriers." The scholar remained hesitant, however, for the entire scheme sounded far-fetched. Then the visitor said, "There is no need for you to have doubts. Let me tell you the whole truth. This is a vacancy in the office of the city god. Your mortal hours are at an end, and you have already been entered into the registry of the dead. But if you will utilize the means available, you may still attain high station in the world of the shades." With that the visitor rose and bid the man goodbye. "Think it over for now. I shall meet with you again in three days." Then he mounted his horse and left.

Suddenly the scholar opened his eyes from what had appeared to his attendants to be a deep sleep. He said his last farewell to his wife and sons and ordered them to bring out his hoard of cash to buy ten thousand paper ingots. This depleted the entire county's supply. The ingots were piled up and mixed with paper figures of horses and attendants. Then, according to custom, they were burned day and night so that they would accrue to their owner's account in the world beyond. The final heap of ashes practically formed a mountain.

As expected, the visitor reappeared on the third day. The scholar produced his payment, and the visitor led him to an administrative office where a high official was seated in a great hall. The scholar prostrated himself. The official merely glanced at his name and, with a warning to be "honest and cautious," approved him. Next this dignitary took a certificate, summoned the scholar to the bench, and handed it to him. The scholar kowtowed, and the thing was done.

Afterwards it occurred to the scholar that as a holder of the lowest literary degree he lacked prestige, and that he needed the pomp and splendor of carriage and apparel to command the respect of his subordinates. So he purchased a carriage and horses and sent an attendant-ghost in a gorgeous carriage to fetch his favorite concubine.

When all was ready Chenting's official insignia and regalia arrived, together with an entourage that stretched half a mile along the road—a most satisfying display. Suddenly the heralds' announcing gong fell silent and their banners toppled. Between panic and confusion the scholar saw the horsemen dismount and to a man prostrate themselves on the road. The men shrank to the height of a foot, the horses to the size of wildcats! The scholar's driver cried out in alarm, "The Divine Lord Kuan has arrived!"

The scholar was terrified. He climbed down from his carriage and pressed himself to the ground with the others. In the distance he saw the great general of ancient times, celebrated for his fierce justice. The Divine Lord was accompanied by four or five horsemen, their reins loosely in hand. With his whiskers surrounding his jaws, Lord Kuan was quite un-like the world's common images of him. But his spiritual presence was overwhelming and ferocious, and his eyes were so wide-set that they seemed almost to touch his ears. From horseback he said, "What official is this?"

"Governor of Chenting," came the reply.

"For this piddling position," said Lord Kuan, "is such a display really needed?"

The scholar shivered, his body hairs standing on end. All at once he watched his own body contract until he became small as a boy of six or seven. Lord Kuan commanded him to arise and walk behind his horse. A temple stood at the roadside. Lord Kuan went in, faced southward in the direction of sovereignty, and ordered brush and paper so that the scholar could write down his name and native place. The new governor wrote what was asked and submitted the paper. Lord Kuan glanced at it and said in great anger, "These letters are miswritten and misshapen. The fellow is no more than a speculator, a shark loose in the official hierarchy. How could he govern the people?"

Lord Kuan then sent for the scholar's record of personal conduct. Someone at the side kneeled and presented a statement to Lord Kuan. The Divine Lord's face grew darker and fiercer than ever. Then Lord Kuan said harshly, "This cannot be allowed. On the other hand, the crime of buying office is yet smaller than the crime of selling it!" Thereupon an arresting officer in golden armor was seen leaving with ropes and collar.

Then two attendants took hold of the scholar, pulled on his official's cap and robes, and applied fifty strokes of the rod. When they expelled him through the gates, the flesh was practically torn from his backside.

The scholar peered in all directions, but there was no sign of his horse and carriage. He could not walk for pain and lay down on the grass to rest. When he raised his head and looked around, he saw that he was not too far from home. Luckily his body was light as a leaf, and within a day and a night he reached his house. The truth of it all dawned on him as he awoke from the dream and lay moaning on his bed.

The members of the family gathered to question him, but all the scholar told them was that his buttocks were sore. It seems he had lost consciousness and was virtually a dead man for seven days. Looking at the assembled household, the scholar said, "Why is my beloved Ah Lien not here?" For Ah Lien was his favorite concubine.

They told him that Ah Lien had been sitting and chatting the previous night when she suddenly said, "He has become governor of Chenting and has sent a messenger to receive me." Whereupon she went into her room, made herself up, and died.

The scholar pounded his chest in bitter remorse. Hoping that she could be revived, he ordered the corpse held and not buried. But after several days there was no sign of life, and they put her in the tomb. The scholar's illness gradually passed, but the bruises on his backside were so severe that they took six months to heal.

Time and again the scholar said to himself, "The sum I had saved to purchase office is gone, and wasted at that, and I have been the victim of punishment by the forces below. Still, I could endure it. But not to know where my beloved Ah Lien has been taken is too much to bear in the cold, quiet night."

· ·

This story provides an example of one that demands a great deal from a storyteller. As we saw in Chapter 4, the issue of story sources and ethics requires a commitment to learning about a set of cultural values that might, at the outset, seem to make little sense to us. However, to present the story to an audience, a storyteller must prepare the audience by explaining why the differences exist. This shows respect for the story and its cultural source.

First, this is a tragic story, and you should prepare the audience to hear it, and perhaps all you need to do is to simply say that there is sadness in the world and this is a sad story. Besides that, however, there are many things to explain. For instance, the idea of using social connections in order to gain benefits one has not legitimately earned will appall some audience members. But in Chapter 3, we learned about such practices in "A Forsaken Wife and Her Unfaithful Husband."

White privilege: Peggy McIntosh, a professor at Wellesley College, first began her studies of male privilege, but contributed to the understanding of white privilege and public reactions to the concept. She describes it as "an invisible package of unearned assets." Part of the discomfort about facing it is that "describing white privilege makes one newly accountable." In other words, once we know that our advantages are oppressive to others, we don't know what to do about it. Among her suggestions to help us face up to white privilege is to give up the myth of meritocracy, or to stop insisting that one's position in life is the result of talent and hard work alone.

Among the specific advantages McIntosh associates with white skin are: "Whether I use checks, credit cards or cash, I can count on my skin color not to work against the appearance of my financial reliability." "I can swear, or dress in second hand clothes, or not answer letters, without having people attribute these choices to the bad morals, the poverty, or the illiteracy of my race," and "I can take a job with an affirmative action employer without having coworkers on the job suspect that I got it because of race."

Solomon, Portelli, Daniel, and Campbell, whose research focused on white privilege in Canadian education, point out that "[t]he continued over-representation of white, female, middle class and heterosexual bodies within faculties clearly belies the increased minority representation in the schools" (149). In other words, the population of the faculty is whiter than the population of the students.

Jennifer Heller insists that a more comprehensive understanding of racial advantage is needed because whiteness intersects with social class and gender to produce psychological and material advantages. "A white racial identity in the USA is associated with numerous psychological and economic benefits, regardless of whether the individual takes an active interest or is aware of the manifestations of white privilege" (112). She calls attention to the overrepresentation of whites in desirable occupations, and reaffirms that many whites assume that "a higher material standard of living is evidence of superior talent and merit rather than the result of structural favouritism."

For white people, the value of understanding white privilege is the ability to understand how people of color view social relationships. Regardless of the struggles of white people to reach their goals, for others, their own struggle is harder and their life chances are more limited.

It's important to be mindful that the presence of two tales addressing social advancement and corruption should not instill in us a stereotype of ancient China that doesn't bear up under further scrutiny. In both stories, severe punishments were afforded to the main character. A strong element of Chinese stories is that nobody gets away with anything. As this lesson is transmitted to listeners, many of them will get the message and take it to heart.

Returning to the concept of life chances, we're reminded that in much of the modern world, whiteness bestows advantage. The idea of white privilege is a difficult one for many of us. It suggests that if we're white, we have unfair advantages that we didn't earn. Acknowledging this reality is a struggle for those of us who are abundantly idealistic and egalitarian in spirit. In the last ten years, scholars have attempted to explain what whiteness means in terms of consequences.

The following African American story, told to collector Richard Dorson, exemplifies the long-lasting position of disadvantage African Americans endured and, in many ways, still endure:

Mistake in Account

It was on a large plantation in Mississippi, all Negro tenants. This man would settle with them seven or eight years. And one Negro. George

Jackson, couldn't read or write. Neither could his wife. But they lived on the main road that led from where most tenants on the place lived, up to the headquarters. So this year the Boss decided to settle. And this particular man, the Boss gave him a statement and a check pinned to the statement for $750. He carried his statement and his check home. He and his wife looked over it. With that being the first settlement they had had in seven years they didn't know what to do with it. Living on the main road where all the Negroes had to pass his house to go down to the headquarters of the office, some of the Negroes could read or write, or could figure. After going home with their statements, several of them found mistakes. They passed back by George Jackson's house going back to have their mistakes corrected. George Jackson being one of the busybodies, he asked everyone that came by, "Hey buddy where you gwine?"

So they would all tell him, "Well I found a mistake in my account, and I'm going back to have it corrected."

And after so many of them had found mistakes, something just told him that there was a mistake in his account. So he went in and told his wife Mandy, said, "Do you know, I believe there is a mistake in our account. You give it here." And he went back to the office to talk to the Boss.

When he walked in the office the Boss said, "Well Uncle George, what's your trouble?"

And he says, "I think there is a mistake in my account."

The Boss knew George Jackson couldn't read or figure. He was just coming back because others were saying they were coming back. He decided to have some fun off him. He took the statement and looked over it for a little while. Called George Jackson over to the desk. He said, "Well Uncle George, I did discover a mistake here." He said, "I find here that I paid you $20 too much."

George said, "I knowed it, I knowed it, I knowed it."

· ·

It's difficult to find the humor in a situation where someone in a privileged position takes advantage of a powerless person. While in this story, an individual character takes advantage, he represents the sort of advantage taken by institutions, often without the conscious intent to oppress. We don't know with utter certainty that the Boss is white, but the context is plantation employment, and so we assume that in this story, white privilege allows the Boss to take advantage.

Finally, we need to understand ways in which discrimination can occur without conscious individual discrimination.

Prejudice and Its Functions

Prejudice is *pre-judgment*, literally, from the Latin root. We generally think of racist prejudice, but there are other kinds, such as religious prejudice, social class prejudice, occupational prejudice, and so on. It is almost always *negative and unfounded* judgment. Prejudice generally influences a person's behavior toward members of the prejudged group. Those behaviors include exclusion, avoidance, hostility, hate speech, and even violence. Just to be clear, even mild-sounding behaviors like avoidance have severe discriminatory consequences in the classroom, the emergency room, or the employment office. Discrimination and social inequality are the result even in cases where prejudice is perceived to be relatively low.

Humans are so adept at prejudice that collectively, we find many ways to develop it. We learn it socially or we develop it as a consequence of social interaction or observation. Humans are also adept at justifying their prejudice, rhetoric, and even violence against generalized groups.

Samovar, Porter, and McDaniel explain that prejudice has functions, and that because they are useful, they persist. The first of these functions, say the scholars, is the ego-defensive function (174). Bad luck or poor performance is blamed on someone else. In cases where employment is involved, an unsuccessful job applicant might blame affirmative action, believing that the program favors unqualified members of minority groups.

The same scholars also say, "The utilitarian function of prejudice allows people to believe that they are receiving rewards by holding on to their prejudicial beliefs. The most vivid examples of this function are found in attitudes related to the economic arena. People often find it very useful, and to their economic advantage, to say, 'Those immigrants have so little education that they are lucky to have the jobs we offer them'" (174). This use of prejudice defends the status quo.

The value-expressive function is used in maintaining moral values. People who express prejudice against people of other religions and social patterns are prejudiced against people with different views.

Prejudice also serves a "knowledge" function. When people categorize and describe others, they construct their perceptions in ways that make sense to them, though their perceptions are often oversimplified, inaccurate, and negative. People are considered not as individuals, but as the labels applied to their groups: "immigrants," "Jews," "these kids nowadays," and so on.

The same set of functions was explained by William Gudykunst and Kim in 1992 (101).

Theories of Prejudice

Contact Hypothesis (prejudice): Gordon Allport, in his 1954 book *The Nature of Prejudice*, thought that contact with others would reduce prejudice because of the increased knowledge that would come out of that contact. Many scholars attribute prejudice to such things as mistrust and fear of the unknown. In such cases, it would make sense that contact would alleviate fear, and therefore, prejudice.

However, there are some conditions that would have to be present throughout the contact. First, the contact must be positive. Second, the people in the groups should be equals. Third, there should be little or no competition between the people. Fourth, individuals should be motivated to break old cognitive habits and act in a nonprejudicial way. Fifth, people should not feel justified in their prejudice.

This does not mean that Gordon Allport was short-sighted or shallow in his treatment of prejudice. In fact, his book, *The Nature of Prejudice*, is considered one of the classic works on the topic, the seminal work upon which other research has been built.

Normative Theory simply says that we learn prejudice from our social surroundings and experiences. As social learning, prejudice is reinforced through family, neighbors, media, friends, and so on.

This theory makes a certain amount of empirical sense to people who have visited places where prejudiced attitudes are pronounced, or are directed at alternate target groups. For instance, in a location where negative attitudes are freely expressed against divorced women, normative theory might explain the formation of the prejudice. However, Normative Theory does not explain why some individuals do not adopt prejudiced attitudes.

Scapegoating Theory says that when people experience misfortune, they might blame it on a relatively powerless group. In essence, this theory says that prejudice is rooted in human nature.

When we think of the Jewish people during the Holocaust, they provide us a clear example of how scapegoating can create prejudice. The limitation to this example is that others in addition to the Jews were also targeted for annihilation: Gypsies, gay people, intellectuals, mentally retarded people, and people with physical disabilities were also targeted.

Japanese Americans were also scapegoated after the bombing of Pearl Harbor. It could be argued that they were not actually blamed, but were simply prevented from carrying out the kinds of terrorist actions that had already been done by their relatives across the sea. As we know, they were not simply prevented from an act they were not planning, but brutally prevented from receiving the rights they deserved as American citizens.

Scapegoating is operative in the case of prejudice and hatred toward "illegal immigrants," who are blamed for underemployment, a stressed economy, and gang violence.

Authoritarian Personality Theory says that a particular kind of personality has the tendency to look upon the world in terms of black and white, right and wrong. They are said to be predisposed to prejudice.

The limitation to this theory is that many people who are capable of more nuanced thinking still embody prejudice. This theory might explain some cases of prejudice formation, but probably not a majority. In addition, discrimination, the result of prejudice, is built right into many of our institutions.

We know that prejudice appears in many forms. High prejudice appears when members of an in-group, such as the Ku Klux Klan and white supremacist groups, decide that members of the out-group are inferior. Symbolic prejudice occurs when people have negative feelings toward others because of differences in values. Examples include anti-gay, anti-Catholic, and other similar groups. Tokenism occurs when members of the in-group have negative feelings against the out-group but don't want to admit it. Behaviors include hiring just one member of the out-group. Arms-length prejudice is when the in-group socializes with the out-group in certain instances, but at the golf course, there is still segregation. Groups with real likes and dislikes are uncomfortable with cultural groups that are noisier, for example. People with low prejudice are more familiar than with the unfamiliar.

The following story from India shows an example of discrimination as a consequence of prejudice. To understand this story, you will need to know that Akbar is Akbar the Great, a 16th-century emperor in India, famous for having encouraged the development of art and architecture, while Bîrbal was one of his nine counselors, a position similar to the American secretary of defense in our own capital. Ahîrs were considered a backward class of people. Secondly, it's important to understand the sense of the word "mean" as conveying a state of lowliness. William Crooke and Pandit Ram Gharib Chaube collected this story.

The Evil of Covetousness (told by Ram Singh, Constable of Kuthaund, Jalaun District)

One day Akbar and Bîrbal were out hunting on an elephant, when Akbar noticed something sparkling on the ground, which looked like a pearl. So he made some excuse and got down. But on touching it, he found that it was only a drop of spittle glistening in the sunshine. Being ashamed, he said nothing; but on returning to the palace, he asked Bîrbal what was the meanest thing in the world. Bîrbal asked for a month's grace to find out, and went and stayed in a village in the hope of learning the answer from the people.

He asked the women what was the meanest thing in the world, and they said:—"Ask our husbands;" and when he asked the husbands, they said, "Ask our women." Then an old Ahîr woman invited Bîrbal to stay with her. So he went and found food ready cooked for the household. When she asked Bîrbal to share their meal, he said:—"How can I, a Brahman, eat with an Ahir?" "What does it matter," said she, "no one will know." But as he still refused, she brought a purse of two hundred rupees and gave it to him. Then he put out his hand to take the food. But she drew the food away from him, saying:—"How evil a thing is covetousness, when a man like you will lose his caste for such a petty sum." Bîrbal was ashamed, and returning to the Emperor, said:—"Covetousness is the vilest thing in the world."

Though the traditional caste system that organized society in India for many centuries has been officially overturned, it still influences the perspectives of many Indians. This is not surprising; we learned that institutions in the deep structures of culture are slow to change. Moreover, if a belief in karma is present, and it also springs from the deep structures, that belief upholds the idea of caste. If someone occupies a lowly social position, it is because of his or her own behavior in a previous incarnation, and hence, they have nobody to blame but themselves. The caste system perpetuates inequality and prejudice, as we saw in this story. The villagers, the Ahîrs, were considered backward, and at first, Bîrbal shrank from eating the food fit for lowly Ahîrs. Offered a sum of money, he relented, only to be chastised by the Ahîr woman, who, to our surprise, asserted the legitimacy of caste.

The story doesn't tell us whether or not Bîrbal confessed his error to Akbar or told him how he came to know that covetousness was the vilest thing, but we are told that he was ashamed. Though our American experience doesn't expose us much to the idea of shame, we do sometimes feel it, and in feeling shame, we decline to share the details about which we feel shame.

But we're left with a curious question about why the Ahîr woman invokes caste when she reprimands Bîrbal. After all, she is the one suffering under its stigma. Why would she want to remind Bîrbal of her lowly position? At least three possible answers present themselves: either she herself is so immersed in the legitimacy of the caste system that she is disoriented by Bîrbal's transgression, or she pounces on the opportunity to criticize the mighty, or perhaps she's working to improve her own karmic merit.

Probably an individual of Indian ancestry would understand more fully the behavior of the Ahîr woman. Ironically, she is the dominant character in the story, for we find that both Akbar and Bîrbal have committed acts that have brought them shame. Yet prejudice against those of lower caste has not been cause for shame. We also know that within our own society, there are prejudiced people who do not know they are prejudiced; they believe they simply observe and understand social realities. When those perceptions are negative, inaccurate, and unwarranted, however, prejudice nearly always lurks beneath those perceptions.

Many scholars have insisted that most people have some prejudice. Gudykunst and Kim explain:

We tend to think of prejudice in terms of a dichotomy; either I am prejudiced or I am not. It is more useful, however, to think of the strength of our prejudice as varying along a continuum from low to high. This suggests that we all are prejudiced to some degree. We also are all racist, sexist, ageist, etc. to some degree. As with ethnocentrism, this is natural and unavoidable. It is the result of our being socialized as members of our ingroups. Even people with low levels of prejudice prefer to interact with people who are similar to themselves because such interactions are more comfortable and less stressful than interactions with strangers. (100)

One area of prejudice left unmentioned in this description is prejudice against particular occupations. At various times, we feel aversion for "dirty" occupations such as manual labor, or at the other extreme, for people possessing what we might view as undeserved obscene wealth. Most people probably have negative feelings toward illegal occupations. Our capacity for prejudice is immense and adaptable, and it reflects well on us when we find ourselves unprejudiced in ways where other people harbor prejudice.

We should not sink into despair at this news, nor should we bristle defensively. For many of us, our degree of prejudice is low, and our targets are limited. Once we are aware of our prejudices, we reduce their power over us and we can govern our outer behavior accordingly. If there is someone you wouldn't date, or someone from whom you would never accept help, or someone like the Ahîr woman with whom you would never have lunch in a restaurant, you have the opportunity to examine your reasons. If you have the courage to confront a prejudice in this way, you are more honest than a good many people, and you can at least be tolerant, if not actually accepting, of others who are different in some respect.

REFERENCES

Bonilla-Silva, E. (2010). *Racism Without Racists*. Third Edition. New York: Rowman & Littlefield Publishers.

Cooke, W., and Chaube, G. (2002). "The Evil of Covetousness," in *Folktales From Northern India*. Santa Barbara, CA: ABC-Clio. (p. 364)

Dorson, R. (Ed.) (1967). "Mistake in Account," in *American Negro Folktales*. Greenwich, CT: Fawcett. (pp. 307–308)

Gudykunst, W., and Kim, Y. (1992). *Communicating with Strangers: An Approach to Intercultural Communication*. Second edition. New York: McGraw Hill.

Heller, J. (February 2010). "Emerging themes on Aspects of Social Class and the Discourse of White Privilege." *Journal of Intercultural Studies*, vol. 31, no. 1, pp. 111–120.

McIntosh, P. (1988). "White Privilege: Unpacking the Invisible Knapsack" excerpted from *White Privilege and Male Privilege: A Personal Account of Coming to See Correspondences Through Work in Women's Studies*. Wellesley, MA: Wellesley College Center for Research on Women.

"Renting a Horse." (1999). *The Emerald Lizard: Fifteen Latin American Tales to Tell in English and Spanish*. Collected by P. DeSpain. Little Rock: August House. (pp. 23–26)

"The Scholar's Concubine." Trans. M. Roberts. (1979). *Chinese Fairy Tales & Fantasies*. New York: Pantheon Books. (pp. 157–161)

Scott, J., and Marshall, G. (2005). *Oxford Dictionary of Sociology*. New York: Oxford University Press.

"Shadowy Lines That Still Divide." Scott, J. and Leonhardt, D. (2005) in *Class Matters*. New York: Times Books.

Samovar, L., Porter, R., and McDaniel, E. (2010). *Communication Between Cultures*. Seventh Edition. Boston: Wadsworth Cengage.

Solomon, P., Portelli, J., Daniel, B., and Campbell, A. (July 2005). "The Discourse of Denial: How White Teacher Candidates Construct Race, Racism and 'White Privilege.'" *Race, Ethnicity and Education*, vol. 8, no. 2, pp. 147–169.

CHAPTER TEN

Ancient Stories and Their Descendants

The relevance of ancient stories is that they do important things for us today. First, they give us a glimpse of where humanity has been on its way to living in this time. We can connect with ancestral perspectives, values, and realities through reading or hearing them. We can learn where we fit into the stream of humanity since the development of language. This alone is an enormous gift, left to us by ancient ancestors we will never get to meet, but from whom we have inherited a rich legacy.

Second, Walter Fisher would say that ancient stories provide us with the setting in which we're able to imagine other times and places. By virtue of the narrative experience, we are transported to another time and place in which we come to new understandings of human experience beyond our individual lives. Perhaps we even begin to care about those other humans, their struggles, their emotions, their achievements, their gods. Perhaps we can imagine ourselves in their place, creating the songs and stories that echoing generations of descendants would learn.

Third, we are invited to join our ancestors with our own voices, bringing our forebears and their wisdom along with us. As we sit in the storytelling circle, they are among us. Perhaps they are pleased that their songs, their words, and their thoughts still have value. Homer, we believe, sang *The Iliad* and *The Odyssey*, but centuries later, we don't know that those were his own words, or whether instead, he was handing down stories from even older storytellers. Likewise, we are the recipients of *The Epic of Gilgamesh,* but not all of it; the fragments that survived the destruction of its clay tablets tell us that it was a story of Everyman, a story of the human condition, a story of yearning, and a story of mortality. *Beowulf,* the Scandinavian epic, reveals an experience in a time when the world was dangerous and unpredictable; it shows us courage, sacrifice, and victory.

Later, in the familiar collection of *Arabian Nights,* we lost connection with any specific culture, but are enriched nonetheless. As Rosalind Kerven explains:

> The stories of the *Arabian Nights* did not come from any one country—many originated in Persia (present-day Iran) and other Middle Eastern countries, and some came from India and China. From about the 7th century, when these stories were being told, most of these countries were linked by a vast empire—the Islamic empire, and many shared a common language (Arabic), a common faith (Islam), and a common way of life. (8)

While we might debate how fully the Middle East, India, and China really shared a common way of life, we should understand that some stories and characters (such as Scheherazade, the beautiful bride who used her wit and her stories to save her own life) have traveled far, have changed through the telling in many voices, and yet somehow still capture our attention and entertain us far into the night.

In other parts of the world, we find the Talmudic and Hasidic masters whose tales confront how humans should live, our flaws notwithstanding. In the 11th century, Lin Yutang anthologized much of the sacred literature from Hinduism, Buddhism, Confucianism, and Taoism. Sometimes we're also elated by the discovery of collections of stories in print, reflecting the amazing variety of cultures. We're fortunate to find a few stories from African traditions in English print, but should be mindful that though some African languages had written form, others did not and still do not. Some stories were transmitted over centuries by memory. Finally, we should consider the probability that in the human diaspora from Africa to Europe, tales were carried to new, fledgling cultures, to be transformed into shapes that are familiar today.

Not all stories are ancient. Younger voices have uttered their own visions. Through the ages, other wise and wily elders have spoken: Chaucer, Shakespeare, Boccaccio, and Murasaki Shikibu, the 11th century Japanese noblewoman who we believe wrote *The Tale of Genji,* a lengthy tale of jealousy and political intrigue.

Whether these newer tales can be considered traditional depends on how we define what we consider a folktale to be. On one hand, folktales, we think, come from the folk, the ordinary people living ordinary lives, and telling each other stories to explain their history, stabilize their communities, convey their values, and entertain each other. Many of the tales collected by Jakob and Wilhelm Grimm were collected from folk, and probably qualify as folktales even though heavily edited at times by the same Brothers Grimm. What about stories of single authorship? Lady Murasaki Shikibu, we suspect, was not ordinary folk. Chaucer, Boccaccio, and Shakespeare didn't toil in the fields either, though at least in the case of Shakespeare, some of the plays were sometimes drawn from folktales. Patrick Ryan and James Mayhew collected a few examples: A folktale they call "The Devil's Bet" was the inspiration for *The Taming of the Shrew,* "Snowdrop" inspired *As You Like It,* "Cap-O-Rushes" inspired *King Lear,* and "Ashboy" inspired *Hamlet*. Hence, we know that we receive stories that have traveled many miles and taken many shapes before we hear them. It may never be known what the origin of a given folktale is. As the Irish story collector Lady Francesca Wilde (mother of Oscar Wilde) explains, "Traditions, like rays of light, take their colour from the medium through which they pass … " (2).

There are also more modern storytellers, spinners of single-author tales, who bring us stories about daily life or inner life. These voices, too, have a place in teaching us about ourselves and others. Mark Twain, Langston Hughes, Nathaniel Hawthorne, Maya Angelou, Sandra Cisneros, James Baldwin, Vine Deloria, Leslie Marmon Silko, and many other powerful writers bring us new expressions of older themes, and with them, the potential for one day taking their acknowledged places next to the ancient, anonymous, ancestral voices.

Tradition is a difficult concept to define. Some traditions are old, but not all. A tradition is a shared way of doing and understanding things, maintained over time among a given group of people. Perhaps it's old, and perhaps not, but it still expresses the motivations, needs, understandings, and realities of the people.

To clarify how this can be so, I refer to the story "The Four Waters," told by Navajo (Diné) storyteller Hoskie Benally. The story was told to him by a medicine man in a sacred sweat ceremony. This is a story of transformation and healing, of the origin of ceremony, and of the return to original teachings. This story is paraphrased from a DVD titled *Circle of Stories*.

The Four Waters

A young man went with his little sister to a corn field where they would play in the daytime. Near the end of the day, they would return to the edge of the cornfield and go home. One day, when they reached the edge of the cornfield, they found that they had come out somewhere else, not in the place they intended. They couldn't see their house.

The young man took a piece of corn husk and said to his sister, "Let's go up to that hill and take a look," so they did, but they still could not see their house. "Let's go up one more ridge." Again, they did, but they still couldn't see their house.

The little girl got scared and started to cry, but her brother said, "Don't cry. Grandpa always told us that when we're lost, we should use tobacco to help us." So he took out the corn husk, rolled some tobacco inside, and smoked, praying for help and direction.

A bird came from the east and brought white water. The bird said, "This is coming. It isn't good for people. Go warn your people."

Another bird came from the south, carrying blue water. This bird said, "This is the only good water. It is pure, and it is medicine."

A third bird came from the west carrying yellow water. He said, "This is coming, and it is not good. Go warn your people."

And from the north, a bird came carrying purple water, saying "This is no good; warn the people."

The young man finished his prayer, and when he stood, he and his sister saw their house.

....

> **Sweat ceremony:** This is a ceremony of physical and spiritual purification, which takes place inside a sweat lodge. The ceremony varies in how it is conducted in different Native American traditions. The ceremony makes use of stories, prayers, and sacred songs.

Hoskie Benally explained that the white water represents whiskey, the yellow water represents beer, and the purple water represents wine. Only the blue water is pure and good. This is a story he uses in the sacred sweat ceremony, when storytellers also say that tobacco is for prayer, and for your mind, and that marijuana is no good. It's his way of warning the people.

This is a new story, perhaps only a few years or decades old. But it speaks to the experience of contact with alcohol and other drugs. The symbolism of the birds is highly significant: Birds make the journey between the ordinary world and the world of spirit, and it is they bringing the young man the message of the four waters. The importance of the little sister is that she will carry the wisdom to the next generation.

It isn't difficult to see how this relatively new story would become a traditional ceremonial tale, which it could, if it becomes known and shared widely in Navajo communities.

Stories used as medicine is not a new idea. In 1978 the power of story was finally acknowledged by the U.S. Department of Health, Education, and Welfare when they published a pamphlet titled "Come Closer Around the Fire: Using Tribal Legends, Myths, and Stories in Preventing Drug Abuse." In focusing on young Native people, the pamphlet tells us, " ... the urban American lifestyle imposes a greater burden. The concepts of harmony with nature, cooperating, sharing, patience, listening, and respect for elders, as well as the importance of the spiritual life are challenged constantly" (2). The emphasis of the pamphlet is on prevention, but it has been found that access to traditional stories and ceremony has a healing effect on Native American prison inmates as well. The healing occurs when they are able to transcend their isolation within in prison walls, become a community again, and reconnect with their cultural identities.

Other traditions also have more recent stories laden with symbolism. One example that appears in collections of traditional Jewish stories comes from 19th-century Eastern Europe, however it was configured at the time. Howard Schwartz's collection includes the following traditional story:

The Golem

....

During the reign of the Emperor Rudolf, a wonder-working rabbi lived in Prague whose name was Rabbi Judah Loew. He had been tutored in these mysteries by Rabbi Adam, whose mastery was unsurpassed. Nor did Rabbi Adam withhold anything from his disciple, and thus Rabbi Loew served as the tzaddik of his generation, as Rabbi Adam had in the generation before him.

One year it happened in the spring that Rabbi Loew had a long and vivid dream, in which he found himself in the Christian quarter of Prague, outside the Jewish ghetto. There he witnessed a terrible crime, in which a child was murdered and thrown in a sack, then carried to the Jewish section of the city, and left inside one of the houses there. In the dream Rabbi Loew saw the face of the murderer; it was the face of the evil sorcerer Thaddeus, a great enemy of the Jews who spent his days plotting ways to harm them. And Rabbi Loew understood that Thaddeus was plotting to accuse the Jews of a blood libel. This terrible accusation, the claim that Jews use blood in order to make matzah for Passover, was a terrible lie. Never had such a thing been done. But the libel had been made in almost every generation, and now the evil priest was planning to accuse the Jews of this falsehood again.

In the dream, Rabbi Loew found himself helpless to do anything when he suddenly heard the sound of beating wings and looked up and saw a flock of birds flying in formation, spelling a word that he read clearly in the heavens. It was God's most sacred Name, which holds the power at the source of all being. And in the dream Rabbi Loew wrote that Name down on a piece of paper, and slipped it into the pages of the Bible he was carrying in his hand. No sooner had he done this, than he looked down at his feet, and suddenly saw the outline of a large body in the earth. Before his eyes the features of the body began to take form, and the word Emet, which means Truth, appeared on its forehead. Just as the eyes of the man of clay opened, Rabbi Loew awoke, the dream still vivid in his memory.

Now the rabbi recognized from the first that he must decipher this dream. For the Name of God was the most sacred word of all, and its appearance in a dream must portend matters of grave importance. He realized that it could have no other meaning than to warn him that Thaddeus was about to accuse the Jews of Prague of the blood libel, which would doubtless unleash a terrible pogrom against them. Thus the dream had come as an urgent warning, but surely it also contained the method by which the plot of the evil Thaddeus could be foiled. But what way was this? Rabbi Loew was uncertain.

Rabbi Loew decided to consult the Torah. He opened the Torah, and when he did, the first thing he saw was a slip of paper with God's Name on it—the very one he had written in his dream! He picked it up in his hand and marveled that it had come to him from the world of dreams. Rabbi Loew thought again of his dream, and of the outline of a man he had seen just before he woke up. Suddenly he had understood that his task was to bring that man into this world. But how could this be done? Surely God would guide him, and make it possible for him to bring that man into being.

There was no time to be lost. Rabbi Loew decided to undertake this mission that very night. Rabbi Loew hurried and awoke his son-in-law, Isaac ben Samson Ha-Cohen, and his foremost pupil, Jacob ben Hayim-Sassoon Ha-Levi, and told them to get dressed and to come with him at once. They wondered greatly what urgent matter had arisen, but dared not ask, knowing that the rabbi would tell them when he was ready. And in fact he said nothing at all, but led them through the darkness to the banks of the river Moldau. There Rabbi Loew told his helpers to dig out enough clay to equal the weight of the three of them. This they did, and Rabbi Loew began at once to shape that formless mass into a clay mass of immense size. The others watched, astonished, as Rabbi Loew created the features, then added the word Emet—Truth—to its forehead, just as he had seen in the dream. Then Rabbi Loew took the slip of paper on which he had written God's Name in his dream, and he put it inside the mouth of the man of clay. He then stood up and walked around the man of clay seven times in one direction, and seven times in the other. As he did, the body of the clay man began to glow, and Isaac and Jacob could barely believe their eyes. After Rabbi Loew completed the seventh circle, he pronounced God's Name, which he, alone in his generation, knew. At that instant the clay man opened his eyes and sat up and nodded to Rabbi Loew. That is when Rabbi Loew realized that he was mute.

Then Rabbi Loew told Isaac and Jacob that the man they had created was a Golem, who would protect them from the evil sorcerer Thaddeus. They were to call him Joseph. Then Rabbi Loew took out the clothes he had brought with him, and a large pair of shoes and gave them to the Golem. The Golem dressed himself, and then joined them as they walked back to town. And Isaac and Jacob marveled that three of them had set out that night, and now four of them were returning!

Rabbi Loew presented the Golem to everyone as a new servant who would be living with them. When they were alone, Rabbi Loew told the Golem that they must set out at once to find where the evil Thaddeus had hidden the body of the child he had murdered. So Rabbi Loew and the Golem walked together through the Jewish Quarter of Prague. The Golem strode swiftly past each house, and Rabbi Loew hurried to keep up with him. At last the Golem stopped in front of a house near the gate of the ghetto, and pointed to the front door. Rabbi Loew went with him to the door and knocked. The door was opened by an old man, a pious Jew, who was very surprised to see Rabbi Loew at his door so early in the morning—and surprised, as well, at this strange companion.

Rabbi Loew hurried inside and asked the old man if there was a cellar in that house. The man said that there was, although it had not been used for many years. He showed Rabbi Loew and the Golem how to get there, and descended the steep stairway with them. At the bottom of the stairs they found the sack Rabbi Loew had seen in his dream, containing the child's body. Just then there was a loud knocking at the door, and when the old man climbed the stairs to answer it, the police demanded to be let inside. In the cellar, Rabbi Loew heard what was happening upstairs, and realized they were in terrible danger, for Thaddeus had no doubt reported the murder to the police and told them where to go. They must know as well, the Rabbi thought, to look for the body in the cellar.

Rabbi Loew turned to the Golem, who seemed to fully understand the danger. Without being told, the Golem picked up the sack with the body in it and led Rabbi Loew to a doorway in the floor of that cellar, hidden beneath a rug. They descended the stairway, closing the door behind them. It led to a dark tunnel, through which they walked for several miles. At last they arrived at another stairway, similar to the first. They climbed it, and found it led to another hidden door in another cellar. Quietly they entered, and heard loud laughter coming from above them. Rabbi Loew instantly recognized the voice of Thaddeus, who was boasting that he had fixed the Jews this time, and that their blood would begin to flow that very day. Then Rabbi Loew motioned to the Golem to leave the body there, and they returned to the dark tunnel.

By the time they had returned to the house of the pious Jew, in which Thaddeus had hidden the body, the police had already searched the whole house, including the cellar. When they found nothing, they departed. Then Rabbi Loew went to the captain of the police and reported a rumor he had heard: a child's body could be found in the cellar of the priest Thaddeus. The captain did not want to take this accusation seriously, but when he saw the Golem towering over him, he decided he had better go there and investigate. He insisted, however, that Rabbi Loew accompany him, for he intended to jail him if his accusation proved to be false.

So it was that the police arrived at the mansion of the wealthy sorcerer. Thaddeus was astounded to see Rabbi Loew and the powerful servant in the company of the police. And when the sorcerer saw the word Emet inscribed on the Golem's forehead, he began to tremble with fear, for he knew that Rabbi Loew had used his great powers to bring him into being. The captain informed Thaddeus of Rabbi Loew's accusation, and Thaddeus scornfully replied that they were free to search his entire house, not only the cellar. But the police said they only wanted to see the cellar, and Thaddeus took them there. Imagine his consternation when he found the body of the child that he himself had murdered, right there in his own home! He sank to the floor in a faint, and when he recovered enough to stand, the police took him into custody and thanked Rabbi Loew for having uncovered this terrible crime. Thus was the evil Thaddeus punished for his sin, and the Jews of Prague were spared the terrible pogrom that would have raged had the body been found in the Jewish Quarter.

After that the Golem remained in Rabbi Loew's home for many years, and every day and night he could be seen strolling through the streets and ghetto, looking for anyone acting in a strange manner who might be trying to bring harm to the Jews. And when the enemies of Jews saw what a powerful protector they had, they ceased to plot against them, for they saw that the Jews could not be defeated. That is how Rabbi Loew and the Golem brought many years of peace to the Jews of Prague, for which they were deeply grateful. And the people gave thanks as well to the Holy One, blessed be He, for protecting them from the enemies of Israel.

....

Tzaddik, or zaddik: A rightly or saintly person by Jewish standards, or a spiritual leader.

Ghetto: "An inner-urban area characterized by the spatial concentration of disadvantage. The term is often associated with particular ethnic groups—for example black North Americans—and was originally applied to the urbanized Jewish populations of Europe ... " (Scott and Marshall. 245).

Pogrom: An organized massacre, generally of a small, defenseless ethnic group. There are many examples of pogroms against Jewish populations, beginning perhaps as long ago as the confrontation between Moses and the pharaoh Ramses.

Pogroms have targeted Native American groups as well in historic times. The attitude was expressed in the often-repeated saying, "The only good Indian is a dead Indian," misquoted and attributed to General Philip Sheridan. While General Sheridan didn't say it, many others did, reflecting a general attitude of hatred against Native people. That attitude fueled several campaigns, or pogroms, against Native villages.

Pogroms are similar to ethnic cleansing. policies based on the attitude that certain

Again, contemplating "The Golem," we find that understanding the sense of the ghetto and the realities of pogroms helps us comprehend the story more deeply. We shouldn't be surprised at the references to the sorcerer Thaddeus in this story of 16th-century eastern Europe. Indeed, there are still cultures where sorcery is taken seriously. Did the Jews of Prague really believe that sorcery was real? It is possible. However, if we interpret the sorcerer as a symbol of an adversarial force against the Jews, the story still works. For an ordinary listener, such an interpretation would be well within the "Messages and Meanings" model discussed in Chapter 2, where meaning is created between the story and the listener. Importantly, the Golem, with the word "Truth" inscribed on his forehead, can be understood as emblematic of a hopeful reality larger than humans, which will rescue Judaism even in the face of blood libel, accusations so heinous that they would almost certainly bring bloody consequences.

The importance of the dream gives us another insight about the people and the time of this story. Contemporary times leave most Westerners in two camps: one side says that it's "only a dream," while the other side believes that dreams do have a function in our mental life. It's believed by some that during our sleep, when we let down our guard and allow our mind to wander outside the lines drawn by social expectations, dreams often solve problems. Thereafter, we either forget the dream, or we are troubled, or we are relieved. Rabbi Loew was relieved, and then guided, by his vivid dream. Indeed, he believed in the truth of his astounding dream so fully that he replicated what he saw in it.

Dreams are understood differently in different cultural settings, and even at different times within the same culture. But we should know that in this story, the dream is important. We find several references to dreams in the Old Testament, the Jewish Bible, in which the credibility of dreams is addressed. In the Book of Daniel, Chapter 2, we find an unfolding story about the king Nebuchadnezzar, who dreamed, and called for Daniel to help him understand the dream. In verse 19, we find that Daniel has also dreamed a dream to strengthen him for his meeting with the king. That passage says:

> 19 Then was the secret revealed unto Daniel in a night vision. Then Daniel blessed the God of heaven.
> 20 Daniel answered and said, Blessed be the name of God for ever and ever: for wisdom and might are his:
> 21 And he changeth the times and the seasons: he removeth kings, and setteth up kings: he giveth wisdom unto the wise, and knowledge to them that know understanding:
> 22 He revealeth the deep and secret things: he knoweth what is in the darkness, and the light dwelleth with him.

Dreams, described as a source of wisdom from God, must not be ignored. In the story of the Golem we find that Rabbi Loew does not diminish the gift of the dream, but acts on it and is rewarded for it.

Stories far older than "The Golem" also provide cultural perspectives and insights. As early as 4000 years ago, cuneiform clay tablets recorded a Babylonian epic of Gilgamesh. In it, the mighty Gilgamesh, it turns out, is still just a man. Here is a fragment of that story, collected by scholar Theodor Gaster.

ethnic groups somehow "pollute" society and should be removed.

Cultural survival: Less than 5% of the earth's inhabitants are indigenous people living on their traditional lands. Because people move about, taking with them their own cultures and practices, many indigenous people are displaced. Cultural survival is not an attempt to preserve cultural artifacts, behaviors, and institutions frozen in time; rather, indigenous and other traditional people have always adapted to new conditions.

Some Caribbean cultures exemplify successful adaptation. However, most indigenous people lack political power, experience all the devastating effects of poverty and poor health, and are targets of racism. In some cases of South American, Australian, Indonesian, African, and some Asian people, industrial development dispossesses them of their land, disrupts their habitat and hunting/gathering territories, and excludes them. However, cultural survival depends on land and language, and both are easily lost.

Indigenous people are underrepresented because of a lack of political power. Some populations are decimated, and some of their languages are extinct. Many Native American survival schools base their curriculums on native language and its traditional meanings, along with the standard kinds of coursework provided in regular public schools. They might also include traditional activities such as harvest ceremonies, dances, and visits to different parts of their traditional lands.

The Adventures of Gilgamesh

Once upon a time there lived in the city of Erech a great and terrible being whose name was Gilgamesh. Two-thirds of him were god, and only one-third was human. He was the mightiest warrior in the whole of the east: none could match him in combat, nor could anyone's spear prevail against him. Because of his power and strength all the people of Erech were brought beneath his sway, and he ruled them with an iron hand, seizing youths for his service and taking to himself any maiden he wished.

At length they could endure it no longer, and prayed to heaven for relief. The lord of heaven heard their prayer and summoned the goddess Aruru—that same goddess who, in olden times, had fashioned man out of clay.

"Go," said they, "and mold out of clay a being who will prove the equal of this tyrant, and let him fight with him and beat him, that the people may have relief."

Thereupon the goddess wetted her hands and, taking clay from the ground, kneaded it into a monstrous creature, whom she named Enkidu. Fierce he was, like the god of battle, and his whole body was covered with hair. His tresses hung long like a woman's, and he was clothed in skins. All day long he roamed with the beasts of the field, and like them he fed on grass and herbs and drank from the brooks.

But no one in Erech yet knew that he existed.

One day a huntsman who had gone out trapping noticed the strange creature refreshing himself beside the herds at the fountain. The mere sight was sufficient to turn the huntsman pale. His face was drawn and haggard, his heart pounding and thumping, he rushed home in terror, screaming with dismay.

The next day he went out again into the fields to continue his trapping, only to find that all the pits he had dug had been filled in and all the snares he had lain torn up, and there was Enkidu himself releasing the captured beasts from the toils!

On the third day, when the same thing happened once more, the huntsman went and consulted his father. The latter advised him to go to Erech and report the matter to Gilgamesh.

When Gilgamesh heard what had happened, and learned of the wild creature who was interfering with the labors of his subjects, he instructed the huntsman to choose a girl from the streets and take her with him to the place where the cattle drank. When Enkidu came thither for water she was to strip off her clothing and entice him with her charms. Once he embraced her the animals would recognize that he was not of their kind, and they would immediately forsake him. Thus he would be drawn into the world of men and forced to give up his savage ways.

The huntsman did as he was ordered and, after three days' journey, arrived with the girl at the place where the cattle drank. For two days they sat and waited. On the third day, sure enough, the strange and savage creature came down with the herd for water. As soon as she caught sight of him the girl stripped off her clothing and revealed her charms. The monster was enraptured and clasped her wildly to his breast and embraced her.

For a whole week he dallied with her, until at last, sated with her charms, he rose to rejoin the herd. But the hinds and gazelles knew him no more for one of their own, and when he approached them they shied away and scampered off. Enkidu tried to run after them, but even as he ran he felt his legs begin to drag and his limbs grow taut, and all of a sudden he became aware that he was no longer a beast but had become a man.

Faint and out of breath, he turned back to the girl. But now it was a changed being who sat at her feet, gazing up into her eyes and hanging intently upon her lips.

Presently she turned toward him. "Enkidu," she said softly. "you have grown handsome as a god. Why should you go on roving with the beasts? Come. let me take you to Erech. the broad city of men. Let me take you to the gleaming temple where the god and goddess sit enthroned. It is there. by the way. that Gilgamesh is rampaging like a bull, holding the people at his mercy."

At these words Enkidu was overjoyed; for, now that he was no longer a beast, he longed for the converse and companionship of men.

"Lead on," said he, "to the city of Erech, to the gleaming temple of the god and goddess. As for Gilgamesh and his rampaging. I will soon alter that. I will fling a challenge in his face and dare him, and show him, once for all, that country lads are no weaklings!"

It was New Year's Eve when they reached the city, and the high point of the festival had now arrived. the moment when the king was to be led to the temple to play the role of bridegroom in a holy marriage with the goddess. The streets were lined with festive throngs, and everywhere the cries of young revelers rang out, piercing the air and keeping their elders from sleep. Suddenly. above the din and hubbub. came a sound of tinkling cymbals and the faint echo of distant flutes. Louder and louder it grew, until at last, around a bend in the road. the great procession wound into sight, with Gilgamesh himself the central figure in its midst. Along the street and into the courtyard of the temple it wove its way. Then it came to a halt, and Gilgamesh strode forward.

But even as he was about to pass within there was a sudden movement in the crowd. and a moment later Enkidu was seen standing in front of the gleaming doors, shouting defiance and barring the way with his foot.

The crowd shrank back amazed, but their amazement was tempered with a secret relief.

"Now at last," each whispered to his neighbor, "Gilgamesh has met his match. Why. this man is his living image! A trifle shorter. perhaps. but just as strong, for he was weaned on the milk of wild beasts! Now we shall see things humming in Erech!"

Gilgamesh, however. was by no means dismayed; for he had been forewarned in dreams of what was about to take place. He had dreamed that he was standing under the stars when suddenly there had fallen upon him from heaven a massive bolt which he could not remove. And then he had dreamed that a huge mysterious ax had suddenly been hurled into the center of the city, no man knew whence. He had related these dreams to his mother, and she had told him that they presaged the arrival of a mighty man whom he would not be able to resist but who would in time become his closest friend.

Gilgamesh strode forward to meet his opponent, and in a few moments they were locked in battle, raging and butting like bulls. At last Gilgamesh sank to the ground and knew that he had indeed met his match.

But Enkidu was chivalrous as well as strong, and saw at once that his opponent was not simply a blustering tyrant, as he had been led to believe, but a brave and stout-hearted warrior, who had courageously accepted his challenge and not flinched from the fight.

"Gilgamesh," said he, "you have proved full well that you are the child of a goddess and that heaven itself has set you on your throne. I shall no longer oppose you. Let us be friends."

And, raising him to his feet, he embraced him.

⋯⋯⋯⋯⋯⋯⋯⋯⋯⋯⋯⋯⋯⋯⋯⋯⋯⋯⋯⋯⋯⋯⋯⋯⋯⋯⋯⋯

Setting aside the issue of accurate translation, we can easily see important perspectives of the Babylonian culture. Early, we find that a goddess, Aruru, was said to have fashioned men from clay, and that she created Enkidu. Many cultures attribute this kind of generative power to women, and some of their worldviews have goddesses, either by themselves or in conjunction with gods, as creators.

It was also a woman who captivated Enkidu. Though she was a woman of the streets, not a socially respectable or powerful woman, she brought him in when the huntsman alone could not. Clearly, we've shifted our attention from the monotheistic culture of Judaism to the polytheistic culture of Babylonia, and in so doing, begin emphasizing the female principle more. The female principle is also a central part of many Native American views, wherein the Mother Earth feeds and nurtures all beings. The union of Father Sky and Mother Earth brings forth new life every spring. Hence, it's the combination of the female and male principles that has generative power. When we consider the cultural differences we encounter in recent times, we can use old stories in an attempt to understand the differences before being tempted to disparage them.

Gilgamesh's dream, interpreted by his mother, is another clue that people considered dreams to be real and consequential. In other translations of *The Epic of Gilgamesh*, the dream appeared earlier in the story, but it was still his mother who helped him understand its meaning.

Sigmund Freud and Karl Jung were among the earliest developers of psychological theory, and both theorized in different ways about the functions of dreams. Their approaches were both Western approaches, but there are other ways to understand dreams. Some people believe dreams are symbolic, while others believe they are prophetic. Yet others believe there is a problem-solving function to dreaming. We aren't limited to the understandings of modern psychology, and as we've seen, people have been dreaming as long as there have been people. When a dream is an element of a story, we must remember that the cultural meanings are the relevant ones. Even though we might not know how a given culture regards dreaming, we should still be mindful that its significance could be far different from what our own Western perceptions might tell us. The very presence of a dream in a story means it's important.

Through storytelling we both inherit from ancestors and bequeath to descendants. From ancient voices, we learn that they were surprisingly intelligent and sophisticated, resourceful and courageous, and we are thankful for who we are. We're especially thankful that we don't have to invent the wheel, harness fire, or develop language from its earliest stages.

We bequeath to our descendants by preserving not only folktales, religious stories, and culturally salient stories, but also by preserving family stories. They will be living artifacts, those stories that instruct and inspire. Our descendants will learn of the grandfather who did the right thing at great risk to his safety, the aunt who prevailed out of love for her children, the uncle who, as a child, pulled his little sister out of a raging fire, and other heroes in our midst.

There are storytellers of great insight: the African griots, the Tibetan storytellers, the gospels, the grandmothers, and the voices like that of Hoskie Benally who teach and warn. For those who want to benefit, or even take their turn in the succession of storytellers, listen with your ears, your mind, and your imagination.

REFERENCES

"The Adventures of Gilgamesh," in *The Oldest Stories in the World*, translated by T. H. Gaster. (1958). Boston, MA: Viking Press. (pp. 21–25)

Circle of Stories. (2010). Philomath Films.

"Come Closer Around the Fire: Using Tribal Legends, Myths, and Stories in Preventing Drug Abuse." (1978). U.S. Department of Health, Education, and Welfare, Public Health Service.

The Holy Bible, King James Version. (no copyright date). Cleveland, OH: World Publishing Company.

Kervin, R. (1998). *Aladdin and Other Tales from the Arabian Nights*. New York: DK Publishing.

Ryan, P., and Mayhew, J. (2001). *Shakespeare's Storybook: Folk Tales that Inspired the Bard*. Cambridge, MA: Barefoot Books.

Schwartz, H. (2009). "The Golem," in *Leaves from the Garden of Eden: One Hundred Classic Jewish Tales*. New York: Oxford University Press. (pp. 292–295)

Scott, J., and Marshall, G. (2005). *Oxford Dictionary of Sociology*. New York: Oxford University Press.

Wilde, F. S. (2006) *Legends, Charms, and Superstitions of Ireland*. Mineola, NY: Dover Publications.

CHAPTER ELEVEN

Animals and Humans, the Stars, the Wind, and the Sea

In this chapter, we take a cursory look at the perspectives of two different cultures: one of the Australian Aboriginal cultures, and a generalized Western scientific culture. Though their cultural knowledge and assumptions are widely different, each is able to understand the perceptions of the other. Both embrace the world as real, but see it through different, fascinating lenses.

While we're accustomed to human characters in stories, we're not accustomed to taking animal characters as seriously, and we might not give any weight to non-animate characters at all. We find, however, that even in the opening tale in the introduction of this book, *The Storytelling Stone*, that Grandfather Stone was a thoughtful, wise character. While it may be difficult for a modern Westerner to grapple with the idea that a rock can embody more knowledge than he or she, another perspective reminds us that not all cultures define life and thought in the same way.

W. R. Smith explains part of a generally shared Aboriginal perspective:

> The greatest time of the year for the aboriginals is the spring-time. It is then that all the great corroborees take place. At these the sacred traditions are chanted or told.

Aboriginal: This is a term that refers to the indigenous people of a region. A loose translation of the word might be "from the origin," or the original people. However, in making a reference to origins, we must be mindful that aboriginal peoples, while often underrepresented, politically disadvantaged, and held in disdain, most often have a sophisticated understanding of the political, economic, and other institutions that impact their communities. For example, in Canada and the United States, Native Americans have taken legal and scientific steps to protect their environments. Likewise, the Torres Strait Australian native people have been proactive in restoring and protecting their rights to self-determinism and to their own land.

All the stars and constellations in the heavens, such as the Milky Way, the Southern Cross, Orion's Belt, the Magellan Cloud, have a meaning. There are legends connected with all of them. The heavens are called Waiirri, and the ruler of the heavens is Nepelle. (22)

Considering Aboriginal Australian conceptions, we find a similarity to Native American thinking. Both have sophisticated conceptual understandings of a living universe. In Aboriginal thought, "every force, form, substance, every creature and thing, is considered to have it own intelligence, its own spirit, and its own language" (Parker, 11). The following story, collected by K. L. Parker, shows us an example.

Where the Frost Comes From

The Meamei, or Pleiades, once lived on this earth. They were seven sisters remarkable for their beauty. They had long hair to their waist, and their bodies sparkled with icicles. Their father and mother lived among the rocks away on some distant mountain, staying there always, never wandering about as their daughters did. When the sisters used to go hunting, they never joined any other tribes, though many tried from time to time to make friends with them. One large family of boys in particular thought them so beautiful that they wished them to stay with them and be their wives. These boys, the Berai-Berai, used to follow the Meamei about and, watching where they camped, used to leave offerings there for them

The Berai-Berai had great skill in finding the nests of bees. First they would catch a bee and stick some white down or a white feather with some gum on its back between its hind legs. Then they would let it go and follow it to its nest. The honey they found they would put in wirrees (bark containers) and leave at the camp of the Meamei, who ate the honey but listened not to the wooing.

But one day old Wurrunnah (fiery Ancestor) stole two of the girls, capturing them by stratagem. He tried to warm the icicles off them but succeeded only in putting out his fire.

After a term of forced captivity, the two stolen girls were translated to the sky. There they found their five sisters stationed. With them they have since remained, not shining quite so brightly as the other five, having been dulled by the warmth of Wurrunnah's fires.

When the Berai-Berai found that the Meamei had left this earth forever. they were inconsolable. Maidens of their own tribe were offered to them, but as they could not have the Meamei, they would have none. Refusing to be comforted, they would not eat and so pined away and died. The spirits were sorry for them and pleased with their constancy, so they have them. too. a place in the sky, and there they are still. Orion's sword and belt we call them, but to the Daens (Aboriginals) they are still known as the Berai-Berai, the boys.

The Daens say the Berai-Berai still hunt the bees by day and at night dance corroborrees, which the Meamei sing for them. For though the Meamei stay in their own camp at some distance from the Berai-Berai. they are not too far away for their songs to be heard. The Daens say, too, that the Meamei will shine forever as an example to all women on earth.

At one time of the year. in remembrance that they once lived on earth, the Meamei break off some ice from themselves and throw it down. When. on waking in the morning. the Daens see frost everywhere, they say: "The Meamei have not forgotten us. They have thrown some of their ice down. We will show we remember them, too."

Then they take a piece of ice and hold it to the septum of the noses of children who have not already had theirs pierced. When the septums are numb with the cold, they are pierced. and a straw or bone is placed through them. "Now," say the Daens, "these children will be able to sing as the Meamei sing."

A relation of the Meamei was looking down at the earth when the two sisters were being translated to the sky. When he saw how the old man from whom they had escaped ran about blustering and ordering them down again, he was so amused at Wurrunnah's discomfiture, and glad at their escape, that he burst out laughing and has been laughing ever since. being still known as Daendee Ghindamaylannah, the laughing star (Venus) to the Daens.

When thunder is heard in the winter time. the Daens say: "There are the Meamei bathing again. That is the noise they make as they jump. doubled up, into the water, when playing Bubahlarmay, for whoever makes the loudest flop wins the game, which is a favorite one with the earth people. too." When the noise of the Bubahlarmay of the Meamei is heard, the Daens say, too. "Soon rain will fall. the Meamei will splash the water down. It will reach us in three days."

Self-determination: This is the principle in international law that says people have a right to make their own decisions in governing themselves. The concept does not indicate any particular form that should be followed. The idea is somewhat related to cultural sovereignty. At least two views of sovereignty are in conflict: In one view, native cultural and spiritual values determine decision making without the influence of external institutions; in the other view, sovereignty is seen as a function of federal Indian law. The Hopi people of the Four Corners in the American Southwest are said to have sovereignty because they have never signed a treaty with the United States. In fact, however, both the U.S. government and American corporations have exerted their influence in deciding where the Hopi can live, how much water they can use, what kinds of educations their children should have, and so on.

The Torres Strait Islanders, one group of Australian natives, have done substantial work in defining their right to self-determination. They define it as a collective (not individual) right to pursue their own forms of economic, social, and cultural development. It isn't an attempt to break away from the existing Australian nation, but instead, to make decisions that affect them.

There are many Aboriginal cultures, languages, and religious practices, just as there are many Native American or African cultures. There are a few generalizations we can make, however, and one of those generalizations is that Aboriginal people saw the Earth as alive. McKay et al. tell us: " ... At certain times the people would sing to the land, singing it into existence. They would go down to their tribal area to sing the land to keep it alive and to let their special stretch of land know that they were there honoring it. Another common belief is that unsung land is 'dead land,' and if the songlines are forgotten, the land itself will die" (14).

The early colonists to Australia looked upon the native people as ignorant, primitive, and superstitious. This is a familiar pattern of assumptions we find in all parts of the world when colonial aspirations lead to conquest. After all, here were aboriginal tribes referring to the Pleiades as girls. Similarly, they spoke of the four brightest stars of the constellation Mirrabooka (the Southern Cross) as sisters as well. What the colonists were unable to understand was the metaphoric expression of a changing Creation. Perhaps it was too different from the concepts that had meaning to them. In a typical pattern of cognitive colonialism, the colonized are held in contempt, in need of rescue from their "primitive" or "savage" ways.

Fundamental differences in perceptions of creation as well as the differences in the languages we use to express those perceptions present us with a challenge to listen. We know that within the United States alone, there are today at least two views: a creationist view and an evolutionist view. In all likelihood, there are distinctive variations within each of these general approaches. In the creationist camp, there are people who embrace a literal interpretation of the Old Testament, in which a divine and intelligent God created the entire universe in exactly six days. Others however, look upon the events in Genesis as metaphors for a lengthier process, in which a day represents a phase in the process of creation. The pinnacle in the process was the appearance of humans, to whom it was said that they are uniquely made in God's image, and "God blessed them, and God said unto them, Be fruitful, and multiply, and replenish the earth, and subdue it: and have dominion over the fish of the sea, and over the fowl of the air, and over every living thing that moveth upon the earth" (Genesis 1:28).

Among Australian people, it is the Dreamtime in which everything was created. Lambert tells us, "Dreamtime stories are myths when one considers the mythic process as a mode of perceiving, experiencing, and expressing the relationships between our visible world and the invisible forces, patterns, and intelligences that have existed since before the world's creation" (6). For Christian creationists, however, these ideas are heretical; they allude to forces and intelligences that existed before Creation.

It's not too difficult to imagine the interpretations that might emerge out of contact with a still-tribal people who don't view Creation as a hierarchy in which humans are near the summit. Greater misunderstandings are possible when people from a monotheistic worldview encounter people who not only view interactive elements as contributors, but view them as intelligent, too.

From yet another perspective, the scientific world, a set of co-cultures in its own right, would be reluctant to agree that frost comes from the Pleiades. Science is an approach to understanding that categorizes and makes distinctions between things. We shouldn't rush to judgment, however. Yes, science does seem to divide the natural world in ways that might seem unnatural. However, if we examine what science has discovered, we find that science has put us in a more intimate relationship with nature than has been possible in the past. Science is one window that helps us see past the surfaces of things. We're amazed at the power of small things: DNA, subatomic particles, molecules, and invisible energy. We also learn that Mother Earth herself has circulatory systems: the hydrologic cycle in the soils, transpiration into the atmosphere, and the motion of liquid magma in the heart of the planet. These are not things we'd be likely to know without science. We find that the knowledge discovered in the scientific process has meaning only within the context of Creation as a whole.

Corroborree: A corroborree is a celebratory gathering of Australian aboriginal people. Activities include sacred songs and dances, and certain ceremonies. "Many of the ceremonies are 'increase rituals.' These rituals aim toward the regeneration of a particular species, but as the ethnobotanist Peter Latz points out, people are not attempting to initiate uncontrolled increase. The goal is to maintain the levels of resources within their country. ... To promote the well-being of animals and plants it is necessary that the appropriate rituals be performed by the correct people (that is, the people whose totem or Dreaming that species is) ... " (*Encyclopedia of Religion and Nature*, vol. 1, p. 7).

Songlines: In keeping with the idea that land must be sung to, songlines were couplets within a tribal song. McKay explains, "A man's couplets from the tribal song were a most important part of Aboriginal protocol. They were his title to his territory, of which he was the temporary custodian. He could lend the songs to others for brief periods and could also borrow other's verses, but couldn't sell or dispose of them. His role was that of custodian until the songs were passed on to the next generation. They belonged to his descendants.

"To the Aboriginal traveler, a song was both a map and a direction finder. Providing you knew the song, you could always find your way across the country. When moving around the country, travelers usually carried a message stick, a small piece of wood incised with marks, to show they had good reason to be where they were. These travelers also needed to know some of the songlines of the territory through which they passed ... " (14).

At the same time, we've come to understand that ancient peoples often had sophisticated symbols and metaphoric ways of representing creation. The following story includes an element of rolling ice—glaciers and hail. This comes from the Quillayute people of the Pacific Northwest Coast in a work collected by Ella Clark.

Thunderbird and Whale

Thunderbird is a very large bird, with feathers as long as a canoe paddle. When he flaps his wings, he makes the thunder and the great winds. When he opens and shuts his eyes, he makes the lightning. In stormy weather, he flies through the skies, flapping his wings and opening and closing his eyes.

Thunderbird's home is in a cave in the Olympic Mountains, and he wants no one to come near it. If hunters get so close that he can smell them, he makes the thunder noise, and he rolls ice out of his cave. The ice rolls down the mountainside, and when it reaches a rocky place it breaks into many, many pieces. The pieces rattle as they roll farther down into the valley.

All the hunters are so afraid of Thunderbird and his noise and his rolling ice that they never stay long near his home. No one ever sleeps near his cave.

Thunderbird keeps his food in a dark hole at the edge of a big field of ice and snow in the Olympic Mountains. His food is the whale. Thunderbird flies out to the ocean, catches a whale, and hurries back to the mountains to eat it. One time Whale fought Thunderbird so hard that in the battle trees were torn up by their roots. Even to this day there are no trees in Beaver Prairie because Whale once fought so hard to keep from being killed and eaten.

At the time of the great flood, Thunderbird fought a long, long battle with Killer Whale. He would catch Killer Whale in his claws and start with him to the cave in the mountains. Killer Whale would escape and return to the water. Thunderbird would catch him again, all the time flashing lightning from his eyes and flapping his wings with a terrible noise. Mountains were shaken by the noise, and trees were uprooted in the struggles.

Again and again Killer Whale escaped. Again and again Thunderbird seized him. Many times they fought, in different places in the mountains. At last Killer Whale escaped to the middle of the ocean, and Thunderbird gave up the fight.

That is why killer whales live in the deep ocean today. That is why there are so many prairies in the midst of forests on the Olympic Peninsula. The prairies are the places where Thunderbird and Killer Whale fought so hard that they uprooted trees.

Consider the structure of the Olympic Peninsula in Washington State. It surrounds the west side of Puget Sound. Its mountains are not overly high, but they are very steep and made of oceanic basalt, unlike the Cascades to the east, which are volcanic. The story of Thunderbird and Whale emphasize the elements earth, water, wind, and fire as major characters. When we actually go to the Olympic Peninsula, we find rock that was once oceanic crust in the backbone of the mountains, and might well wonder how it got there. There is a geological explanation, and there is a mythic explanation, and both views contribute to our enriched relationship with the Earth. In a very direct way, the story of Whale and Thunderbird reminds Native people that creative power is to be found in the combination of things. Whale and Thunderbird might be held as ancestral spirits, but we live with wind, fire, earth, and water every day.

Whale: Water   Thunderbird: Wind and Fire   Olympic Peninsula: Earth

One last story illustrates how ice and fire become characters in a mythic tale, and it shouldn't be surprising that it's a Norse story. The following is a portion of a tale collected and retold by Kevin Crossley-Holland:

The Creation

Burning ice. biting flame; that is how life began.

In the south is a realm called Muspell. That region flickers with dancing flames. It seethes and it shines. No one can endure it except those born into it. Black Surt is there: he sits on the furthest reach of that land, brandishing a flaming sword: he is already waiting for the end when he will rise and savage the gods and whelm the whole world with fire.

In the north is a realm called Niflheim. It is packed with ice and covered with vast sweeps of snow. In the heart of that region lies the spring Hvergelmir and that is the source of eleven rivers named the Elivagar: they are cool Svol and Gunnthra the defiant, Fjorm and bubbling Fimbulthul. fearsome Slid and storming Hrid, Sylg, Ylg, broad Vid and Leipt which streaks like lightning, and freezing Gjoll.

Between these realms there once stretched a huge and seeming emptiness; this was Ginnungagap. The rivers that sprang from Hvergelmir streamed into the void. The yeasty venom in them thickened and congealed like slag, and the rivers turned into ice. That venom also spat out drizzle—an unending dismal hagger that. as soon as it settled. turned into rime [frost]. So it went on until all the northern part of Ginnungagap was heavy with layers of ice and hoar frost. a desolate place haunted by gusts and skuthers of wind.

Just as the northern part was frozen. the southern was molten and glowing, but the middle of Ginnungagap was as mild as hanging air on a summer evening. There, the warm breath drifting north from Muspell met the rime from Niflheim; it touched it and played over it, and the ice began to thaw and drip. Life quickened in those drops, and they took the form of a giant. He was called Ymir.

Ymir was a frost giant; he was evil from the first. While he slept, he began to sweat. A man and woman grew out of the ooze under his left armpit, and one of his legs fathered a son on the other leg. Ymir was the forefather of all the frost giants, and they called him Aurgelmir.

As more of the ice in Ginnungagap melted, the fluid took the form of a cow. She was called Audumla. Ymir fed off the four rivers of milk that coursed from her teats, and Audumla fed off the ice itself. She licked the salty blocks and by the evening of the first day a man's hair had come out of the ice. Audumla licked more and by the evening of the second day a man's head had come. His name was Buri.

Buri was tall and strong and good-looking. In time he had a son called Bor and Bor married a daughter of Bolthor, one of the frost giants. Her name was Bestla and she mothered three children, all of them sons. The first was Odin, the second was Vili, and the third was Ve.

All this was in the beginning, before there were waves of sand, the sea's cool waves, waving grass. There was no earth and no heaven above; only Muspell and Niflheim and, between them, Ginnungagap.

The three sons of Bor had no liking for Ymir and the growing gang of unruly, brutal frost giants; as time went on, they grew to hate them. At last they attacked Ymir and killed him. His wounds were like springs; so much blood streamed from them, and so fast, that the flood drowned all the frost giants except Bergelmir and his wife. They embarked in their boat—it was made out of a hollowed tree trunk—and rode on a tide of gore.

Odin and Vili and Ve hoisted the body of the dead frost giant on to their shoulders and carted it to the middle of Ginnungagap. That is where they made the world from his body. They shaped the earth from Ymir's flesh and the mountains from his unbroken bones: from his teeth and jaws and the fragments of his shattered bones they made rocks and boulders and stones.

Odin and Vili and Ve used the welter of blood to make landlocked lakes and to make the sea. After they had formed the earth, they laid the rocking ocean in a ring right round it. And it is so wide that most men would dismiss the very idea of crossing it.

Then the three brothers raised Ymir's skull and made the sky from it and placed it so that its four corners reached to the ends of the earth. They set a dwarf under each corner, and their names are East and West and North and South. Then Odin and Vili and Ve seized on the sparks and glowing embers from Muspell and called them sun and moon and stars; they put them high in Ginnungagap to light heaven above and earth below. In this way the brothers gave each star its proper place; some were fixed in the sky, others were free to follow the paths appointed for them.

This story goes on for some length, adding details about the earth and skies, frost giants and rock giants and their offspring, of whom one was a giant daughter named Night. Eventually, the first woman and the first man appeared, and creation took shape around Yggdrasil, a giant ash tree that is the Tree of Life, and holds together the separate homes of the gods (Asgard), the humans (Midgard), the realm of the dead (Niflheim), the home of the giants (Jotunheim), and the home of the Norns, the rulers of human destiny.

Clearly, this story is incompatible with what would then or now be considered children's stories. It's full of blasting heat, brutal cold, venom, hatred, violence, and gore. Norsemen established themselves in Scandinavia around 800 A.D., and as John Grant puts it, "They lived in lands which were not particularly hospitable to life—the summers were short and the winters long, and always the glaciers in the north seemed threatening. They tried to explain the things they saw around them. The crashing of thunder must be Thor throwing his mighty hammer, Möilnir, at the frost giants ... " (7). So, in this story, we find the explosive encounters between fire and ice, and we find that even the rivers seem foul-tempered.

The raw power of heat and cold combined with the elementals is evident in the geography of Iceland, where in April 2010, the volcano Eyjafjallajökull began erupting. The eruption was described as an effusive eruption in which a series of explosions resulted from the meeting of ice, water, and lava. Lightning was seen in the billowing smoke, and air travel in many parts of continental Europe, more than 1000 miles away, was disrupted for several days in April and again in May.

This series of events echoed the eruption of an earlier volcano, Hekla, in the year 1104, when there was another cultural view of such events. Christians saw Hekla as a doorway to the underworld, and the historian Sigurdur Thorarinsson wrote:

> Great is the power of the Prince of Darkness. Now he has flung open that horrible inferno Eclafeld [another volcano] out of Hyslandia, where the souls of the damned in flames of eternal fire, never thence to return, except when from time to time Satan drags them from the flowing embers to cool them in the piercing chill of the polar ice enclosing that dreary island, lest them become too inured to the fires of Hell.

What we know of the Vikings is that they were farmers, explorers, and fearless (we are told) seafarers. We also know of many accounts wherein their encounters with others were nothing less than brutal. Yet the power of the elementals, especially the Icelandic icecaps sitting over the mid-Atlantic rift zone, shaped their mythology and their creation stories. "Burning ice, biting flame; that is how life began" is the opening to the Norse creation story, and it isn't difficult to understand the preoccupation with the power of the elementals, not only to destroy, but to create as well.

The contrast between the worldview in Norse mythology and the Judeo-Christian worldview of Creation could hardly be more stark. Whereas the Judeo-Christian tradition has Creation as including a nurturing place created for humans, Norse Creation is hostile. Reflecting on the cultural experience of these two general groups, it is no wonder each had the worldviews they did. Microbiologist René Dubos once said, "The statement that the earth is our mother is more than a sentimental platitude: we are shaped by the earth. The characteristics of the environment in which we develop condition our biological and mental being and the quality of our life ..."

Did the Norse people literally believe the world was created as the story said? Did the Quillayute believe that a giant thunderbird and a giant whale shaped the Olympic Peninsula? What about the Australian natives? We have no way of knowing the answers. But the stories and the sacred spirits are still remembered even now that both groups are well informed in the sciences.

Winona LaDuke, a woman of Anishinaabeg (Ojibwe) ancestry, writes of the wind:

> I am standing on Porcupine Butte, near a village with the same name on the Pine Ridge Reservation in South Dakota. The KILI radio station stands next to me, blasting 50,000 watts of power across the prairie, with everything from Lakota talk shows to almost any imaginable kind of music. KILI is an amplifier for the heartbeat of the Lakota Nation. The winds, or Taté (pronounced "taa-tay"), are blasting as well; my hair heads out in all directions in sort of an Albert Einstein 'do.
>
> It is February, and the wind speed at KILI Radio clocks in at around 17 miles per hour, strong and prime for a wind generator. That is why I am here. A consortium of KILI Radio, Honor the Earth, the Intertribal Council on Utility Policy, NativeEnergy, and the Midwest Renewable Energy Association is putting up a wind turbine. We plan on having the turbine operational by 2006. A couple of bluffs over, a second wind turbine should be up and running in 2005 on the land of the White Plume tiosapaye ("extended family") along the banks of Wounded Knee Creek.
>
> From Porcupine Butte, the rest of the world seems distant—the politics of Washington, D.C., and the seats of state governments—but it is here that some of the most dramatic potential for transforming America's energy policy is emerging. The Lakota are looking to harness Taté and play their part in moving us from combusting the finite leftovers of the Paleozoic into an era of renewable energy. It is all part of a strategy by Native people across the Great Plains to power their communities in an environmentally sound manner and to, over time, build an export economy based on green power ... (239–240)

As people who live indoors most of the year, we may not often contemplate the wind as an actor in human events. Fortunately, as we've just seen, Native people, with the support of environmental scientists, understand that it can help us in very direct ways. In this reading, we found a blending of technically accurate knowledge with respect for the sacred wind, Taté. Littleton reminds us that "Spirits of nature in Native American belief vary considerably in their power and significance. Some are seen as vast and even universal potencies, while others may hold sway over more specific aspects of the world, such as the wind, the sea, the rain or the animals" (504).

Wind is a complicated character, both in traditional tales and in our lives. On the one hand, wind carries voices to us—songs, pollen, and scents. It's the highway for birds and insects and the audible vibrations that tell us they are alive. The wind cools us and fills our sails. Wind carries life-giving rain and floods, it churns the sea and shapes the dunes. But the wind also dries the land and drives the wildfire, dangerous and cleansing. Wind seems both random and purposeful. When traditional Native American people think about wind turbine projects, they aren't just thinking of themselves: they're thinking about the spirits of Mother Earth and the generations that will follow theirs, so they invite the wind.

The Native-owned turbine was completed and its dedication ceremony was held July 31, 2008—"Indian time," as it were. This expression, "Indian time," is often mistaken as a slur, but it refers to the reality that all things happen in their time: births, harvests, rain, and so on. These are not things that can be scheduled with a calendar or a clock. The wind turbine began operations when it was ready, no sooner.

The knowledge in traditional tales is compatible with our known world. We need to keep in mind that scientific investigation has brought us into a more intimate contact with nature than we previously knew, albeit far different from the natural relationships emphasized in Aboriginal conceptions of Creation. Perhaps the old stories persist because they embody the sacred meanings of Creation, something not emphasized in the sciences.

We may think of science as a process of systematic investigation, except when it isn't. For instance, there are times when discoveries emerge that seem not to be the direct result of research. The discovery of penicillin, for example, has been said to be serendipitous, sort of a lucky accident, as it were. However, the development of penicillin happened in a systematic way. Many of us have a view of science in which things, processes, and concepts are classified, categorized, and isolated from other variables. Through this lens, we might begin to feel that all of nature is being dissected, separated from everything that keeps it alive. The goal of science, however, is to discover and explain how things work within the context of the whole. When the Lakota on the Pine Ridge Reservation have a dedication ceremony, it acknowledges the wholeness, the matter-and-spirit wholeness that makes us alive.

In considering scientific communities as important co-cultures, we find that they are not so removed from the wholeness after all. Dr. Lewis Thomas, a physician, researcher, and one-time president of Memorial Sloan-Kettering Cancer Center wrote in his 1974 book of essays called *The Lives of a Cell*:

> We are told that the trouble with Modern Man is that he has been trying to detach himself from nature. He sits in the topmost tiers of polymer, glass, and steel, dangling his pulsing legs, surveying at a distance the writing life of the planet. In this scenario, Man comes on as a stupendous lethal force, and the earth is pictured as something delicate, like rising bubbles at the surface of a country pond, or flights of fragile birds.
>
> But it is illusion to think that there is anything fragile about the life of the earth; surely this is the toughest membrane imaginable in the universe, opaque to probability, impermeable to death. We are the delicate part, transient and vulnerable as cilia. Nor is it a new thing for man to invent an existence that he imagines to be above the rest of life; this has been his most consistent intellectual exertion down the millennia. As illusion, it has never worked out to his satisfaction in the past, any more than it does today. Man is embedded in nature.

The biologic science of recent years has been making this a more urgent fact of life. The new, hard problem will be to cope with the dawning, intensifying realization of just how interlocked we are. The old, clung-to notions most of us have held about our special lordship are being deeply undermined ...

To further exemplify and acknowledge the capacity of native peoples to understand the sciences, LaDuke cites a specific case:

In 1994, the U.N. Declaration of Human Rights enacted Article 29, which recognized the developed knowledge of indigenous peoples, saying, "Indigenous people are entitled to the recognition of the full ownership, control and protection of their cultural and intellectual property. They have the right to special measures to control, develop and protect their sciences, technologies and cultural manifestations including human and other genetic resources, seeds, medicines, knowledge of the properties of fauna and flora, oral traditions, literatures, designs and visual and performing arts." (Declaration of the Rights of Indigenous Peoples, Article 29, August 1994)

Finding that beneath the "colorful" customs of underrepresented people there is a body of intellectual knowledge, knowledge of medicine, of music, of astronomy, of the intricate fabric of the natural world, can perhaps open our eyes to our own ancient ancestors. The celestial calendars that guided their seafaring journeys in the South Pacific and the planting of crops in North America were more than folk beliefs; they were elements of survival, and we are the beneficiaries.

REFERENCES

Crossley-Holland, K. (1980). *The Norse Myths*. New York: Pantheon.

Dubos, R. (1990). *The World of René Dubos: A Collection of Historical Writings*, Ed. Gerard Piel and Osborn Segerberg, Jr. New York, Henry Holt. (pp. 386–387).

Encyclopedia of Religion and Nature, vol. 1. Ed. by Bron Taylor. (2005) New York: Continuum Books.

Grant, J. (2002). *An Introduction to Viking Mythology*. Edison, NJ: Chartwell Books.

The Holy Bible, King James Version. New York: the World Publishing Company.

LaDuke, W. (2005). *Recovering the Sacred: The Power of Naming and Claiming*. Cambridge, MA: South End Press. (pp. 239–240)

Lambert, J. (1993). "Introduction," in *Wise Women of the Dreamtime: Aboriginal Tales of the Ancestral Powers,* collected by K. L. Parker. Rochester, VT: Inner Traditions International.

Littleton, C. D., Ed. (2002). *Mythology: The Illustrated Anthology of World Myth and Storytelling*. San Diego: Thunder Bay Press.

McKay, H., McLeod, P., Jones, F., and Barker, J. (2001) *Gadi Mirrabooka: Australian Aboriginal Tales from the Dreaming*. Englewood, CO: Libraries Unlimited.

Parker, K. L. (1993). "Where the Frost Comes From," in *Wise Women of the Dreamtime: Aboriginal Tales of the Ancestral Powers*. Rochester, VT: Inner Traditions International. (pp. 44–46. Copyright is held by Johanna Lambert)

Smith, W. R. (1930). *Aborigine Myths and Legends*. London: Random House.

Thomas, L. (1974). *The Lives of a Cell: Notes of a Biology Watcher*. New York: Viking. (pp. 3–4)

Throrarinsson, Sigurdur. Iceland: Fire and Ice. http://volcano.oregonstate.edu/oldroot/legends/iceland/iceland/html Retrieved Aug. 17, 2011.

"Thunderbird and Whale," in *Indian Legends of the Pacific Northwest*. (1958). Collected by Ella E. Clark. Berkeley and Los Angeles: University of California Press. (p. 163)

CHAPTER TWELVE

Becoming the Voice

We can use our voices toward good, and to do so, we must do all we can to be sure our perceptions of the world are correct. We don't have many good role models for this practice. Our political history is laden with vitriolic accusations, name-calling, racist derogatory words and even lies, though the people uttering these things might be convinced that saying them was the right thing to do.

We can't have perfect knowledge, and we shouldn't stay silent simply out of fear of making a mistake, but we do have to be mindful that different worldviews understand things in different ways. In applying good judgment, we can present a narrative that will have positive value to the audience. We would probably like to tell a powerful story, a story that rivets audience attention and dazzles them all with drama and vivid imagery. We like a story told with a lot of kinetic energy. However, a powerful story doesn't have to be dramatic. A powerful story can be one that helps us make a decision, or find a solution to a problem. A story can be powerful if it has particular meaning for you. A story might be powerful if it changes something in the way you experience your life—a change in perspective, perhaps. A powerful story can be simple and straightforward, but in the days and weeks after hearing it, a listener recalls the story and thinks about it.

The following story comes from the Inuit people and dramatizes the juxtaposition of raw survival and human emotion. The story comes from S. E. Schlosser:

The First Tears

Once long ago, Man went hunting along the water's edge for seals. To Man's delight, many seals were crowded together along the seashore. He would certainly bring home a great feast for Woman and Son. He crept cautiously towards the seals. The seals grew restless. Man slowed down. Suddenly, the seals began to slip into the water. Man was frantic. His feast was getting away.

Then Man saw a single seal towards the back of the group. It was not moving as quickly as the others. Ah! Here was his prize. He imagined the pride on Woman's face, the joy in Son's eyes. Their bellies would be filled for many days from such a seal.

Man crept towards the last seal. It did not see him, or so Man thought. Suddenly, it sprang away and slipped into the water. Man rose to his feet. He was filled with a strange emotion. He felt water begin to drip from his eyes. He touched his eyes and tasted the drops. Yes, they tasted like salty water. Strange choking sounds were coming from his mouth and chest.

Son heard the cries of Man and called Woman. They ran to the seashore to find out what was wrong with Man. Woman and Son were alarmed to see water flowing out of Man's eyes.

Man told them about the shore filled with seals. He told how he had hunted them, and how every seal had escaped his knife. As he spoke, water began to flow from the eyes of Woman and Son, and they cried with Man. In this way, people first learned to weep.

Later, Man and Son hunted a seal together. They killed it and used its skin to make snares for more seals.

The absence of personal names for the three characters opens the possibility of this story as a metaphor for humanity. In fact, we find a number of Inuit and Yupiq stories in which the characters are central, but are not named even when they achieve extraordinary things. In keeping with collectivism, its, the community, not the individual, that counts. And in the harsh climate of Arctic Siberia, Canada, and Greenland, Man must hunt or Woman and Son will die. The collective need is desperate. The confrontation between human and animal is a struggle, on both sides, for survival.

A point of reflection about the story is that "every seal had escaped [Man's] knife." We know, of course, that Inuit people have used projectiles: spearheads, arrowheads, fishhooks, and the like. But in this story, Man must face a seal in an immediate way. It's well worth noting that the Inuit believe that all living things have souls, and so that the taking of a life of any kind is weighty. It's done in order to continue the life of one's family, and in this story, it's done up close, with a knife.

In the land inhabited by Inuit people, crops can't be grown for food, and there are no trees for building materials or fuel. In older times life was tentative, and nature is still uncontrollable. One is not likely to escape from an encounter with a polar bear. Life is uncertain, and difficult. In our story, Man wants so much to make Woman and Son happy, and he wants so much to live, that he encounters his emotional self: his frustration, his desperation, his love for Woman and Son, and the tears came. They cried together and became human, and in becoming fully human, they learned to hunt together, and they learned to make snares for seals.

We might end up feeling that this tale is as old as the Arctic, and might not be much mistaken. Much has changed since subsistence was entirely from hunting and fishing. After World War II, more and more contact with non-Inuit people occurred, and with that contact came disease. Further, children were pressed into the kind of a public education that emphasized white values, not traditional ones. The land alone can't provide for all the Inuit people living now, and their small communities too often languish under unemployment, alcoholism, and poverty. This is not a good cultural trajectory for a people who were once courageous, resourceful, spiritual, and strong. It's painful to see their small, isolated communities wracked with poverty, poorly educated, poorly housed, unhealthy, and all too often, alcoholic. This is one of those times when we should guard against ethnocentrism, stereotyping, and prejudice.

In Arctic regions, Native material culture is

> **Ethnocentrism:** This is the biased view that one's own culture is or should be the standard by which other cultures should be compared and judged. One's own cultural ways are perceived as normal or sensible, and the behaviors of other cultures are judged by their degree of conformity to one's own norms.
>
> Members of virtually all cultures are at least somewhat ethnocentric. On the positive side, ethnocentrism contributes to social cohesion and coordination, strong group identification, and the impulse to protect and assist "one's own." Positive self-image is one of the outcomes. On the downside, though, ethnocentrism is often a barrier against members of other cultures when it comes to housing, employment, social inclusion, and treatment at school and on the job. In the United States, we witness an emphasis on American lives, American jobs, and American interests when we read or view the news. Without implying that the needs, lives, and interests of others have no value, our institutions do seem to imply that American concerns always should come first. These phenomena suggest a general quest for group survival, a need served in part by ethnocentrism.

sparse; there simply aren't enough resources to generate the voraciously materialistic, individualistic culture we witness in the United States. Often, people are dismayed to see the low quality physical conditions Inuit people live in. It's important not to blame the victims. In collectivist societies, what befalls one befalls many. A single instance of alcoholism, for example, has a devastating impact on an entire village. Often, the village not only loses a fisherman and the benefits of that economic activity, but we also see that a family incurs legal costs even if they get free representation. They also find that their reduced income results in worse health for children, who then miss school.

Humans must make inferences, or assumptions, about the world, what they see, and what they expect to see, but don't. We make inferences in order to decide our own survival strategies; we make inferences about what our professors want so we can do well; we make inferences about noises (gunshots and sirens, for instance) so we can say alive; we make inferences about what our own family members will and won't

Fundamental Attribution Error: Frequently when people observe and interpret the behavior of others, there is a tendency to make the fundamental attribution error, the error of assuming the worst of others while assuming the best of themselves and others like themselves. The cause of the behavior is seen as either internal or external. For instance, if someone similar to you does a good thing, we tend to attribute it to his or her good character, courage, or intelligence (internal cause). If the behavior is bad, we tend to attribute the cause as external: the situation was unfair, the actor was under enormous stress, and so on.

However, if someone different from us does something we perceive as good, we tend to see the cause as external (they were just lucky, they had a lot of help), but if the action is perceived as bad, then we tend to attribute it to an internal cause (his own fault, his irresponsibility, his attitude, etc.) However, not everyone makes this error. It's a tendency, though. Some people make the fundamental attribution frequently, some occasionally, and some rarely.

Klyukanov further explains, "Notice how Self always looks good ... while blame is shifted to the Other. ... We always want to perceive our own culture in a positive light, and the fundamental attribution error allows us to do so by manipulating dispositional and situational factors—always in our favor. With this reasoning, what can go wrong? A lot!

"The fundamental attribution error is still an error of perception, and it is truly fundamental. It prevents us from seeing ourselves the way we really are and people different from the way they really are ..." (222).

appreciate so we can behave appropriately. It's impossible to know every relevant thing, so we must make some inferences. Similarly, we make attributions, or judgments, about what we know little about. Therein lies the risk of getting it wrong by making the Fundamental Attribution Error.

The following conceptual map (opposite) is an oversimplification of the tendency to make the fundamental attribution error, and the point is to clarify the relationship among our perceptions, others, and ourselves.

Returning to the example of Inuit people who are unable to conform to the standard of living expected by many U.S. citizens, it would be easy to blame their living conditions on them: they don't try hard enough, they don't care enough, they don't see how backward they are, for instance. The truth is more complicated. First, in their Arctic and subarctic environments, they never presumed that they had the right to own expensive things. Second, economic opportunities are virtually nonexistent for many of the Inuit people. Third, their public educations aren't helpful enough. Education does not create jobs and careers that don't already exist. Moreover, many youngsters in schools are learning coursework that is framed in the perspectives of the dominant Anglo group of teachers and writers, not from the perspectives of Inuit culture. "The First Tears" provides us with a tiny glimpse into their reality.

If "The First Tears" has narrative power, it is partly the power that gives us permission to feel weak, the power to shed tears, the power to come undone, and the power to pull together again and thrive. It's the kind of story that may not be dramatic by our usual definitions, but later, when we feel as overwhelmed as Man, the story returns and we contemplate it again.

How would you go about telling a story like "The First Tears?"

To be an effective storyteller of any story, you must like your story. The more enthusiasm

FUNDAMENTAL ATTRIBUTION ERROR	PERCEIVED <u>POSITIVE</u> BEHAVIOR OR DISPOSITIONAL TRAIT	PERCEIVED <u>NEGATIVE</u> BEHAVIOR OR DISPOSITIONAL TRAIT
Actor is similar to us.	Internal cause of behavior: the individual is a hard worker, honest, and intelligent, e.g.	External cause of behavior: the individual is treated unfairly, is traumatized, was lied to, e.g.
Actor is dissimilar.	External cause of behavior: the individual has advantages, an easy workload, or a lucky break.	Internal cause of behavior: the individual is disrespectful, lazy, and opportunistic, e.g.

you feel, the more engaged you can become in preparing to present the story. Of course, the story must not be so epic that it far outstrips your level of skill, but you should be willing to try to stretch your experience by beginning modestly, and then growing. Here are some tips:

1. Learn about the culture from which the story comes. Knowing something about the culture should provide you with some insights about messages embedded within the story. You can come to a new understanding about when and how to use nuance, how to use emphasis, how to use gestures and facial affects, and how to effectively use vocal attenuation.
2. Learn the story as fully as possible. Don't attempt to memorize the story as a sequence of words. Instead, try to visualize the unfolding of the story, and then recall that story as though you were there when it happened. Then practice your story out loud, on people. Perform the story at a laundromat where you will have a captive audience. Practice on the people who share your residence. Rehearse with others in your class. Get accustomed to having an audience—even a small one.
3. Set the tone for the story in your introduction (see Chapter 4). You shouldn't have to generate audience enthusiasm. Your audience is there because they're already interested. Setting the tone prepares the audience for the kind of story you will tell. There are all kinds of stories: love stories, heroic stories, ghost stories, humorous stories, spiritual stories, and many others. It's important for your audience to know what to expect. This becomes an inescapable responsibility if you're telling a story that might be disturbing.

There are some disturbing stories that should be told if we hope to use our voices for good. We shouldn't avoid stories about the enslavement of humans, for instance, or stories about greed, arrogance, or the violence that can emerge from ignorance and hatred. But we should handle these stories carefully without assigning blame or ing motive. It's by examining these things in the light of history, truth, and rea we learn.

4. Use simple language whenever you can. This is not a time to show off your vocabulary; it would confuse some listeners. Instead of using more words, try using fewer. It's not a good idea to elaborate on stories from other cultures anyway; we run the risk of introducing culturally inappropriate elements or turning the story into nonsense. Tell the story in a straightforward way. The feedback you receive during your practice sessions will probably tell you if you've accidentally dropped an important detail.

5. Try not to become too concerned about stumbling over words during your presentation. Even some of the most famous storytellers occasionally have to correct themselves. The audience might notice it when it happens, but if they're there to find out what happens in the story, they might not be counting the number of times you stumble. It often happens that after a bit of a rough start, a storyteller begins to become very articulate. Audiences tend not to remember the stumbles until you mention them. Instead, they will remember the story.

6. Refrain from faking an accent. When you're ready to try it, you can use distinctive speech styles to distinguish between two characters, but you should not attempt an accent. This is not a matter of whether or not you can do it well. The matter is that various audience members might perceive the accent as a method of mimicking them or making fun of them.

7. Find a way to achieve psychological closure at the end of the story. Avoid trailing off, or saying, "That's it," to indicate that the story is over. Instead, make use of vocal cues, pace, pitch, volume, gestures, or body position so the audience will know when the story is over and they can applaud.

Here is a model that might be useful in making decisions about such presentation strategies as volume, pitch, and pace.

Cite the source:

This story is from the Inuit people of the Pacific Northwest Coast. It tells us "How Raven Helped the Ancient People." It's found in a collection titled *The Storytelling Stone: Traditional Native American Myths and Tales*, by Susan Feldman.

Say something about the culture:

The Inuit have traditionally lived in one of the harshest climates. They therefore had to know much about the land, the animals that roamed about and migrated across it, about the qualities of snow and ice, and about weather patterns. Ignorance or inattention could put one's life at risk. We often think of Inuits as people who live in igloos, domes made of blocks of snow, but in these times, those are temporary shelters used during hunting and food gathering expeditions that take them far from home.

Help the audience understand the meanings of the story:

Raven, the hero of this Inuit story, is considered a trickster/creator. Often preoccupied with his own wishes, he nonetheless manages to produce some benefit for humans and other animals.

STRUCTURE AND PRESENTATION:

"How Raven Helped the Ancient People," an Inuit story from *The Storytelling Stone: Traditional Native American Myths and Tales*, by S. Feldman.

[The layout of this model represents a general story structure showing the waxing and waning intensity in both the narrative itself and in the presentation by a storyteller. Many stories fit this model.]

EVENTS IN THE STORY	STORY STRUCTURE	PRESENTATION
Grey Eagle was guardian of the sun, moon, stars, fire, and water, which he kept away from humans.	The context is established. The narrator sets out the time and place.	The narrator uses an animated, but moderated, tone and pace to describe the setting.
Grey Eagle had a beautiful daughter and Raven fell in love with her.	Characters are introduced.	The narrator begins to establish vocal distinctions between characters.
Raven changed into a white bird, and he pleased Gray Eagle's daughter, who invited him into their lodge.	Motivations become evident.	Vocal nuance emphasizes the motivations.
There in the lodge, Raven saw the sun, moon, stars, and water.	A discovery is made.	The narrator begins using more gestures and physical stances to typify reactions.

He knew what he must do. He waited for his chance.	Characters respond to a crisis, each in keeping with distinctive personality.	Narrator involves the audience by vocally hinting at secrets or by giving other information to build suspense.
He grabbed the sun, moon, stars, water, and a brand of fire, then flew away through the smoke hole.	Dramatic action occurs. In some stories, a courageous stand is taken.	As the story pace picks up, so should the pace of the vocal delivery.
Quickly, Raven hung the sun in the sky. When the sun set, he fastened the moon, and hung the stars.	This is a turning point. What happens now determines the final outcome of the story.	Vocal pace and variation are used to dramatize action, or to relax the audience prior to a surprise.
In the light of the next day's sun, Raven flew over the land and dropped the water he had stolen.	The reason for, and the importance of, the event begin to become clear.	A narrator should use timing to hold suspense and not "give away" the ending too quickly.
He flew on, carrying the firebrand in his bill; the smoke blew back over his white feathers and turned them black.	A small but important detail conveys special meaning..	The pace begins to slow.
Raven dropped the firebrand. Fire struck the rocks and went inside; fire will drop out if you strike together two flints.	A change comes, and order is restored.	Narrator returns to a tone similar to the tone used at the beginning of the story.
Raven never became white again.	This is the end of the story.	The narrator uses vocal cues to provide a satisfying ending. The audience knows the story is over.

As we can readily see, this model could also be used for telling "The First Tears":
In this story, we might feel that we are "left hanging." What about Grey Eagle's daughter, whom Raven, we thought, loved? Some of us are culturally conditioned to

expect a Walt Disney ending where two characters fall in love, get married, and live happily ever after. Chapter 5, however, reminds us that other experiences are more often the pattern. In this story, we find that the interpersonal attraction felt between Raven and Gray Eagle's daughter was merely the opportunity Raven needed in order to fulfill his purposes. It is as much of a challenge for others to understand our way of thinking as it is for us to understand the perspectives of others.

Here is another example of Raven's agency in shaping the world.

Introduction: Cite the source:

This story is called, "Raven Steals the Light." It's a story from the Northwest Coast, told in many cultures in that region. I found this story in a book titled *Handbook of Native American Mythology*, by Dawn Bastian and Judy Mitchell.

Say something significant about the culture:

Native people of the Northwest Coast have highly developed artistic representations of their mythical characters and their totems, which they call moieties. Most of us have seen the giant "totem poles," elaborately carved and painted. These carvings signify the ancestry and moiety of the people in the houses where they appear. Moreover, the houses themselves often have elaborately carved and painted fronts. People on the coast also carved huge canoes, often rowed by 20 or more men. Some of these were "war canoes," and some were used in whale hunting.

Raven Steals the Light

Long ago, while everything was still dark, there was a great chief who kept light hidden away in three boxes. Raven, who had been busy forming the land and seas, decided that he needed light to proceed with his work. So Raven set off on his quest to steal the light, but he could not figure out how to get inside the chief's house undetected.

One day when the chief's daughter left the house to fetch water, Raven devised a plan. He changed himself into a small leaf and floated into the girl's drinking water. The girl was very thirsty. She drank the water quickly but didn't realize she had swallowed the leaf. Inside her body Raven transformed himself once more and caused her to become pregnant. Raven grew as all babies do and eventually the girl gave birth to a son. No one suspected that this was not an ordinary little boy.

The grandfather was delighted with this new grandson and began to spoil him from the very first day. As the baby grew he became more and more demanding, his mother and grandfather tried to keep him entertained and happy by giving him anything he wanted. One day Raven, disguised as the baby, put his arms out as if trying to reach the boxes that stored the light. The adults tried to distract him by giving him other toys to play with, but Raven just threw those things across the room.

Raven cried and cried until his grandfather finally took down the first box. The old chief told the little boy that he could play with the box, but he was not allowed to open it. Raven took the box and played quietly. When no one was looking, he opened the lid and out flew the stars. They ascended high in the sky and are there to this day. The old man scolded his grandson for disobeying, but later when Raven demanded the second box, he took the box down and gave it to the boy.

Again, Raven played quietly with the second box and waited for the right opportunity. When it came, he opened the lid and out flew the moon. Now the grandfather was more than a bit upset. But sometime later, when Raven began crying and demanding to be allowed to play with the third box, his grandfather eventually relented and handed the box to the little boy on the condition that he would never open it.

Raven quickly changed back to his raven form, and with the box in his beak, flew out the smoke hole and into the starlit sky. When he was far away from the chief's house, he opened the lid of the third box and immediately a blazing ball of light appeared in the once dark sky. The light was much too bright for many of the people. They ran away, some to live in the forests on the mountainsides, some to live in caves, and some to live under the water. That is how the different animals came to be.

....

Help the audience understand the meanings of the story:

Many stories are the property of a clan or individual, and are told only by their owners, but others can be told by anyone. This story can be told by anyone who learns it. It's a story of Raven, the trickster and transformer. He is a complicated character, often resorting to sneaky strategy and manipulation in order to get what he wants. But Raven is also an influential force in shaping the world. What Raven wants is often to the benefit of the people. Raven is sometimes considered the father of the first people.

Out of Raven's selfish wiles and manipulation came consequences that contributed to the tapestry of Creation. That's often how it goes with tricksters, and storytellers who find the trickster easy to forgive can tell a story in such a way as to allow the trickster a fair hearing. One of the themes we might discern is that nobody's perfect. Some characters might be tragically imperfect, but others are unduly lucky. Raven is one of the lucky ones.

So, how shall we go about telling stories in a respectful, sensitive way?

Much of the time, a theme within a folktale presents itself to the teller, who can emphasize that theme when they introduce the story, and again as they are telling it. Some of the common themes we might find in stories are:

- The world of humans, the natural world, and the world of spirit intersect and interact.
- Some realities can't be negotiated.

- Bad behavior ultimately brings bad consequences.
- Nobody is exempt from social rules.
- Ignoring the wisdom of elders can bring trouble and regret.
- The easy way is not always the best.
- You should not abandon your friends.

Julius Lester says, "A tale is a thing of wondrous mutability. Just as water assumes the shape of whatever container it is poured into and yet its essential properties are not harmed or changed, so does the tale. A folktale assumes the shape of its teller, and through the teller's voice colorations, vocal timbre and rhythms, gestures, a sparkle in the eye, a cocking of the head, the tale is recreated and made new" (ix).

But we should not strive to change, modify, or modernize a tale. They have integrity as they are. Even songwriters who express songs in a bardic tradition, much as Homer did so long ago, respect the story and the people from whom it came.

REFERENCES

Bastian, D., and Mitchell, J. (2004). *Handbook of Native American Mythology*. New York: Oxford. (p. 158)

"The First Tears." Retold by S. E. Schlosser. http://americanfolklore.net/folklore/2010/the_first_tears.html Retrieved Aug. 23, 2011.

Lester, J. (1969). *Black Folktales*. New York: Grove Press.

"How Raven Helped the Ancient People," in *The Storytelling Stone: Traditional Native American Myths and Tales*. Collected by S. Feldman. (1965). New York: Dell Publishing. (pp. 90–91)

Klyukanov, I. (2005). *Principles of Intercultural Communication*. Boston: Allyn and Bacon.

GLOSSARY

The following are important concepts for understanding cultural experience and respecting cultural differences. What is it like to be an Inuit woman or an African American man? How are their lives shaped not only by their own culture, but also by the dominant social system that surrounds them?

The following are brief explanations of some key terms. Be aware that they are incomplete treatments of realities that deserve more thorough examination. These concepts should be useful in two ways: first, you should be able to identify them at work, and second, you should be able to use some of these terms in your writing assignments.

Alabama Literacy Test: In 1965, the year after the passage of the Civil Rights Act of 1964, election officials in Alabama administered this test to Black people, who had to prove they could read before being allowed to vote. Whites were not required to take the test. All the questions had to be answered correctly. Answering incorrectly meant that the test-taker didn't have the reading ability required for voting. There were 68 questions. Among them were:

8. When the Constitution was approved by the original colonies, how many states had to ratify it in order for it to be in effect? _____
15. If a vacancy occurs in the U.S. Senate, the state must hold an election, but meanwhile the place may be filled by a temporary appointment made by _____.
28. The electoral vote for President is counted in the presence of two bodies. Name them: _____.
42. The only laws which can be passed and apply to an area in a federal arsenal are those passed by _____ provided consent for the purchase of land is given by the _____.

The purpose of this test was to limit the number of Black voters.

Archetypes: These are symbolic characters found in many stories. Many Native American stories feature the trickster Coyote, the archetypal character who symbolizes the foolishness of humans. He is curious and full of mischief, leaves a trail of disorder behind, defies injunctions against foolish behavior, and often gets away with it. Sometimes, however, Coyote finds that foolishness can backfire. Another general archetype is the hero, beholden only to his or her principles. It is often the decision or the action of the archetype that determines the outcome of the story.

Archetypal characters in stories embody a coherent and predictable set of characteristics. Sir Galahad, for instance, was the virtuous knight of the King Arthur cycle of stories. His presence in a story meant that certain things could be counted on: no evil would go unchallenged, no truth would remain hidden, and no duty would be neglected.

Attitudes: See beliefs, attitudes, and values

Beliefs, attitudes, and values: These are the core motivations of cultural members. A belief is the conviction that something is true. For instance, I might believe that my behavior has more to do with my health than God's will, in contrast with what a member of another culture believes. An attitude is a predisposition to respond to something favorably or unfavorably. For instance, I might take the individualist attitude that "to the victor go the spoils," while a member of another culture takes the attitude that resources should belong to everybody, a clearly collectivist attitude. Finally, a value is one's conceptions of right, worthiness, and good. For instance, I value equal rights, education, and so on, while a member of another culture values submission to God. The term belief can be confusing because of the linguistic quirk whereby one says he or she "believes in" the things they value.

Because people in different cultures believe and value different things, they behave differently and are often misunderstood by others.

Brown v. Board of Education: In the early 1950s, race relations in the United States were dominated by segregation. The doctrine of "separate but equal" meant that public schools were racially segregated. The case *Brown v. Board of Education*, which took place in the U.S. District Court in Topeka, Kansas, was brought by Oliver Brown, whose third-grade daughter attended one of the segregated Black schools. During the trial, the NAACP claimed that segregation in the schools sent the message that Black children were inferior to white children and that their schools were inherently unequal. They also claimed that school segregation denied Negro children the equal protection of the law guaranteed by the Fourteenth Amendment, even when the schools' physical and tangible facilities were similar.

Dr. Hugh W. Speer said, " ... If the colored children are denied the experience in school of associating with white children, who represent 90 percent of our national society in which these children must live, then the colored child's curriculum cannot be equal under segregation." The court heard arguments that segregation and the sense of inferiority affect a child's motivation to learn.

The U.S. Supreme Court struck down the "separate but equal" doctrine and decided for the desegregation of schools across America. The decision did not, however, abolish segregation in other public areas.

Civil rights: This term refers to the rights belonging to people by virtue of their citizenship and the protections guaranteed by the Constitution and laws. In particular, the

United States often considers civil rights to be concerned with equal opportunity and treatment for members of underrepresented (minority) groups. See also Human rights, which are concerned with a different set of human experiences.

A confounding problem concerning equality of opportunity has been that many times, this equality has been more theoretical than real. Although legislation specifically calls for equality of opportunity, the real opportunities exist in meager numbers for members of underrepresented cultures, or exist only for a group with the "right" credentials. This form of meritocracy has been only one of the obstacles in a vicious cycle of needing education so that opportunity would be within reach, but needing work opportunities in order to be able to pay for appropriate educational access.

Civil Rights Act of 1964: This act outlawed major forms of discrimination against Blacks and women. Under the act, racial segregation was illegal, as were the unequal voter registration requirements. At first, the act was weakly enforced, for the very next year the Alabama Literacy Test was deployed against Black citizens.

Collectivism: See Individualism.

Colonialism: Colonialism is an exploitative relationship. It is a process whereby one state or corporate entity exerts power over the territories of another state through the use of military means, missionaries, media propaganda, or economic strength. The subordinate group is most usually of another race, language, and culture. Colonialism benefits the dominant power. Typically, the subordinate group has resources that are valuable to the dominant group. Under colonialism, the subordinate group loses control of those resources.

Even where colonialism is thought to provide some benefit to the colonized people, those benefits are likely to be extremely small compared to the losses (in culture, self-determination, autonomy, well-being, and access to their own natural resources, especially land and/or hunting grounds) and also extremely small compared to the benefit derived by the dominant state.

The process of colonialism creates the dependence of the subordinate state on the dominant one, and militates toward *un-development*, a term coined by Jacqueline Goodman-Draper to denote the way in which the values of the colonized people are subverted. Traditional social relationships and institutions that once defined them as a people disappear or are replaced by new ways.

Goodman-Draper's research among the Mohawk exposes that the white fur trade broke up the collective household, emphasized trade and sale rather than contribution to the collective, and encouraged the separative values of private property, materialism, and individualism. Moreover, the idea of male superiority was imposed—an idea that flew in the face of the clan mothers and formal women's councils that appointed the traditional chiefs and made other crucial decisions. The process of colonialism brought about the deterioration of a highly developed society into a ruined one. The harms are enduring. Only through steadfast determination have the Mohawk been able to reconstruct the body of their traditions before they were lost.

The removal of native people from their ancestral and economically desirable lands to arid lands has occurred with astonishing frequency. Colonial powers wanted good land for farming and railroads, furs, and gold. The discovery of any of these resources would result in the suspension of treaties that promised an end to the displacement of native people. In addition, sometimes the federal government would appoint tribal leaders who they felt would serve the agenda of the government, not the native people. Other examples are abundant in African history. In the Congo, King Leopold II of Belgium, who never went to the Congo himself, sent others to brutally extract work from native peoples and riches from resources (killing nearly all the rubber trees) from the land. (Read "King Leopold's Ghost," by Adam Hochschild.)

Crone: An elderly woman, generally in possession of a special power such as wisdom, magic, or the ability to help. However, there were also frightening and dangerous crones, such as Baba Yaga from traditional Russian tales. When they are present in a tale, they are of central importance; they are needed in order to bring the story to the right ending. In many stories, malicious and benign crones can symbolize dimensions of human nature. Leeming tells us that "the figure of the crone has a number of connotations. In fairy tales, a crone can be a witch-like woman who brings bad luck or difficulties to the hero or heroine. Yet as Joseph Campbell notes in *The Hero with a Thousand Faces*, "For those who have not refused the call, the first encounter of the hero-journey is with a protective figure ... " (127).

Cultural mosaic: See Melting pot.

Cultural survival: Less than 5% of the earth's inhabitants are indigenous to their land. Because people move about, taking with them their own cultures and practices, many indigenous people are displaced. Cultural survival is not an attempt to preserve cultural artifacts, behaviors, and institutions frozen in time; rather, indigenous and other traditional people have always adapted to new conditions. Some native Caribbean cultures exemplify successful adaptation in the face of conquest. However, most indigenous people lack political power, experience all the devastating effects of poverty and poor health, and are targets of racism. In the case of South American, Australian, Indonesian, African, and some Asian people, industrial development dispossesses them of their land, disrupts their habitat and hunting/gathering territories, and excludes them.

Indigenous people are underrepresented by virtue of poverty, powerlessness, lack of good education, poor health, and isolation. Some of their populations are decimated, and some of their languages are extinct. Many Native American survival schools base their curriculums on native language and traditional meanings, along with the standard kinds of coursework provided in regular public schools.

In some cases, there is disagreement about what to call a given cultural group (e.g., African American, Black, Negro; or gypsy, Rom, traveler; or Sioux, Lakota). Cultural identity is at stake in the struggle for cultural survival.

Culture: "Culture consists of the shared cognitive and material items that force a group's identity and ensure its survival. Culture is created, shared, and transmitted through communication ... " (Samovar, Porter, and McDaniel, 140).

"Sociologists and anthropologists use 'culture' as a collective noun for the symbolic and learned, non-biological aspects of human society, including language, custom, and convention, by which human behavior can be distinguished from that of other primates. Cultural anthropology takes as its special province the analysis of the culture of human societies. Anthropology recognizes that human behavior is largely culturally and not genetically determined ... " (Abercrombie, Hill, and Turner, 59).

Discrimination: An expression of prejudice in which one group is treated differently from others, and unfairly. For instance, the "separate but equal" doctrine excluded African American people from participating in society as freely as whites. Samovar, Porter, and McDaniel tell us, "Often in cases of discrimination, we observe ethnocentrism, stereotyping, and prejudice coming together in a type of fanaticism that completely obstructs any form of successful intercultural communication" (175).

Environmental justice: This term refers to the fair treatment of people of all cultures, races, social groups, and incomes with respect to the conditions in which they must live, work, and go to school. The concept rose out of the disproportionate number of radioactive and toxic dumping grounds found near poor communities where many people of color live. In more recent times, the concern about the high rates of asthma and other respiratory disease among children of color has led to a movement toward environmental justice.

In addition to the salience of race and culture, poverty is a feature of the apparent injustices in the distribution of polluting materials. It is costly to address this issue. For instance, Jonathan Kozol, in his book *Savage Inequalities*, shows the brutal conditions in which schoolchildren in four school systems attend classes. Somehow, there is never enough money available to improve conditions to an adequate level. Inevitably, the children themselves know they are marginalized and that other, more privileged children go to schools that are clean and safe. Another source is *Environmental Inequalities: Class, Race, and Industrial Pollution* in Gary, Indiana, 1945–1980, by Andrew Hurley.

Ethnocentrism: This is the idea that one's own culture is the standard or norm by which other cultures should be compared and judged. One's own cultural ways are perceived as normal or sensible, and the behaviors of other cultures are judged by their degree of conformity to one's own norms.

Fisher's Narrative Paradigm: This is a paradigm, conceptualized by Walter Fisher, which insists that "all forms of human communication need to be seen as stories—symbolic interpretation of aspects of the world occurring in time and shaped by history, culture, and character ... " (57). Fisher acknowledges the existence of a rational-world paradigm that values scientifically fact as the only source of truth, but insists that there are human truths that can't be expressed in terms of science. They are expressed in the stories we tell about ourselves. Moreover, he says, Longinus in *On the Sublime* was right: "The effect of elevated language is not persuasion but transport ..."

Fisher insists that people are motivated by concepts other than facts. We are motivated by love, beauty, desire, imagination, courage, and many other things that are not measurable. His paradigm allows us to be transported by literature, mythology, rhetoric, music, and other nonscientific human creations.

Much of storytelling meets this description. We tell stories as accounts of immediate events, but also to transport our audiences to places far away in distance and time.

Freedom Riders: In 1961, an integrated group of college students began a Greyhound bus trip to cities in the Deep South. Their purpose was to challenge segregation and racial inequities at bus stations and lunch counters. In a political climate focused almost exclusively on international relations, the Freedom Riders were able to gain some attention for racial injustice in the south. They were often refused service at lunch counters, and were threatened and even beaten severely during their bus odyssey, but they did not yield to threats and brutality.

Fundamental attribution error: Frequently when people observe the behavior of others, there is a tendency to make the fundamental attribution error, a perceptual error of assuming the worst of others while assuming the best of themselves and others like themselves. The cause of the behavior is seen as either internal or external. For instance, if someone similar to you does a good thing, it is seen as a result of his or her good character, courage, or intelligence (internal cause). If the behavior is negative, the cause is seen as external; the situation was unfair, the actor was under enormous stress, and so on. If someone different from yourself does something perceived as good, the cause is often seen as external (e.g., they were just lucky, they had a lot of help), and if the action is perceived as negative, then the attributed cause is internal (e.g., his own fault, his irresponsibility, his attitude). Not everyone makes this error.

Griot: A storyteller and historian. Originally noted in French-speaking countries in West Africa, their role was complicated. Thomas Hale tells us that a griot is also a genealogist, a raconteur, a musician, an adviser, a spokesperson for a family or clan, a diplomat, a mediator, an interpreter, a teacher, an inspirational speaker, an exhorter, a warrior, a witness, a ceremonial participant, and a praise-singer. This individual had enormous importance and influence among his people. He functions wholly within the oral tradition.

Hate speech: This is speech that is intended to threaten, belittle, insult, or disparage people on the basis of race, ethnicity, religion, age, sex, sexual orientation, or any group in which membership is not voluntary. This applies also to mobility impaired, cognitively impaired, and other impairments as well.

Hate speech does real and lasting harm. Richard Delgado, in his paper "Words That Wound: A Tort Action for Racial Insults, Epithets, and Name Calling," argues convincingly that verbal abuse can lead people to doubt their own worth. "Minorities may come to believe the frequent accusations that they are lazy, ignorant, dirty, and superstitious. Further, responses to hate speech include isolation, fear, humiliation, and self-hatred. Some affected people seek escape from anxiety in alcohol, drugs, or other kinds of antisocial behavior, thus leading to the pernicious self-fulfilling prophecy.

Achieving good socioeconomic status does not diminish the psychological harm done by prejudice, and successful achievers do not enjoy the full benefits of their hard-earned status.

There are also physical harms that result from verbal abuse. They include hypertensive disease and stroke. Many sufferers do not have the health insurance they need to treat these chronic conditions.

Most disturbing, children discern at a young age that they are labeled. They begin to "exhibit self-hatred because of their color ...

"A few examples readily reveal the psychological damage of racial stigmatization on children. When presented with otherwise identical dolls, a black child preferred the light-skinned one as a friend; she said that the dark-skinned one looked dirty or 'not nice.' Another child hated her skin color so intensely that she 'vigorously lathered her arms and face with soap in an effort to wash away the dirt'" (Delgado et al., *"Words That Wound": Critical Race Theory, Assaultive Speech, and the First Amendment*, 93).

Early Native Americans were also portrayed as "wild and savage people" to their profound harm. Alexander Tsesis, in *Destructive Messages*, tells us, "A linguistic framework developed side by side with the noble savage depictions that negatively stereotyped native inhabitants and eased European consciences about encroaching on aboriginal lands. Indian haters relied on dehumanizing images to encourage conflict" (51). For instance, in the words of Samuel Purchas in 1625, "bad people, having little of Humanitie but shape, ignorant of Civilitie, or Arts, or Religion; more brutish than the beasts they hunt, more wild and unmanly than that unmanned wild Countrey, which they range rather than inhabite; captivated also to Satan's tyranny in foolish pieties, mad impieties, wicked idlenesse, busie and bloudy wickednesse" (51). These instances of hate speech were the kind of speech that continues to have influence on the present status of Native American people.

Human rights: In 1948, the United Nations adopted the Universal Declaration of Human Rights, which set out what they believed to be appropriate guidelines for all the people of the world. They address a set of ideal conditions under which they believe every human should live in dignity and fairness. However, certain of the guidelines have a distinctly Western bias that ignores some cultural differences. For instance, Article 21 says:

1. Everyone has the right to take part in the government of his country, directly or through freely chosen representatives.
2. Everyone has the right of equal access to public service in his country.
3. The will of the people shall be the basis of the authority of the government; this shall be expressed in periodic and genuine elections which shall be by universal and equal suffrage and shall be held by secret vote or by equivalent free voting procedures.

Article 21 may seem ideal to us, but it overlooks the ways in which the remaining monarchies and chieftainships work. Overall, however, the Declaration of Human Rights provides a good set of attitudes and values with which to define an ideal human state in which a person has some influence on his own destiny.

Immigration: Human migration is an ancient social phenomenon. People move to places where they are not citizens for many reasons: economic survival, religious asylum, political asylum, and others. A reasonable generalization is that people who leave behind all that is familiar to go to a place that will seem alien is that they badly need change in their lives, and see migration as the best chance they have to meet those needs.

How immigrants are treated depends on many variables. The economic conditions and political realities where they seek new residence are among the most important. Perceptions about whether or not immigrants enter the United States legally are probably a diversion from the actual concerns about how much it might cost American taxpayers to have immigrants here, or how much Americans like or dislike the incoming group. Some of these concerns are rational; others are not.

Discrimination becomes more acute when economic times are difficult. When Irish immigrants came to this country during the potato famine, they sought scarce jobs, and often succeeded in finding employment desired by others. Even with employment, Irish immigrants remained in poor urban enclaves. The diversionary discrimination became the hatred of Catholics in general instead of the Irish in particular.

In contemporary times, there seems to be little backlash against Asian immigrants, who are seen as a nonthreatening people who can and do make social contributions. It was not always this way, however. In the days when the railroads were first being built in the American West, many Chinese were employed in this physically demanding and dangerous work, but the Chinese Exclusion Act meant that these men were not allowed to send for their families. Later, in WWII, Japanese American citizens—full citizens—were rounded up and detained in "relocation centers," where the conditions were crowded and inadequate against winter weather. In the end, all these Japanese American families lost their businesses and their homes while they were incarcerated.

The irony of discrimination against immigrants has to do with the fact that the most conspicuous discriminators are of European ancestry, and immigrated to this continent and took over, victimizing Native Americans with cruel political tactics and a systematic and intentional military program to annihilate them. They now discriminate against other immigrating people for real and imagined threats that amount to a great deal less offense than their own ancestors perpetrated.

Individualism and collectivism: This is best represented as a continuum along which members of societies tend to cluster by preference. Some societies tend to prefer individualism (the "I" orientation, independence, mobility, competition, freedom, and privacy), while others tend to prefer collectivism (the "we" orientation, interdependence, stability, cooperation, restraint, and respect).

No culture exists in pure or extreme forms of individualism or collectivism; they tend to prefer one or the other most of the time. However, even the most individualistic person might feel compelled to cooperate with his or her community in times of emergency. Many examples of the shift from individualistic behavior to collectivistic occurred after Hurricane Katrina, when volunteers flooded into New Orleans. Many were college students who traded their spring break for the opportunity to help clean up and rebuild.

Sometimes the cultural orientation can be detected in the way people speak of themselves. For instance, one person might say, "I'm an engineer and I live in Chicago ... " while another says "My people are Okanogan and we live in Saskatchewan ... "

Here is a standard model:

Individualism < - - - - - - - - - - - - - (continuum) - - - - - - - - - - - - - -> Collectivism

"I"	"we"
equality	equity
emphasis on personal success	emphasis on relationships
independence	interdependence
individual well-being	group well-being
competiton	cooperation
mobility	stability
direct conflict	mediated resolution
freedom	restraint
privacy	respect

These descriptors name some of the general tendencies (not rules) of collectivist and individualist societies. Much of the time, Americans gravitate toward the preference for individualism. There are, however, many situations that produce behavior that is clearly collectivist.

Institutional discrimination/racism: Institutional discrimination is the unfair and unequal treatment that is so entrenched in basic social institutions that it defies change. A couple of examples here will be helpful:

Hypothetically, a company is relocating to an industrial park in the suburbs. The cost of their operations will be cheaper there than inside the city limits. It's a financial decision. However, in order to get employment there, you need a car. If there is no public transportation from the city center or other location where disadvantaged people live, they are once again excluded from the opportunity to work because most haven't worked for a high enough income to get a car and insure it. The company managers do not consciously decide to exclude people of color or the persistently poor, but the discrimination is built into the location itself.

One of the most brutal forms of institutional discrimination occurs when banks and other mortgage lenders give favorable terms to white borrowers and unfavorable terms to applicants of color. For instance, white borrowers typically get lower interest rates and pay a lower down payment. The impact of even a small difference in interest rate means a difference of many thousands of dollars over the life of the mortgage. Furthermore, home buyers of color are generally steered toward more or less segregated neighborhoods.

This means that even without individual personal bias, discrimination still occurs.

These examples illustrate the "American Dilemma," about which Gunnar Myrdal wrote in 1944. In his book, *The American Dilemma*, he examined the social and economic problems of Black people in the United States and the failure of our society to substantially improve their status and their rights since the Civil War. Ideals had not been translated into practice nearly enough. However, Myrdal didn't believe that government institutions were to blame, but he did blame the racism of white Americans.

Institutions: This term is widely used to describe social practices that are regularly and continuously repeated, are sanctioned and maintained by social norms, and have a major significance in the social structure. Five major complexes of institutions are conventionally identified:

1. Economic institutions serve to produce and distribute goods and services. Here we find business, banking, credit, and taxes.
2. Political institutions regulate the use of, and access to, power. This includes politics at all levels, law, law enforcement, military, and the courts.
3. Stratification institutions determine the distribution of positions and resources. Here we find jobs, status positions, prestige, education, wealth, and family status.
4. Kinship institutions regulate married people, the family, and the socialization of the young.
5. Cultural institutions are concerned with religious, scientific, and artistic activities. They include churches, music, entertainment, the arts, all branches of medicine, and scientific research. (Abercrombie et al., 1988)

Stratification institutions are of particular interest. In the United States, the level and quality of education serve to decide who attains position, pay, prestige, and privilege. In other cultures, other determinants influence status. For instance, kinship with important families, valor during war, age and wisdom, or a valuable contribution to the collective might influence the organization of social status.

Jim Crow laws: Jim Crow laws prohibited contact between white and Black people in the Southern and border states between 1876 and 1965. They enforced the "separate but equal" policy. Although facilities for Black people were legally required to be equal to white facilities, they weren't. (For specific examples, read *Black Like Me*, by John Howard Griffin.)

Jim Crow laws were overruled by the Civil Rights Act of 1964. However, this act did not stop de facto segregation, which could still be achieved through rules about neighborhood school attendance, for instance, in many cities.

The earlier Civil Rights Act of 1866 gave freedmen some legal rights, but not the right to vote. The 14th and 15th Amendments to the Constitution guaranteed civil rights and the right to vote. However, as late as 1965, even after the Civil Rights Act of 1964, other measures were used in order to prevent the Black vote. The Alabama Literacy Test was required of Black citizens. The test was long and asked for several obscure answers about American government. Wrong answers were taken as evidence that the individual could not read sufficiently well enough to vote. This test is no longer used.

Kluckhohn and Strodtbeck's Worldviews Model: Scholars Florence Kluckhohn and Fred Strodtbeck published a model (*Variations in Value Orientations*, 1951. Evanston, IL: Row, Peterson and Company) that explained cultural differences along five social dimensions: human nature, man–nature relationship, time sense, activity, and social relationships. Values are emphasized.

In this model, the cultural variation of each dimension is presented as a range. For example, their man–nature relationship dimension includes subjugation to nature, harmony with nature, and mastery over nature. However, the table visually implies that the three variations are bounded categories. This may not be what the researchers meant to imply. It seems more realistic to see the variations as placed on a continuum along which humans can move back and forth.

The model below should be read in rows, not columns.

Kluckhohn and Strodtbeck's Worldviews Model

ORIENTATION	RANGE		
Human Nature	Basically evil Mutable Immutable	Neutral Mixture of good and evil Mutable Immutable	Basically good Mutable Immutable
Man–Nature Relationship	Subjugation to nature	Harmony with nature	Mastery over nature
Time Sense	Past-oriented (tradition-bound)	Present-oriented (situational)	Future-oriented (goal-oriented)
Activity	Being (expressive/emotional)	Being-in-becoming* (inner development)	Doing (action-oriented)
Social Relations	Lineality** (authoritarian)	Collaterality*** (collective decisions)	Individualism (equal rights)

*Being-in-Becoming—The personality is given to containment and control by means of such activities as meditation and detachment, for the purpose of the development of the self as a unified whole.

**Lineality—Lines of authority are clearly established and dominant-subordinate relationships are clearly defined and respected; a system of rights according to rank.

***Collaterality—Man is an individual and also a member of many groups and subgroups; he is independent and dependent at the same time.

Kluckhohn and Strodtbeck offer us examples of the three variations in the Man–Nature Orientation. Of the subjugation to nature orientation, they said that in the American Southwest, Spanish-American sheepherders in the early 20th century believed that "there was little or nothing a man could do to save or protect either land or flocks when damaging storms descended upon them. He simply accepted the inevitable. In Spanish-American attitudes toward illness and death, one finds the same fatalism. 'If it is the Lord's will that I die, I shall die' is the way they express it, and many a Spanish-American has been known to refuse the services of a doctor because of the attitude" (12).

In the harmony with nature orientation, "there is no real separation of man, nature, or supernature. One is simply an extension of the other, and a conception of wholeness derives from their unity." The attitude is reminiscent of many Native American, Masai, and Chinese outlooks.

In the mastery over nature position, "natural forces of all kinds are to be overcome and put to the use of human beings. Rivers everywhere are spanned with bridges; mountains have roads put through and around them; new lakes are built, sometimes in the heart of deserts; old lakes get partially filled in when additional land is needed for building sites, roads, or airports; the belief in man-made care for the control of illness and the lengthening of life is strong to an extreme ... " (12).

Liberation theology: This is a school of thought that focuses on Jesus as the liberator of the poor and oppressed. It says that Christians should work toward justice for the poor through political action. According to Philip A. Howard in his paper "Liberation Theology," "The liberation-theology movement was partly inspired by the Second Vatican Council in the 1967 papal encyclical Populorum progression. ... The liberationists have received encouragement from the Latin American bishops, especially in resolutions adopted at a 1968 conference in Medellin, Columbia; others in the Roman Catholic church have objected to their use of Marxist ideas, their support for revolutionary movements, and their criticisms of traditional church institutions ..."

One important undertaking of South American liberation priests was restoring peasants to their own lands after losing them to corporations.

Both Pope John Paul II and Pope Benedict XVI reprimanded individual liberationists and rejected what they viewed as Marxist or socialist goals, even though they also rejected rapacious forms of capitalism.

Life chances: The likelihood, given a person's circumstances, for him or her to achieve his or her goals. For instance, if an individual is poor, female, and Black, her life chances will tend to be less than those of someone who is wealthy, male, and white.

Literary tradition: When societies shift from being predominantly oral to being predominantly literary, they begin insisting on faithful repetitions of "original" word sequences. These repetitions become conventions. While we must credit the literary tradition with having preserved some works that might otherwise have been lost (e.g., portions of *The Epic of Gilgamesh*, a Sumerian or Babylonian epic recorded 3000 years ago on clay cuneiform tablets), there are some difficulties. First, "living" (orally transmitted) stories adapt to the needs of the communities they serve. Wilhelm and Jakob Grimm acknowledge that adaptation, even as they committed to writing several versions of some stories and adapted them to different audiences. Second, it can be difficult or even impossible to identify an "original" version of a story. Some Native American and Cajun stories are found to have widely different versions because they were transmitted orally, not in print.

Melting pot versus pluralism versus cultural mosaic: The term "melting pot" refers to the idea that when people from other places enter the United States, they adapt to American language, institutions, social expectations and realities, and eventually assimilate. In doing so, they cast away characteristics associated with their old culture and become more like "typical" Americans. The problems with this idea are that first, this isn't usually what happens, and second, the expectation that they immediately assimilate shows contempt for their cultures of origin and implies contempt for those who do not assimilate or who do so slowly.

"Pluralism" refers to the idea that many cultures exist side by side, each observing their own practices and values, with each regarded as equally valuable. While this is a nice idea, we know this isn't what generally happens.

"Cultural mosaic" refers to the idea that many cultures and fragments of cultures all exist within a region, interacting with the mainstream culture and with each other to various degrees. In this view, some cultures are fully developed and vigorous while others are still budding and perhaps others yet are weakening in vitality, perhaps losing their languages or other cultural practices. This idea seems most in keeping with reality.

NAACP: The National Association for the Advancement of Colored People. Founded in 1909, its purpose is to promote political, educational, social, and economic equality and to reduce the barriers of racial discrimination.

Oral tradition: This is the widespread social practice of gathering in groups, face to face, to tell stories. Within this practice, a great deal of cultural teaching, history, entertainment, and social cohesion are achieved. The oral tradition began in pre-literate societies and continued after the availability of books and public schooling.

It's important to note that stories were thought to be "alive" in the sense that they served a community. In the interpersonal and inter-generational passing along of stories, we find that stories have been mutable, allowing them to serve the changing needs of the societies in which they're told. Stories are also "alive" in the sense that they responded to the teller and to the audience. It is the literary tradition, not the oral tradition, that insists on having "original" versions and accurate wordings at the expense of the transaction between the story, the telling, and the audience.

Pluralism: See melting pot.

Political correctness: This term usually refers to an effort to produce the least offense when speaking to an ethnic, racial, religious, or other group. For instance, people who want to be politically correct try to call others by the names those other people prefer. A certain group of Native Americans, for instance, prefer to be called Lakota.

The disdain for political correctness we sometimes hear could arise for several reasons: (1) Much political correctness is euphemistic, that is, indirect and unclear. For example, the term Native American sometimes invites confusion, leaving some to believe they are Native American because they were born here. (2) Using politically correct language does not guarantee that the referent people are actually treated well as a result. Using a term such as "mobility impaired" instead of "handicapped" does not substantially enhance anyone's inclusion in activities most people take for granted. (3) The least charitable possibility is that there are people accustomed to calling people insensitive names and don't care to be corrected. Many in this group believe political correctness is basic dishonesty.

Poverty: This is a scarcity of resources, usually material sources needed for maintaining a dignified life. Some poverty is relative poverty, which compares the resources of the group to the resources of other members of society. However, absolute poverty refers to a state in which someone lacks the bare minimum resources for survival.

Definitions and statistics generally fail to provide a picture of the emotional experience of the poor. Often blamed for their poverty, the poor struggle to improve their condition in a social system that makes it extremely difficult to gain economic and social footing. The misery of the poor was confronted by Joseph Riis, a social reformer and photographer who lived from 1849–1914. He photographed people in the tenements of New York in order to promote social change.

Within folktales, a character who is poor often represents someone who has been victimized, either intentionally or by bad fortune. A form of social organization that keeps poor people poor is often implied. Poor widows, for instance, can improve their lot only by marrying wealthy men; their society offers no opportunity for her successful entrepreneurship. Orphans are usually bereft unless adopted, or unless there's a miraculous revelation that they are the inheritors of a deceased wealthy person. In neither case can the poor individual advance through their own efforts.

Only recently has there been any open acknowledgement of the emotional effects of contemporary American poverty, and it has been expressed as a "misery index."

Prejudice (theories): Prejudice is pre-judgment, literally, from the Latin root. We generally think of racist prejudice, but there are other kinds, such as religious prejudice, social class prejudice, occupational prejudice, and so on. It is almost always negative and unfounded judgment. Prejudice generally influences a person's behavior toward members of the pre-judged group. Those behaviors can include exclusion, avoidance, hostility, hate speech, and even violence. Just to be clear, even mild-sounding behaviors such as avoidance have severe consequences in the classroom, the emergency room, or the employment office. Discrimination and social inequity are the most likely result.

Humans are so adept at prejudice that collectively, we find many ways to develop it. We learn it socially or we develop it as a consequence of social interaction, interpretation, or observation. Humans are also adept at justifying their prejudices.

Contact Hypothesis is introduced by Gordon Allport in his 1954 book *The Nature of Prejudice*. Allport thought that contact with others would reduce prejudice because of the increased knowledge that would come out of that contact. Many scholars attribute prejudice to such things as mistrust and fear of the unknown. If this is true, it would make sense that contact would alleviate fear, and therefore, prejudice.

However, there are some conditions that would have to be present:

- First, the contact must be positive.
- Second, the people in the groups should be equals.
- Third, there should be little or no competition between them.
- Fourth, individuals should be motivated to break old cognitive habits and act in a nonprejudicial way.
- Fifth, people should not feel justified in their prejudice.

This does not mean that Gordon Allport was short-sighted or shallow in his treatment of prejudice. In fact, his book, *The Nature of Prejudice*, is considered one of the classic works on the topic, the seminal work upon which other research has been built.

Normative Theory simply says that we learn prejudice from our social surroundings and experiences. In social learning, prejudice is reinforced through family, neighbors, media, friends, and so on.

This theory makes a certain amount of empirical sense to people who have visited places where prejudiced attitudes are pronounced, or are directed at alternate target groups. For instance, in a location where negative attitudes are freely expressed against divorced women, normative theory might explain the formation of that kind of prejudice. However, it doesn't explain why some individuals do not adopt prejudiced attitudes.

Scapegoating Theory says that when people experience misfortune, they might blame it on a relatively powerless group. In essence, this theory suggests that prejudice is rooted in human nature.

When we think of the Jewish people during the Holocaust, they provide us a clear example of how scapegoating can create prejudice. The limitation to this example is that others in addition to the Jews were also targeted for annihilation: Gypsies, gay people, intellectuals, mentally retarded people, and people with physical disabilities were also targeted. Scapegoating theory doesn't explain the many other groups that were victimized.

Japanese Americans were also scapegoated after the bombing of Pearl Harbor. It could be argued that they were not actually blamed, but were simply prevented from carrying out the kinds of terrorist actions that had already been done from across the ocean. On the other hand, it still appears that they were punished. As we know, they were not simply prevented, but brutally prevented from receiving the rights they deserved as American citizens.

Scapegoating is operative in the case of prejudice and hatred toward "illegal immigrants," who are blamed for underemployment, a stressed economy, and gang violence.

Authoritarian Personality Theory says that a particular kind of personality has the tendency to look upon the world in terms of black and white, right and wrong. They are said to be predisposed to prejudice.

The limitation to this theory is that many people who are capable of more nuanced thinking are still capable of prejudice. This theory might explain some cases of prejudice formation, but probably not the majority. In addition, discrimination, the result of prejudice, is built into many of our institutions.

Race and racism: Race is most often the categorization of people based on their appearance (skin and hair color, facial characteristics, and so on) rather than on any legitimate genetic differences. These categories might possibly have useful applications in explaining patterns of poverty, health, employment, and other social experiences. They are not useful, however, in predicting characteristics such as intelligence, personality, attitudes, work ethic, or other values.

A frequent error is committed in confusing the concept of race with ethnicity. Even more frequently, errors are made in stereotyping people according to their so-called race. These errors can lead to the further problem of active discrimination based on a social construct that has very limited to no validity.

Racism, simply put, is the belief in the inherent superiority of a particular race and the inferiority of others. The expression of racism takes various forms: hate speech, hate crimes, avoidance, discrimination, racial "jokes," and tokenism.

"Reasonable" racism: This is also known as subtle racism or modern racism. This is a pernicious type of racism, wherein an individual denies being racist while having racist attitudes. It occurs as much among educated people as among the uneducated. People who deny that they are racist have learned how to verbalize their prejudice in a "reasonable" way.

One example of reasonable, or subtle, racism occurs with the desegregation of schools in some cities where busing is proposed as a way to distribute cultural and racial diversity among several schools. Parents might say that they support diversity but oppose busing their children (often to largely Black schools) because they don't want their child spending so much time on the bus.

Another example occurs in some cases of prejudice against immigrants. No objection to race or ethnicity is overtly expressed, but opposition to non-English speakers or illegal aliens is expressed and defended. Scholar Neil Brick explains that one place where modern ("reasonable") racism appears is in the English-only movement. He says that movement "justifies racist and nativist biases below a cover of American patriotism." Nobody argues against the usefulness of knowing the language spoken where you are. However, the English-only emphasis provides an undeserved barrier to those who have not yet had a realistic opportunity to learn the language. Other instances of modern racism occur when people express the misguided opinion that "aliens" pay no taxes, but only burden our schools and welfare system.

Reservation system: In the United States, reservations are areas of land set aside for Native Americans, but not owned by them. They are held in trust by the U.S. Bureau of Indian Affairs. Reservation lands have been managed in a variety of ways: Some lands have been sold, leased, and allotted to Native American families. Reservation lands amount to less than 3% of the lands that once belonged to Native Americans, and are often seen as the least desirable land.

Initially devised as a way of containing and controlling Native people, reservation lands are often now seen as a place where like-minded people live, and where Native traditions are still alive. Some Native people stay on reservations, for a variety of reasons: they can subsist there, their ancestors are buried there, they have no place else to go, they want to remain near their families, they can't afford to move to a town, and so on.

However, the discovery of resources on reservation lands can change the picture substantially. Two examples show how such change can occur. The Black Hills of South Dakota were once protected for the sacred and ceremonial use of the Lakota. When gold was discovered there, non-Native people rushed in for access to the gold, which many Lakota called "the yellow metal that makes white men crazy." The other example is the Navajo Reservation where coal and uranium were discovered. Navajo families subsisted by sheepherding and agriculture. In 1985 the U.S. Congress undertook to re-allot the Hopi and Navajo areas in the Four Corners area, opening up new areas to the Peabody Coal Company. Navajos were expected to leave, and those who did so experienced immeasurable hardship and misery, and many died.

Segregation: The separation of groups. For instance, in the segregation of the Jim Crow South, there were separate public toilet facilities for Blacks and whites. School populations were largely either Black or white. Bus station waiting rooms, as well as buses themselves, were divided between Black and white areas. Medical facilities were also separated along racial lines.

There were many opportunities to keep the races separate: Churches, lunch counters, neighborhoods, and even businesses found ways to segregate. Not all traces of segregation have disappeared. In some places, Black employees are relegated to the dirtiest, most dangerous, lowest status, and lowest paid areas of a business or institution.

Self-determination: This term refers to a principle that groups of people ought to be allowed to determine their own governments and make their own decisions free from the influence of outsiders. Historically, colonized people have lost their right to self-determination, though some are taking steps to regain it.

Self-determination is not the same as independence. Many groups strive toward self-determination without demanding independence or separation from the dominant society. An example of a group effectively seeking self-determination is the Torres Strait Aboriginal people of Australia. Other groups that have achieved self-determination are the socialist republics that were once subsumed within the USSR, Taiwan, East Timor, the Kurds of Iraq, and various Native American tribes that are said to have sovereign status.

Moving in opposition, Tibet, which once was a nation in its own right, has a government-in-exile in Dharamsala, India, since the Chinese takeover in 1959.

The goal of self-determination is tremendously complicated by issues of interdependence, citizenship, and territory.

Slavery [excerpted from *Dictionary of Sociology*, 1988, Abercrombie, Hill, and Turner]: "As an institution, slavery is defined as a form of property which gives to one person the right of ownership over another. Like any other means of production, the slave is 'a thing.' Slave labor has existed under a variety of social conditions—in the ancient world, in the colonies of the West Indies and in the plantations of the southern states of America. ...

"While slavery was the basis of classical societies of Greece and Rome, it also flourished in the plantation system of the Americas. Cotton produced by slave labor in the southern states of North America played a crucial role in the development of American industrial capitalism. ...

"In a comparative perspective, it has also been argued that slavery in North America was far more repressive than in Latin America. There are a number of reasons for this. (1) The Protestants of North America regarded the slave as sinful and in need of sexual restraint, while Catholicism in South America was more tolerant. (2) The ethnic diversity of Latin America was extensive and therefore the division between black and white was less sharply drawn. (3) It was possible for slaves to purchase their freedom in South America, but this was uncommon in North America. Although the American Civil War put an end to slavery, the legacy of racial hatred has been a decisive influence on contemporary politics in North America."

While this definition is accurate and important, it ignores the cruel treatment perpetrated against many enslaved people. Certain rules were generally practiced: Enslaved people had no rights; enslaved people could not marry; they were not allowed to learn to read; they had no recourse when treated with cruelty or violence. And enslaved people could be bought and sold in groupings that separated mother from infant.

Southern Poverty Law Center: This is a nonprofit civil rights organization founded in 1971 by two lawyers. The organization his become internationally known for its activities to seek justice for the underrepresented. They've opposed the activities of the Ku Klux Klan and prosecuted other violent racially motivated crimes. They also distribute, for free, a Teaching Tolerance program that includes documentary films, books, and lesson plans that promote tolerance and respect.

Stereotypes: When we refer to stereotypes, we refer to a generalization about a group that is easily identifiable by virtue of race, language, age, sex, or other discernible characteristic. Because the human brain is designed to process information in categories, we form stereotypes. For instance, rather than collecting data about each of 300 African American 15-year-old males over six feet tall, we create a stereotype that links and confines this generalized group to sports. We also learn stereotypes from our families, neighbors, and media.

Everyone has stereotypes, but this does not mean that stereotypes always make our decisions for us. For instance, most of us have a stereotype about used car salesmen even though we have never met one who matches the stereotype. We still buy used cars, despite the image. Stereotypes resist change even in the face of substantial evidence that should debunk them. (See Archetypes)

Storm Fool: A traditional storyteller from certain Eastern Woodland cultures, especially around the Great Lakes area. He travels through harsh winter weather to reach the villages where people await his arrival.

Stratification: Stratification is systematic inequality between groups. This outcome is not always conscious or intended, but may be built into the social arrangements as they traditionally exist. Usually, stratification refers to inequality of power (wealth), opportunity, and life chances. This status quo is maintained by the way in which society is organized. One's social status is often linked to that of her or his parents. For instance, an individual born into a professional middle-class family (doctors, lawyers, scientists, teachers, business owners) will tend to have easier access to educational opportunities such as study abroad, music lessons, travel, and other advantages. In contrast, an individual born into a working-class (blue collar) family will tend to have much more difficult access to the same advantages. Being nonwhite complicates access for people in all socioeconomic groups.

Taboo: A taboo is something forbidden. We learn from Scott and Marshall that a taboo is "a social and often sacred prohibition put upon certain things, people, or acts, which render them untouchable or unmentionable. The most famous taboo is the near-universal incest taboo, prohibiting sexual or marriage relations between particular categories of kin." However, some taboos are specific to particular cultural groups, such as the taboo against eating pork for Jews and Muslims. Social or other consequences are attached to breaking a taboo.

Tolerance (racial or religious): Enduring the presence of others and restraint from harassment. Clearly, tolerance is not the same as acceptance, a condition wherein the presence of others is welcome.

Trickster: Leeming tells us that the trickster is a "dual-natured figure prevalent in oral traditions around the world. The trickster is usually male, lecherous, a cheat, careless about taboos, amoral, and outrageous. He can be human, semi-human, or take on an animal form. … Tricksters clearly represent chaos and disorder. However, tricksters are also inventive and creative culture heroes who are often a great help to human beings" (465). Some familiar tricksters are Anansi, Coyote, Br'er Rabbit, Iktomi, and Raven. Some modern tricksters include Bart Simpson and Captain Jack Sparrow.

Within the context of narratives, tricksters represent the unpredictable and untrustworthy, but not the malicious. Generally, they symbolize human foolishness.

Underrepresented groups: These are groups that have distinctive cultural characteristics that have been used to exclude them from full participation in social, economic, political, legal, and educational institutions. These cultural characteristics are usually ethnic or religious. It is a safe bet that all these groups have rich repertoires of stories that embody values and meanings that are important to them.

In the United States, the underrepresented groups include African Americans, Native Americans, Native Alaskans, Native Hawaiians, Latinos, Cajuns, Creoles, American Jews, American Rom (gypsy), American Arabs, Asian Americans, Amish, and ethnic immigrants.

Values: See beliefs, attitudes, and values

White privilege: Whiteness in this country means that an individual is privileged. This reality is uncomfortable for many white people with a sense of fairness, or who fear they will be held accountable for it. White people are advantaged in ways that elude members of other groups. For instance, white people are not generally stopped by the police for "driving while Black." Whites are less often stopped and searched, and are less often perceived as behaving suspiciously. When white people seek a loan, a bank will usually give them desirable terms if their credit ratings are good. When white people want to move into a nice neighborhood, realtors are less likely to discourage them than nonwhites. The advantage also moves up the educational-career chain; whites are more likely to get promotions and raises at work. They are also more likely to be included in gifted educational programs.

Answers to the Alabama Literacy Test

8. Nine states had to ratify the Constitution.
15. The governor appoints a temporary senator to a vacant seat until an election is held.
28. The electoral vote is counted in the presence of the House of Representatives and the Senate.
42. Congress passes laws applicable to areas in a federal arsenal, but state legislatures must consent.

If you had to take the Alabama Literacy Test, would you be considered literate, and could you vote?

REFERENCES

Abercrombie, N., Hill, S., and Turner, B. (1984). *Dictionary of Sociology*. New York: Viking Penguin.

Brick, N. (Oct. 2008). "Modern Racism and Its Psychosocial Effects on Society—including a discussion about bilingual education." http://bilingualeducationmass.wordpress.com/category.modern-racism-and-its-psychosocial-effects-on-society-including-a-discussion-about-bilingual-education. Retrieved on 31 August 2011.

Delgado, Richard (1993). "Chapter 4: "Words That Wound": A Tort Action for Racial Insults, Epithets, and Name Calling," in M. Matsuda et al., *Words that Wound: Critical Race Theory, Assaultive Speech, and the First Amendment*. San Francisco: Westview Press.

Fisher, W. (1989). *Human Communication as Narration: Toward a Philosophy of Reason, Value, and Action*. University of South Carolina Press.

Hale, T. (1998). *Griots and Griottes: Masters of Words and Music*. Bloomington: Indiana University Press.

Hurley, A. (1995). *Environmental Inequalities: Class, Race, and Industrial Pollution in Gary, Indiana, 1945–1980*. Chapel Hill: University of North Carolina.

Kluckhohn, F., and Strodtbeck, F. (1961). *Variations in Value Orientations*. Evanston, IL: Row, Peterson and Company.

Kozol, J. (1991). *Savage Inequalities: Children in America's Schools*. New York: HarperCollins.

Leeming, D. (Ed.) (1997). *Storytelling Encyclopedia: Historical, Cultural, and Multiethnic Approaches to Oral Traditions Around the World*. Phoenix, AZ: Oryx Press.

Samovar, Porter, & McDaniel (2007). *Communication Between Cultures*. Boston: Wadsworth Cengage.

Scott, J. and Marshall, G. (Eds.) (2005). *Oxford Dictionary of Sociology*. New York: Oxford University Press.

Tsesis, A. (2002). *Destructive Messages: How Hate Speech Paves the Way for Harmful Social Movements*. New York: New York University Press.

STORY CREDITS

Daryl Cumber Dance, "I'll Go as Far as Memphis," *Shuckin' and Jivin'*: Folklore from Contemporary Black Americans, p. 174. Copyright © 1978 by Indiana University Press. Reprinted with permission.

Zora Neale Hurston, "John Outruns the Lord," *Mules and Men*, pp. 70-71. Copyright © 1990 by HarperCollins Publishers. Reprinted with permission.

Dori Jones Yang, "The Brother Who Gave Rice," *The Brother Who Gave Rice*, pp. 5-32. Copyright © 2007 by Cengage Learning, Inc. Reprinted with permission.

Jeremiah Curtin & J.N.B. Hewitt, "Godasiyo the Woman Chief," *Seneca Fiction, Legends and Myths*, pp. 537-538. Copyright in the Public Domain.

Sharon Creeden, "The Fisherman and the King's Chamberlain," *Fair is Fair: World Folktales of Justice*, pp. 43-44. Copyright © 1994 by Sharon Creeden. Reprinted with permission by Marian Reiner Literary Agency.

Inea Bushnaq, "The Price of Pride," *Arab Folktales*, p. 19. Copyright © 1987 by Random House, Inc. Reprinted with permission.

Virginia Hamilton, "How Nehemiah Got Free," *The People Could Fly: American Black Folktales*, pp. 147-150. Copyright © 1985 by Random House, Inc. Reprinted with permission.

S.E. Schlosser, "How Selfishness Was Rewarded," AmericanFolklore.net. Copyright © by American Folklore. Reprinted with permission.

Haiwang Yuan, "A Forsaken Wife and Her Unfaithful Husband," *The Magic Lotus Lantern and Other Tales from the Han Chinese*, pp. 97-100. Copyright © 2006 by ABC-CLIO Inc. Reprinted with permission.

Richard Erdoes & Alfonso Ortiz, eds., "Coyote Steals Fire," *American Indian Trickster Tales*, pp. 18-19. Copyright © 1998 by Penguin Group Inc. Reprinted with permission.

Barbara Diamond Goldin, "The Midwife and the Cat," *One Hundred and One Jewish Read-Aloud Stories*, pp. 173-175. Copyright © 2002 by Black Dog & Levanthal Publishers. Reprinted with permission.

Roy C. Amore & Larry D. Shinn, "Savatri and the God of Death," *Lustful Maidens & Ascetic Kings: Buddhist and Hindu Stories of Life*, pp. 28-33. Copyright © 1981 by Oxford University Press. Reprinted with permission.

S.E. Schlosser, "Pele's Revenge," AmericanFolklore.net. Copyright © by American Folklore. Reprinted with permission.

Roy C. Amore & Larry D. Shinn, "The Prostitute Who Lost Her Charm," *Lustful Maidens & Ascetic Kings: Buddhist and Hindu Stories of Life*, pp. 39-40. Copyright © 1981 by Oxford University Press. Reprinted with permission.

Jilali El Koudia, "The Sultan's Daughter," *Moroccan Folktales*, pp. 15-18. Copyright © 2003 by Syracuse University Press. Reprinted with permission.

Doug Lipman, "The Three Laughs," HasidicStories.com. Copyright © 1997 by Doug Lipman. Reprinted with permission.

Nathan Ausubel, "The Woman Who Buried Three Husbands," *A Treasury of Jewish Folklore*, p. 173. Copyright © 1989 by Random House, Inc. Reprinted with permission.

Wolfram Eberhard, "Faithful Even in Death," *Folktales of China*. Copyright © 1965 by University of Chicago Press. Reprinted with permission.

John Bierhorst, "St. Theresa and the Lord," *Latin American Folktales: Stories from Hispanic and Indian Traditions*, pp. 118-120. Copyright © 2003 by Random House, Inc. Reprinted with permission.

Jean Russell Larson, "Piccolo," *The Fish Bride and Other Gypsy Tales*. Copyright © 2000 by Shoe String Press, Inc. Reprinted with permission.

Jane Yolen, "Knee-High Man," *Mightier Than the Sword: World Folktales for Strong Boys*, pp. 36-38. Copyright © 2003 by Houghton Mifflin Harcourt Publishing Company. Reprinted with permission.

Barry Lopez, "The Eye-Juggler," *Giving Birth to Thunder, Sleeping With His Daughter: Coyote Builds North America*, pp. 59-60. Copyright © 1990 by HarperCollins Publishers. Reprinted with permission.

Fredrick Hyde-Chambers, Audrey Hyde-Chambers & Kusho Ralla, "The Creation," *Tibetan Folk Tales*, pp. 1-4. Copyright © 1981 by Shambhala Publications. Reprinted with permission.

Michael J. Caduto & Joseph Bruchac, "The Earth on Turtle's Back," *Keepers of the Earth: Native American Stories and Environmental Activities for Children*, pp. 25-26. Copyright © 1988 by Fulcrum Publishing. Reprinted with permission.

Harold Courlander, "Obassi Nsi and Obassi Osaw," *A Treasury of African Folklore: The Oral Literature, Traditions, Myths, Legends, Epics, Tales, Recollections, Wisdom, Sayings, and Humor of Africa*, pp. 255-256. Copyright © 1996 by Perseus Books. Reprinted with permission.

Richard Erdoes, "Buffalo Calf Woman Brings the First Pipe," *American Indian Myths and Legend*, pp. 47-52. Copyright © 1985 by Random House, Inc. Reprinted with permission.

John Bierhorst, "Death and the Doctor," *Latin American Folktales: Stories from Hispanic and Indian Traditions*, pp. 81-82. Copyright © 2003 by Random House, Inc. Reprinted with permission.

A.K. Ramanujan, "A Plague Story," *Folktales from India: A Selection of Oral Tales from Twenty-two Languages*, pp. 51-52. Copyright © 1992 by Random House, Inc. Reprinted with permission.

Norma J. Livo & Dia Cha, "The Origin of the Shaman," *Folk Stories of the Hmong: Peoples of Laos, Thailand, and Vietnam*, pp. 38-39. Copyright © 1991 by ABC-CLIO Inc. Reprinted with permission.

Charlotte Leslau & Wolf Leslau, "The Midwife of Dakar," *African Folk Tales*. Copyright © 1963 by Peter Pauper Press. Reprinted with permission.

Pleasant L. Despain, "Renting a Horse," *The Emerald Lizard: Fifteen Latin American Tales To Tell In English And Spanish*, pp. 23-26. Copyright © 1999 by Pleasant L. Despain. Reprinted with permission by Marian Reiner Literary Agency.

Moss Roberts, trans., "The Scholar's Concubine," *Chinese Fairy Tales & Fantasies*, pp. 157-161. Copyright © 1980 by Random House, Inc. Reprinted with permission.

Richard M. Dorson, "Mistake in Account," *American Negro Folktales*, pp. 307-308. Copyright © 1967 by Patti Freeman Dorson. Reprinted with permission.

William Crooke & Pandit Ram Gharie Chaube, "The Evil of Covetousness," *Folktales From Northern India*, p. 364. Copyright © 2002 by ABC-CLIO Inc. Reprinted with permission.

Howard Schwartz, "The Golem," *Leaves from the Garden of Eden: One Hundred Classic Jewish Tales*, pp. 292-295. Copyright © 2008 by Oxford University Press. Reprinted with permission.

Theodor Herzl Gaster, trans., "The Adventures of Gilgamesh," *The Oldest Stories in the World*, pp. 21-25. Copyright © 1958 by Beacon Press. Reprinted with permission.

K. Langloh Parker, "Where the Frost Comes From," *More Australian Legendary Tales*, pp. 73-75. Copyright in the Public Domain.

Ella E. Clark, "Thunderbird and Whale," *Indian Legends of the Pacific Northwest*, pp. 163. Copyright © 1958 by University of California Press. Reprinted with permission.

Kevin Crossley-Holland, "The Creation," *The Norse Myths*, pp. 3-6. Copyright © 1980 by Random House, Inc. Reprinted with permission.

S.E. Schlosser, "The First Tears," AmericanFolklore.net. Copyright © by American Folklore. Reprinted with permission.

CPSIA information can be obtained at www.ICGtesting.com
Printed in the USA
LVOW09s2026110815

449739LV00004B/13/P